DEAD GAME

A JOHN MARQUEZ CRIME NOVEL

DEADGAME

KIRK RUSSELL

CHRONICLE BOOKS
SAN FRANCISCO

Library of Congress Cataloging-in-Publication Data:
Russell, Kirk, 1954-
Deadgame : a John Marquez crime novel / by Kirk Russell.
p. cm.
ISBN 0-8118-5078-1
1. Marquez, John (Fictitious character)—Fiction.
2. California. Dept. of Fish and Game—Fiction.
3. Government investigators—Fiction.
4. Sturgeon fisheries—Fiction.
5. California—Fiction.
6. Poaching—Fiction. I. Title: Dead game. II. Title.
PS3618.U76D43 2005
813'.6—dc22
2005013530

Manufactured in the United States of America

Designed by Affiche Design, Inc.

Cover photo © Bill Denison/Veer

Distributed in Canada by Raincoast Books
9050 Shaughnessy Street
Vancouver, British Columbia V6P 6E5

10 9 8 7 6 5 4 3 2 1

Chronicle Books LLC
85 Second Street
San Francisco, California 94105
www.chroniclebooks.com

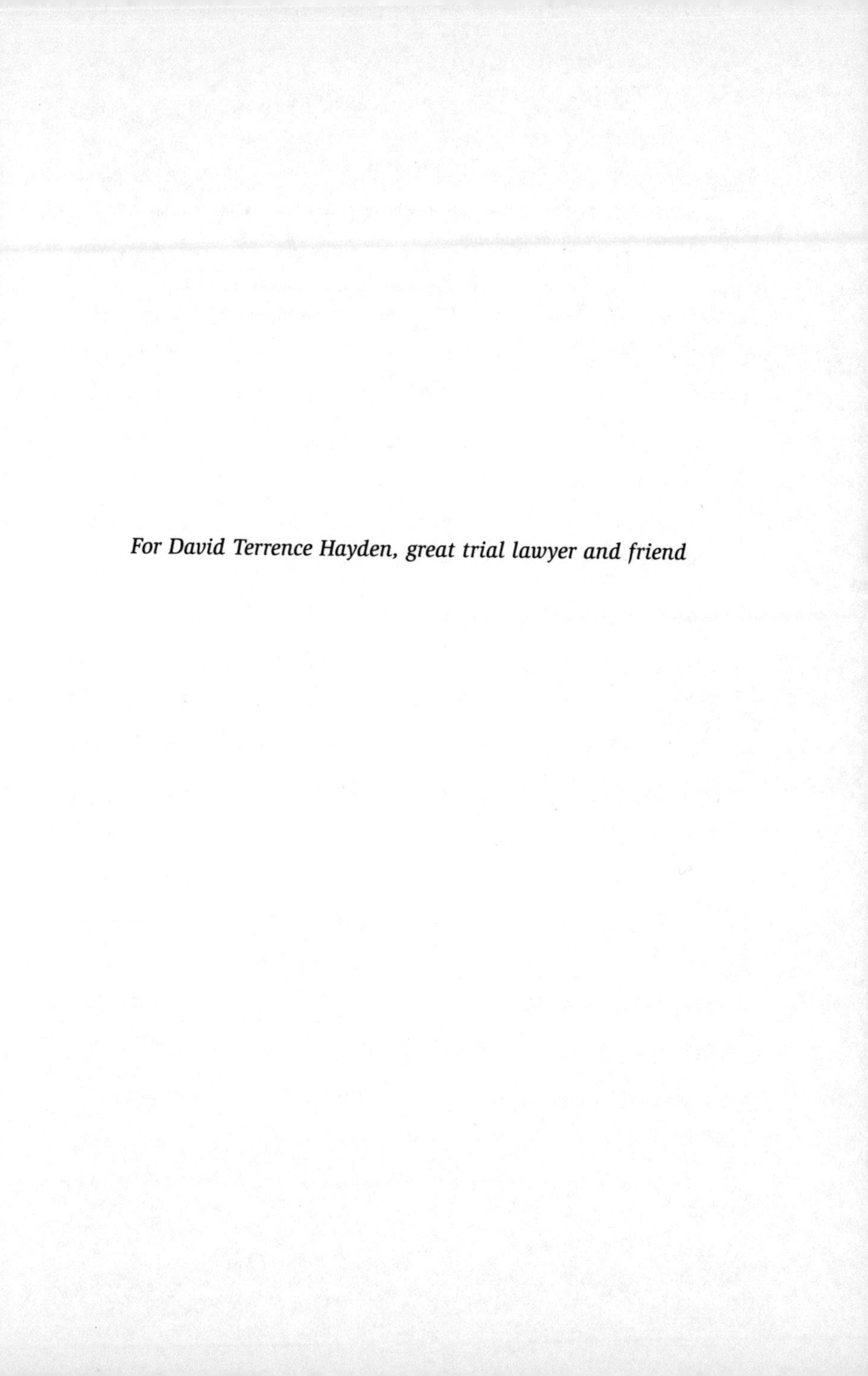

For David Terrence Hayden, great trial lawyer and friend

1

Raburn climbed back up the muddy bank, shielding his eyes from the headlights as he looked at Marquez. He smiled and scraped mud from his boots. He was happy about what he'd found.

"She's still alive," he said. "We're okay."

He went to his pickup, started the winch, and Marquez stood near the edge of the levee road looking down at the dark water of the slough as the steel cable tightened and the sturgeon's head broke the surface. With the pickup's pale headlights shining from behind him, he could just make out the gray-white shape as it was dragged toward the bank. He heard Raburn calling to him over the pickup engine and winch.

"Is she out of the water yet?"

"Almost."

"Tell me when."

As the cable pulled the heavy fish from the water, the sturgeon rolled onto its back, and spiny scutes, the armor on the sturgeon's back, dug into the bank mud. It plowed through the low brush, began climbing, and was every bit as big as Raburn had claimed, probably close to eight feet, as big as any Marquez had seen poached in the delta in the years he'd run California Fish and Game's undercover team. It was hard to watch but, without turning, he held his left hand out, thumbs-up to signal Raburn that it was on its way up.

The pickup engine revved as Raburn tried to give the winch more power. The sturgeon's ascent slowed and the winch cable sawed through mud at the edge of the levee road, but the heavy treble hook in its mouth did not pull free and the fish continued an upward slide. When it crested the road, Raburn hurried over. He clapped Marquez on the back.

"Look at the size of her!"

They worked the fish onto a plastic sheet spread in front of the truck. It gasped. Its tail flopped as Raburn rummaged in his truck. He returned with a knife and a sledgehammer, and handed Marquez the knife.

"Your baby," he said, "unless you want me to cut them out for you."

Marquez had made the buy for eleven hundred dollars. He wore a wire and had recorded the haggling they'd done in Isleton before driving out here, and he had shown Raburn, the fish broker, the money but hadn't paid him yet. They'd made several buys from Raburn, had more than enough to arrest and charge him, yet couldn't seem to get him to talk about another suspect they were trying to get close to, a Russian immigrant named Nikolai Ludovna, or "Nick," as Raburn called him.

The traditional way to make caviar was to cut out the ovaries while a sturgeon was still alive. After death, the body's enzymes altered the chemistry and tainted the taste of caviar made from the roe. But they weren't going to keep it alive tonight. The fish had suffered enough, hooked and brought here, tied off on the tree for two days, and now pulled alive up the slope.

"Go ahead. Kill her first," Marquez said.

Raburn smiled, didn't comment, didn't want to do anything to mess up the sale. He was a good-sized man, limber and strong, a middle-aged gut on him, but still agile and he swung the sledgehammer easily. One blow wasn't enough, and each made a flat hard wet sound striking the fish. Marquez watched the fish die, then leaned over her belly and slit her open. He removed the ovaries and rested them on ice in a cooler.

Now they would find out what they had, and he waited for Raburn to reposition the flashlight, then gently squeezed eggs from an ovary as Raburn held the light above him. The eggs were black and slimy and not mature enough for caviar. That had always been the risk with this one. The main sturgeon run in California's Sacramento/San Joaquin River delta was months away in April, and though sturgeon varied, it was only late November.

"She was already on her way into the delta so I thought when I caught her she was further along," Raburn said. "Remember, I called you and told you I caught her in the delta."

Raburn was afraid he'd back out of the deal. Marquez glanced at Raburn then back at the sturgeon. He figured the sturgeon was close to fifty years old, same as himself and Raburn. He'd let Raburn kill the fish and now he had to make this work.

"You connect me to Nick Ludovna and the deal stays the same," he said.

He watched Raburn pick up the cooler, walk it over to the side of the slough road, then dump the ice along with the ovaries. Raburn pushed an ovary with his boot to get it to roll down the embankment toward the slough and away from any warden who might find this site later. He kicked at the mound of ice.

"Garbage," he said, as though they'd been cheated.

2

Raburn was good at gutting and cleaning. He carved the sturgeon into chunks, which they lifted onto the ice in the pickup bed. They covered the chunks with a tarp, drove slowly back through the fog, and it was almost dawn when Marquez got dropped at his truck.

Later that morning he met with the other two wardens on his undercover team, Carol Shauf and Sean Cairo. Sitting in Shauf's minivan they listened to the tape of last night's conversation with Raburn, then drove back out the slough and took photos. In the midafternoon Shauf and Cairo drove back to Sacramento. They'd stay at the safehouse tonight, and Marquez would remain in the delta. He rented a room at Lisa's Marina and at dusk carried a beer out on the deck and waited. A confidential informant was on her way here to meet him.

She was helping unravel another thread of the poaching ring, how the poached sturgeon roe that became caviar was getting sold. She didn't have anything new for him tonight, but he hadn't seen her in a couple of weeks and she was passing through the delta anyway, so it was a chance to touch base. That she was late didn't bother him. He was tired, and it was nice to stand out here with a beer and take a break from the operation, even if the beer was warm. Long lines of cars like convoys swept past up on the levee road. When his phone rang, he guessed it was Anna.

"Lieutenant?"

"I'm here."

"I screwed up."

"How?"

"I agreed to meet Don without calling you first."

She sounded like a little girl confessing and not like herself. Marquez set his beer down on the railing cap.

"Where are you?"

"At the fishing access up the road from the Rio Vista Bridge, and I'm scared. Don wanted to meet me here, but he hasn't showed up and now these other guys have. It was like a big deal and a favor he'd owe me for. He said he had something he wanted me to hold and give to a friend of his tomorrow, but now he's forty minutes late and these other guys have pulled in and parked next to my car, even though the whole rest of the lot is empty."

"Are you in your car?"

"No, I got out to walk around and I don't want to go back to my car because of the way they're watching me. I'm sorry, I know that sounds crazy."

"Doesn't sound crazy. How far are you from them?"

"About fifty yards."

"I'll drive to you," he said. "But why don't you walk up to the levee road and wait for me there?"

"I'm really sorry, Lieutenant."

"There's no reason to be."

The fishing access lot was down by the river, rectangular, bordered on the road side by the levee embankment, on the other by an asphalt path and a row of oak trees. He could picture her car in the middle of the lot.

"Should I just run down to my car and get in fast? Am I making a problem out of nothing?"

Probably, because there was a pretty good chance the two men in the car were there for no reason other than the lot was free, along the river, and it was Friday night, the day after Thanksgiving on a long weekend. There to kick back, drink, smoke, listen to music.

"Not if they scare you. The safest thing is to go up to the road, and I'll stay on the phone with you. I'm going to walk to the truck now. If we lose connection I'll call you back. Tell me what you can about the men and their car."

"They're like middle-aged white guys, but I can't see them that well. The car is newish and looks expensive. It's a black four-door."

"What model?"

"I don't know cars, but like one of those airport cars."

"Like a limo?"

"No, smaller than that, a black four-door, modern looking."

A late-model black four-door didn't sound like a couple of guys hanging out at a fishing access, but still, it was no reason to worry, and Anna wasn't that deep into their operation. Yet it was troubling because it didn't make sense that Don August, the suspect she was helping them with, had anything for her to hold for him. He couldn't see August trusting her to hold something overnight for him. He didn't know her that well.

A nervous energy started in Marquez. The feeling of relaxing with the beer was gone, but at least the beer would finally be cold when he got back, and he'd buy Anna dinner here after retrieving her. Christmas lights came on around the bar windows as he crossed the marina deck. Through the windows he saw the same three fishermen at the bar, the owner, Lisa, bartending.

"I can't walk up to the road because I was really stupid. I left the car unlocked and my purse is in there. As long as they can see me on the phone they know I can call 911."

So she wasn't that scared. He registered the difference as he got in his truck and thought about her waiting this long to tell him about the purse in the unlocked car.

"It's going to take me fifteen to twenty minutes with the fog to get there." When she didn't answer he repeated, "Anna, walk up to the levee road and wait there. You have a bad feeling about these guys—you can watch from up there."

He drove up to the road and turned downriver. Anna was big-boned, athletic, high cheekbones, cheeks pocked by acne, brown eyes, nothing demure about her, a river rat who guided boat tours and mountain expeditions for a firm called Adventure USA. They were legit, had been around awhile, and Anna's face was in their brochure and on their website, an experienced river guide, diver, and climber. The website carried a picture of her on the saddle of a Himalayan mountain. They'd checked her out every way they could, including her credit history, as they chased a rumor about her kiting checks. From Immigration they'd gotten record of her moving here from Russia with her mother twenty years ago.

She'd climbed some serious peaks and guided trips on Class IV rivers. She'd told him tales of stuff that had happened to her in remote places, in particular because she was a woman. She'd struck him as tough, not easy to intimidate, and he'd never heard her talk about being scared of anything. Now, suddenly, her voice was lighter and louder. She laughed.

"Guess what, I really am a total idiot, they're leaving. They're backing out. They're going to pass me here in a second."

Marquez heard a car engine idling somewhere near her, then Anna's startled, "Wait, oh, no," and a man's voice calling, "Come here, bitch."

"Anna, run!"

But she answered the man instead, her words unintelligible to Marquez.

"Get your ass over here before I use this on you." The man's voice was abruptly much louder, closer. "Don't move, don't make any noise. Drop the fucking phone."

She screamed. The phone clattered and died. Marquez jumped on the accelerator. He reached for his radio. He was still ten minutes away.

3

Anna's green Honda was in the middle of the lot, passenger door wide open, contents of a purse dumped on the seat. Marquez shined the flashlight beam into the wheel well at a soft leather purse turned inside out, lying like a rag in the corner. He went back to his truck and talked to the Sacramento County watch commander again. Far away, out across the delta, he heard the first siren. He read off the license plates and told the watch commander he recognized her car.

"I'm going to take a look out along the water."

But he swept his flashlight over her car again first. In the backseat was a nightstand, a desk lamp in an IKEA bag, sandals, running shoes, clothes folded and stacked on a seat as though she planned to carry them from the car to a drawer. He knew she was moving back to Sacramento, the company she worked for no longer willing to contribute rent toward a San Francisco apartment.

"Anna!"

He'd called her name when he'd gotten here and called for her every twenty yards as he moved away from her car now. He stepped into the reeds, the flashlight beam fracturing as it shined through them. He walked the path out to the river, checked between driftwood logs, picnic tables, the reeds and brush and swept the light across the dark water of the river. Across the river the lights of Rio Vista shone hazily through fog. Seals barked out on a buoy. She was a strong swimmer, but the man's voice had been right there. The phone had hit something hard, clattered. The voice had been so close he didn't see her running away.

A CHP unit, its light bar milky, siren loud, dropped down from the levee road, and Marquez lifted his badge as the officer put a light on him. County units began to arrive. They gathered near her car, and one CHP officer recognized it. He turned to Marquez.

"Dark-haired woman, right? I pulled her over a week ago. She was close to a DUI. How'd you end up working with her?"

"She's helping us on a sturgeon poaching case."

He left it at that and organized a search. Through the incident command system, until someone with higher rank and more experience arrived, Marquez was in charge. They covered the reeds and brush, the embankment up to the road and into the field on the other side. A Sacramento County deputy found a crushed cell phone in reeds not far from the picnic table.

Forty minutes later a Sacramento County detective named Brian Selke took over, and a K-9 unit from Contra Costa crossed the Antioch Bridge and dropped into the delta. Marquez related the phone conversation to Selke and gave him what he had for addresses and phone numbers on Anna Burdovsky and Don August. He gave Selke license plates and a description of August's Porsche.

"Are you going out with an All Points Bulletin?" he asked.

"Not yet."

Selke was a solid-looking guy, balding, broad nose, thick wrists, shoulders rolled forward. He stood close to Marquez as he asked his questions, then left him when a dog found a wallet in the brush. Selke bagged the wallet, waved Marquez over.

"Let's look at this together." He opened the evidence bag so Marquez could see the wallet and asked, "Why was she meeting you tonight?"

"It just worked out that she was coming through the delta. I haven't seen her in a couple of weeks, so it was really just to touch base."

"Are you married?"

It took Marquez a moment to register what he was being asked. He nodded and said, "Yeah, I've got a wife and stepdaughter. There's nothing between Anna and me."

"If she was going to stay in your room tonight, now would be the time to tell me."

"Nothing like that."

Selke showed him the contents of the wallet. An REI card, Macy's, membership in the Wilderness Society, a couple of folded Visa receipts, both from gas stations, three photos, one that was probably her mother, one of a much younger Anna standing in snow with a building behind her and a young boy, a toddler in a coat that came down to his shoes standing next to her. A man was alongside her. The third photo was of a landscape, a lake and green-blue forested mountains climbing behind it. Marquez lingered on that photo a moment.

"You said she speaks Russian and that's important in this investigation of yours."

"Some of the people we're looking at are Russian immigrants."

"Was this photo taken in Russia?"

"I've never seen the photo before, but I know Anna left Russia and came here with her mother when she was a kid."

Marquez studied the photo again. In it Anna looked nineteen or twenty. If it was Russia she must have gone back when she was older.

"Do you recognize the man?"

"No."

"What about the boy?"

"No."

He watched Selke walk back over and talk to the dog handlers. Earlier, when Selke had refused to do anything about August yet, Marquez had called Shauf at the safehouse and she'd driven to San Francisco. A few minutes ago she'd called to say she was down the street from August's apartment. He'd told Selke that, and Selke had asked for Shauf's phone number.

Now Selke walked back to where Marquez waited. He picked up the photo again, held it steady, studying the black-haired man with a mustache, wearing a shirt open at the collar, older than Anna in the photo by at least a decade, black leather coat down to his thighs, smiling down at the kid who looked a little like Anna. No other photos but more receipts, and an old W-2 from Adventure USA and another plastic card in Cyrillic that Marquez guessed was a Russian ID of some sort.

"Let's go talk in my car," Selke said.

After they got in his car Marquez listened to Selke go back and forth on the radio, and he was still having a hard time understanding Selke not going out with an APB on August's car, or getting the warrant application going, getting in touch with the on-call judge in San Francisco. He watched Selke type into a Blackberry, his thumbs thick on the small pad. He couldn't watch this much longer.

"What business is this Don August in?"

"He owns three specialty-food stores, one in Seattle, one in LA, one in SF, all named August Foods."

"So what's he going to tell me when I ask why he was in the delta today?"

"He buys product from small producers, artisanal food products. We're pretty sure he also buys sturgeon roe that's been processed to caviar out here and gets that repackaged as Caspian beluga. The eggs are similar in size and color, gray and about like a little glass bead. All his labels have the proper stamp, but we think they're either forged or bought."

"What do Customs and U.S. Fish and Wildlife think?"

"Everything appears legit."

Selke surprised him. "But you've checked DNA and it's not?"

"What we've checked is legit, all from the Caspian."

Selke's cell rang. The radio crackled at the same time. He answered the radio call, which was to tell him a vehicle stop was in progress—two white males in a black Lincoln sedan just north of Patterson, about fifty miles from here. They waited, talking about August until more information came in. The officer who'd made the stop had run the driver's license and then called for backup. The individual was wanted on a felony drug charge. Marquez listened to the names spit out of the radio and shook his head. He didn't know them. Then his cell rang.

"August is home," Shauf said. "The lights just came on; I can see him through the window. There's a woman with him. Where are you?"

"Still at the fishing access but about to leave here." He saw Selke react to that. "Hang on a minute."

He turned to Selke. "August is home."

Selke was quiet, looking through the windshield, watching the dog getting loaded back into the K-9 car. Half the officers standing around were gossiping. There was nothing left to do here.

"All right, Lieutenant, we'll go knock on his door."

4

Shauf slumped back against the driver's door, blond curls flattened from the headrest, a Diet Coke resting on her left thigh. Selke and a San Francisco homicide inspector were up on August's porch. Two SFPD patrol units were on the street, their light bars reflecting off the white-painted stairs. Getting to the on-call judge and getting a warrant had delayed Selke's arrival, and lights were no longer on in the front rooms of the apartment. Through binoculars Marquez watched Selke hit the bell a second time.

"Selke called me on his way here," Shauf said. She took a sip of Coke. "He wanted to know if you and Anna have something going on."

"He's got to ask."

"Not the way he does it."

The front door opened, and August moved onto the threshold, silhouetted by the light from behind him. Selke badged him, showed him the warrant, and August handed it back to him. He stroked his goatee and smiled.

"Why does he remind me of the devil?" Shauf asked as August stepped aside and ushered the detectives in. "The woman he came home with is also in there. She looks like a kid, but he had his arm around her when they went up the stairs, and I think I've seen her in his store here. I'm pretty sure she works there. She's got a little ruby stud in her nose." After a pause, Shauf added, "The guy is a scuzzball."

The door closed and Marquez laid the binoculars down. The street was mostly commercial buildings, shops, boutiques, a Tully's Coffee at the corner. Two blocks down the street was August Foods, the neon script with the store name not unlike the neon over his wife's two coffee bars, Presto on Union and Presto on Spear, a third about to open down near the wharf.

"Did you talk to Chief Bell?" Shauf asked.

"Yeah, after the BOLO went out."

"How'd he take it?"

Bell had immediately assumed it was their fault, that the *be on the lookout for* going out meant the SOU had somehow screwed up. But Marquez didn't volunteer that yet. It was the kind of information Shauf was fishing for, and he didn't want to get into that with her tonight.

"He wants me in his office tomorrow morning."

"He's going to say the operation is blown."

He'd all but said it tonight.

The front door opened and they watched Selke come back outside alone. He held his cell phone under the porch light to punch in numbers. Seconds later Marquez's phone rang.

"Does Anna Burdovsky have a cat?" Selke asked.

"She does."

"Could you describe it?"

Marquez pictured the cat. He'd been to her apartment here in San Francisco after she'd called CalTIP saying she might have information on sturgeon poachers. But that was about four months ago.

"It's black and white, a male, it looks a little like a Holstein cow. The name is Jim or Pete, something like that."

"Bob."

"That's right, it's Bob. What does the cat have to do with anything?"

Selke turned to face the street. He seemed to like delivering the bombshell.

"Mr. August says Burdovsky and her cat have stayed here for the last week. He told her she could stay with him a week or two and showed us the room she's been staying in. The cat is part of the deal and I don't know what else is, though August's friend here is sure she knows and she wants to leave, but we're holding her because we want to get a statement, otherwise you'd see her stomp down the stairs. Have you ever been up here?"

"No."

"Do you know, he's got four bedrooms? How much money is this guy making? This place has to be worth a couple million bucks minimum. It looks like a magazine and I can see why Burdovsky would want to stay here. There are clothes and items he says belong to her and we're welcome to take. He also admits talking to her today but it was closer to noon and they argued because he told her he wanted her stuff and the cat out today. He told me the cat's next home is the Humane Society if she doesn't show up by tomorrow. Is any of this making sense to you?"

Marquez didn't have to answer that.

"Well then, try on this idea, Burdovsky isn't who you thought she was. Mr. August is very cooperative. Anything we want we can have. Even the sheets off the bed or his phone records, whatever we want. Hell, he'd give us the cat if we had a carrier. He's also coming in tonight to sit in an interview box."

"Where?"

"The Richmond Station." Selke waited a beat then continued. "The young lady he's with works at his store here in the city and told us August was in the store from 10:00 this morning forward. I don't think she's lying, particularly since she can't wait to get out of here. Either way it's easy to check. She says they left the store together and went to a bar at around 5:30."

Selke walked over to the edge of the porch and looked down the street, perhaps trying to locate them.

"I also called the number you gave me for the apartment Burdovsky is moving out of and got the ex-roommate who just got back from Chile two weeks ago. She's not a big fan of Burdovsky. She told me she got back from Chile and found the cat in her bedroom with a litter box and food. Apparently, whenever Burdovsky was gone for a day or two she put the cat there. The room smelled like a litter box and the rent hadn't been paid in two months. She claims Burdovsky lied about paying it, was supposed to have sent the check and didn't do it because she didn't have her half. There was an eviction letter on the kitchen table, and Burdovsky had some story about her employer owing for the rent. She's thinking of taking Burdovsky to small claims court, so she's right there with you, she wants her found."

"We'll see you at the Richmond Station," Marquez said.

"Sure, you're welcome to listen in."

At the Richmond Police Station they watched Selke and the

SFPD homicide inspector go into an interview box where August was already waiting. Coffee sat untouched in front of August, and he'd changed clothes. He wore a dark green cashmere sweater, gray slacks, polished loafers.

"My ex-wife loves your store," Selke said. "She always ran up a big bill. I ought to lock you up just for that."

The SF inspector laughed. August smiled. Selke smiled back at him.

"We appreciate you coming in."

"Frankly, detective, I think you know I only came down here because I lied to you earlier. You asked if I was sleeping with her, and I couldn't tell you with Dara there."

"So you were sleeping with Ms. Burdovsky?"

"Yes, but I told her yesterday I wasn't interested in continuing the relationship. She got hysterical and told me she was falling in love with me, so maybe you ought to dredge the river. Maybe she got lovesick and threw herself in."

Selke walked August through the past few days, where he'd been, whom he'd talked to, who else knew anything about his relationship with Anna. The interview ended at 12:17. Shauf left to drive back to Sacramento, and Marquez stayed to talk with Selke and the SFPD inspector.

"It's going to turn out that she was staying there," Selke said. "We've got a downstairs neighbor that recognizes her and has seen her come and go with August. We showed the neighbor photos, and she said they had their hands all over each other. You've got to face the very strong possibility Burdovsky burned you." Selke looked at the SFPD inspector, then back at Marquez. "We have to ask you something."

"Go ahead."

"How is it she's staying with your suspect and you don't know about it?"

It was a fair question and not easy for Marquez to answer. Watching August interviewed he'd realized Anna most likely had burned them.

"My team is down to three wardens, and we've had our hands full in the delta."

Selke nodded. Sure, that explained it. The SFPD inspector nodded in understanding, but the answer didn't cut it for either of them. It stank of incompetence. Selke studied his face, looking for a further answer there, then backed off.

"What is it about sturgeon?" Selke asked, smiling again. "Isn't that what Scott Peterson said he was doing that night, going sturgeon fishing Christmas Eve?"

Selke and the SF inspector had a laugh over that. Marquez left them there, the two of them still joking about Peterson and sturgeon fishing as he walked down the corridor and out the door.

5

At dawn Marquez stepped over crime tape at the fishing access with a tightness in his chest he hadn't felt since his DEA career ended more than a decade ago. The tape sagged with condensate from the fog. The sandy path out to the water was dark, the morning cold. He walked the parking lot and then out to the river, as though seeing it again would provide a reason for Anna to stage an elaborate scam to disappear.

After he left the fishing access he stopped at a diner in Isleton and ate a breakfast of scrambled eggs, bacon, and toast soggy with a commercial butter spread that dripped through his fingers onto his pants. Later in the morning when he walked into Chief Bell's office, Bell's eyes went immediately to the stains the butter had left. Bell didn't like undercover work, didn't really like the idea of wardens out of uniform, and equated neatness in appearance with clear thinking.

"Take a seat, Lieutenant."

It was Saturday, the rest of the floor empty, the building quiet, Bell making the point he'd come in just for this. He made a second point, that he'd talked with Selke and understood Burdovsky had burned them.

"Where do you think your operation goes now?"

"We've got one suspect I want to try to flip. If he'll work with us we can make several arrests in the next few weeks and then it doesn't all go to waste."

The faintest smile started on Bell's face. "Lieutenant, all August has to do this morning is pick up the phone. Won't he call everyone he's bought illegal sturgeon or roe from?"

"We don't connect all of the suspects with August. There are other people."

"You don't know if August is working with or buying from these other suspects, and in fact, what you don't know has been highlighted in the last eighteen hours. Let's face the music, Burdovsky identified you for August. She blew the operation. It's over. You're done. I'm meeting with Chief Baird in an hour to discuss the SOU because I think we've also reached that door."

"What door is that, Chief?"

"Last night was an embarrassment." He paused so the importance of that wasn't lost on Marquez. "The question I'll raise with Chief Baird today is whether the SOU is viable in its current configuration. I don't believe this would have happened if your team had been at full strength. You would have known she was staying with August. Keep your phone with you today. I'll call."

Marquez left Sacramento and drove back into the delta on Freeport Road. He talked to Shauf and Cairo, told them where to meet before taking a call from his stepdaughter, Maria, who was with her mom in Boston. Though his wife, Katherine, and his stepdaughter had been gone on a college tour only a single day, it felt like weeks.

"What colleges have you seen?"

"Boston College and Tufts. We're on our way to Harvard Square. We're going to BU this afternoon. Mom wants to see it."

"You don't?"

She breathed hard into the phone as she walked. He tried to picture them in Boston, white sky and cold when he'd checked Boston weather on the Internet.

"Dad, this trip is more about her."

"Have you told her what you told me?"

"Not yet. Where are you this morning?"

"In the delta on a sturgeon poaching case, but don't change the subject."

A month ago, Maria had lightened a streak of her hair from dark brown to a pale gold sheaf falling down her left temple, similar to her mother's streak of white hair. She'd done that despite arguing nearly continually with Katherine for the past six months. What she'd talked to him about on Thanksgiving was her plan to take a year off before college.

"I'll talk to her today or tomorrow," she said. "She's going to get really upset."

Katherine had gone one semester to a college in Vermont twenty-five years ago and had loved being away from home and in college. Then her mother had been diagnosed with ALS and she'd had to drop out, return home to help care for her and get her younger sister through high school. She'd signed herself up at the local junior college. Now what she hadn't had she wanted for Maria.

After hanging up with Maria he drove into Freeport and parked across the street from a restaurant the SOU used occasionally as a rendezvous point. He bought three coffees to go, walked up to the levee road, then down the wood stairs and around the old building to the marina dock. Gusts shoved two plastic chairs around, and he caught one to sit on. He propped the other so it couldn't move and rested the coffees on a splintered dock board at his feet. He tried to drink his but found his gut was already churning.

He looked out over the river. The fog was gone and cirrus clouds were running ahead of the forecast storm. Shauf and Cairo were still fifteen minutes away, and he thought back to the first contact with Anna and his first meeting with August. Because of the smaller size of his team he'd done something he wouldn't ordinarily do, made direct contact with the suspect, visiting August at his San Francisco store under the guise of opening a catering business.

Marquez had bought tiny olives imported from a boutique Spanish producer, capers from the Aegean Islands, ghost shrimp from the delta that August advertised with the old line, "So fresh you can't see them." He'd bought Caspian caviar that the Ashland, Oregon, wildlife lab had tested and come back negative on for Pacific white sturgeon DNA, though the SOU was fairly sure August was buying poached sturgeon roe from the Sacramento/San Joaquin delta and repackaging it as Caspian beluga, or mixing it with Caspian beluga. Unfortunately, "fairly sure" was as far as they'd gotten with August, which was why Anna had seemed like such good luck.

He'd given August his card with the name John Croft, told him he was a cook going into business on his own, starting a catering business called Three Bridges Catering, meaning he'd go anywhere in the San Francisco Bay counties. You build a cover story, make it whole enough to stand up, make it so it wears like a comfortable shirt.

August sold walnut oil, honeys, tins of sardines, dried fishes and seaweed, balsamic vinegars, olive oils, a whole vocabulary of artisanal products. He spoke seven languages, made a point of telling Marquez that, eyes glittering, the kind of guy who needs you to be impressed by his credentials, wants you to think he's superior to you. He claimed to travel the world looking for "what was left," and Marquez didn't doubt that. Some of the best of what was left of sturgeon was in the Sacramento/San Joaquin delta, and August certainly had been there.

Marquez had stood on the polished chestnut floor of August Foods, handling tins of Iranian caviar, talking business, August memorizing his face while explaining that he was working through his stock of the 2003 harvest of Caspian caviar. He didn't know what he would do next, because the UN through CITES had banned any commercial trade in sturgeon roe from the Caspian Sea. They'd shut down the 2004 harvest, blaming the poaching for decimating sturgeon stocks. But that was in September. By October CITES had reversed itself, and the ban was lifted. Go figure.

Now Shauf and Cairo walked around the corner. Marquez handed out the coffees and Shauf freed the other plastic chair. She sat across from him in the chair, the wind at her back, and Cairo sat on the dock.

"So when do we get the word?" Shauf asked.

"Bell told me to keep my phone close this afternoon."

"We may as well go home."

"No, with Baird there's a good chance he'll want to think it over this weekend, so I'm thinking we'll go see Raburn tomorrow, and see if we can flip him. It'll shock him hard when he sees my badge."

Shauf shook her head, saw the reasoning but had a hard time with it. She'd handled the surveillance of Abe Raburn. She had him nailed for commercial trafficking in sturgeon, and they'd hoped to take him down along with the rest once they'd built the full case.

"This is all so wrong," she said. "If it turns out Burdovsky is alive I want to see her do time."

Marquez looked to Cairo, who'd been quiet through all this. Cairo nodded. He was for giving it a try with Raburn.

An hour later Marquez was on the phone to Jo Ruax, the lieutenant who ran the DBEEP boat. They'd worked in pieces with the Delta-Bay Enhanced Enforcement Program crew. He figured from the way Bell had talked this morning he'd already called DBEEP, possibly Ruax directly. He followed Ruax's directions and parked along a road on San Pablo Bay, then walked down the trail and found her sitting between trees, binoculars focused on a boat on the bay. Her lips were chapped, her cheeks red from the cold wind. She smiled a tight smile, handed him the glasses, and behind her the horizon carried the dark gray band of the approaching storm. She was a hard-charger and had wanted to direct the surveillance on the sturgeon operation. She'd argued against bringing in the SOU.

"I heard this morning you're going to get shut down," she said.

DBEEP was funded by both the U.S. Bureau of Reclamation and the California Department of Water Resources. Their focus was the fisheries, and Ruax knew a lot more about sturgeon than he did. What she didn't know more about was undercover work.

"If that happens we'll get together, and I'll make sure you've got everything on everyone we've been watching. Did my chief call you?"

"He did. He wanted to know if I'd ever met Anna Burdovsky and what I thought of her. I told him what I told you."

"That you think she's a flake?"

"Yeah."

In a lot of ways he liked Ruax, and he had a lot of respect for DBEEP. They had an identity, knew who they were, and Ruax was tough and serious and good at what she did.

"We're supposed to get the word this afternoon, Jo. If we go down, I'll call you."

"What happens otherwise?"

"We're going to try to flip Raburn and take another run at it."

He caught the faint shake of her head. "Good luck," she said. "He's just about the last guy I'd want to have to rely on."

6

Bell never called, and the next morning Marquez led the way down a muddy path in the rain. Off to their right was a rotting dock, then a clot of willow, cottonwood, and bay trees. Beyond that was a row of houses, each with river access and a modest dock, and though he lived near them, Abe Raburn wasn't really part of their community. He moored his houseboat in a small cove beyond where the road ended. His work boat, the *Honest Abe,* was tied off on a buoy near shore. His old Ford pickup was parked between eucalyptus trees well above the river. Shauf called the cove "Raburn's homestead."

Raburn saw them coming, and if he recognized Marquez, gave no sign of it. He was outside on the rear deck of the houseboat standing over a barbecue under a blue plastic tarp he'd rigged from the roof of the houseboat out to shoreline trees. Smoke from the barbecue swept violently sideways in gusts. White cotton line had been strung through the corner grommets of the tarp, but little had been done to cinch the tarp tight, and it snapped and pulled against the lines so hard it was just a matter of time before the tarp ripped loose, not unlike the way Raburn's life was about to change.

"Hey," Raburn said, "good to see you, and I've got plenty of fish and beer. I was about to watch a football game." He looked quizzically at Marquez, his joker's expression frozen for a moment. "Who are your friends?"

"My friends are game wardens, Abe." Marquez showed his own badge. "We're here to talk to you."

"I'll be damned." He shook his head. "Sonofabitch. I should have known."

Raburn wore sandals, shorts, and a T-shirt under a windbreaker. Stenciled letters on the back of his windbreaker announced a police golf tournament in '92. Hairs on his legs glistened with rain. He was a gregarious man, but you didn't have to look through the windows of the boat very long before you knew he lived alone. He did his business in bars, used them as offices, and watching him Marquez had decided that Raburn also needed to be among people before coming back here at night alone to his boat.

"We've got a proposition," Marquez said. "We're not in a hurry. We're here to talk with you."

Raburn tried to catch his stride again. He took a pull of beer that was on a shelf near the barbecue.

"Anybody else want a sandwich?"

"I'll take you up on that," Marquez said, "but I think you'd better lay off the beer until we finish."

Cairo shook his head no. Shauf never answered the question, and Raburn laid another piece of fish over the coals. He went inside, cleared magazines and newspapers off his table, grilled bread and finished making the sandwiches, offered Marquez a beer, and found another couple of chairs for the table. Then, inside, in the small space around the table, tension gathered. Through the windows the tarp swelled and lifted as if the houseboat was in an America's Cup race.

"We're going to offer you a deal," Marquez said. "The best one we've offered anyone in a long time."

Raburn was fifty-one, bloodshot eyes, salt-and-pepper hair, three or four days' stubble of beard going gray, an eccentric in a part of California that prided itself on eccentricity. They'd followed him over hundreds of miles of delta waterways, told him that now, let him adjust to the truth that he'd been under surveillance for months.

"I don't know much about sturgeon."

"Maybe you wouldn't poach as many if you did," Marquez said and took a bite of sandwich. "You seemed to know a fair amount about it the other night." He held the sandwich up. "Thanks for this. What we want you to do is switch sides and start working with us. In return we won't charge you and arrest you. That'll keep you out of prison. Here, take a look at some of the videotape and photos." Marquez wiped his hands, checked the camcorder, and then showed Raburn how to operate it. "If we arrest you, then anything we negotiate would have to go through the DA, so we thought we'd try to work it out with you first and keep the District Attorney out of this. But if you feel like you should hire an attorney and defend yourself, that's your call."

Raburn didn't answer and picked up the camcorder. He played it back and then dismissed it.

"I can't tell anything. It's not clear enough."

He laid the camcorder down.

"I can't even tell if that's me."

"Do you think it could be your brother?"

He scowled and said, "Isaac's not involved. He doesn't know anything about it."

Raburn's twin brother, Isaac, owned a pear and apple orchard in Courtland called Raburn Orchards. It wasn't far from here. The word was Abe and Isaac's father had been a TV preacher who'd given his twin sons biblical names, then raised them with the brutality the self-appointed righteous seem to have such a gift for. The brothers had run away from home in their teens. They'd come to the delta and been here since, and even now, better than thirty years later, they lived just a short drive apart.

As far as the SOU knew, Isaac wasn't involved in sturgeon poaching. But there was a twist. Isaac boxed and shipped pears from the packing shed in the orchard. He also produced organic apple and pear butter, and Marquez had seen the pear butter in August Foods.

"Okay, Isaac's not involved, so it's all you, and I can tell you it's fairly certain we'll get the sentence we want. Most likely three years, though you may only do a year to eighteen months. Then a fine for each felony count. The fines can get pretty big." He laid a finger on the first photo after sliding it across the table to Raburn. "I was there for that one," he said, waited, looked out at the rain on the river, caught Shauf's eye as Raburn went through what they'd decided to show him.

"You work on the DBEEP boat," Raburn said to Shauf from across the table, taking it to the next level, trying to sort it out, figure out where he'd screwed up.

Once again, Shauf didn't answer, preferred to glare at him, and Marquez answered for her.

"No, we're not part of DBEEP, though they're good. They know the delta salmon, sturgeon, and striped bass a lot better than we ever will. We're undercover officers for Fish and Game, part of a special operations unit, the SOU."

"I've never heard of you."

"Well, now you've met us, that's even better."

Marquez finished the sandwich as Raburn picked up the camcorder again. He turned the camcorder in his hands, probably looking for the erase button and the way out of this mess. Marquez had learned over the years that you can lay it all out for them, read them the riot act, but they still have to come to it on their own.

"Sometimes I loan my boat out."

That got the start of a smile from Shauf, improved her day. Raburn's twenty-three-foot Chris-Craft was tied off on a buoy just upriver from the houseboat. It left a persistent stain of blue smoke anywhere it went, and Shauf had joked about expecting to see it sink one day. Raburn pointed across the rain-pocked river at his boat. Marquez pointed at two sturgeons in a photo.

"See, there you are, and you look good there, relaxed, the sun on your face, nice day. You don't want to celebrate your next three birthdays in a prison cell."

"That's what my father said would happen."

No one fielded that. They didn't want any part of his childhood this morning. He was a complex man, cunning, a born smuggler, Shauf claimed. He earned part of his living brokering fish to a handful of markets in Stockton and Sacramento and lived modestly, but he had to be putting away cash with the amount of roe and sturgeon he was moving. He did other work as well, repaired appliances, did odd jobs, and they'd watched him install lights on a marina dock and tap into a PG&E line to draw illicit power for a friend living up a slough. He sold T-shirts with names like New York, Steamboat, Cache, or Terminous Slough across the front. Under the hundred or so shirts he routinely carried on his boat were two blue plastic coolers used to transport poached fish.

Marquez rested an open hand on the file. "Either we cite you, arrest you, and take you in, or we try to see if there's some way you can help us shut down the sturgeon poaching operation you've been selling into. If you do help us, we'll forget the charges against you."

"I may as well kill myself."

He made his big face look sorrowful.

Only Marquez heard Shauf's whispered, "Sounds good to me."

"Who are you afraid of?" Marquez asked.

"Will I be going into the Witness Protection Program?"

This time Shauf spoke up. "Oh, sure, and live on a clear blue lake in a nice new cabin," Shauf said. "How would Lake Tahoe be, or is that too close to the guys who will want to do you?"

"We don't have Witness Protection," Marquez said. "That's more a Federal deal. It takes a lot of money to relocate people. You'd still be here on your houseboat when it was over." Marquez looked behind him across the small galley kitchen and at the thin wall of the bedroom. He realized the fish smell in here was probably permanent. "Still, this is bigger than any cell I've seen. Who exactly is going to kill you?"

"Ludovna."

For a moment Marquez was unsure whether Raburn was gaming them, then realized he was serious. Raburn picked up a heavy fish hook lying on the table, a treble hook with three hooks joined together. Trebles were used to snag bottom feeders like sturgeon.

"I saw him get angry at a guy selling sturgeon."

"Saw who get angry?"

"Nick Ludovna, because the fish he came to buy was old, and he thought he was getting ripped off. But it was just a Mexican guy with no money who screwed up. He caught the sturgeon and he didn't have any way of moving it, so he'd tied it off to a tree in a slough, just like the one I sold you the other night." Raburn touched his gut. "It was full of eggs and on its way up the river last April. Anyway, this Mexican called me first, and I went out and took a look at it because I've bought from him before. When I checked it the fish was fine and still alive." He shook his head. "I told him not to kill it, but I think he got scared the fish was going to get away so he clubbed it to death. Then he lied to Nick about when he killed it, and Nick knew he was lying and got real mad. It was out of the water by then. They'd dragged it up on the bank and there was a treble hook still in its mouth, and Nick worked the hook out. He wanted to see the eggs so they cut it open and took out the ovaries. They were filled with eggs and they would have been perfect for caviar, except that the sturgeon had been dead for too long. Nick got mad because he'd paid him already. He wanted his money back and the Mexican kept arguing and saying it had died just before they got there."

Raburn turned the treble hook in the air, gestured toward Shauf, sweeping it through the air slowly in her direction though nowhere close to her.

"Nick took the treble hook and swung it at his face." He gestured toward Shauf again. "Like that, and it went right through his cheek and he pulled him in like he was fish. He took his money back while the Mexican was screaming and trying to get the hook out."

"And what did you do?"

"He told me to leave. He said go back to my boat and forget about it, so I left."

"Did you call the police?"

"No."

Marquez had a hard time with that. It wasn't difficult to picture what a treble hook could do, and there were plenty of fishermen poaching sturgeon who were poor and without work or money.

The tarp tore loose and blew back over the roof of the houseboat. It covered the four windows on the river side and steam hissed off the barbecue. Raburn looked at the tarp but didn't react to it and looked back down at the table.

"I want to work with you," Raburn said, "but I'm afraid of him, and I'm not ashamed to say it. He scares me sometimes. It's like he's okay and then he just blows up."

"We'll deal with Ludovna, but you'll have to testify."

"I don't know about that either."

"We can set it up so it's done in the judge's chambers."

Marquez flipped a page in the file, slid more photos over. He knew the treble hook story might have been made up for them, but he didn't think so.

"We want to meet Ludovna and we'll want to sell to him. We'll take a ride this afternoon, and you show me your whole routine when you go to deliver to him. Then you'll have to convince him you trust me and that I supply fish to you. After that I'll cut you out of the business."

It took all of them to tie off the tarp before they left. While they were doing that, Shauf leaned into Marquez and, with rain running down her cheeks like tears, said, "He should be more scared of us. He should be more afraid of losing his boat and going to prison. I get the feeling he's already working us."

"He's all we've got."

"Then maybe it's not worth it."

7

Raburn's cell phone played "Take Me out to the Ball Game" with each ring. He pulled the phone from his windbreaker as they followed the river road toward Sacramento.

"Don't answer it," Marquez said.

"It's my brother."

"He'll still be your brother after he leaves a message."

The phone stopped playing, and the windshield wipers slapped back and forth. It rang again a few minutes later, and Marquez looked at mist low over the fields and asked, "Are you and Isaac close?"

"We're twins, but he's the hardworking one."

"And what are you?"

"The fuckup."

Raburn smelled of fish and stale clothes. When Marquez lowered his window a crack the rain found its way in. A lot had to be going through Raburn's head, but he probably didn't see himself as a fuckup. Earlier he'd made a little stab at being a victim of his own ineptitude and alluded to ignorance of the game laws, but he wasn't that guy either.

"What's your brother going to say about this?"

"There's no reason he needs to know."

"You work out of the pear packing shed, and we're going there. He's going to find out."

"He doesn't have to, and he's got enough problems already. Leave him out of it."

They drove through Courtland, and, as they neared the sign for Raburn Orchards, Marquez slowed. But he didn't turn down the steep road. Below on the levee island were long rows of pear trees, some still with fall leaves, wet red-brown, turning in the storm wind. They looked like a fire burning across a field. Between the rows, the soil was dark from rain. Pears had all been picked before the end of July this year, Bosc and Reds last. A hundred yards from the road was the pear packing shed, a big wooden building with a gable face that Raburn worked out of.

There were other outbuildings, an equipment barn, two aluminum prefab structures, and the main house in the distance, a big three-story wood frame with a sagging roof. Half an hour later they drove past Ludovna's one-story ranch house in the Land Park area of Sacramento. Brick wainscoting. Painted redwood siding. Lawn out to the street. A good-sized but ordinary house in the suburbs. On one side of the garage was a white BMW 330i, the car's polish gleaming through the rain.

"Ludovna's car?"

"He has a lot of cars."

"Is he into cars?"

"I don't know what he's into."

"Fair enough, but when we made the offer to you, Abe, we did it because we believed you know enough to help us. If it turns out on the drive that you don't remember anything, we'll have to rethink it all."

Marquez jotted down the plates as though it was new information, but it wasn't as if he'd never seen this house. There was a man who worked for Ludovna who drove this car. They called him Nike Man because his standard outfit was a running suit. The BMW was registered to Ludovna's fish brokerage business. They'd assumed Nike Man was both an employee of Ludovna's Sacramento Fresh Fish and a bodyguard. In the last month they'd steadily tried to gather more information on Ludovna, but their focus had been August, Raburn, and a dozen poachers who were feeding sturgeon to Raburn and a couple of other suspects. He turned back to Raburn.

"How much does Ludovna pay you?"

"A dollar fifty a pound for meat, fifty dollars a pound for roe. Sometimes I freeze the eggs, sometimes I make caviar."

"How did you find him?"

"I didn't."

"He found you?"

"Right." He stared out the windshield. "His guy just showed up at my boat one morning, and I could barely understand him. Ludovna speaks English okay, but not the guys that work for him. They're all from Russia or places like that."

"How many of them are there?"

"Including the guys who work at the shop, I guess about

five. They like vodka and they like to play cards. They all wear black clothes."

Marquez kept questioning him as they drove back into the delta and past the houses of a couple of guys who fished weekends and worked construction during the week. Guys who supplied him. They crossed the Sacramento River and drove toward Main Street in Rio Vista where Raburn said he routinely sold to the owner of Beaudry's Bait Shop, a place Marquez knew. According to Raburn, the former owner, Tom Beaudry, had sold out over a year ago to an ex-con named Richie Crey. Sold the sport fishing business, the boat, everything.

"Crey never wants to deal directly with me. He has a couple of guys who pick up the fish."

"What's he do with it?"

"I don't know where he sells it. I don't even know how he heard about me."

"Maybe from the same people we heard from."

Raburn didn't see the humor. He rubbed the whiskers alongside his jaw.

"You don't know where he goes with the sturgeon?"

"No, but somebody is buying. Last spring I could have sold all the roe in the world. Somebody wants everything there is."

"Ludovna?"

"No, it's not him. I think he buys from me and sells to them."

They recrossed the Sacramento River on the Rio Vista Bridge and drove upriver past the fishing access where Anna had disappeared. They followed the levee road, winding through the delta towns until they reached Courtland and Raburn Orchards. Then they made the steep drop down to the levee island. A graveled road ran out through deep puddles to the packing shed. Marquez pulled inside under the roof and left his headlights on.

"My room is in back."

As Raburn went to turn the lights on, Shauf's van eased into the big shed. She got out as Raburn walked back, and he seemed uncomfortable with her presence. He kept glancing over at her as they started back toward the room his brother let him use. They walked past conveyer belts and sorters and an ancient box machine.

"Does your brother own his packing equipment?" Marquez asked.

"He leases."

Water dripped through holes in the corrugated roofing twenty feet over their heads, and they dodged that and worked their way around old wooden fruit boxes. Raburn unlocked two tall wooden doors, swung them open. He hit a light switch, and they were looking at two long wooden tables, dirt floor, stainless-steel sinks, stainless-steel pans, a hose, freezers, always a freezer, but not the pots and seines for producing caviar that Marquez was looking for. He opened a freezer and found sturgeon fillets wrapped in white butcher paper. On the end of one of the tables was a scale.

Shauf worked her way around the room with the camcorder. She was the one designated for recording all evidence. If it went to trial she'd be the one called. That was their practice, have one officer designated to avoid having several pinned down by the same trial.

When they finished, Marquez drove Raburn back to the houseboat and dropped him near his pickup. The rain had stopped, though heavy droplets still fell from high in the eucalyptus branches and struck like pebbles on top of the truck cab.

"I'm supposed to buy a sturgeon in the morning," Raburn said.

"I'll ride with you to pick it up."

"You don't believe me about Nick, do you? You think I'm bullshitting you."

"I'm hoping you're not bullshitting us. I'm putting faith in you."

They had set up surveillance on Ludovna's house this afternoon. Cairo was there now.

"We'll meet tomorrow," Marquez said. "I'll see you in the morning."

Driving away, he returned a call from Cairo, and he'd worked enough years with Cairo to know the differences in his voice. There was a way Cairo's voice got both quiet and intense.

"Ludovna just got here, and it looks like he's leaving again. There's a woman with him, Lieutenant. He pulled up in a midnight-blue Cadillac that looks black in this light. It could be Anna's airport car. From across a parking lot in the fog it would look black. It's late-model, maybe last year's. He's pulling out now. What do you think?"

"Stay with him. I'm on my way."

8

Ludovna came down the street with his date, right hand resting high on her ass before slipping down and up under her skirt long enough to feel the slide of nylon on both legs. His arm was around her shoulders as they went into a restaurant, and Marquez waited until they were at a table in the corner and he could see a waiter opening a bottle of wine.

"You're good to go," he told Cairo, and Cairo slid onto his back at the curb and shimmied under the front of Ludovna's Cadillac. He attached a GPS unit to the engine block, taking his time with the battery pack. He was still under the Cadillac when the waiter returned to pour more wine.

The rain started again as Ludovna and the woman stood up from dinner. When they walked outside Ludovna draped his coat over her narrow shoulders, and rain soaked through his shirt and blew against his face, but he didn't seem to care or be worried about that or anything else. He held the woman near his chest and sheltered her body as they walked to his car. He was half bald, the remaining black hair slick in the rain, his eyes checking the sidewalk ahead, checking his car, cars passing on the street, checking everything.

Marquez watched them pull away in the Cadillac, an Escalade, an '04, last year's model. He drove toward his Land Park house but stopped at a bar on the way.

"The night is young," Marquez radioed.

Cairo had run the Cadillac plates and gotten the name Sandy Michaels and a Ventura address for the owner. The digital clock on Marquez's dash moved toward midnight. He could see the Cadillac under a light in the parking lot and thought about Raburn's story of Ludovna and the treble hook. Shauf drove up, and he watched her get out and walk up to his truck. She got in on the passenger side, and they talked in darkness.

"My friend Cheryl in administration called me today," she said. "She told me a story about Bell that might explain why he's been all over us."

"Must be a good story to call you on a Sunday."

From her tone it didn't sound like it was going to be a happy story, at least not for Bell. Marquez glanced over at her. He'd probably sat through more surveillances with Shauf than with anyone else in his years with the SOU. It was still less than a year since her sister had died of cancer, and, though she seemed like she was doing better, there was still a quiet to her that filled the cab at times.

"This happened the day before Thanksgiving," she said. "A kid showed up with a pizza delivery for Bell at headquarters. You know how Chief Baird doesn't like anything brought in, so Bell's pretty snippy about it when they tell him his pizza has arrived. He's got to stop what he's doing, writing a memo to God or whatever it was, and leave his office and tell the pizza kid he made a mistake. So he comes down the corridor and tells this kid he didn't order any pizza, and what's more would never order pizza to headquarters. But the kid checks the name again and hands Bell the tag. Pizza is from Bell's wife. She called it in and sent it there, or so the kid insists."

"Bell's wife sent him a pizza?"

"Right, and that's what Bell can't figure out. He doesn't even like pizza."

Shauf's face turned in the darkness. She was getting to the punch line, and the streetlights reflected her smile. But in her face he saw her anger at Bell.

"The pizza kid has one of those candy-cane striped shirts and a hat. I wish I could describe him like Cheryl did, but anyway he's a pimply-faced college kid, and Bell asks, 'What kind of pizza?' The kid goes, 'This kind,' and opens up the box. He's a process server, not a pizza guy, and he's got divorce papers from Bell's wife. He hands them to Bell and says, 'Enjoy your lunch.'"

Marquez felt bad for Bell as he listened to the rest. Bell had stood there reading, making no attempt to hide what it was about, and according to Shauf's friend he didn't move for twenty minutes.

"Hard story," Marquez said.

"Well, don't forget all those times he went somewhere with his wife and then chewed our asses for working through the weekend and wasting overtime dollars."

Marquez remembered Bell coming in Monday morning after a weekend in Aspen or LA, having gone to some party at the Getty Museum, remembered one Monday morning in particular when

Bell had flown back early from LA. With his wife, Bell did things that were complete fantasies for Marquez and Shauf on their salaries. More than a few times Marquez had walked out of Bell's office angry, but he'd never begrudged Bell his lifestyle and forgave him his need to talk about it. He read it as Bell's desire to look like something he wasn't, but the truth was, Bell's wife made the money. No one working for Fish and Game made any more than just enough to get by. The Bells lived in a big house in Sacramento with a wide lawn and a huge garden that went two lots deep in the back. Among the roses were a circular brick pavilion and a koi pond lit with underwater lights that threw soft colors into the water.

Working in a bureaucracy where the pay scale is low, you tended to hear rumors of who's having more fun. The Bells entertained quite a lot, and those parties were, or so the rumor went, often thrown to further Bell's career. For several years Bell worked out every day at lunch, and it always seemed like he was readying himself for some anticipated promotion. He got his hair cut at a beauty parlor, and the manicures were a running joke among wardens. He kept his skin tanned and his uniforms well pressed. In many ways he was the antithesis of a game warden, but not at a summer cocktail party where he could regale a group with tales heard from the SOU or wardens in the field and almost make it sound like he'd been there before he'd been promoted. At those parties where his tan skin and athletic pose suggested a man accustomed to the outdoors, he portrayed the image of an officer on the rise, a man who had it all.

He also worked hard and had kept doing so through the low morale of the budget morass. Few people had advanced much in the last four or five years. The Fish and Game Academy had been shut down, a hiring freeze went into effect, and the department had hunkered down for the ride as the state deficits ballooned. The SOU went from ten to seven to five, now three.

"Cheryl says he went in his office, closed his door for an hour, and then left for the day."

"I wouldn't have hung around either."

It wasn't that long ago that he and Katherine had a rough couple of years, and she had wanted to separate. He hadn't realized until much later how numb that had made him.

"I hate him for making this thing with Anna the reason for closing us down," Shauf said. "I can understand deciding three wardens isn't enough for the team. It's not enough. I know it isn't; you know it isn't. What I hate about Bell is he has to make us look like bad guys first. We embarrassed the department. That's the kind of pure bureaucratic bastard he is."

Marquez was listening but distracted now by a man working his way through the parked cars. At first it seemed he was looking for his car, but now he was stopped alongside Ludovna's Cadillac.

"Do you see this guy coming across the parking lot?"

Shauf stopped her riff on Bell.

"Where?"

"He just got in Ludovna's car. He must have had a key."

The Cadillac lights came on a few seconds later, and the car backed out and started hard for the street. Marquez turned to Shauf, but she already had her door open.

"We go with him. Cairo can stay with Ludovna."

Shauf went for her van, and Cairo read out the position of the car on GPS. Within minutes they were behind it on I-5 southbound, Shauf quietly calling it out over the radio.

"Lane one at seventy-five."

Then they were into agricultural land the subdivisions hadn't yet reached. The Cadillac exited, crossed under the freeway, and went eastbound on a county road. It started showering, and Marquez hit his wipers. The Cadillac lights blurred in the distance, and he went back and forth with Cairo as they figured out that the Cadillac was following a dirt road running between planted fields and a railroad bed.

"We're trying to figure out where the car is. He went out a road following the rail bed, and his lights are off now. We can't see him. He may be out there stripping it with a buddy or still driving."

It was several minutes before Cairo came back. "I've got him stationary. You don't see him?"

"No."

"He's about a mile and a half off the road."

"Hold on, we've got lights coming at us, but from farther away."

"The Cadillac isn't moving."

It took a couple of minutes to sort that out. The car stopped, and its lights were small dots out in the dark open fields. Marquez hit his wipers again. He lowered the window and used his binoculars as Cairo guessed that the other car was an accomplice, then cut himself off and said, "Ludovna is outside the bar with the babe. He's looking around for his car and just pulled his phone like it's a gun. Who are you going to call?"

"It'll be the police to report it stolen. This was planned."

Marquez used his scope and wanted to drive down the access road for a better position but figured he couldn't risk it. He watched car lights start to move again and went back and forth with Shauf.

"Which car is moving here?" she asked.

"Car number two." The lights swung away from them. "Turning around."

"He may have gotten away fast, but he didn't strip it that fast. So what's going on?"

Marquez didn't have an answer, but they were looking at taillights as the other vehicle moved away. He gave them another minute. They were moving fast.

"Let's go recover our GPS unit," he said.

He started down the access road. On his right was the elevated railway bed, and fields were planted on his left. About a quarter mile in he saw Shauf's headlights follow, then ahead, a flash of light, white and quickly orange-yellow, a ball of fire and a low heavy whump as the sound reached his truck. Gasoline. Ludovna's car burning, the fireball ballooning, then straightening. He knew that the kid who'd brought the Cadillac out here and whoever had picked him up were also watching and would see Shauf's and his headlights approaching. But their headlights could be anybody, police, someone who saw the fire and got curious, anybody.

He drove fast but knew it was too late. When he got there, flames curled out of the interior and around the roof, the heat like a hand pressing against his face. The burning shell blocked the road and the rain did little to slow the fire. Even with the cold wind and rain, the air was thick with the odor of burning plastic, leather, the stink of paint frying. It illuminated the wet rail bed. With Shauf he watched the car burn and a twenty-thousand-dollar GPS unit with it. Marquez watched the flames and could think of only one reason for Ludovna to have his car intentionally stolen and burned.

9

The blue tarp was folded back onto the roof of the houseboat and weighted down with cinder blocks. It glistened in sunlight. The river was smooth, and Raburn held a garden hose in his left hand, a Corona beer in the other as he washed duck guano off his decks. He turned the water off and poured the rest of his beer into the river, his sandals squeezing water out of the Astroturf as he walked back across the deck. He was less nervous today, close to flip and a little devil-may-care, as though life had tossed him a curve and he was just going to make the best of it. He'd also been drinking with his lawyer last night.

"My lawyer told me not to agree to anything until I have something signed by your superiors."

"That's not going to happen."

"That's what I told him. Let me get the boat, I'll be right back."

He untied a dinghy to row over to his boat and then couldn't get the *Honest Abe* started. The engines sputtered, died, and when they finally caught he over-revved them before they'd warmed up. He yelled back across the water again.

"These engines are junk, but I haven't had the money to do anything about it."

As they went upriver Raburn talked about his brother. "What Isaac should do is tear out the trees and put in vines. Everyone in the delta is doing that."

"That might be a good reason not to."

"The money isn't in pears."

They left the river and turned into a slough. They passed under a small bridge and, after rounding a bend, were in the quiet of the slough.

"Look, I've got to know for sure I'm not going to get prosecuted later. Do you really have the authority to do this?"

"I do."

They came around another bend in the slough. Along both banks the trees leaned over the water. In the cold clear chill on the slough this morning, Raburn wasn't such a bad guy. He obviously cared for his brother and his brother's family. He pointed up ahead.

"It's not much further. One of these guys got laid off from work and he's got a kid sick with leukemia so he fishes sturgeon to pay for medicine. The fish they called about isn't huge but he says it has roe."

"How many times have you bought from them?"

"I don't know. Enough."

Raburn cut the throttle as they came through the bend. The bow dropped, and they slowed.

"Let's talk about Beaudry's Bait Shop," Marquez said. "What else you know about Richie Crey?"

"He did time for drug dealing and he doesn't want to go back in. That's the thing you've got to know about him. He won't deal directly with you. He's got these two guys who work for him who handle the fish."

"What are their names?"

"I don't remember."

"Did Beaudry know he was selling to an ex-con?"

"He must have."

The last time Marquez had been in Tom Beaudry's shop a faded Goldwater bumpersticker had been tacked up in a corner up behind the counter. If you asked about it you'd wish you'd brought a bag lunch, because Beaudry had a lot of theories to share. According to Beaudry, when the country went for Johnson over Goldwater in 1964, that was a turning point. He felt sure that if Goldwater won, he would have nuked Hanoi and the war in Vietnam would have been an easy win afterward.

For years, in addition to the bait shop he'd also run a sport fishing boat out of Benicia and occasionally called CalTIP to report poaching. He was one of the first sport fishing captains with a website and sold custom sturgeon hooks and bait mixes off it. He also posted his political opinions on the website, along with the essays of other deep thinkers who proposed ideas such as defoliating Humboldt County in northern California to put the dope farmers out of business. From what Marquez remembered, Beaudry had a problem with all drug use, so it didn't make much sense he'd sold his shop to an ex-con who'd been in for trafficking.

"Basically, I didn't know Beaudry well," Raburn said. "I stopped there and bought bait from him once, and he wouldn't even let me use his bathroom—told me to go up the street to a bar."

Ten minutes later, they met up with the two fishermen, and Raburn introduced him to the pair, one a blond kid, with a chrome-plated construction toolbox bolted down in the back of his pickup, and an older Latino carpenter. It took all four of them to get the sturgeon into the boat. Marquez's hand slid along the bony armor, the gray skin. He felt the abdomen for eggs and helped Raburn cover it before talking to the guys. Raburn pointed at Marquez.

"He's your new money. I can't afford you anymore. You call his cell phone from now on."

Marquez shook hands with both. He scribbled down a number to call him at.

"Good to meet you guys, nice-looking fish. Call me when you land another like it."

When they got back to Raburn's houseboat a neighbor kid helped hump the fish up to Raburn's truck. At the truck Raburn gave the kid ten bucks, and Marquez followed Raburn down to the pear packing shed where they took the ovaries out and made the call to Ludovna.

"He wants it," Raburn said as he hung up with Ludovna. "But not until tomorrow."

"Didn't sound like you told him you're bringing a friend."

"I didn't."

"Why not?"

Raburn didn't answer at first, instead lifting the heavy knife and hacking into the sturgeon again.

"Because you don't understand this guy at all, and I don't want anything to happen to me."

10

Marquez walked with Chief Baird from headquarters to an Italian restaurant that Baird liked. It was early for lunch, and there wasn't anyone in the dark room other than a bartender doubling as a waiter, sitting at a table folding napkins. He led them to a booth, took an order for two draft beers, and dropped a couple of heavy leatherbound menus on the table. Baird waited until he was behind the bar pulling the drafts.

"I think you know what I'm going to say, but what you don't know is how proud I am of what you've done with the team in the past decade."

So they were done. Marquez looked from Baird to the bartender drawing two pint glasses of beer.

"Lieutenant, you know my heart is in the field, always has been, that's where our real job is."

What Marquez knew was last year he had a one point one million–dollar budget to work with and this year 13 percent of that.

Next year was slated to be less again and with no equipment upgrades. He had vehicles with 275,000 miles on them, but Baird was telling him that didn't matter anymore. He wouldn't need them.

"I don't agree with Chief Bell that we can fill in the gap with uniform wardens," Baird said, "but I agree we're taking too many chances without sufficient backup. This event with the informant wouldn't have happened if the team was at its former strength."

"It depends on what happened."

"The point is we're stretched too thin."

"Take everything that's happened in the last decade, Chief, and this sturgeon poaching operation we're up against now is the most organized and efficient we've dealt with."

"This Raburn character is efficient?"

"No, but getting to the traffickers beyond him is hard. From the rumors and the number of CalTIP calls coming in, we know a lot of sturgeon is going out. We may be starting to feel pressure from the collapse of the Caspian Sea stocks."

"You don't really have any evidence to back that up, do you?"

"We know the overall poaching has heated up."

Baird was quiet and watched the bartender return with the beers. He obviously wanted to do this in a way Marquez could accept.

"You've always spoken highly of DBEEP," he said.

"Sure, they're great. But they're not enough."

Baird took a sip of beer and Marquez looked at his own but felt no desire to pick it up. He listened to Baird order a meatball sandwich. When the bartender turned in his direction, Marquez shook his head. He didn't have any appetite.

"Maybe you should work with DBEEP," Baird said after they were alone.

"Give me another month, Chief. Let's see if it works out flipping Raburn. Give us until the first of the year. The storms are coming through and that kicks up the bottom and gets the sturgeon biting. We can use the fog to our advantage." He heard himself plead, couldn't believe it had come to this. "We've got some new contacts and leads." He told Baird the story of Beaudry, the bait shop, Richie Crey.

The bartender tried again to take an order from Marquez and finally gave up, refilled the bread sticks, brought Baird's meatball sandwich, and the chief couldn't find a way to take a bite out of it. The meatballs were too big. He had to cut them.

An hour later Marquez had until Christmas to make whatever arrests he could, and he'd told Baird the focus would be on Ludovna, August, and this Richie Crey who'd bought Beaudry's Bait Shop in Rio Vista. Leaving the restaurant with Baird, he felt a strange mix of gratitude and emptiness. Big picture, it was over, no more SOU. Three more weeks and then finished until new money could be found. That after a decade of running the team.

As they walked back toward headquarters Marquez asked for one more thing. "Let me get some of the old team back."

"Who?"

"Brad Alvarez and Melinda Roberts. Roberts has been bouncing around, and she's up in the Region IV office right now. Alvarez is back in uniform down along the central coast, but I know he's got a vacation coming up that he's planned for a while."

"You want to talk him out of his vacation."

"I'd like to talk him into postponing it. You'd have to give him the time off later."

"All right, if they're both willing, you can have them both."

Baird slowed as they neared headquarters. He stopped and faced Marquez before going back inside the Water Resource Building and up the elevator, and for a moment Marquez thought he'd changed his mind.

"John, you are the finest field officer I've ever known. I want you to know that, and I don't want you to quit when we close down the SOU."

"I don't know if there's a place for me here, sir."

"We'll make a captain out of you."

Marquez nodded toward the building. "You wouldn't want me in there."

He thanked the chief and watched him go inside. From his truck he called Alvarez, then Roberts.

"Sounds like fun," Roberts said. "I heard these sturgeon poachers are kicking your ass."

"Who'd you hear it from?"

"Alvarez."

"He's going to spend his vacation with us."

"I guess the fun never stops."

"We need you."

"And I miss the SOU. Tell me where to be and when."

"Pick up the gear you turned in and start with the computer. We're trying to find out everything we can on a Nikolai Ludovna. We're calling him N-I-C-K, but I think the Russians leave out the C, so you're looking for a N-I-K L-U-D-O-V-N-A, or N-I-K-O-L-A-I. He may have been a former KGB officer. We haven't had time to check that out." He briefed her on what they had learned. "See what you can find out about former residences, what he did before moving here, who sponsored him, anything at all. Start there and we'll meet at the Sacramento safehouse tonight."

Marquez met Shauf now outside the dirty stucco apartment where Anna rented a two-bedroom unit. It was where she'd told him she was moving back to. They went in to meet the manager, a sarcastic kid who seemed annoyed at their presence, chattering about how many police officers had already been in her apartment as he walked them up a flight of concrete stairs. When he started to go inside with them, Marquez stopped him, told him they'd bring him back the key.

The apartment looked like it had been tossed. They found a window wide open in one of the two bedrooms.

"What did the county take from here?" Shauf asked.

"Selke told me he pulled a computer, photographs, and a record of bills she'd paid. He said he took everything he thought might help locate her, but I don't see him leaving it like this."

"I don't either."

Marquez started in her bedroom, a mattress on the floor, no sheets, no covers, but a sleeping bag and pillow. In the bathroom only a Crest toothpaste tube and a frayed toothbrush in a drawer. He heard Shauf in the kitchen opening cabinets, and he moved into the second bedroom, the one Selke had described as resembling a Big 5 Sporting Goods store. Where a bed might have gone were two kayaks, one bright yellow, the other green, each with significant scrapes along the sides and bows. Several sets of oars, an O'Brien water ski board, a wake board, snow skis, a snowboard, a backpack, cycling equipment, assorted helmets, and a whole lot of other equipment and clothing.

"This is some nice stuff in here," Shauf said and lifted a ski. "These are new. I looked at them myself this fall."

"Are you starting to ski again?"

"I would if I could afford to. Over six hundred bucks for these, and that's a new board she's got there too, not the surfboard, the snowboard. What sport doesn't she do?"

They moved into the kitchen/dining/living area. Shauf had already been through the kitchen, but Marquez felt the need to work his way along checking the cabinets, listening to the hollow slap of their doors shutting again. He hadn't told Shauf yet about the lunch with Baird and needed to tell her. Wasn't sure why he hadn't yet.

He checked the refrigerator. Empty, but the manager had told Marquez the Sacramento police had advised him to clear it out. There was a round dining table with a simulated wood top, a tired white sofa, a TV. The rest of the room was green-brown carpet and an aluminum sliding window without a drape. It was hard to picture a river rat like Anna living here. She'd told him the year she was twenty-six she didn't sleep a single night under a roof. Either was in a tent in a national park or wilderness area or was under the stars, and that was the year her mother had died, the year she said she realized she had no one. Which in some ways was a connection between him and her, a feeling that he'd thought he understood. He'd once checked out of everything and hiked the Pacific Crest Trail alone, a long hike that hadn't healed him but did give him the time he needed to figure out how to fit in again.

He walked back to the room with the sports equipment. Anna's identity was in that room. There were trophies that he'd only glanced at on the first pass. Most of them were from playing in a softball league. He went through the contents of the backpack again, a couple of empty suitcases, knelt on the floor and shined a flashlight down each end of each kayak. The stop at the end of the flotation compartment in the bow was a different color than the one at the stern. Probably no big deal and from a repair, but since he was here to check everything he prodded at the bow compartment. He couldn't reach it to touch it, but after shining the light on it and then studying the edges and the proportion, comparing it to the stern, he began to wonder if there was a false piece there ahead of the real flotation compartment. Shauf walked in, and he found an oar they could slide in and poke at it. It moved but didn't pop free.

"Let's flip the boat over," he said. "You hold the bow end up, and I'll reach up there."

"You're too big, better let me do it, but you know all that's going be in it is more gear. This girl has more gear than anyone I've ever seen."

Marquez gripped the bow and felt her weight as she leaned in and reached toward the bow. He heard something give, a scraping, and she came out holding boat booties. But also a waterproof pouch and, inside it, a package of documents they opened up and started going through. Anna's face on photos. A different name and her face on a Russian passport. Photos taken of her at nineteen or twenty, he thought. Snow on the ground around her, a man next to her, the same guy who'd been in the photo in her wallet. The passport name was Anastasia Illyach.

"So an alias," Shauf said.

"Or maybe her real name, her father's name."

There was a pale blue ink handwritten letter in Cyrillic that he unfolded, then another and more small photos, a few that were black-and-whites, faces that could be relatives though, from the clothes and age of the photos, probably were long dead. He studied the photo of a small boy standing on snow, with Anna's hand resting on his shoulder. The photo was black-and-white, and they were both looking directly at the camera. He opened the passport while Shauf turned another photo in her hand. Passport stamps indicated Anastasia Illyach left Moscow in September 1994. In December she'd returned. She'd flown to Tokyo twice and Stockholm once. He looked at the rest of the stamps, guessing that she'd traveled to Moscow on an American passport, then traveled from there under this passport.

"When did she and her mom immigrate here?" Shauf asked.

"In 1989, when Congress upped the amount of Russians who could come over."

Marquez did the arithmetic, calculating years. "Look at this closely," Shauf said. "What do you see? You see it, right."

"Sure."

"I bet she's four and a half to five months." She touched her own belly as if she were pregnant, and Marquez focused on the man standing next to Anna. "She's just starting to really show." She looked up at Marquez's face. "So where's the kid? Is that the little boy in this other photo?" She picked that one up again.

"There was a photo that came out of the wallet found at the fishing access. Selke showed it to me. There was a kid in it, young, a toddler or a little older. That looks like him."

"Did she ever say anything to you about a child?"

"No."

Shauf angled the photo to study it again.

"Well, she's definitely pregnant in this.

11

Late in the afternoon Marquez pulled into the lot alongside Beaudry's Bait Shop. He was still on the phone to Ruax of DBEEP as he parked. She was giving him her take on Richie Crey.

"Crey looks like one of these geeks who screw up the way they look trying to figure out who they are. He's tall and probably weighs over two hundred. Got a shaved head and tattoos running down his arms, you know, real prison sleeves, not the hip variety you see kids running around with. What else? Let me think, oh, he's got a couple of silver rings in one ear. Look for torn jeans, cowboy boots, leather coat, kind of like a biker playing businessman. But he does know the delta."

"Where'd he learn it?"

"Oh, he's homegrown. He's one of ours," and Marquez remembered that she was from Isleton. "I think he was raised in Rio

Vista, though I'm sure no one was holding their breath waiting for him to get out of prison and come back. His family is from there. What's up with him?"

"We're going to try to sell him some sturgeon. He's bought a couple of times from Raburn. Do you know anything about two guys who work for Crey?"

"No, but you know what they say about shit and flies."

Like many bait shops, Beaudry's sold cold drinks, maps, a medley of hooks, sinkers, and various bait. It was also a source of advertisements and newsletters, a gathering spot for finding out where anyone was getting a bite. Marquez smelled crawdads when he walked in. He picked up a Pepsi and paused near the maps. He opened a copy of the *Fish Sniffer,* and a young Asian American girl came out to the counter and asked if she could help him. Behind her, silhouetted in the doorway of the old office, was the guy Ruax had just described.

"I'm looking for Tom Beaudry." The man behind her moved toward the counter. "I'm John Croft, a friend of Tom's."

"You're a year late," the man said. "I guess you're not that close a friend."

"Well, he's such a mean old bastard I wasn't in a hurry to get back."

"So you do know him." Crey smiled a big yellow-toothed, affable smile, though his eyes were flat. He looked at the card Marquez had handed him. "I bought his business, but why are you looking for Beaudry?"

"We used to do a little sturgeon business on the side." Marquez waited a beat to see how that registered and added, "I've been out of it for a while, but now I'm getting back in."

Crey pointed toward the door and the pale sunlight outside on the lot. He patted the girl on the rear and stepped around the counter and led Marquez out.

"You and me, we don't know each other," Crey said, "and I don't know what people have told you about me, but I messed up and did some time for it a few years back. One thing I'm not going to do is end up inside again."

"Abe Raburn said he'd call ahead."

"Raburn is going to vouch for you?"

"He was supposed to call this morning."

Crey's smile was sarcastic. "Then that's one strike against you already because Raburn can't keep his mouth shut about anything."

Marquez gauged Crey. "I've got a fish to sell."

Crey frowned at that, and Marquez wasn't sure which way this was going to go. He knew Crey was close to telling him to take off.

"You ever been inside, done time?"

"No."

"Then you don't understand what it means to not go back. What I'm leading to is I don't do business with people I don't know."

"That's why Raburn was supposed to call you."

"Raburn is like the town clown with his little boat with the happy stern. Lincoln is rolling over in his grave. He's doing fucking cartwheels."

Marquez spoke slower. He wanted this to work.

"I'm not Raburn, and Raburn is getting some heat from the Gamers, or at least he thinks he is, so I'm not selling to him right now. I don't take those kinds of risks."

Marquez let Crey study a face a good fifteen years older than his, and one that had seen more sun and water than his had.

"People seem to respect you, Richie. I can sell you caviar for two hundred bucks a pound."

"That's another strike against you. That's way fucking high."

"Then let's get a beer and talk about it. Or if you want, I'll call you when I have another good one."

Crey didn't say yes or no to any of it. He didn't even say he'd ever done a deal with Raburn. He smiled the affable smile again and said, "Sure, we'll have a beer sometime."

They shook hands before Marquez walked up the street to a bar Beaudry used to hold court in. He slid onto a stool, looked at what they had on tap, and ordered a Sierra Nevada Pale, then sized up the handful of people in the premature twilight of the room. A couple of women who looked like bikers, a couple of old boys who might know something, and a middle-aged black-haired man Marquez was pretty sure he'd seen around some other dock, maybe on the north coast when the SOU had worked an abalone poaching case.

One of the two old boys down at the other end called to the bartender and, when the bartender didn't turn fast enough, got to his feet, wondering aloud what had happened to Mac, the former bartender, and then limped toward the restrooms. Marquez left his beer and followed the man into the restroom, used the urinal next to him, asking, "How long has this kid been tending bar?"

"Not goddamn long enough."

"Where the hell is the old bartender and where's Tom Beaudry? I went into the bait shop, and there's some asshole there who says he bought Beaudry's shop."

"Stole it is more like it."

Marquez washed his hands slowly and took time with the paper towel, and, like many older men, this guy's flow wasn't what it used to be. Took him a while but after that he had no problem explaining what he meant.

"Don't go saying I told you this, but something funny went on when Tom sold the bait shop and his boat."

Marquez wadded the paper towel he'd dried his hands with and threw it away. The old boy hitched his pants and leaned toward him, turning his head a little bit like he could see better that way.

"That kid that bought it sure as hell didn't earn the money to buy Tom out."

Now Marquez sat on a torn leather bar stool between the old men. He bought a round of drinks, a gin and tonic for one and a scotch with a splash of soda for the other.

"Rumor is Tom didn't want to sell, but then he did it anyway because he had to. In fact, had to sell so bad he couldn't choose who to sell to."

When Marquez thought of the bait shop, a single blue neon sign, BAIT, BEER, ICE, faded markers, the dusty windows in a building that listed like a shipwreck, the idea seemed absurd. Beaudry kept his boat in good repair, made a point of saying that's where the money should be spent, yet even the boat wasn't worth forty grand. It had to go deeper than that. Marquez took a pull of beer, turned the bottle so the label faced him as he put the beer down. He picked at the label with a fingernail.

"Either of you have a phone number on Beaudry?"

"Hell, no, but he's up along Lake Berryessa. He's got a house across from the lake. I bet you can find him if you really want to."

Marquez laid another twenty on the dark wood bar. "A final and then I've got to take off."

"Well, as long as you're buying let me tell you another story that went around. Tom Beaudry had a sister who died in a fire down in Henderson, Nevada. Her house burnt up with her in it, and the rumor up here was Tom borrowed money from the wrong people and couldn't pay them back fast enough, so they killed his sister. There was a retired FBI fellow who used to live around here who told us that."

"Is he still around?"

"No, he moved to the desert. He knows things about Roswell, New Mexico, that the government has been suppressing. He's going to write a book about it so he's got to be somewhere they can't find him first."

Marquez thanked the old boys and left enough money for yet another round. He walked out into a cold wind, and from his truck he called the Las Vegas police and ran the arson story by a captain he knew there, who as it turned out knew about the fire and the controversy. He gave Marquez the name of an officer in the Henderson PD that he said was a pretty straight-up guy, but he suggested Marquez call the FBI first.

"Why would I want to screw up my operation?"

Heard the laugh on the other side, the understanding, then got the explanation.

"Because there may be an organized crime angle and that's the Feds' turf."

"What kind of organized crime?"

"The new boys in town are Russians, and that was the rumor."

Marquez thanked him and sat in his truck still holding his cell phone before deciding against a cold call to the FBI in Vegas. He was holding the phone when Shauf called. She'd followed Ludovna and another man to a café on old Main Street in Isleton. She sounded angry or disturbed or both.

"Guess who just pulled up, parked, and went inside a café here to meet Ludovna." She didn't wait for his answer. "Raburn is at a table with Ludovna and the running suit. Did he call you and say anything about meeting Ludovna?"

"No."

"They're in there laughing, John. Ludovna is sitting close enough to kiss him. Does that seem right?"

12

When Marquez knocked on Tom Beaudry's door, morning sunlight was high on the rounded hills behind the house. It hadn't been hard to get an address on Beaudry, a little police magic, but looking around at the other houses and the lake across the street it seemed a surprising place to find a guy who'd scratched out a living with a bait shop and a sport boat. When the door opened he saw recognition, brief shock, then a tightening around Beaudry's eyes at the invasion of his privacy.

"I'm retired."

"That's what I heard."

"What are you doing here?"

"You used to help us, so I thought you might again. I've got some photos of people I'd like to run by you."

Beaudry had lost weight. His hair had whitened. His skin, though permanently tanned, had paled as though he no longer spent any time outside.

A woman's voice called from another room, "We have to leave right now, Tom." Then she appeared in the hallway, a large purse hanging off her shoulder. "Who's he?"

Marquez stepped aside as she went past him. He slid photos out of a manila envelope that included several miscellaneous faces, a few with features similar to Raburn's, Ludovna's, and August's. He had a single photo of Anna. Because Beaudry's hands were deformed by arthritis, Marquez held each so he could read them, then moved slowly to the next.

"Well, that's Abe Raburn, the fool. He and his brother were runaways who showed up in Isleton must have been thirty years ago. In those days whether they ate dinner or not depended on how much fish they caught. They told everyone they were eighteen but they couldn't have been more than fifteen and spent half their time hiding out. I know for a fact neither one of them had a legal driver's license until they were in their twenties." He tapped a gnarled finger on Ludovna's face. "This man is a foreigner and a communist, one of the Russians that came over after Reagan finally brought those bastards to their knees. He was out on my boat a couple of times bragging how important he was in Russia."

Marquez showed more photos, including a profile of August taken at fifty feet and not easy to read. Down in the car Beaudry's companion honked the horn twice, leaning on the horn with the last burst.

"No, I don't recognize anyone there."

"How about her?"

In the photo Anna had hair pulled back. She wore sunglasses and a dark blue tank top showing tan shoulders and arms.

"Sure, she worked as a river guide and bartended in Rio Vista at night. Nice girl and cute. You're not going to tell me she's poaching?"

"What I'm wondering is whether you remember ever seeing any of these people together."

"Now her mother was a Russian, wasn't she?" The horn sounded again, this time a longer blast, and Beaudry yelled, "Goddammit, stop that."

Marquez nodded. "Her mother was a Russian who immigrated here. She worked at UC Davis as a scientist. She and Anna lived in the delta."

"You're wondering if I ever saw her with this other Russian?"

"Did you?"

"Not that I can remember, and I can't believe she'd be mixed up with sturgeon poachers. That's what this visit is all about, isn't it?"

"That's right."

"What I remember of her is she loved to be on the water. She worked for one of those guide businesses, but you know that already."

The horn sounded again, and Beaudry touched Marquez's arm. He closed the front door and without a word moved toward the steps, calling back to Marquez after he'd started down.

"I've got to go."

Marquez slid the photos back into the envelope and followed him down the steps. He was surprised how unsteady Beaudry was. When they reached the car Marquez asked his last questions.

"Who'd you sell your business to?"

"A young man whose father I knew very well. The boy isn't made of the same stuff as his father, but I needed the money and I wanted to see him try to make a new start. Sorry I couldn't be of more help to you."

Marquez was still at the top of their driveway as Beaudry and the woman drove away. He knew as he got back in his truck that he was going to call the FBI, and that meant starting with someone he trusted. He found his address book and then the number for Charles Douglas, who as far as he knew was still in the FBI Field Office in San Francisco. He'd worked with Douglas twice before, most recently trying to take down a drug smuggler who'd branched into abalone poaching. But it was the first time he'd worked with Douglas in '98 that had marked him most. That was during an FBI search for a child abductor who was working California coastal towns the SOU knew well.

"Good to hear your voice," Douglas said.

"Likewise. How's your war on terror coming?"

"Until we figure out what the other side really wants it's going to go on a while. But my kids are growing up, and my wife got her law degree."

"Congratulate her for me."

"I will." Douglas let a beat pass. "But you're calling."

"I'm chasing sturgeon poachers, and there was a fellow who used to own a bait shop in Rio Vista named Tom Beaudry. Beaudry had a sister who died in a fire in Henderson, Nevada, and there may have been some question about whether it was a homicide or an accident. I understand the FBI got involved, that the Bureau may have questioned Tom Beaudry about a loan made to him that may have been Russian mob money."

"We call it Eurasian Organized Crime nowadays. EOC."

"That's fine, but the story I heard was that these were Russians."

"And where'd you hear all this?"

"I called a friend."

"Okay, let me ask it a different way, what's this have to do with sturgeon poaching?"

"I'm not sure yet, but we're looking at the guy Beaudry sold his bait shop and boat to. I know it's a long shot that you can help me, Charles."

"It is a long shot, but I'll check for you. No promises, okay? Is this the number to get you at?"

"It is."

Marquez hung up with Douglas and turned the heater on high as he left Berryessa. He still couldn't shake the cold that felt as though it had reached down to his bones. The sun was bright when he reached the valley, and he drove toward the delta on Route 12, running out through the low rolling hills where the B-52s had practiced touch-and-go landings for years, their shadows darkening the sky as they lumbered toward Travis Air Force Base. Douglas called back before he'd crossed through the low hills and reached Rio Vista.

"How long would it take you to get to San Francisco?"

"A little over an hour if I turn around now."

"The head of our Eurasian Organized Crime unit would like to talk with you. Ask for me when you get here."

"See you there."

13

"Do you remember two Lithuanians picked up in Miami trying to sell nuclear weapons and anti-aircraft missiles? There were about forty missiles, and these weren't the handheld fire-and-forget variety either. We think most ended up in Iran. Fortunately, the nuclear deal never went down. This was in 1998."

Ehrmann watched Marquez's face for any reaction, probably wondering whether a Fish and Game officer would track something like that. Douglas had introduced Stan Ehrmann as their local EOC, or Eurasian Organized Crime, expert and Marquez as a warden who'd once swum from a poacher's boat out in the bay and climbed out over the rocks in Sausalito like Godzilla. That while trying to break another poaching ring, and, though he hadn't meant it to, Douglas's telling made Marquez sound ill prepared, just escaping the boat with his life. No doubt Douglas briefed Ehrmann on the SOU and their friendship and what they'd worked on together.

• • • • •

Ehrmann was a tall man, reedy, professorial, not a guy you looked at and thought FBI. But then many of the Eurasian criminals he was chasing didn't fit traditional stereotypes either. Some were Ph.D.s and highly educated.

"We estimate there are two to three hundred of these Eurasian crime groups active in the United States. There is some cooperation and communication with other Russian groups, but not any shared structure. You can't compare them to the Italians. EOC groups are closer to terrorist cells. Some speak their own code within their language, so we have a hard time penetrating with undercover officers. You have to remember there are fifteen republics now where there was once the Soviet Union, and there are many different dialects. In California they're into money laundering, drug trafficking, extortion, identity and credit card theft, car rings, prostitution, murder, and a whole list of other things. Do you remember the five bodies dumped in San Pedro Dam?"

"Sure."

"The word we use is *liquid,* and I don't mean the water in San Pedro. They're very liquid as organizations. They'll put together the group they need for a criminal enterprise and dissolve when they're done. So, who would they need for an illegal caviar business?"

"A network of fishermen and a way to broker the fish, transport it, and with caviar the means to produce caviar from roe, package and ship it. The people selling may or may not know what's going on."

"Are any Russian immigrants suspects?"

"We're looking at a Nikolai Ludovna."

"I've heard his name before." Ehrmann wrote Ludovna's name down. "Let me see what I can find out." Now he cleared his throat and got to it. "The Bureau investigated a fire resulting in the death of a woman named Sally Beaudry. Arson investigators determined it was deliberately set, and we got involved because we had her brother, Tom Beaudry, on tape with known associates of Russian organized crime trying to arrange a loan to pay gambling debts. We had a possible motive for killing his sister in that he was beneficiary on her life insurance policy. The payout would have more than cleared those debts.

"He was in the habit of visiting his sister and gambling after she'd gone to bed. He'd fly down from here, stay with her, and drive into Vegas at night. What I think happened, and this can't leave this room, is Beaudry backed out of a loan with the Russians and somehow they became aware of the life insurance policy. Maybe he told them she was sick and to wait a couple of years for their money. I hate to think he did, but whether they hacked it or he told them, they figured out it made more sense to keep him alive and collect when she died."

"I'm sure you sweated Beaudry."

"Like sweating a small hard stone. He's also got a lot of opinions about the government. He'd built up a debt he couldn't service running his boat as a cash business and skimming the profits. The bait shop didn't make any money, and he'd maxed out his credit cards. The sister had disability payments and a little bit of a retirement stipend, so he couldn't go to her, and he sure as hell couldn't go to a bank. He had to go to a unique lender and start negotiating, except that he wasn't in a position to negotiate.

They reached terms, but then he backed out of the loan, and we think he realized they were going to end up owning his business in short order."

"You got this through wiretaps?"

Ehrmann nodded and continued.

"About two weeks later the fire kills Sally Beaudry. When the insurance company balked at paying, he hired a lawyer and fought them. In the end he got paid most of the policy value, and the Russians stopped looking for him soon after."

"Have you ever looked at the guy who bought the bait shop and boat?"

"No. Give me his name."

Marquez watched him write down Richie Crey. He wrote it without hesitating. He wrote like he didn't have any question about how Crey was spelled.

"It's possible," Ehrmann said, "that organized crime fronted Crey the money to buy out Beaudry. They may have told Beaudry what the price would be as part of the whole package of getting forgiven on his late debt payment. You'd have to tell me that sturgeon poaching is worth the effort, if that's what you're saying they'd want the business to front for."

"Over time it could be worth it. Crey's an ex-con, and I've talked to a few people who wonder where he got the money to buy. There's also a rumor Beaudry sold too cheaply."

"A connection may have been made with Crey in prison. That happens. These deals have a way of getting complicated."

Now Ehrmann glanced at his watch. He leaned forward and faced Marquez.

"We're eighteen months into an investigation of a Ukrainian group operating along the West Coast. One of the locations we've had under surveillance is in Sacramento. We believe there's some possibility of overlap with your sturgeon poaching investigation."

"Are you telling me we're tracking one or more of the same people?"

"No, and unfortunately I can't talk much about our investigation. I have to leave things vague today, and I'm sorry about that. But if there's an overlap we don't want any confusion. I'm going to give you a phone number for me and would appreciate one in return that I can always reach you at."

"Where would we overlap?"

"I can't do this with you, Lieutenant. I'm sorry, I wish I could." Ehrmann's gaze went to Douglas. It was about to end. They'd called him in to put him on notice, and about everything else he could draw his own conclusions. "I hope this conversation has cleared up some of your questions."

Ehrmann walked out, and it was just Douglas and him again.

"What's the bottom line here?" Marquez asked.

"You may get backed off of whatever you're doing in a hurry. He wanted your phone number so that all he has to do is call you and say quit. They've got a lot of time into the investigation he's talking about, and they're close to a bust."

Marquez stood, and they looked at each other for a few seconds. He'd been sucker pitched with a promise of information about Beaudry, but either way they would have communicated the possible overlap, the blue-on-blue problem. In which case whatever they were doing always superseded any other agency or department. That's what it meant to be top dog.

"Remind me never to call here again."

Douglas laughed. "Good to see you. We've got to get together. How are Katherine and Maria?"

"Back east looking at colleges."

"That's where she wants to go?"

"She doesn't know."

"But her mom has an idea."

"That's about right." He looked at Douglas again before leaving. "How close are they with their investigation?"

"They don't tell me anything. Call me and let's get the families together."

14

Raburn had cleaned the sturgeon and bedded it on ice in the pickup. He had a special refrigerator set to twenty-nine degrees Fahrenheit, the temperature Ludovna wanted caviar stored at, so he didn't get the cooler out until Marquez arrived. It wasn't until they got on the road that Marquez smelled whiskey.

"Do you always get lit up before you go see Ludovna?"

"I had a couple of drinks waiting around for you."

"Might be a good night to have a clear head."

"Look, if I wanted someone to nag me I would have gotten married."

"Why don't you pull over and I'll drive."

Marquez ground the old pickup into gear. At Sacramento Fresh Fish they drove around back to the loading bay. The white BMW was there. Raburn used his cell phone instead of knocking on the door. A rolling door slowly rose after he hung up. An employee wearing a butcher's apron waited on the other side and didn't do much more than grunt as he helped unload the sturgeon. When Ludovna walked in he was wearing a dark blue suit and looked like he was on his way to a wedding. Cologne mixed with the smell of fish, and he was careful with his shoes as he walked through the shop.

"This is my friend I told you about," Raburn said, and Ludovna looked at Marquez without saying anything. He pulled his suit coat back so it didn't brush against the stainless-steel table and the fish they'd unloaded. He leaned over to smell the sturgeon.

"It's old," he said.

"No, it's not," Marquez answered, giving it back to him, reading him as a bully.

"Who the fuck are you again?"

"John Croft, and it's great to meet you. Sorry we're late. The fish was on ice as soon as it came out of the water. Then it was in Abe's freezer."

"Are you going to tell me I don't know fish?"

"I don't know anything about you, so I don't know what you know or don't know. But I know about this sturgeon."

"Yeah, yeah, you know about this sturgeon." He stared hard at Marquez. "Where's the caviar?"

The cooler was behind the seats in the pickup, and Raburn went to get it. He carried it in and put the cooler down on a stainless-steel counter, opened it, removed the bowl with the caviar, and peeled back the Glad wrap. Ludovna dipped a finger in the eggs.

"Tastes like mold, like shit."

"Let's just load it back in the truck," Marquez said to Raburn, saying it evenly, meaning to disrupt the show here. "I don't need this tonight. I've got plenty of people I can sell to."

He didn't wait for an answer from Raburn and picked up the bowl and resettled it in the cooler before starting toward Raburn's old Ford.

"Stop the fuck where you are and bring it back."

When he turned, Marquez saw Ludovna pointing a finger at him, and Nike Man with a gun showing but still tucked in his waist. Meanwhile the employee lowered the rolling door. Marquez set the cooler down on the concrete, and Ludovna registered that but turned to Raburn.

"You're a drunk and you're stupid. You think you can fool me, but I have a dog smarter than you. You don't deserve anything, but I'm going to pay some money tonight. I'm going to give you half, then you leave, and if this happens again then we never do any more business."

Marquez looked to his left at the big sinks they rinsed fish in, drains that could handle fish guts. He looked at the small amount of money on the table representing all the sturgeon species was worth tonight, looked at the men who were destroying it, and crossed to where the money lay on the stainless-steel counter. He picked up four one-hundred-dollar bills, clean new notes Ludovna had counted out. One bill fluttered to the floor.

"Pick it up," Ludovna said. "You take two bills and leave the rest. Pick the one you dropped up."

Marquez picked up the bill off the floor and laid it on top of the other three, then walked back over to the cooler, everyone watching as he carried the cooler to one of the big sinks and sloshed eight pounds of caviar into the sink. Repackaged as Caspian beluga in two-ounce jars it might have brought fifteen thousand dollars. He swiveled the spigot, the water gushed, and a stream of gray eggs flowed toward the drain. They rolled and swirled in the water and sucked down the drain as Ludovna yelled and Nike Man pulled his gun.

"Keep your money. We'll take the sturgeon home with us, too."

Marquez swept the eggs with his hand and washed another pound down the drain, the water a torrent getting the upper hand now. Soon the sink would be clean. Eggs popped against his palm. Ludovna crossed to him, saw the last go down the drain, and drove an open palm into Marquez's shoulder, pushing him back. His face was dark red. A shine had started on his forehead, and Nike Man held the gun with both hands, aimed at Marquez's head.

"What the fuck did you just do?"

"We're not selling anymore. You didn't like my caviar, so I threw it out. I'm the one taking the loss, so tell your goon to put his gun down."

"He'll shoot you and we'll feed you down the drains."

Ludovna said something in Russian, and the goon racked the slide. Marquez froze, his wet hands flat on the stainless-steel table. "You fuck," Ludovna said. "You make one step and he's going to kill you. Put your head in the sink. I'll wash your blood down the drain, you fuck."

"I don't cheat people. I don't sell bad product, but how good did you expect it to be this time of year?"

Ludovna turned abruptly to Raburn.

"I should kill you both." Then to Nike Man, "Search him, and if he moves, shoot him."

Nike Man checked him for a wire, doing it quickly and efficiently from behind. Ludovna waited until that was done.

"The caviar was moldy."

Marquez gauged the change in Ludovna.

"It wasn't the best," Marquez agreed.

"It's shit."

"I did the best I could with it."

"It's still shit."

Ludovna moved over close to him. He was close enough that Marquez could feel his breath and smell the cologne again.

"You keep two hundred dollars tonight."

"I don't want any money, and you can keep the sturgeon. It was all a mistake. It was a mistake asking Abe if he knew anyone who'd be interested in doing business long term. I'm interested in a relationship. I want someone I can call without a lot of complication when I have a fish to sell."

Ludovna smiled, repeated Marquez's words, making them sound weak. "A relationship." He put a hand on Marquez's shoulder and squeezed too hard. "That's what you want, a relationship. Okay, next time we'll have a drink together. You come to my house." His voice changed, was quieter. "You want to do business with me, then I have to know who you are, okay?" He massaged Marquez's shoulder, rubbing the skin between his fingers. "You come to my house."

"Sure."

"You get another fish and you call me."

"All right."

"When you come to my house you come alone."

Marquez nodded. Ludovna continued to stare at him, his breath on Marquez's face. Then he stepped back. He insisted Marquez keep two hundred dollars. He smiled and patted Raburn on the back, and all the problems were over.

15

Marquez rented a room at Lisa's that night. She had four rooms side by side up the road from the marina building. He parked his truck where he could see it from the window and brought his gear in. The confrontation with Ludovna had taken something out of him and left him tired. The main marina building was down the road a hundred yards, and he could see part of the roof and a corner of the deck. The lights were off in the bar, or he might have walked down and sat for a little while. He was hungry, but that could wait too.

The door squeaked as he unlocked it and went in. He put his gear bag down, showered, and lay on the narrow bed. The foam mattress wasn't much, but it was enough tonight. He lay on his back looking out on the darkness, thinking about what had happened, and then about Katherine and Maria, wondering how the trip was going. Katherine wouldn't mind the SOU coming to an end. She might even buy a bottle of champagne to celebrate. His head turned with images of the confrontation with Ludovna, Nike Man racking the slide. Before falling asleep he decided he'd bring some gifts when he visited Ludovna next. The guy's anger was mercurial, but he could probably get through to him. He did not remember falling asleep, but his cell phone woke him at 2:15.

"Hold for a second," he said, found his pants, his coat, and walked out barefoot to his truck. It was Selke.

"Where are you, Marquez?"

"At Lisa's Marina."

"You're not far from us. We're around the back side of Dead Horse Island. You'll see the lights and the vehicles."

"What's there?"

"The body of a woman. The body isn't in good shape, but I want you to take a look at her."

Selke's voice seemed to come at him from a distance. He'd talked himself into believing she hadn't been abducted. He packed his gear, swung the small pack onto his shoulder, and the neighbor's fist hammered the shared wall as Marquez tried to get the door lock to work. A man's muffled swearing carried into the night, and Marquez didn't turn his headlights on until he got up to the main road.

He drove through thick fog, overshot the slough, had to backtrack, and now he drove out the dirt road on the levee above the slough. He saw the lights up ahead, counted eight vehicles and a coroner's van. A deputy stepped out and blocked the road as he got close.

"Selke's up there," the deputy said. "You'll see him."

"When did they find the body?"

"I heard there was a tip or something a couple of days ago, and one of the detectives drove out here this afternoon and saw where the riverbank was torn up, so they got a diver out and he found the refrigerator after dark."

A small crane had been brought in, and as Marquez parked and walked up, the crane operator was leaving. The road was lit with klieg lights, and the light reflected brightly off the fog. A sheet of thick clear plastic had been unfolded on the dirt road, and a white household refrigerator lay on its back, door open in the middle of the plastic, the effect almost comical. Selke stood with a group of men near it but not too close, as a county photographer worked his way around it.

If it was Anna, Marquez wasn't ready yet and looked from the men back to the refrigerator, then stopped. The open door of the refrigerator made him think of a coffin. He made out the darker color of the body inside. He listened to the men talking and the hum of the klieg lights and a sound in his head like ocean waves breaking on a shoreline.

When he started forward he saw metal banding, the type used to bind pallets or a load of lumber, and guessed that the refrigerator had been banded shut when they craned it out. He didn't want anyone to tell him or talk to him yet. He acknowledged Selke and lifted a hand to let Selke know to hang on another minute. He didn't understand the camaraderie of detectives. He just wanted to look and if it was her, take it in alone. Selke walked over.

"Take your time," Selke said. "No hurry. Her face is so badly damaged you won't recognize anything, but there are other identifying marks you may be able to help with." He added quietly. "I hear you've seen bodies before."

"Who told you that?"

"I don't remember."

"No one I talk to seems to remember anything. How was she found?"

"A couple of fishermen who haunt this stretch for catfish snagged on the box and knew it hadn't been there long. One of them is a diver, and since they didn't like what it was doing to their trolling he went down for a look. He saw the bands and of course he knew about Burdovsky being missing, so because of the bands we came out. We figured with the banding it was more than the old tradition of throwing old appliances in the river."

"Do you believe these two men?"

"I had the same reaction, but we're talking about some fifty-something guys that everyone around here knows. The one who went in the water was a Navy diver in Nam. He's kept on diving so it was no big deal for him to go in. Neither one of them has any money." Selke looked at him. "You ready?"

Marquez's legs felt weighted, and from the way Selke held himself he knew Selke believed it might be Anna. As he followed Selke, he felt like he was floating away from his body and looking down into the refrigerator cavity from a height where he saw her folded, head tucked to her knees, lying on her side. The black hose of a small pump curled over the refrigerator, and he realized they'd drained the water and saved it. Her hands were shrunken, gray and curled like bird's claws, her face destroyed, nose and eyes gone, a knife taken to her cheeks and lips. Someone had started to scalp her, then stopped. Part of her scalp and hair lay to one side, the hair wet and twisted like something cleaned from a drain. There was no face to identify, but Selke pointed at a small tattoo on the back of her neck.

"That would have been up under the hairline," Selke said.

"I don't remember seeing a tattoo there on Anna."

"What about a little tattoo on her right breast?"

Marquez looked at the breast tattoo, a butterfly, shook his head. "Never saw this part of Anna." He felt a need to touch her, and Selke stopped him. He couldn't shake the sense of being outside himself, his shock at the brutality, but he didn't know if the body was Anna Burdovsky's. He backed away, walked down the road away from the group with Selke, listening to him recount again how they found her, as if in the retelling a truth would reveal itself.

"If you had to guess," Selke asked.

"I'd guess it's not her. Shoulders don't seem right. The body is heavier."

"I can tell you've seen this kind of thing before."

Marquez nodded. "Cartel wars," he said. "Yeah, I saw some bad stuff when I was DEA."

More than enough for a lifetime. Enough to where he'd lost his tolerance for it, and he knew Selke was probing for more than that reason. Selke had wanted him to see the body just to watch his reaction. He had wanted to point out the breast tattoo and gauge Marquez's face. The guy was pure detective.

"Can you see someone doing this to her over sturgeon poaching?"

He wasn't sure he needed to answer. The young woman was badly mutilated, and that was more than hiding her identity. It was rage, and Selke knew that better than he did.

"No, I can't. It looks to me like they quit when their anger got spent."

Selke just nodded, left it at that. They walked toward Marquez's truck.

"I've got something for you as long as you'll scan the photos and email them to me. We found these in Burdovsky's Sacramento apartment."

Marquez got in his truck and got out the evidence bag. He unfolded it and got out the passport and photos, told Selke about his meeting with the FBI and the possibility they could help him with Burdovsky. He gave Selke Stan Ehrmann's name but not the phone number Ehrmann had given him. Selke could start with the duty officer, and Marquez didn't doubt Ehrmann would talk to him.

"Ehrmann is very interested in Russian immigrants. He'll call you back."

An hour later Marquez helped get the corpse out of the refrigerator. They slid her into a body bag, and the refrigerator got loaded onto a truck, and the police vehicles left one at a time, Selke last and slowing alongside Marquez's truck, asking him why he was still here.

Marquez stayed until dawn. He slept a few hours in his truck. When the sun rose he looked at the ruts on the slough embankment the refrigerator had made sliding down the steep slope. It wouldn't take Selke long to find out what kind of banding tool was used, who made it, and where the bands came from. Then he'd find out who sold it, and they'd trace the refrigerator back. They'd be able to say how she died and how long she'd been dead. But the kind of mind that butchered a face that way, you couldn't find the answer for that anywhere.

He knew it wasn't Anna but felt a need to prepare for the possibility it was. He thought of August's coming in and sitting for a videotaped interview, no lawyer, combative and unconcerned.

August had no problem admitting she'd stayed at his apartment, even suggested she was lovesick and that Selke "dredge the river." Whatever the sarcastic comment had been about Anna drowning herself. Marquez turned these things in his head as he watched morning light come to the slough. The water was very calm and dark green. He watched a mallard fly the length of the slough. It was clear and cold, and he stood on the bank and watched another duck go past before walking to his truck. It was unlikely, he thought, that in the history of the world there had ever been a species crueler than his own.

16

"It's cold," Katherine said.

"Where are you?"

"In Vermont looking at Middlebury College."

The way she said it made it sound like that wasn't necessarily fun. Maybe it was the cold.

"How are the roads?"

"Oh, they're fine. It was snowing this morning but it's stopped. White sky, cold wind, it all makes me remember why I moved to California. I was hoping she'd like Middlebury, but it's the wrong time of year."

"What has she liked most so far?"

"Shopping in Boston."

"What about you, Kath? How are you?"

"I've been better. Maria is in looking at the library, then we're going to get lunch in town."

"And then north to Colby?"

He'd memorized their circuit, or thought he had.

"South." There was too long a pause before Katherine said, "We're headed to Vassar."

"I don't remember Vassar on the list."

"It wasn't, but now that she's told me what she told you a month ago we're abbreviating the trip." This was the quiet moment where he knew he was supposed to explain, but his heart wasn't in it. "You don't have to explain," Katherine said. "I know she asked you not to say anything, so I understand."

"But your feelings are hurt."

"Wouldn't yours be?"

He looked at the dark almost black line of Mount Diablo and the high concrete curve of the Antioch Bridge, the three-bladed white windmills with the dark blue sky beyond them. His feelings probably would be hurt, but it was still Maria's to explain, not his. He'd respected her wish not to say anything, and Maria had procrastinated. You kept your word to Maria, he thought. Let her take her own heat; she's old enough.

"Oh, she's told me some things," Katherine said. "Like she's not going to college next year and we're wasting our time on this trip. She wants to live with her two friends in the city, keep working at Presto, and go clubbing every night. How much trigonometry do you think she'll remember after a year of clubbing, excuse me, after taking a year off to recover from the rigors of high school? I raised a kid who is so selfish she thinks she's doing me a favor to come back here. I would have given anything to have what I can give her. Why did she wait to tell me?"

"I don't think she knows her own mind yet, Kath."

"Well, she's not going to spend next year screwing around in San Francisco. What's life going to do to her if she can't handle high school and needs a break to recover? I need you to help me bring her around, and I don't understand why you're defending this idea of hers."

"I'm not defending anything, but Maria is seventeen going on eighteen, and the days when we can tell her what to do are almost over."

"So is she going to start paying her way?"

"You can't make her want to go to college."

"No, I really can't, and now I'm wondering if she even sent all her applications. I didn't read her essays. Did you?"

"If she said she sent them in, she did."

"Here she comes. I'll call you later."

She hung up, and he drove, thinking about how he might help close the rift between Kath and Maria. He had interrupted several of the fights and tried to mediate and had heard about the worst ones when he wasn't there. Maria was as stubborn as her mother, and each time she got punished she came back harder, and yet she continued working for Katherine at Presto on Union, rather than try to find a different job.

When he hung up with Katherine he returned a call from Ruax, and she was cheerful this morning.

"I've got a fish for you," she said. "You're becoming quite the dealer."

"Any roe?"

"I can't promise roe."

"It's got to be fresh or I won't take it."

She chuckled, and they picked a spot to transfer the sturgeon to his truck later that morning. He called Richie Crey.

"Do you want it? It's just out of the water."

"Okay, guy, let's give it a go. Let me tell you where to take it. Guys that work for me will be at the house when you get there. It's not far from my shop. You take it there. They'll know what to do."

Marquez picked up the fish from Ruax and drove over the bridge to Rio Vista. He planned to cut through these two front men and sell directly to Crey. In their remaining three weeks they were going after Crey, Ludovna, and August, and they'd need to deal face-to-face with Crey to generate enough evidence to build a case the DA would accept. Now he circled the block once. He parked and knocked twice before a man opened the door.

"I'm looking for Lou Perry."

"That's me. Are you the guy with the fish eggs?"

Marquez nodded and saw a second man on the sofa watching TV. Stale air flowed from inside, bad breath, dust, the sweet smell of dope.

"What's your name, Mr. Fish Eggs?"

"John. What's yours, sport?"

"Lou."

Marquez smiled as though the name Lou was funny sounding. He wanted to make it clear early on that they weren't going to be friends.

"Okay, where are the eggs?"

"They're in my truck with the fish. They come as a package."

The guy didn't get it, took it as a straight line, said, "Back into the garage."

A beat-up gold-colored Le Mans sat out in front of the house. It was rusted down along the base of the doors, and the ass end was humped from a rear-ender and sloppily sprayed with primer. It looked more like it had been tagged than painted. Someone had also done a hand job painting black stripes on the hood, and Marquez figured it could be either of the two men inside.

After the garage door went up, the second man drifted in, and Marquez got his name. Liam Torp. He offered his hand for Marquez to shake. Everybody was a businessman this morning. This was the business of trying to get a sturgeon deal done without missing too much of the show on TV that Torp had been watching.

"Is it worth the hassle, man?" Perry asked, face serious, doing his own risk/reward analysis.

"Is what worth the hassle?"

"Dealing sturgeon and fish eggs."

"Sometimes it's worth it."

"Yeah? What kind of money can you make? Maybe I'll get into it."

"It's messy. You deal with a lot of fish guts, and you've got to watch out for the Gamers all the time."

"Richie says there aren't that many of them."

"Well, he ought to know. He's your boss, right?"

Marquez had the cooler top taped down with duct tape. He peeled that off and showed them the eggs. Explained how to make caviar and answered more questions. It was like conducting a seminar. He looked at Perry, deciding that insulting him might be the easiest way to get rid of him.

"We'll trade you some weed for your eggs," Perry said.

"No, you won't."

"You don't have to smoke it, man. You sell the weed, you'll make more than you'd make the other way. Want to take a look at it? You're welcome to a hit." He turned to Torp. "Where's that stub you had earlier?"

"Look, I just want to get paid and take off."

"At least take a look."

"What's up with you guys? Does Crey know you're offering this trade?"

Perry had a red birthmark along the back of his neck. His wiry friend, Torp, needed a change of clothes and had a way about him that bothered Marquez. In fact, they both annoyed him. Now, after standing around watching and saying nothing, Torp suddenly felt like he had to lower the garage door. Shauf and Roberts had been videotaping, and the lowering ended that.

"What are you doing, I've got to get my truck out. Open the door again."

"Chill, man," Perry said. "We just want to show you the weed. Wait here a minute." He came back with a bag of weed. "Put your nose to it. If you don't like what you smell we'll shut up."

"Then I don't like it."

"Smell it."

"I'm not interested."

"You'll make more money selling the weed."

"You're the dope dealers; I sell fish." Marquez figured that either they were comfortable enough with Crey to screw around with his deal or Crey said check him out, push him a little, see what happens. "How about you call Crey and tell him we're done and I'm ready to get paid?"

Perry got a hold of Crey on his cell, cradling the cell with his chin, a couple of days' growth of whiskers holding the phone in place. He described the eggs, tasted them when Crey told him to. When he hung up he said, "He'll pay you when he sees you."

"You're kidding me, after all this you guys don't have the money?"

"Hey, you could have had the dope."

They gave him the address of a bar on Main Street where Crey would meet him, and Marquez talked with Shauf before going into the bar.

"I've got to cut this pair out of the picture."

"They just got into an old Le Mans out on the street."

"Run the car, let's find out what we can about them."

Marquez was inside the bar on Main Street, waiting for Crey to show up. The bar was empty, no daylight drinkers yet, the bartender glancing up at the light flooding in from outside but not really paying Marquez any attention, maybe registering a big man occupying a stool at the far end. Then Perry and Torp came in the door. Perry waved at him and started toward him. They took stools next to him on either side. Perry drummed on the bar to get the bartender's attention.

"We got to thinking since you're the man with all the money this morning, maybe you should buy a round," Perry said.

"I guess that means there aren't any more cartoons on TV."

Perry leaned over the bar, looking past Marquez at his friend. "Hey, Fishman made a joke," he said. Then more seriously to Marquez, "Liam doesn't like people laughing at him."

"Who does?"

When Crey arrived he stopped to say hello to the bartender as though he'd just returned to his office and wanted to know what had happened while he was out. Torp oozed off the seat next to Marquez, and Crey took it. He slid a hand onto Marquez's thigh.

"I'm not feeling you up. Reach down, I've got something for you."

"Better not be pills or dope." Marquez reached down, felt the money, and said, "This is a lot of work for one fish."

Roberts walked in, took a seat at the far end of the bar near the door, and ordered before they did. Crey's team studied her, Perry, on Marquez's left, immediately saying, "I'd do her."

The bartender came over, took drink orders, Marquez asking for a Coke, saying he'd drunk too much last night. Marquez laid one of the hundred-dollar bills on the bar top.

On his left Perry said, "A Coke? That's pussy-assed, man," and ordered himself a draft beer and a vodka chaser. The hundred-dollar bill got broken and change spread in front of Marquez like a poker hand, the bartender fanning out the twenties. Marquez talked fishing with Crey and watched Perry down the vodka, get up from his stool, move halfway down the bar, and summon the bartender. The bartender drew four more drafts and carried one over and put it in front of Roberts, who already had something to drink. The other three he brought to their end and asked Marquez if he wanted a refill on the Coke. Marquez shook his head, turned to Crey.

"This is disrespect. What's this little greaseball doing ordering drinks for himself and his friend with my money?"

"Next time they'll buy."

Perry lifted his glass to Roberts. She lifted hers, acknowledging the gesture but not touching the beer.

"I'm out of here," Marquez said, "and these guys need to apply for welfare. I can keep the sturgeon coming, but I can't deal with these losers."

Torp heard that, though Perry didn't because he was down the bar, trying to hit on Roberts.

"Don't go yet," Crey said. "Let's you and me talk a little more."

Whatever Roberts said, Perry didn't like. He came back a few minutes later and leaned on the bar near his stool, looking past Marquez and Crey at his friend Torp. He looked angry.

"I'm not good enough for the bitch," he said to no one in particular, though Marquez answered him, saying, "Makes sense to me," and then turning back to Crey. "It depends on the bite, but with the storms forecast it could be good fishing this next week."

They negotiated some more, but it all felt lowlife. Roberts got up to leave before they did, and before she reached the door Perry was off his stool. He reached around and tapped his friend on the shoulder.

"We're going too," he said, "catch you later, bro," to Crey.

"Those two are going to end up back inside," Crey said as the pair went through the door.

"Whatever. But either way I don't want them around when I deal with you. They stick out too much."

Crey looked into his drink, thinking it over, then agreed, "They've got some rough edges. But how polished do they have to be to hump a fish around?"

"They're the wrong type of guys. What were they in for?"

"Perry for robbery and Torp did time for rape, only it was a lot worse than what they were able to pin on him, and there were others they didn't get him for. Problem is I owe Perry, and he's trying to get back on his feet."

"He tried to trade me dope for the sturgeon. Did you tell him to do that?"

Crey didn't answer, and his eyes kind of glazed over. It told Marquez that Crey had known the offer to trade would get made. He could read the pores on Crey's nose, see every mark on his face, but couldn't read much in his eyes, and the feeling came out of nowhere, that he wouldn't miss having to deal with guys like this.

They finished their drinks now and walked out into daylight.

"I did four years and I'm not going back inside," Crey said. "You want to know about me, that's all you need to know. If I've got to use some help like Lou and Liam, that's what I've got to do then. The boys aren't so bad. I know Torp has got some problems, but sometimes I need their lifting power. And they can deliver shit. All they have to do is drive a car, right? You don't have to talk to them." He saw he wasn't getting anywhere with Marquez and added, "I can handle a sturgeon a day if you can do it."

"Why not live straight? You've got your sport fishing business and the bait shop. Why risk it all?"

"Kind of funny of you to ask that."

"Yeah, well, we're talking straight, so I'm asking."

"The answer is I've got some other obligations."

Marquez nodded and saw Crey was tracking the Le Mans, which was heading toward the bridge.

"Look at them," Crey said. "They're trying to follow her home, and you can bet they'll go back there some night. That's about the only way either one of them can get close to a woman." He picked at something on a tooth, adding, "I swear to God sometimes I wish I could just start all over."

17

"The Le Mans is registered to a Sherri La Belle. Stockton address," Shauf said, and then read off the address to Marquez. "They're still on her."

Roberts cut in. "They're on me, and they're not doing a bad job of it. They're staying with me, Lieutenant."

"What's your location?"

"Just passing the Ryde Hotel, coming up that side of the river. They're hanging back about a third of a mile."

The pink art deco hotel with the water tower behind it was a straight run up that side of the river. If they stayed behind her they'd be very visible and easy to track.

"Let's try to turn it around on them and see what we learn. How are you doing for gas?"

"I'm good for a couple hundred miles."

"Okay, stay on that side of the river, and let's see if they follow you into Sacramento. Then let's get them out on the freeway and get photos of each of them and the car, and meanwhile we'll run them through NCIC. We can ask the CHP for help."

Shauf fell in behind the Le Mans. Marquez talked to a highway patrol dispatcher and told her two suspects were trailing one of their wardens.

"We want to slow them down while our officer loses them. Can we get a CHP unit to come off an overpass and run alongside them?"

Perry and Torp wouldn't chase with a CHP unit alongside them, and Roberts could hit it hard and put some distance between herself and this pair that Crey called "his boys." Shauf would sit on their tail and turn it around on them. It was a twist to the afternoon no one had figured on, but at least a deal had gotten done with Crey, and more would follow. That there was friction between Marquez and Torp and Perry might ultimately build some credibility with Crey. It wouldn't look so much like he was trying to ingratiate himself. Marquez went back and forth with both the CHP dispatch and Roberts. She continued up the river road, chatting now about the Rio Vista bar.

"What did Perry say to you?" he asked her.

"That he was the gentleman who'd sent the beer."

"Did he tell you I was the gentleman who paid for it?"

"No, because I told him I hadn't noticed any gentlemen in the room."

"Come on, how can you say that? You must have seen me down there."

She laughed, and he liked hearing her. The last cutback, the one that took out Roberts and Alvarez, had been the worst.

They used to have a pretty good time together even on the long surveillances.

"Now he wants to go home with you."

"Yeah, lucky me."

But nothing about them trailing her was funny. Roberts worked her way through the outskirts of Sacramento, and they were quieter because the opportunity was there for Torp and Perry to catch up. She moved into a part of town with more traffic and stoplights, and they got ready in case the Le Mans closed on her. But other than race lights a couple of times to avoid losing her, Torp and Perry hung back. When Roberts turned onto 80 eastbound toward Reno, the heavy Le Mans swung onto the on-ramp behind her, its engine a deep roar as it accelerated onto the freeway.

"Take the Roseville exit," Marquez said.

"Roger, that."

Half an hour later Roberts did a slow figure eight through a large shopping center off the freeway in Roseville. She stopped briefly, went into a store while the Le Mans idled in the lot, waiting. Then she got back on the freeway and ran it up to eighty-five as the CHP unit dropped down alongside the Le Mans. Torp and Perry kept glancing over at the CHP officer, waiting for him to go ticket her, but the officer just rode alongside them, his sunglassed eyes turning from time to time to return their stares. Eventually, they slowed even more to get away from him. When they did that they had to let Roberts go.

In Sacramento Roberts switched vehicles, then caught up to Shauf, who was with the Le Mans at a Sacramento McDonald's, watching Perry and Torp eat in their car in the McDonald's lot.

"You're on your own with them," Marquez said, "I'm going to stop in at Lisa's Marina and see if I can find her."

He figured Selke had already blown his cover with the owner of Lisa's Marina, so why not come clean with her and find out if she saw anything? If Anna's vanishing act was schemed, then she would have needed to know he was at Lisa's before going forward with it. That had caused him to wonder about the fishermen who'd been at the bar that night.

When he walked into the marina bar it was empty. The tall windows looked out across the river, and this part of the building was one story with a high ceiling. But there was a second story that covered half of the building and held Lisa's office and apartment. He thought about calling from the bottom of the stairs, then spotted her out on the deck.

"Hi," she said, "Sorry to keep you waiting. I was cleaning. Do you need a room tonight?"

"No, I'm here to talk to you, Lisa, if you have a few minutes."

She brushed a strand of hair back from her forehead.

"I wondered when you'd come explain, or whether you ever would. The detective came by and asked a lot of questions about you and the woman they've been searching for. I haven't been able to sleep through a night since that happened. I think about Anna all the time."

"You know her?"

"Sure, it's the delta. There aren't that many of us."

"She's probably fine."

"That's what the detective said. He thinks she faked it. But why would she do that?"

"Do you have time to sit down?"

They took a table out on the deck, and it was warm in the sun. The mention of Selke's name conjured the body last night, an image he pushed away when Lisa asked if he wanted coffee. Now he watched her come back outside with two coffee mugs. She had rose spots on her cheeks from cleaning the rooms. She had a wisp of hair that kept falling over her forehead and she kept pushing it back.

"Sometimes at night I just like to sit here and listen to the river," she said. "I've been here twelve years this coming March. I moved here from Florida after my husband died in a boating accident."

"Is he the one in the photos on the wall inside?"

"He's the one driving the boat."

Marquez knew she'd been a waterskiing star in Sarasota, Florida, when she was younger. Photos of her cutting through slalom courses, trick ski shots, and jumps were framed and on the walls outside the restrooms near the pay phone.

She took a sip of coffee. "So you're not a research biologist."

"No, I run an undercover team for California Fish and Game called the Special Operations Unit. Our mission is to stop the commercialization of wildlife. Right now we're working a sturgeon poaching operation. Anna was working as an informant for us."

She moved the strand of hair off her forehead again.

"What's your real name?" she asked.

"John Marquez."

"So it is John."

"Yes."

"Is Marquez Spanish?"

"My grandfather came here from Barcelona. My grandmother was English. They met in San Francisco."

Undoubtedly, she had Selke's voice in her head and was evaluating him as they talked, wondering about the things Selke had asked her. When she finished with questions about him, he brought out his mug shots and photos. He reconstructed Friday night, the three men sitting at the bar while he was outside on the deck with a beer. When she couldn't tell him much about the fishermen he brought out photos of August, Crey, and Ludovna. She picked up Ludovna's photo, black-and-white, grainy.

"He's been here, though not in a while. He drives a white BMW, or a friend of his does. I remember that because I've always wanted one of those." She tapped August's face. "I don't know about him." Her expression changed, remembering something, a fingernail moving to Ludovna's face. "This guy I think is a Russian immigrant. He said he was going to buy the marina from me, give me a big price, but he was drunk that night."

"What would he do with it?"

She laughed, moved the strand of hair off her forehead again. "Lose money, I guess. Sit up nights trying to figure out how to get people to come here. Give free power and water to the boats that stop to use the bathrooms, but I'm whining."

"Would you sell?"

"At the right price."

"Did he know that?"

"No, I don't have anyone to talk to, and I don't gossip at the bar, but I was born in the Keys and I miss Florida. I'm ready to move back." She seemed to feel she owed some further explanation.

"I was towing my husband waterskiing, and he hit a piece of waterlogged lumber that was submerged." He saw her take a breath. "It broke his leg and the bone severed the femoral artery. He died before we got to shore, and I just couldn't stay in Florida after that." She touched Ludovna's face again, almost tenderly. "He is Russian, isn't he?"

"Yes, but he became a U.S. citizen in '97."

"And I know Richie Crey," she said. "I mean, there aren't that many people in business in the delta. He brings his sport boat here sometimes, you know, with the fishermen. I'm supposed to let him drink for free in return, but he sure can run up a bar tab. Sometimes it works out for me, but Richie can drink a lot. He's still got problems. He's not real happy, sort of like a big kid with tattoos and a record. It's like he can never get away from some types of people he shouldn't associate with anymore. But this guy, the Russian, scares me. I don't mean he scares me like I'm afraid he would do something to me, but there's something cruel about him. He kind of looks right through you."

"Looks through you?"

"I mean it."

Marquez nodded. "Lisa, I want to give you a number to call me at if any of these men come back here."

"Then, what? What are you going to do if I call you?"

"We're just trying to put some pieces together and keep track of them."

"Is Richie getting in trouble again?"

"He's trying to."

"That's too bad. I'm not surprised, but it's too bad."

Marquez thanked her for the coffee and told her he'd be back to stay soon. He talked with Shauf and Roberts as he drove away, checked in to see where they were at with Torp and Perry.

"They're in about the seediest bar in south Sacramento," Shauf said. "So maybe they're on their way home to Sherri La Belle's in Stockton. Or maybe this is home. This place is called Tommy's. Have you ever heard of it?"

"Yeah, I know Tommy's." He heard her say to Roberts over the radio, "He knows it. What did I tell you?" Then Shauf was back, talking to him. "Are you coming here now?"

"No, I'm on my way to headquarters."

"What's going on there?"

"Bell called while I was meeting with Lisa and wants me to come in."

When Marquez walked into a conference room at headquarters he was surprised to see Ehrmann talking with Bell and Baird.

"This is about an officer named Jo Ruax," Ehrmann said. "I understand she runs the DBEEP boat." Ehrmann said that like he knew what it was, so maybe he did. Maybe the FBI was working in the delta. "We've had wiretaps in place on individuals who have referred to Ruax in their conversations. Some of the conversations are disturbing, and we know her residence has been cased. There's a lot of chatter about an undercover team of wildlife officers that they think she runs. Take a look at these, Lieutenant."

Ehrmann walked a transcript over, acted like he'd worked here all his life. He laid an inch-thick record of conversations down in front of Marquez and watched him start flipping through. A lot of blacked-out sections in the first pages and then whole sections twenty, thirty pages blacked out.

"Can I read the blacked-out sections?" Marquez asked. "Because there's not much else here."

"Keep turning pages. The sections I want you to look at are highlighted in yellow."

He flipped through five more pages and was looking at a conversation.

"Donny will come see you."

"He didn't show up last time. He called and said he was coming and then didn't show, the fuckhead."

"There was a problem."

"Ah, there's always a problem with him. He makes the problems and we take care of them. Now he's all worried again."

"He says you're the problem."

"Fuck him. He doesn't know anything. Tell him to stay in his store. Besides, we've information on some of the others. We'll deal with it."

"Then back off Donny. It's working so leave him the fuck alone."

"He made the problem with her."

"No, he didn't and anyway it's over. Forget about it because you don't know what the fuck you're talking about anyway."

Marquez read the conversation twice and flipped through the next stretch of blacked-out pages. He glanced at Ehrmann.

"There's too much blacked out."

Ehrmann shook his head. "Sorry."

"Another one of them is a woman. The unit is called DBEEP."

"What does that mean? Besides, how do you know it's about caviar and not LA?"

"Because they work off a fucking boat."

"What's going on in LA?" Marquez asked and then flipped through another run of blacked-out sections. The transcript might be an inch thick, but it could be five inches thick and with this much blacked out he still wouldn't be able to tell what the conversations were about. But, of course, Ehrmann knew that.

"In LA?" Ehrmann asked, and Marquez glanced at him, wondering why he didn't just say. "In LA it's car theft, but let's talk about DBEEP." He addressed his next comment to Chief Baird. "You should consider pulling that team for a while," Ehrmann said. "This is a bad group."

"Are we talking about organized crime?" Marquez asked.

He was sure everyone in the room knew they were, but Ehrmann hadn't said it, and he wanted to hear him say it. Ehrmann gave a faint nod, and Marquez put one piece together.

"You've known for a while they're buying sturgeon roe."

"We've had some idea, yes. What I'm here about today is to communicate that Lieutenant Ruax and possibly her crew are in some danger. We think you should shut that unit down."

"Shut it down for how long?" Baird asked.

"I can't answer that, but I will say we intend to move soon." He nodded toward Marquez. "You may want to pull your team back as well."

"Do we show up in the transcripts?"

"Not unless they're referring to a different woman warden than Ruax. They're concerned about an undercover team they think Ruax is part of. They've done the work to find out where she lives, so that means they're serious about her. It may be they think Ruax is connected to you."

"But now you're speculating?"

"Yes."

They went back and forth on that for a few minutes, and then Ehrmann got tired of it. He looked at his watch, must have figured out he was done here. He picked up the transcript and thanked them.

After Ehrmann left, Baird closed his eyes as if meditating. When he opened them he asked, "Should we pull the SOU?"

"Absolutely," Bell said.

"No," Marquez answered. "The SOU isn't mentioned."

"Just that Ehrmann has come here to warn us is reason enough to pull back and evaluate, I think," Bell said.

Marquez didn't respond. He kept his focus on Baird, waited for the chief to decide.

18

The Le Mans drifted north along a frontage road, then doubled back and drove into a residential area and parked down the street from an elementary school. They didn't stay long, pulled away from the curb a few minutes later, and turned into a gas station about a mile up the road. Marquez watched Perry fill the tank and Torp walk down the street and go into a drugstore. Then they cruised by the school again as it was letting out.

Minivans and SUVs were lining up, kids getting on buses. Some of the kids started walking home, and a few of those were alone as they went past the two men in the car.

"So maybe one of them has a kid here and lost any custody rights when he went to prison, but I wouldn't bet on it," Shauf said. "I'm going to call the locals. What do you think?"

"Yeah, make the call."

Not long after she did the Le Mans moved again. Torp and Perry drove north on 5 and then worked their way to west Sacramento and a failed industrial park called the West Sacramento Commerce Center.

Only a handful of the buildings had been completed. The three-story low-income units were framed and wrapped in lath, but stucco had never been applied and the black paper under the lath had faded in sun and storms, windows broken out. There'd been articles in the *Sacramento Bee*, a fraud indictment, new owners, an appeal for city money, and Marquez remembered hearing something about some of the spaces being leased. They were looking at one of those right now.

The Le Mans bounced across a wide asphalt lot and ran toward a long cinder-block building at the rear of the industrial park like a bad dog coming home. A sign on the building read Weisson's Auto Body and Repair. The car pulled into an open bay, and Marquez looked at the twelve-foot, razor-wired fence surrounding the building and protecting the rows of vehicles with body damage waiting for repair. From here the fence looked like a moat.

"Maybe they're going to get the Le Mans cherried out," Shauf said. "They seem like classy guys."

The building was at least two hundred feet long, twenty feet tall, paved all around, the chain-link fence standing away from it forty yards. Marquez spotted four police vehicles waiting for bodywork, so they had the right prices or an in with somebody at the city. The police vehicles suggested the place was at least legit. Shauf drove around back to check out what was there and found another road leading out and more open bays.

"It's a big building," she said. "A lot of bodywork going on in there. I didn't even know about this place."

Marquez checked out the rest of the industrial park again. The retail shops had never opened. Their glass faces were dusty, sterile. The big three-story low-income housing with its broken windows and unfinished exterior looked like it had already lived out its life rather than never having started it. Temporary fencing surrounded it. Fences seemed to be a theme.

He took a call from Selke while Shauf scouted the opposite side of the building. "It's definitely not Burdovsky. We got Burdovsky's dental records and blood type. No matches. She's a Jane Doe at the moment, and though it doesn't change the fact that somebody did that to her, it must make you feel better. I saw your face out there. I know you wanted a call. Thanks again for coming out last night."

Shauf's voice crackled over the radio. She was around the back side still, down near a PG&E substation, following a road she'd turned around on.

"Lucky thing I turned around. Perry and Torp switched vehicles and just pulled out this side in a white Econoline van. I'm behind them. You're going to have to go around the building and come out this other road, unless you want to let them go."

Her question was, was it worth still following them? Probably not, but Marquez decided they'd stick a little longer. They followed the van onto 80 westbound and an hour and a half later were in the Bay Area working through heavy traffic along the east shore of the bay.

Marquez took a position two lanes over, two hundred yards back. On the bay a kite surfer skimmed along. Ahead, traffic jockeyed for position in lanes that weren't going anywhere fast. When the Spanish got here all this land close to the bay was marsh. They wrote of the skies darkening when millions of birds took flight. Grizzlies fished from pockets of water left at low tide. There were times when Marquez felt like his team, what the SOU was doing, was just part of the slow fading away of wildlife that had begun when we separated the wild from ourselves. The cities kept growing and every year got more complicated. Just the dance of traffic alone was a game of timing and nuance, but compared to the wild it was still simple stuff. None of what we'd ever made had the complexity of what we were giving up.

Torp and Perry crossed the Bay Bridge and dropped into San Francisco. No one said anything except to call out their own position or that of the van. Then, as they got closer, Shauf voiced it.

"Is this possible?" she asked. "These two spitballs."

August Foods had Christmas lights up and a holiday display of Belgian chocolates and Italian cookies and breads in brown paper wrappers near the entry. Torp and Perry had pulled into a yellow zone, and Torp stayed with the van while Perry went inside. He spotted August in the middle of the store holding an olive oil bottle, talking to a couple, and began to move toward him. Marquez shifted his binoculars to August's face, saw him raise a hand above the head of the woman he was selling olive oil to and stop Perry's approach. When that happened Perry went back out to the van, leaned against it, and fired up a smoke. Inside, August had disappeared.

"We may have just caught our break," Marquez said to Shauf. "Here comes August's Porsche."

The van side door slid open, and Perry lifted out a carry-on suitcase that he brought around to the passenger side of August's car and rested on the seat. August pulled away. He drove south, and the SOU followed him off the airport exit and then into the short-term parking garage at SFO. He crossed to the terminal, checked in at one of the United computer stations, and was in the security line before Marquez reached anyone at SFPD who could direct him to their airport security chief. Meanwhile, August walked toward a gate with his carry-on, which had run through X-ray with some questions but no delay.

"Do you want to follow him or watch him on camera?" the security chief asked.

"Both."

"How many of you are there?"

"Three, and I'd like to get at least one of us to the gate where he is."

"Will you possibly be boarding a plane?"

"I don't think so."

Shauf followed August out to the gate and watched him sit down. They had his flight. United 1375 to LA. Marquez watched Shauf in grainy black and white on the airport video monitors as she talked to him on her cell.

"He's about an hour early," she said. "Why? Who gets here early to go to LA?"

August sat with his legs crossed, arms folded as he looked out the windows at the planes coming in.

"Who is he?" the security chief asked, and Marquez gave him a quick recap. "We're pretty sure he's repackaging illegal caviar and selling it out of his stores. But he's got a system for moving it we haven't figured out."

Maybe they were in the process of figuring it out. Another man entered the screen and sat down near August, leaving the gap of one seat between them. He also had a carry-on, similar in type.

He started talking with August. Stocky man, fleshy face. Marquez asked the security chief if he could get sound.

"God no, we can't even get cargo holds X-rayed."

He watched August's lips. Twenty years of undercover and some training and he was pretty good at this, but he didn't think it was English they were speaking. When August got to his feet, the other man stood as well. They left the gate, then went into a restroom, and Marquez looked to the chief.

"I guess I've got to ask what I've been wondering all these years. How much can you see?"

"You don't want to know. Follow me." He led him to a secluded screen, and they had a top-down view of the toilet stalls and urinals. August was at a sink, his carry-on against a wall near the exit. He slowly washed his hands while keeping an eye on his bag. Then the other man used the urinal, his carry-on parked next to August's.

Shauf asked, "What are you seeing?"

"Man number two at the urinal, August at a sink. The two bags are next to each other. Now August is leaving and the other guy has moved to the sinks."

"Did you catch that?" the security chief asked quietly off to Marquez's side.

Marquez relayed what they'd just watched onto Shauf. "They traded bags in the restroom."

Forty-five minutes later the unknown man had a name and was on a flight to Seattle. Instead of flying to LA, August drove back to San Francisco. He went to his apartment and carried the bag upstairs while Marquez talked to Washington Fish and Wildlife and then U.S. Fish and Wildlife in Seattle, trying to get the inbound man tracked. They decided to follow the man rather than stop him in the airport with the carry-on, and toward dusk the bad news came.

"I'm sorry," the Washington warden said. "We're not even sure how he did it, but we've lost him."

"He's gone?"

"Like he was never here."

19

Two women sat on a big black leather couch in Ludovna's living room. One wore skin-tight jeans and couldn't have been more than eighteen. The other wore a short skirt and a top that had to be a little cold tonight. Marquez handed Ludovna the bottle of vodka he'd brought him. He looked around the room. The sliding door to the backyard was open, and chill December air flowed in. Steam rose from the hot tub in the backyard.

"You didn't tell me it was a party," Marquez said, and then "Hello" to the women. The call had come from Ludovna, and he'd left Shauf and Roberts and driven from San Francisco. In the corner of the room an old Western movie played silently on a high-density screen.

"These are my friends." Ludovna looked at them. "You girls go outside."

He poured two vodkas, handed Marquez one. From the backyard the smell of dope drifted in through the door.

"The first thing I bought in America was a house, even before a car. A car is bullshit. You can always get a car."

"You must have had some money when you got here."

"Someone stole my car a couple of nights ago. I was out with one of the girls and someone stole it. It was a beautiful Cadillac, and they stripped it and burned it, so now I have to get a new car. But a car is no big deal. A man should have a place of his own. Where do you live?"

"Here, in Sacramento. But now I want to move in with you. You've got girls, a big house, and plenty to drink."

Ludovna smiled and refilled their glasses. He downed his and gestured for Marquez to do the same. But Marquez didn't kill his drink. He looked from Ludovna's face to the big room and the fireplace, heard the women giggling outside.

"If you want a house like this, get me a thousand sturgeons."

"Sure, I'll catch a thousand tomorrow."

"Here everyone wants to make a lot of money. In Russia I was a KGB officer in charge of interrogating foreigners, and now I sell fish and real estate in the land of opportunity. You get me good sturgeon, and we'll make you rich."

Marquez lifted his glass, toasted, "To catching every last sturgeon."

Ludovna refilled the glasses and expounded his theories on money and America as Marquez watched the two women in the backyard. A low deck surrounded the hot tub. The backyard was deep with a lawn and low-voltage lights along the back fence. It was landscaped. He watched one of the women bend over the hot tub to test the water. She kept her legs straight and arched her back for them.

"You like her, you can have her tonight," Ludovna said.

"Thanks, Nick."

"You need to wear something when you're with her."

"Yeah?"

"I caught something from her once."

The women came back in, and Ludovna told one to get some caviar for his friend. He poured the women vodka and said to the younger one, "After you bring the plate, you should get in the tub."

She made a show of saying that was going to be fun. She touched one of her nipples, and yet it didn't seem like she was looking forward to the tub. Ludovna waited until they were in the kitchen.

"How do you know so many guys catching sturgeon?"

"I don't know so many guys."

"You said you did."

"I exaggerated because I want your business. It's what we do in America. First we exaggerate to sign you up, and then we tell you how it's going to be."

"No one knows you. I asked around and no one knows you."

"Raburn knows me."

"So why does he help you fuck him? He sells to me. Why would he want you to get any of the business?"

"Because he owes me money."

"Raburn owes you?"

"Yes."

Ludovna thought about that. He was quiet, and then his eyes returned to Marquez's face.

"Do you know how to make caviar?"

"Sure."

Ludovna refilled the glasses again, and the young woman with skin-tight jeans came out with a plate of caviar, little crackers, and sliced lemon. She'd lost her top in the kitchen and sat down next to Marquez after putting the platter on the table. She snuggled close. Her breast was rock hard, but it didn't hurt.

"We're talking," Ludovna told her, "you and her go in the tub."

"I want to sit here."

Ludovna's voice hardened abruptly. "Go in the tub," and Marquez wondered if he was sitting with a small-time hood moving a little bit of stolen fish and whatever else, or whether Ludovna was as organized as they imagined he might be. When he gave Ehrmann Ludovna's name, Ehrmann had acted uninterested, and maybe the FBI had already checked him out. The new Bureau could get all phone numbers on a suspect very quickly and send them to their Special Operations Division in Virginia. The computer there would track any hit on any of those numbers. His guess was the Feds had already looked at Ludovna and didn't see anything to go after.

The women stripped their clothes near the sliding door and walked out to the tub, both men watching as they dipped their feet in the water and then climbed in. Ludovna gestured toward them with his glass.

"They're good for me. I don't have a wife anymore. In my last year in the KGB I taught interrogation. If you interrogate a wife about sex, it's very complicated. But not with these women. With them it's very simple, and for now that's okay for me."

"You were KGB?"

"Yes, and I was very good at knowing when I was being lied to. That was my talent. Yesterday, I read in the newspaper that the FBI told the military not to torture the prisoners in the

Guantanamo Base. The military didn't listen to the FBI, but the FBI was right. It's easier to get them to talk if you don't torture them. The important thing is to scare them deep inside, but not make them hate you. You want them to talk, of course. I could take a man like Raburn and make him tell me everything he has ever done. A man like that is easy to break. You see the way he is nervous. I could break him down so he shakes all the time the rest of his life. The brain is very delicate."

"That's an interesting story."

"It got me here."

"What got you here?"

"What I knew got me here. Everything is information. That's what everyone is trading. I could put you in a chair in a room, and it would take days, maybe weeks, but in two weeks I promise you would want to make me happy. If I told you to smile, you would smile. If I told you to urinate in a cup and drink it, you would do that too. You would drink my piss."

"I don't think so."

"You don't know, but I know. This is what I was good at. Where is your house in Sacramento?"

"What?"

"Where do you live? What street?"

"I'll invite you over, and you can come see how we live. We don't drink our urine, but we have a good time."

"When do I come to your house?"

"How about later this week? Let me check with my wife and I'll call you."

Ludovna seemed okay with that. He reached for the bottle again, then built a cracker with caviar, asked Marquez to eat it and tell him where the caviar was from.

"From here," Marquez said after taking a bite.

"You're right." He leaned forward, got closer. "I don't like your friend Raburn, but I understand him. I know the ways he is weak, but you I don't know yet. You hide things."

"Who doesn't?"

Ludovna refilled Marquez's glass. They ate different caviar, small black beads of sevruga, flavor bright and intense. Marquez lifted his vodka and downed it.

"All the bullshit in this country," Ludovna said. "I started with an American wife, like Raburn's brother, only in reverse. I didn't have to mail for mine; she was already here."

"So what happened to her?"

"She went off the road into the river in her car in the fog." He pointed at Marquez's hand. "Why don't you wear your ring?"

"It catches on fishing gear."

"See, all the bullshit." Ludovna smiled. "Everybody has the answer ready. Everything is bullshit. In this country there are people who want to save every kind of animal, but with the sturgeon it's the United States who helped to get the ban on Caspian sturgeon lifted. No other country eats so much caviar, not even the French. The U.S. wants to make better relations with Iran so they are willing to let the poachers kill the rest of the Caspian. They're helping the wrong poachers. They should help us ban everything from the Caspian so the price will rise here."

Marquez looked at his watch. "Nick, I've got to take off, but I'll call you and invite you over." Marquez stood. "Thanks for the drinks. Enjoy your girls."

"No, sit down, don't go yet."

Marquez started to move out from around the coffee table. He stopped at the end of the couch, knew Ludovna had to control the situation.

"You stay for one more drink. We are almost finished talking, but I want you to understand."

"I think I do understand, but I don't want to recite my Social Security number or tell you all the places I've lived or the people I know so you can check on me. It's not worth it to me."

Marquez moved back along the couch and sat down, and Ludovna moved over and sat alongside him. Their thighs pressed against each other. Ludovna refilled the shot glasses.

"I won't hurt you," he said, then pretended to backhand Marquez's face. "Sometimes you have no choice but to use force. With a woman I hit one side, then the other. Always the back of my hand, okay. Never hard enough for her to lose consciousness, but always I wore a ring that tore the skin. Women don't like to lose the way they look. Even the ones who are very tough hate to lose that. Even the ugly ones." He brushed knuckles across Marquez's face. "Never too hard, but scarring each time until I get a specific answer. That was my other career before fish and real estate, before I came to America."

He sat back. The vodka had reached him, opened his tongue, reddened his cheeks and the starburst of capillaries on his nose. The attempts at physical intimidation didn't mean much to Marquez, but he felt the touch of paranoia he'd felt when he'd walked in tonight. Ludovna would work hard to find out everything he could about him. Ludovna leaned back, his leg still pushed against Marquez, stone-washed jeans, soft leather shoes.

"Raburn is lying. I know this, and if you are not who you say you are, you should leave now and nothing will happen to you."

"I'm just trying to make some money."

"Okay, I want to hear you talk about what you know. Tell me about the land of the delta, the seasons, what you know about the sturgeon."

So he did, talking for another twenty minutes but drinking little more, drawing an image of the Sacramento River coming from the north, San Joaquin from the south, the Consumnes, the Mokelumne, the levees and sloughs branching, where the tide ran, the brackish water, the shifting through the year. He named fishermen he knew, people Ludovna knew or could check out or wouldn't know how to approach and who'd rebuff him anyway. He made up a couple of names and put people in boats they didn't own and along Montezuma Slough and fishing between the Mothball Fleet.

Sometime later, after the women were back in the house complaining that they were lonely, a car pulled into the driveway. Marquez heard doors slamming, voices. The doorbell rang, and Ludovna greeted a friend who introduced himself as Mickey, which he said was short for Mikhalov. Mickey had four two-ounce jars of caviar with August's import label on them, and Marquez felt Ludovna follow his eyes to the labels.

"Time for you to go," Ludovna said, walked him out and then to his truck on the street. "If things are not right, then Raburn and his brother are responsible. Do you understand?"

Marquez wanted to ask about the brother but didn't want to reveal he didn't already know. "I hear you," he said, got in the truck, and Ludovna was still standing in the road as he drove away.

20

Brad Alvarez had left the SOU in April. By then they'd heard the first rumors of the poaching ring they were after now. Alvarez had returned to the central coast as a warden, and Marquez hadn't seen him since June, so it was great to walk in and spot him in back in a booth. Alvarez already had a beer and was watching a cook make pizzas, fire them in the wood-burning oven.

"Did you drink him under the table?"

"No, Ludovna can put away the vodka, but I did my part."

"How are you feeling?"

"A little buzz, but I'm okay." Marquez looked around. "Hungry."

It smelled like cheese melting in the open wood-fired oven. Alvarez had grown a goatee again. He looked like the resistance leader of a guerrilla unit who'd come out of the jungle for a beer.

"It's time to check out the KGB story, and he told me tonight he had a wife here who went into the Sacramento River in her car and drowned. Doesn't seem very troubled by that."

"Where are we at, overall?"

"Not much closer with August. Not any closer, really. We've documented sales to a Richie Crey and Ludovna, though some of the videotape is sketchy. We'll need several sales to make a case. Burdovsky is an open question."

"Cairo told me she burned us."

"Looks like it."

They ordered a pitcher of beer and a pepperoni pizza. Alvarez filled a glass for Marquez and refilled his own after the pitcher arrived.

"Long drive here," he said. "I'm starving. Hey, what's the deal with the FBI?"

"They're getting close to making a bust and they're nervous. They're not saying what it's about, only that it's Eurasian Organized Crime and there's a possibility we might go blue on blue, in which case we get backed away."

"So is Eurasian the Russian mob?"

"Yeah, and it sounds like these guys are Ukrainian."

"Where's Ludovna from?"

"Moscow. They haven't said what this group is into, but the FBI has wiretaps where Jo Ruax of DBEEP is mentioned. They also claim her house was cased. DBEEP is being pulled back."

"You mean, like off the water?"

"Yeah."

"No kidding."

"So there's some sort of overlap. And we have until Christmas."

"I would have been in Mexico."

Marquez lifted his beer glass to Alvarez. "Good that you're here instead."

They ate the pizza, and the beer was quickly gone, but it was nice to sit in the warmth and firelight from the oven. When the bill came they paid and Marquez said, "See you back at the house."

At this late hour he didn't expect a call from Maria or Katherine, but he got one from Maria. It was after 1:00 on the East Coast.

"We went to Vassar."

"Yeah, how was it?"

"The library is beautiful, but now we're in New York City. We went to dinner at some place called Bellavitae tonight that mom thinks is the greatest."

"What did you think of it?"

She paused and admitted, "It was good. It's new and like a crostini-and-wine-bar type thing."

"How was the crostini?"

"Do you know what it is?"

"Yeah."

"It was really good but you kind of have to drink wine."

"If you go to college they hand out fake IDs when you register. So where are you tomorrow?" He tried to remember. He parked outside the safehouse and tried to remember. "Cornell?"

"We're skipping the tundra. We would have to fly up there anyway."

Marquez listened to the clipped answers, the grudging explanation of why they'd changed their schedule, the sort of bitchiness that drove Kath crazy but never really got under his skin. Maybe it was one advantage of being a stepfather. Perhaps that role made it easier to see her as a separate person. He read through the sarcasm and saw a teenager still sorting out who the enemy was. It definitely wasn't her mother.

"Okay, then where? Columbia?"

"Mom probably should since she wants to go back and finish her college degree some day. It might be a good school for her. For me it's a 'reach school,' and I'm already applying to enough reach schools."

"You don't think you'd get in?"

"I definitely wouldn't."

"You've flown all the way back there. Walk the campus."

He could add, the money has been spent to send you back there for this special trip that very few kids get to make and the walk wouldn't be any more than you'll make in your average shopping mall. What Maria needed was her world shaken up, and he'd have to find the words to reach her, but he didn't have them tonight.

"I have to say good night," Maria said.

"Try to connect with your mom."

"Right."

The next morning Marquez drove into the delta to meet Ruax at Mel's in Walnut Grove. There were a couple of tables inside and they were empty, but any room would have been too small for her today. She'd gotten the word last night. He bought a coffee to go while she waited outside in the wind. By the time he walked out she'd crossed the road to the river and looked like someone who'd come out of a movie theater and found her new car had been totaled. She wanted to be angry but was still too shocked.

"I can't believe they made the decision without talking to me," she said. "Why were you at that meeting and I wasn't?"

"Because I'd already been to the FBI Field Office in SF and met Ehrmann. He heads the Russian mob squad there, but no one told me he was coming to Sacramento and I didn't know he'd be there when I got there. My chief called me in, and you didn't miss anything. He brought a blacked-out transcript so we'd have something to hold when he told us they want DBEEP pulled. The idea was to make it seem like Chief Baird's decision."

"Okay, then will this Ehrmann blow me off if I call him?"

"No, he'll talk to you. He's not shy. I'll give you a cell number, and if you want you can try him."

He wrote the cell number down and watched her fold the paper and jam it in her pocket. She exhaled and looked away, looked down at the dark green roll of the river.

"We've got a bunch of things we're working," she said. "You're going to have to take a ride with me. I'll have to show you where we're at." She shook her head, reminded him of Shauf with Raburn. "I can't believe this is happening."

"We can take my boat," Marquez said. "It'll get us where we need to go."

"What boat do you have? I didn't even know you knew how to drive one."

Marquez let it go, let her lash out without coming back at her. He'd worked with DBEEP before, had worked well with them and figured he would again.

"I've got a Fountain I bought damaged at a DEA auction years ago. The bow got a hole punched in it when the driver rammed a boat with a couple of DEA agents onboard and tried to sink it.

I bought it on the cheap and then it sucked all my savings into the repair. It's not for sneaking up on people, but we won't look like surveillance either. It's docked down in San Rafael at Loch Lomond. We'd have to meet there."

They set a time, and he left her and drove across the river. The palm trees in Ryde were framed against a white sky. The river was muddy green and running with whitecaps. The Sacramento/San Joaquin drainage formed the largest delta facing the Pacific on the northern or southern hemisphere. It drained two thirds of the water that left California. The web of sloughs, the agricultural land along the levee islands, wasn't like any other place he knew of in the state. There were relatively few buildings, and he drove past deep orchards of pear and apple and vineyards that stretched as far as he could see.

On the drive home he talked again with Selke, who'd been talking to Ehrmann.

"I ran the photos by Ehrmann that you found in her kayak as well as the photo we found in her wallet. He told me Burdovsky had a short marriage and a son she doesn't see anymore because he was kidnapped by the father. The photo from her wallet was taken outside Moscow. That's her ex in the photo, the same guy who kidnapped the boy. His name is Alex Karsov, and according to Ehrmann, he started with computer crime but went on to become a big wheel in arms dealing. For years Burdovsky made trips back to Russia to try to find her son. The deal was her ex didn't want his boy to disappear to America, didn't want him to grow up fat wearing baggy pants falling off his ass and watching TV when he's not playing videos. Forget that last part about the kids, Marquez; I've got some issues with my ex-wife."

"Are the Feds looking for Anna?"

"It's not clear, but Ehrmann talks like she's alive and they might know where she is. I told him you were very worried about her. I played it up. You haven't slept at night since she vanished. You're consumed with guilt, that kind of thing. I'm trying to get him to tell us more, so this is your heads-up on that." He chuckled. "You cry every night over Burdovsky."

"When did the father run with the boy?"

"She was in school in Moscow, got pregnant, married, and then things went south. He didn't want her to take their son, so he grabbed the boy and took off. Russia was a mess so there was no one to go after him, or he was connected enough to keep it from happening."

Ehrmann had formed the boundaries of an imaginary tumor with his hands as he'd described the malignancy Eurasian Organized Crime represented. He wasn't against the word *mob* but said it didn't cover it.

"I think Ehrmann will tell us more if we both work him," Selke said. "They've got their investigation and there's more overlap than he's let on. He's returning calls too quickly. I just get that feeling. We need to play off each other when we work him."

Marquez doubted that either he or Selke would work Ehrmann successfully for information. And he wasn't even sure he wanted to know what Ehrmann saw when he looked at a county detective and an undercover warden. But neither did he really care. He knew why his team was here. They weren't shutting down arms traffickers, but they were trying to protect a species that had been on this earth since the dinosaurs. An arms trafficker might come up with an elaborate rationalization for how the arms they sold actually helped the oppressed, the same as market poachers taking bear might claim to feed a market for traditional medicines. Fundamentally, both were about greed, and he had the feeling Ehrmann was sympathetic to what the SOU was trying to do because he understood the commonality.

But, like Selke, Marquez felt the hand of the Feds brushing closer. He knew if the stakes were high enough with this arms trafficker, then the FBI might even be listening in on the SOU conversations. Unlikely. Still, he turned the idea as he drove home to Mill Valley.

21

When Marquez pulled up to Loch Lomond Marina, Ruax was sitting in her truck. He backed the boat trailer down the ramp, and the Fountain slid into the water. He waited until Ruax was on the boat and the engine idling, then eased the boat trailer back up the ramp and parked. Calm water broke smoothly off the bow as they headed out the channel.

"I brought a thermos of coffee and picked up some cinnamon rolls on the way in," he said. "They're from a bakery in San Rafael."

"I don't eat that kind of stuff."

"I know you drink coffee; I've seen you do that."

"I had a cup earlier."

He poured her one anyway, and they came slowly through the buoys, keeping to the five-mile-per-hour limit. He opened the bakery bag, showed her the cinnamon buns, fresh, still hot and sticky, and she shook her head, a look of disgust crossing her face.

"Take the coffee, Jo. It'll keep your hands warm even if you don't drink it."

He wasn't much of a pastry eater himself, had only a bite or two, and checked out the bay ahead, looking for other boats. Ruax fixed her gaze on the seismic work underway on the Richmond/ San Rafael Bridge. Sparks flew from welding work. Then they were out of the channel, turning the stern to the bridge and San Francisco Bay behind it. He bumped the speed, and they ran across the gray water toward the red light at the horizon.

The sky streaked with pink and magenta. Marquez tapped the throttle gently forward, and the bow rose. A deeper roar came from the engine, and Ruax wouldn't have to talk now. She could look through the windshield at whatever she was thinking about and brood. He pushed the speed past fifty, adjusted the flaps, and the boat began to plane across San Pablo Bay. Along the east shore commuter traffic was already thick. Ahead, the new span of the Vallejo Bridge stood like a gray sentinel, and the sun began to rise through delta fog. They left a white wake under the bridge, swept past Benicia and into the wide shallow upper bays.

He cut their speed, clicked on the baffling system to dampen the engine noise, slowed more as they left the last sunlight and moved into fog that at first was thin wisps, then wrapped thick around them, cold on their faces. He steered around a log floating off to their left, a branch from it extending like an arm reaching for the sky.

Now they started passing sloughs, Cache and Steamboat, and he saw a few fishing boats out. No one liked a powerboat at dawn. They drew looks. He got sarcasm from Ruax.

"Not as quiet as you think," she said.

But neither would anyone likely associate the Fountain speedboat with law enforcement. As the river narrowed and fog thickened, Marquez slowed more. He offered Ruax more coffee, poured himself some.

"What are you going to do with the time off?" he asked.

"Take a vacation while they figure it out."

"Use your vacation time?"

"No, Baird says they'll do something about all that."

"How'd your crew take it?"

"They're angry. Everyone wants more explanation, and we had a lot of things we were working on."

"Our operation isn't just in the delta. You could still work with us."

"I'm supposed to stay away from anything associated with sturgeon poaching. That was the advice of the FBI for all of my crew."

"*Advice* is the word they use when they can't step in and control. *Strongly advise* is one of their favorites. They're also the largest single buyer of black marker pens."

That last bit went by her, but then, she hadn't seen the transcripts. Passing Riera's Marina not all the buildings were visible, still wrapped in fog. Marquez avoided a ship coming downriver and watched Ruax pour herself more coffee, her face changing even as she didn't want it to, and he could tell she loved the river, loved being out here this morning. She turned to him.

"We were on the water when those concrete bridge pieces came downriver from Stockton. They were huge."

"Pieces for the new Bay Bridge?"

"Yes." She described the barge and the pieces for the new eastern span of the Bay Bridge going past her DBEEP boat. "You turn in up ahead not too far," she said. "These guys were taking sturgeon before you showed up. That's why you haven't heard about them before now."

"You didn't owe us anything. You were working your own things before we arrived, and you'll have new ones when we leave."

"We knew they were dealing with Raburn, and we knew he'd sold sturgeon in Rio Vista. His brother's wife rode with him a couple of times, but we never tied him to the new owner at Beaudry's like you did. I should have told you those things."

Marquez nodded. He understood completely. The SOU had cases they worked and didn't talk to anybody about until they needed to. Ruax had taken a wait-and-see attitude on the SOU operation and hadn't risked cases that DBEEP was building. Anna's disappearing would have only reinforced that, and Ruax didn't have to apologize for any of it.

"How much do you know about Isaac's wife?" she asked.

"Not a lot. Raburn told us she does some gutting and cleaning but doesn't know anything about the illegal business. He says she doesn't even know the laws. How did you get onto her?"

"Followed her."

The boat punched slowly up the river. Up off to the left Marquez made out the water tower behind the Ryde Hotel, then the red lights of the TV tower marking the location of Walnut Grove. Without the light you'd see only gray fog.

"Okay, you followed her, and then what?"

"On three instances we saw her drop the kids at school and drive to Ludovna's house. Never checked her rearview and she wasn't delivering anything, but each time she was inside about an hour."

"What's your guess?"

"What's yours?"

The answer was supposed to be sex, but if that was the answer he wasn't there yet. He'd had a hard time seeing Isaac's wife in that role. Didn't think she'd interest the Ludovna he'd met, and she and her husband looked pretty tight. As near as he could tell she worked all the time with either the pear farm or taking care of the two kids.

"Maybe she cleans fish or processes roe at his house," Marquez said.

"I should have told you weeks ago about her." Bitterness showed again. "But I didn't want to give up what we'd been working on, and besides, you're the legend. I wanted to see what you'd come up with on your own."

"You don't really mean that last, do you?"

"No, I'm sorry, John. It's not you. I guess I'm just generally pissed off."

"That I can understand."

She turned quiet again, and they entered the slough. When she next spoke it was to explain what was ahead.

"There'll be someone glassing you as soon as you come around the bend up ahead."

"How many of them?"

"Four, and they look like dorks but they're smart. Usually, they like to sit off the Mothball Fleet, particularly when there's a moon like this week, but they'll move around also and camp up a slough like this. Two will fish and two will watch for us or the other wardens. Those two always have binos and usually one of them is on land."

"Not like the good old days when the poachers would smoke dope, drink, and hang ten rods on the stern."

"I don't know much about the good old days. I'm only thirty-two."

"Is that one of them up there along the bank on the right?"

"I don't see anybody."

"Third tree in. You see a little bit of a head poking around the trunk."

"I can't tell that's a person."

She lifted a small set of binoculars after settling back into her seat. Marquez continued to stand and steer, one hand on the windshield, the slough up ahead narrowing. Ruax was subtle as she swept the binos along the bank, hiding the shape of them with her hand.

"You're right," she said, "and he is looking at us. He's hoping we break a shaft on a submerged log. Up ahead here is an old boat that's been docked about fifteen years."

"I know the boat."

"The Army Corps tried to get it towed out of there years ago, but the owner fought them and won. These guys are using it to camp out in."

"I came in here with Raburn."

"That's what I was saying, he buys from them. So he brought you here?"

"Yeah, and I guess you and I haven't been communicating enough." When she didn't answer, Marquez said, "There's a woman across the river up ahead on our left."

"I see her."

"You've kept your distance since we got here, and I guess we have too."

"We don't really need any help with the delta, and you've got enough problems with abalone, bear, and everything else."

"What do you think of the Russian mob idea?"

"I'd like to see some proof. But there's always been sturgeon poaching, and, sure the Russian community loves caviar, but the mob talk is a lot of noise so far even if the Feds show up after you start asking questions." The abandoned boat was visible now. "We call this Camp Sturgeon. They're here all the time."

Marquez kicked it into neutral and eased into reverse. The bow swung around, and he could feel them watching as he made a show of struggling with getting the boat turned around like he didn't really know how to manage the craft. Someone hooted from somewhere on the bank.

"Camp Sturgeon," Marquez repeated, then added, "You've got a good crew."

"'Most everything is in my log, and I'll copy it off for you."

"I need your help with this operation, Jo. We only get a few more weeks ourselves, and either we're going to make one or two busts or we're going to crack this thing."

"My orders are I'm off the river and away from sturgeon poaching."

"I want to talk to Baird, see if he'll let you work with us, unless you want a break from it all."

"Well, you've got all the pull with Baird."

"Yeah, I begged for an additional three weeks after Burdovsky disappeared. That's the kind of pull I have." He looked over at her again. "We need your help."

"If I'm so good how come I haven't noticed anyone watching me, and I don't mean some bogus mob, but some dipshit Fed in a suit in a white sedan trying to figure out what's going on."

"The Feds can be pretty damned good when they want to be."

"Right, the Feds are invisible, and the Russian mob just invaded the delta in a submarine they stole from the old Soviet navy."

They turned out of the slough and onto the river again. There were more gaps in the fog as they headed downriver, and Marquez figured the day would turn pretty. He liked the smell of the cold mornings when they just started to warm on the river. You could tell the time of year in the way it smelled. Water slapped against the bow as they ran through patches of sunlight on the water. Ruax hadn't said anything since they came under the trestle bridge, her bitterness overwhelming her again.

"You didn't have any of the cinnamon rolls. Do you want to get something to eat?" he asked.

"There's a place up here ahead where you can dock, and it's good for breakfast."

"Is the coffee good?"

Ruax smiled and her face lit up. "No, we joke about it. The coffee is terrible, but they've got an egg scramble that's great."

Marquez kicked the engine up, and they crossed the river. He turned to Ruax as they slowed, approaching the dock.

"What do you say we eat and figure out how we can work together?"

22

Marquez pulled the Fountain from the water at Loch Lomond, and after he'd parked the boat and unhitched the trailer, Ruax followed him to San Francisco. She went in to have a look at August Foods, and he left her there and was on his way back to the delta when he took a call from dispatch. Two duck hunters had found a strange dumping ground. One hunter had left a phone number, and Marquez called and talked to the man, who then agreed to meet him. He scribbled directions and turned toward the rice fields where the hunter said he'd be waiting in a white Ford pickup.

Marquez got there ahead of the hunter and talked with Shauf while he waited. More had come in on Torp and Perry. Shauf had made it her project to find out.

"Torp did five years for his part in a gang rape. He and a friend fed Liquid X to two high school girls in Hayward. Roofies and GHB.

Both were found in his apartment, and his friends testified he'd participated in two rapes. DNA matched semen found on both girls, but somehow the evidence got tainted and Torp ended up with a light sentence. He got picked up on suspicion of rape in Washington about two years before that."

"Anything with children?"

"I can't find anything. Perry graduated from burglary to grand theft to aggravated assault, did two for a robbery. He was Richie Crey's cellmate in Lompoc."

"What about sex crimes?"

"None, but another thing about Perry is he broke three of his stepfather's ribs after getting released last time."

"Where'd you get that from?"

"A deputy in Bakersfield. The stepfather brought charges, then dropped them and called it an accident. It would have put Perry back in." She was quiet a moment. "Can I talk to you about something completely different? My brother-in-law is supposed to be here this weekend with the kids." If she was wondering if she could get time off, they'd find a way. "If he gets here, I want to have them over for dinner, and when our operation ends or we get shut down, I'm going to go stay with them for a couple of weeks."

When her sister died the family was living in Folsom, and she had thought she'd play a much bigger role raising the kids, but her brother-in-law Jim found he couldn't stay in the same house and had taken a job in southern Cal last March. Since the move she hadn't seen much of the kids.

"When I talked to Jim last night he said he had to tell me something before I came to stay with them. He's started seeing someone. He's got a girlfriend who sometimes stays the night. He wanted me to know she might be there when I'm staying with them. I didn't say much. What am I going to say anyway? It's his life, and I know how hard it has been for him, but I'm having a real hard time with the idea of staying in the house and someone there taking my sister's place."

"She's not taking her place, is she?"

"I know he's got to go forward and all that, but for me it just doesn't feel like it's been very long and now the anniversary is coming up. I didn't think it would affect me as much as it has. I was shaking all day today. I don't care how nice she is; it's just too soon for me. But if I don't sleep there I won't be around the kids when they wake up in the morning. I want to be there Christmas morning if I can, if we're not watching these bozos. I want to bring a trunk full of presents and see their faces."

"You'll be there, and the other part, he's got to go about it his own way. No one else can know what it's been for him."

She didn't say any more, and the duck hunter drove up. Marquez followed him out to the blind. They crossed a large tract of private property and went through several gates. Then, out beyond a duck blind at the spot where a dirt road ended, there was a pile of fish heads and tails. Marquez knew before he got out of the truck that they were all sturgeons. A biologist had once told him that a sturgeon today fit almost perfectly into fossilized imprints its ancestors left two hundred fifty million years ago.

"When did you find these?"

A few of the tails were large. He began counting, and the hunter pointed.

"About a week and a half ago we were out at the blind down there. The dogs smelled this, and we came down here."

Marquez had counted better than sixty so far, all sturgeon. He turned back to the duck hunter, a young guy, overweight, earnest.

"Were you the one who called CalTIP?"

"Yes."

"Why did you wait to call?"

"I don't know. We thought they were for the rice for next year's crop. You know, maybe to fertilize it or something."

"Did you know they were sturgeon?"

He nodded. "One of the guys I hunt with goes sturgeon fishing."

"Then he knows about the legal size limits."

It was called the slot size. A legal sturgeon was between forty-six and seventy-two inches. Some of these were way over and some under. If the friend fished sturgeon then he must have realized that.

"It wasn't really any of our business."

"It's everyone's business. Part of why this is dumped out here is someone figures no one will bother."

"Look, I called it in."

"I'm not riding you about it. I'm just telling you we need help from everyone." Marquez pointed at the pile. "There are more poachers than wardens. Call it in right away next time."

Marquez finished the count and followed the white Ford back out. He knew the duck hunter probably felt like he'd tried to do some good and had gotten lectured for his efforts. But it was going to take a lot of help from the public to save some of these species. He relayed to Shauf the eighty-two sturgeon heads he'd counted.

"Someone like Raburn," she said. "Where are you headed now?"

"To pick up one of the older cars and go by Weisson's Auto. Maybe the one Alvarez hit the tree with chasing those bear poachers up in the Trinity."

"The Scout?"

"Yeah."

"It still runs?"

"It runs okay. Where are Torp and Perry at?"

"Rio Vista. The bait shop. Torp just bought a bag of Cheetos and a six-pack of Bud, so they're having lunch. Then it's back to the office and a busy afternoon for both of them."

Marquez smiled. Shauf knew that after what Torp and Perry had connected for them with August, it was worth staying with them. But later, if they went down, despite their prior records the DA would likely allow a plea bargain reduction from a 17B felony to a misdemeanor conspiracy charge. They might get sixty to ninety days of jail time, but more likely home time with a bracelet, which probably would force them to scratch out a living making dope and meth deals from Crey's house.

Now Marquez drove the old Scout toward Weisson's Auto. The engine ran raggedly. It coughed blue smoke, and the transmission ground into gear when he pulled away from stoplights. When he drove up, the fence gate was open. He drove past an old yellow diesel Mercedes and a battered Ford van, vehicles they'd watched get moved at closing time a couple of nights to positions partially blocking access to roll-up doors on this face. They'd picked up on some of the habits of the owner of Weisson's.

After he parked, Marquez checked out the rest of the building and doubted the developer put in anything like the heavy-gauge steel the bay doors were made out of. The fence with the razor wire, the floodlights on the tall cinder-block building, gave the place a prison look and said something either about vandalism and theft in the area or about what went on inside. Body shop workers in blue coveralls. Plenty of them. He caught the eye of one.

"Can I help you?" the man asked.

"Yeah, some asshole hit my Scout." Marquez walked him over and pointed at the damage. "I'd like to get a price to fix it."

"Looks like it happened a while ago."

"It did."

"Go talk to the estimator, but if you want my opinion the cost to fix it is probably more than this bucket is worth."

"It's just a fender."

"You've got a rust problem."

"I know, but I'm going to drive it at least another year."

The man shrugged and pointed him toward the estimator's office at the far end of the building. When he got to the estimator's office Marquez found a heavyset guy with a cluttered desk. They walked back together, then back down to the office, and the estimator consulted a computer and came up with $1,854. Marquez expressed his shock, folded the estimate, and said he'd call. He walked back slowly, found the guy he'd first talked to.

"He give you a price?"

"Way over what I can afford. I just want to knock out the dent and throw some Bondo on it." Marquez handed him a card. "What I want doesn't need to be done in a shop."

"How much you want to pay?"

"Three hundred."

"If I call you tonight are you going to be around? I might be able to do it for you."

"I'll be around."

"I get off work at 6:00. You'd have to bring it to me."

"That's fine."

"I'll call you when I get off."

23

Auto body Ray checked in a little after 5:30. He was off early and wanted to get started.

"You're going to stop at an ATM on the way here, right?"

"Don't worry, I'll have the money to pay you."

"I can't take a check."

"I'm not writing one. I'll have cash, but what I need right now is an address."

He copied down the address and made a stop on the way, at a convenience store for beer and a bag of potato chips. But it turned out Ray didn't want to drink while working, and he dismissed the potato chips.

"You eat the grease, man. I get enough at work."

But then as the Bondo dried they opened a couple of beers. They sat on the curb. Ray had plugged in an extension cord in his garage but hadn't wanted to work there because Bondo dust would get all over everything stored inside. Out here on the street the wind would take care of the dust.

"That's a big operation there at Weisson's," Marquez said. "How many employees?"

"Something like a hundred."

"Come on, not that many."

"I'm not shitting you. Sometimes they run twenty-four hours a day."

"How long have you been there?"

"Two years too long."

Marquez nodded as though he understood that. He let a beat go by.

"When I was there today I saw some guys carrying a big cooler like they were going to a tailgate party. What do you have to keep cold in a body shop?"

"The boss is a big fisherman."

"He brings his fish to work?"

"Naw, they deliver to him there. You know, he'll catch something on the weekend, drop it off to have it cleaned and cut up, and then they'll deliver it to him." He smiled at some memory. "We get fish deliveries all the time, and he does all kinds of trades for that. You wreck your car, and Al will end up owning your boat before it's over."

"The way that shop is running he probably could afford a fleet of boats, especially if the estimates are like mine was."

"He's got three businesses in there. One shop is union so he can get some of the city and county contracts. And he's got a specialty shop with a different crew. They don't talk to us, and they do a lot of custom shit. The building is divided up, and they're off by themselves. You've got to have the lock code to even get in there, but, yeah, the shop does a lot of business, runs overnight on the bodywork sometimes. They got mechanics, detailers, upholsterers, a lot of work going on. He buys and sells cars like no one's business, wrecks out of auctions, that kind of work. Why do you want to know?"

"Just got curious walking through today. You wouldn't really know it from the outside, but it's a big deal once you get inside."

"Damn straight, and low pay for lousy hours."

He crumpled his can. Bondo had dried on his fingers, and he picked at it. He stood and tried to get a crick out of his neck.

"Look, I got to get going," he said.

Marquez went around to the driver's side and got his wallet. He counted out the twenties and said, "I saw a gold Le Mans parked in there. Kind of a beater but I wouldn't mind having it. Cars like the Le Mans were right about my time."

"Too late, man. Car's going to be rebuilt and sold as a classic. The guys who brought it in traded for a van. I'm supposed to do some work detailing a couple of things on it in the morning. They got a high-mileage piece of shit, a '99 Ford E-150, half ton with a V-6 for trade, but if you ask me they wanted to get rid of the Le Mans."

"Get rid of it for what reason?"

"You've got me, I don't know."

At the safehouse that night Marquez cooked dinner with Roberts and Cairo. Too often they ate fast food. That was just the way it was with surveillances. But late this afternoon Roberts had bought a bass from a commercial fisherman she ran into at the Benicia dock. She had cleaned the fish, salted and oiled the fillets. Coals glowed in the grill in the backyard. But it was Cairo who'd taken the real interest in eating better, and when the SOU had been larger they had pooled their per diems and had given him the money to work with.

One of the things about moving around California undercover was they saw what was for sale along the road in the different seasons. Marquez knew where to buy Gravenstein apples in August in Sonoma and when the best tomatoes showed up in the farmers markets, or when Last Chance peaches came down from Donner in October, right about the time the bear hunters were gearing up. If you worked for the department you could always find out where the boats were bringing in the first salmon or crab. He knew which towns had farmers markets and when, and from time to time he'd stop and buy apples because Maria loved the tart ones, or tomatoes, something on his way home to Mill Valley, and in some ways undercover for the SOU was the perfect job for knowing where to find the best produce and fruit.

But it was most fun when the team was still ten wardens, and on a given night six could make it to dinner at a safehouse. It became a way to relax and step away from an ongoing operation. Information and ideas got passed around.

"Are we going out again tonight?" Roberts asked.

"No, we're down."

"Good, I bought some wine."

"Open it up."

They grilled the fish, roasted potatoes and red bell peppers, and drank the wine, which was smooth going down and left him wishing he was home with Katherine tonight. There was some existentialist quality to being here, as if they weren't legit anymore because they were going to get shut down. He listened to Roberts talking about working at headquarters and in the Region IV office, and the changes she saw coming inside the department. Then there was gossip about Bell's divorce papers and a more earnest discussion of Cairo's dry-farming tomato idea, which none of them, including Cairo, knew much about. But he had books on it, loved tomatoes, and he had a friend already farming tomatoes who wanted a partner.

A team couldn't be on all the time. You couldn't sit night after night on surveillance without going flat, and one of the harder things to juggle as the team shrank was picking and choosing where they put the energy. Tonight as the wine was gone a quiet settled over them. The moon blurred in fog. The coals burned down, and it got colder outside, the near-winter damp cutting through their clothes and the warmth from drinking wine fading to tiredness. Roberts and Cairo called it a night, Shauf not long afterward. Marquez stayed outside and waited until the coals burned down.

He dreamed of Anna that night. She had a bullet wound at her right temple. Her body was folded into the refrigerator that had held the body of the unknown woman. She wore a blood-drenched shirt and in the dream struggled to get out of the refrigerator. When he helped her climb out her face was gray, hair matted, and she had another wound high on her forehead. A stone bench appeared in sunlight along the slough road, and as he sat down she sat next to him. He saw then that a large piece of the back of her skull was missing.

"Who was it that did this to you?" he asked.

"There's nothing wrong with me. I'm fine. That's why I'm sitting here talking to you. I told the detective the same thing. I feel fine. Quit worrying about me."

When Marquez woke it was just before dawn. He dressed and made a pot of coffee, opened the door to the back patio and let the cold, damp with the smells of the wet grass and the fallen leaves, chill the kitchen. Roberts walked in barefoot as he was watching the coffee drip through.

"Are we going to get somewhere today?" she asked.

"Today is the day we take them all down and roll up the whole poaching operation. Do you want to start with coffee or vodka?"

"I'm going to make tea. Where's Cairo? Out planting tomatoes?"

"I'm right here."

Cairo had come in quietly, and Marquez got down another mug and, as he poured coffee for Cairo, had a thought he'd had many times before, that they were all from completely different walks of life and separated by years in age. In his late forties now, he had better than fifteen years on Roberts, twenty on Cairo. Only Shauf was his contemporary and she was forty, so eight years younger than him. But for banding together for this cause, they never would have met each other. He handed Cairo half a mug of coffee and watched him fill the other half with milk. None of them had to be here. He took a sip of coffee. Looking at them filled him with pride.

24

The next morning a tall gold-colored SUV sat in the spot between the eucalyptus trees where Raburn usually parked. The man in the driver's seat turned to stare as Marquez pulled in between two trees. When Marquez walked up to the edge of the trail to look down the muddy path to the river and Raburn's houseboat, he heard the man coming up behind him. Before turning to talk to the man he realized that the houseboat windows were broken.

"What happened?"

"Raburn's boat got shot up."

"Is he okay?"

"He's fine. It's always the drunks that survive the wrecks. He's hiding at his brother's."

"You're not a friend of his."

"Are you?"

"He called me yesterday and said he had some fish for me. I said I'd stop by this morning. When did all this happen?"

"Late last night. I'm Barry Gant. I'm with the volunteer firefighters. My sister-in-law lives right here. She's got a four-year-old daughter. Any one of those shots could travel a mile and kill somebody. Whoever came here and did this is here because of him. He draws that element here."

Gant walked down the muddy path behind Marquez. A line of bullet holes pocked the painted plywood walls of the houseboat, but there were no holes in the flotation, which was interesting, assuming they knew Raburn wasn't home and wanted to cause maximum damage. He walked the length of the boat, then stepped onto the deck while Gant ranted.

"That dumb sonofabitch had a gallon of gasoline next to a corner outside on the deck. A bullet came within an inch of it."

Marquez nodded, had seen the plastic two-gallon container each time he'd been here, though he didn't see it right now. The walls of the boat were nothing more than two-by-fours on two-foot centers with a skin of plywood and a mix of glass and Plexiglas windows. The Plexiglas panels had degenerated under years of bright sunlight and turned cloudy, and now they were marked with bullet holes. The glass windows had been shot enough times to shatter, and he guessed a dozen or more bullets had passed through the boat, probably ricocheted off the rock embankment across the river. Marquez poked his head, looking inside.

"Don't go in there. The county crime people are coming out."

"Was there a police report?"

"Last night."

"Did they find casings on the bank?"

"How do you know all that?"

Marquez decided to let the conversation end. He'd made a guess about trajectory, deciding that the gun had been fired from a position almost level with the boat, a slight downward trajectory so probably just a few steps up the bank, and he looked for footprints but couldn't find anything definitive. It did not look like the spray of an assault weapon, and he pictured someone standing on the bank pumping shots into the houseboat. Someone who knew Raburn wasn't inside. Someone unconcerned about the noise the shots made. Ludovna's guy came to mind. Here to make a not-so-subtle point. The county wouldn't waste time with this because there were no witnesses and no one was hurt. He turned to Gant.

"Raburn is at his brother's?"

"A deputy found him down there last night."

"Okay, I'll check there. Thanks for all your help."

The wet corrugated metal of the packing shed roof reflected the morning sunlight brilliantly. The remaining leaves of the pears looked more tattered and bare than just a few days ago. He drove past the equipment building, and the old Scout bounced hard in a pothole. Isaac's big blue Ford F-350 was in front of the house, parked near the older Volvo his wife, Cindy, drove. Raburn's truck was hidden from the road and covered with a tarp, so he was either scared or making a show of it. Marquez pulled up alongside Raburn's pickup, got out, and walked up to the house.

It needed paint. The porch creaked under his weight. He knocked and stood near the railing cap, listening for a moment inside and looking out through the rows of fruit trees. He smelled damp earth, the fall. On the porch railing under his hand, paint had peeled and cracked like a dry riverbed and small beads of water had pooled between the cracks. He knocked again, and the door rattled loosely. The house was probably in need of more work than the money you could make selling apples and pears in a dozen years of good harvests, and Raburn was probably right about his brother's chances.

It wasn't until his third knock that Isaac's son opened the door, then went to get his father. But it was Abe who came to the door rather than Isaac. He stepped out onto the porch and shut the door, his face pale, combative, anxious. He smelled like a hangover, and ashen half-moons of pouched skin sagged below his eyes.

"Lucky I wasn't home when it happened."

"Who did it?"

"It's got to be him. He must know who you are." Raburn tried to give him a hard stare now. "Either way I'm done with Fish and Game. You can go ahead and arrest me this morning because this sure as hell isn't worth dying for."

"I can understand you being scared."

"You don't understand shit. I'm fifty-two. I got here when I was sixteen. Do you really think you know more about the fish species that live in the delta than I do? You sure as hell don't, and there's no problem with sturgeon. The problem is you trapped me and you've made some people angry and if you keep it up you're going to get me killed just like I told you the first day."

"Let's take a drive together and get some breakfast. You look like you need some food."

They drove up the river to Freeport, and Raburn put away sliced ham, three eggs, potatoes, and coffee. He asked for another order of toast and concentrated on the food, head down, eyes out the window whenever he looked up. Something about the shooting didn't fit. Raburn's answers were too dodgy. The accusatory tone, how Fish and Game had entrapped him, had a staged air to it.

"You can arrest me, but I'm going to tell the jury I did everything I could to help and finally got scared."

"That sounds like your lawyer talking."

"I've done everything you asked. You can't ask me to risk my life."

They weren't offering him any protection, and the DA would roll her eyes and say, look, he's done enough, we're not bringing any case against him. They'd plea-bargain something, and Raburn would get a slap on the wrist.

"So you think shooting up your boat was a message from Ludovna?"

"I already said that."

Marquez handed the waitress a twenty and looked at Raburn again, caught Raburn studying his face.

"One problem with all this is you haven't given us what we need to take Ludovna down. You say you don't have records of sales."

Raburn was scornful. "No one keeps records. Who's that stupid?"

Marquez drove him back to his brother's, and Raburn didn't say a word during the ride. He got out of the Scout.

"Don't shut the door yet," Marquez said. "Here's what I'm going to do. I'll give you a day to think about everything. You're hungover, you were up all night, and like you said, anyone would be scared. Think it over. We'll talk tomorrow."

"I've already thought it over. If you want to bust me, go ahead. I know someone else who disappeared, and it isn't going to happen to me. I got warned last night, and I don't need to be told twice."

"Who do you know that disappeared?"

He could see Raburn regretted having said that. He didn't answer, let the door fall shut, and Marquez watched him go up the porch and into the house.

25

"How'd it go with Dishonest Abe?" Shauf asked.

"He says we can arrest him whenever we want."

"Nothing would make me happier. Want me to talk to the DA this morning?"

"Why don't you meet me in Walnut Grove and we'll get a cup of coffee and talk about where we're at instead."

He got into Walnut Grove ahead of her and took a call from Ehrmann while he waited, parked on the side of the road.

"Lieutenant, Stan Ehrmann here." Marquez picked up on the formal tone right away. "We've got the problem this morning I warned you about. You've crossed into our operations, and I'm going to back you off."

"Where did we do that?"

"At Weisson's Auto. How many times have you been there?"

"I've been in the building once, and we've been by the building a number of times."

He related the events with Torp and Perry, then listened to Ehrmann.

"It's a chop shop. What the Russians call a *patsani* gets a few hundred bucks to steal a car and deliver it. You've seen the totaled cars in the fenced-in area. Most of those totals are late-model cars that were sold cheap at auctions by insurance companies. You can make pretty good money if you have stolen cars to get the new parts from and you rebuild a cheap total. We're looking for several individuals who periodically visit Weisson's, and we'll shut down their operation at the same time. We've been there awhile, and I don't want anything happening that has any chance of arousing any suspicion."

"We'll stay away. Is that your surveillance in the unfinished three-story building off to the left?"

"Excuse me."

"I saw something going on in that building on the third floor."

"And why did you think it was surveillance?"

"I've been doing this a long time, and I saw what I thought was a reflection off glass."

It was more than that. He'd spotted what he'd thought might be surveillance but hadn't wanted to start asking questions yet. Chop shops weren't unusual, and he'd figured it could be a Sacramento Police team. If by some chance he'd spotted an FBI team, it shouldn't have happened. He listened to Ehrmann clear his throat.

"Why don't you come to work for me, Marquez?"

"The Feds would never have me, but I think you know that. I'm sure you've read up on me."

"I'd like to hear your side of it sometime."

"My side is the leak came from somewhere inside DEA. Someone got bought, and I was lucky enough not to be home when they came around to kill everyone. Did you read about the drug killing outside Cancun, Mexico, a couple of days ago? Nine dead, two of them Federal agents, two more agents found wounded yesterday. It was a lot like that."

"I'd still like to hear the story." Marquez left it at that, and Ehrmann said, "I sent you more information on Torp. It'll be at DFG headquarters by noon."

He said, "Thanks," and meant it. Ehrmann didn't have to and no doubt had gotten them more than they could ever get from NCIC or WSIN, the Western States Information Network.

"What's happening here is you're doing your job so well we may have to stop you from running over the back end of us."

"We won't go near Weisson's. We've got a buyer in Rio Vista. We'll work him, and we're getting somewhere with the Nick Ludovna I talked to you about. But I'm going to ask again, is Nikolai Ludovna part of your investigation?"

"Not at this time."

"You've looked at him before?"

"We have."

He bought coffee with Shauf, and she rode with him out Walnut Grove Road past the tractor business and the fields of young pears, past Giusti's and out beyond tomato fields ready to be tilled under and grapevines bare with the late fall. She looked at the tomato fields and said, "I guess we can't let Cairo see this. He'd be down on his knees, running earth through his fingers."

They turned off the main road and then drove out to a stand of oaks, parked, and got away from the truck. They walked out to a log and sat down well away from anywhere anyone could hear them.

"Look at us," Shauf said. "Ruax gets her house bugged so we're not even sitting in the truck."

This was the other thing Ehrmann had told him. They'd swept Ruax's house and come up with bugs. That was happening now. They were seeing more counter-surveillance, and suspects had gotten smarter about cell phone use as well. They favored the stolen chip and the prepaid card.

"So where are we at this morning?" she asked. "Dishonest Abe wants out. Anna is gone. Ludovna is sitting on his toadstool, and prison bait isn't calling you back. We're nowhere on August even though we watched the airport handoff."

"Crey did call me back. I'm going to meet him tonight, but the trick there is still to cut Torp and Perry out of the picture."

"That's what I mean, nothing is quite working. We've got a bunch of pieces and nothing whole. Do you think we're bird-dogging for the Feds?"

"Do you want to roll it up?"

"No."

"Does Cairo?"

"No. Neither does Roberts or Alvarez, but you've got to be as frustrated as everyone else."

"It'll come together."

"What do you think is going on with the Feds?"

"I think they're waiting to see if our operation turns up anything that'll help them."

"So we are bird-dogging for them. You think there's a tie-in with August and what we watched come out of Weisson's and go to him? These guys trafficking in sturgeon are also moving other stuff."

"Good chance of that. Let's focus on Crey the next several days and see what more we can learn from the FBI about their investigation."

He sat with Shauf another hour, bringing up past operations as they tried to find parallels. There'd been a bear bust, a twisted guy named Ungar, it had taken them a while to figure out. The operation had gone several directions before they took Ungar down.

When they got ready to leave, Shauf threw out, "You know, the shutdown is hanging over everybody, and I don't mean the Feds. I mean the end of us. What'll happen with you and me?"

"I'll put you up for captain, and I'll go plant tomatoes with Cairo."

"Yeah, everybody is going to be a captain. But really, what are you going to do? Are you really thinking of hanging it up? What would you do then?"

"Go to work for the Feds; they've got all the money."

"Isn't that the truth? Or the Highway Patrol. Every time I think about what they make compared to us it pisses me off."

Marquez knew he wouldn't quit on this case. He'd find a way to shut down these sturgeon poachers, and if it meant doing it without his badge, he'd cowboy it and find a way to stay legal. He felt a strong rush of emotion.

"I've got to know what happened to Anna. I want the truth there. And I'm not walking away from these poachers. I'll sink a few boats first."

"Great. I'll visit you in prison. Maybe you can bunk with Torp, Perry, or Crey when they get back in."

Marquez's phone rang, and he smiled at Shauf. "It's Crey."

"What's going on, big man?" Crey asked.

"Not much, just sitting around."

"Are we still on for tonight?"

"Nothing has changed on my end."

"See you at Lisa's around dark. We'll get it all figured out tonight. We're going to make some money, bro. Life is a big rock candy mountain."

"I was just thinking that. See you there."

Marquez hung up. He held the phone in one hand and smiled at Shauf.

"What's funny?"

"Nothing. Let's get out of here."

26

Marquez found Lisa down on her dock replacing a couple of rotted deck boards. He helped her cut and screw into place a new pressure-treated piece of two-by-six. The last gold reflection off the river caused her to squint as she stood and faced him, and she wiped chips of the arsenic-laced wood off her cheeks. He rolled up her power cord as they talked.

"Richie's friends are already here," she said. "Or they were half an hour ago. They were asking about you again. I was going to call you as soon as I finished this. They said they're meeting you here for dinner. Their last names are Torp and Perry. They make me uncomfortable."

"They should. Did they rent a room?"

"One room for the two of them. I put them as far away from you as I could."

"What about Crey?"

She shook her head, and that said it all. Marquez had told Crey he was staying here, and Crey had told "the boys." No doubt they figured to get the chain of command straight tonight with Crey standing off to the side and innocent. Marquez walked up from the dock with Lisa. He prepaid his room, then moved his truck up there. He'd switched out of the Scout. He talked to Shauf again from the room.

"I just heard Bell quit," she said. "He handed Baird his badge and a letter of resignation this morning, then walked out. I'm surprised he didn't stick around to watch us twist in the wind."

Had to be about his divorce, Marquez thought, and listened quietly, thinking about people who'd left. Who you thought would stick didn't and vice versa. He knew he'd be gone too when the SOU shut down.

At dusk he left the room and walked down to the marina. Crey, Perry, and Torp were already at the bar. Torp spotted him first and nudged Perry as Marquez walked in. Might as well warm it up right away, Marquez thought.

"I didn't know it was a party," he said to Crey. "Or weren't you able to get a babysitter?" He looked at Torp and Perry. "Just kidding, guys, and I'll buy you a drink if you take it outside."

Maybe they were here to vet him for Crey. Crey was moody and quiet, so it was possible it had rained on the big rock candy mountain this afternoon.

"Man, you are some kind of asshole," Perry said.

"You two bring it out in me."

Crey settled it down, and they moved from the bar to a table and ordered drinks. Lisa turned on the Christmas lights, and the different colors lined the windows and cast a glow on the deck.

Two couples came in for dinner as it got darker, and right around the second round of drinks or maybe their third, Perry got interested in the young woman who worked nights as a waitress. He waved her over.

"How'd you like to dance on my lap?"

Marquez leaned over to talk to Crey, though he made sure Perry and Torp could hear. "Can't you feed him outside and then put him in the car until we're done? There are people in here trying to eat, and I can't think with him around."

That lit up Perry. Anger was bright in his eyes. He pointed a finger at Marquez.

"This is going to get squared up."

"Sounds good to me."

Perry lifted the empty bread basket and waved it. "Chiquita. Bread."

"Get him out of here," Marquez said.

"You boys go to the bar," Crey said to them. "The man and I are going to talk."

They didn't move, so Marquez stood and said he was going to use the restroom, figuring that would give Crey time to sort it out. In the hallway on the way, there was a poster of Anna Burdovsky. "Missing." "Feared Abducted." When he got back Crey nodded toward Perry and Torp standing at the bar.

"These guys don't get why you're all over them. Why not give it a rest?"

"Why are they staying here tonight?"

"Is that what this is about?"

"You tell me. Are they here because I'm here?"

"You've got to make your peace with them, my man. However you do it, it's got to happen. They're part of my crew."

"You don't need them."

"They're all I've got to put between me and anyone watching. I'm not a big operation. I'm not like the Russians."

"Right, and I keep hearing about these Russians. Maybe I should be doing business with them."

"You don't want to deal with them."

The waitress returned and took their dinner orders. Marquez saw Lisa handing Torp and Perry menus. They'd taken seats at the bar.

"What do you think of the chick that runs this place?" Crey asked, following his eyes.

"I like her."

"Yeah, she's cute." Crey sighed. "You've got to back off a little, man. You're not a bad guy but you're making problems I don't need."

"I keep saying the same thing over and over; I'd rather deal straight with you."

"Lou is pretty quick with a knife, and you've got him angry. I want you to apologize tonight. Why do you have such a hard-on for them?"

"Why'd you ask me about Lisa?"

"Because she's alone here and she's got to be lonely." Crey gave him a sly smile. "She needs somebody to keep her warm at night."

In his room before walking down to the marina deck, Marquez had read through what Ehrmann left for him at DFG. Torp was a registered sex offender who had to report his whereabouts. The home address for him was Sherri La Belle's address in Stockton. She was the owner of the gold Le Mans Perry and Torp had traded for the van.

"Here's what bothers me," Marquez said. "They stick out. Like that car of theirs."

"The Le Mans is gone. They traded it for a van."

"But you know what I mean."

Torp also had two strikes, and Marquez wasn't much of a fan of California's three-strike system. There wasn't enough flexibility in the way the law got applied. In some cases the application of the law was immoral. In the case of a man named Santos Reyes, for example. Reyes had perjured himself on a driver's license application and taken the test for a cousin who couldn't read so that his cousin could work as a roofer. Reyes had two priors, one for robbery a decade before, and a burglary as a juvenile in '81. He got his third strike for the driver's license fiasco, and in consequence twenty-six to life.

"It's more complicated than you know about. Liam is a good mechanic. He works on my charter boat, and I need him."

"But look at them right now, both trying to hit on her. They stand out. Cops will pick up on them." Marquez added, "I've done business for a long time by not sticking out."

"They're who I've got right now. Later, we'll figure it out differently."

"I'm on record about them, okay?"

"Man, you are too loud and clear on record. Chill."

The waitress brought more drinks, and Crey bought another round for the guys at the bar. Lisa put a burger in front of Torp and spaghetti in front of Perry. She brought more bread. She gave them what they asked for and otherwise ignored them, pretending to be too busy, and Marquez kept an eye on the bar. He took the conversation at the table back to the Russians.

"So if these guys exist, have you done business with them?"

"I've done some. I heard about it when I was inside. I heard they were into sturgeon so I made contact when I got out. But you don't need them, you've got me. I can take whatever you've got to sell."

"And what do you do with it? Do you sell to them?"

"Don't worry about who I sell to. My money is good. That's all you need to know."

Marquez kept drinking beer. Crey switched from hard liquor to wine, ordering another glass as Marquez looked around at what Lisa had here.

Twelve tables with wood tops, big A-frame windows looked out on the deck and the river. He'd seen Lisa on a ladder with a caulking gun a couple of times, trying to find leaks. The floor was old wood plank and worn. There were water stains and grooves worn in the flooring around the bar. Bathrooms were clean but needed to be redone, and Lisa had told him she just got by. Made just enough to justify keeping the doors open. The space was warm when sunlight came through the windows. It was a comfortable place in the good parts of the year, and the rest of the time she had to hustle more. He watched Torp and Perry follow her movements down the bar and didn't have to guess to know what they were thinking. Crey swirled wine in his glass, trying to be something he wasn't. Then he surprised Marquez, pulling out a two-ounce glass jar of caviar with August's import label from his coat.

"Take a look at this. It's some good beluga. The largest one of those ever caught ran fifty-three hundred pounds. Man, you wouldn't know how to move something like that."

"You've got that right."

"You'd have to cut the ovaries out right there on the riverbank and kick the thing back in the water."

"Hack off a little meat too."

"Make you rich, wouldn't it? How many pounds of eggs are in fifty-three hundred pounds?"

"Enough."

"You know it."

Crey twisted the top, broke the vacuum seal. He handed it to Marquez to taste.

"If you eat caviar the alcohol doesn't absorb as fast," Crey said. "That's the God's truth. I heard it from a Russian."

"Okay, so where are these Russians from?"

"They put the word out about a year ago. They've got some guys working the middle for them, so when you sell to them you drop stuff off. You never deal direct, kind of like what I'm doing with the boys." He used his wineglass to gesture toward the caviar. "That's some good shit, isn't it? It's what the jar says that matters. The label, man. Things keep heating up with the Iranians, and Congress will be cutting off the caviar they ship here, but those fat-ass bankers in New York are still going to want caviar, and that's where you and me make the money."

They ate dinner and talked sturgeon haunts, different baits, the best holes for finding the big sturgies. Ghost shrimp. Grass shrimp. Eel/shrimp combos. Pile worms and eels. Crey favored grass shrimp. He liked to fish the Big Cut and would eat bass or halibut or crappie over sturgeon because he found sturgeon too oily.

"I learned to fish with my old man and Tom Beaudry. But I never liked Beaudry. He was an asshole to work for and a lying fucker. He'd look those Fish and Game people right in the eye and lie his ass off. Let me tell you, we were big time over-limit so many times I can't remember how many. But he taught me, man, that's the one good thing he did. Well, actually, two good things because he sold me his shop way too cheap."

"Why'd he do that?"

"He wanted out."

"Hey, I knew him. That's bullshit."

"Okay, let me put it this way. He owed money, and I was connected with the people he owed it to. They got the deal done for me, and I'm paying them a little on the side."

"Are we talking Russians again?"

"That's it for tonight, man."

Crey stood and, with a long bow-legged stride, cowboy boots clicking on the flooring, left after talking to the boys. Marquez watched the backs of Torp and Perry and finished his drink, thinking over what Crey had told him. He'd said that Beaudry taught him the two big rivers and the bays, where to take the sport boat, and he still fished Cache Slough, Steamboat, and Chain and Decker Islands. The Mothball Fleet was always reliable for sturgies. Meeks Hole. Mare Island. Montezuma Slough. The PG&E plant, the power lines, Ryer and Sherman Islands, though not in the wind. Lots of times he'd check out sturgeonfishing.com. The whole online thing was good for fishing.

It was a short walk from here back to the room, and Marquez thought he'd call Katherine before going to sleep. The waitress cleared his table. Lisa turned a couple of the lights off when there was nobody left in the room but himself, Torp, and Perry. She came over to his table and sat down after Perry and Torp moved out onto the deck to smoke.

"One of those two came into the kitchen tonight and scared me."

"Which one?"

"The thin one with the dark hair. I think his name is Liam."

"What did he want in the kitchen?"

"He said he used to work as a cook and he's looking for a job again, but when I asked him about it, it didn't sound like he knows how to cook. He was a short-order cook or something like that in Florida for a few weeks once, and I don't even believe that. He says he was in Sarasota but can't remember the name of the restaurant he worked at."

"He got Sarasota from your waterskiing photos on the wall."

"I don't like the way he looks at me. It makes me feel like I need to take a shower."

Perry and Torp watched through the windows as he talked with Lisa. Then they came back inside and up to the bar. When Lisa got up to go serve them Marquez also stood.

"Last call, gentlemen," she said.

"We'd like to buy a bottle of Jack Daniels," Perry said, and pointed at Marquez. "Put it on his room."

Lisa turned to Marquez. "That okay with you?"

"No."

"Thought you were going to buy us a drink," Perry said.

"Sure, give them a last drink on me."

"And one for him too," Perry said.

"I'm done."

"Stick around because we've got something to say to you."

"Say it now."

"It's got to wait for outside."

Lisa poured two Jack Daniels and turned the bar lights off.

"Take them out on the deck," she said. "I'm going upstairs."

Marquez led the way out to the deck. It was late but cold and clear. The deck chairs had dew on them. Cigarette smell lingered from when Torp and Perry had been out here earlier.

"Richie is a real good friend of mine so I didn't get into it with you earlier, but you treat me like that ever again I'll kill you," Perry said.

Marquez waited. Nothing more came.

"That's all you have to say?"

"You wouldn't be the first either."

"I'll remember that. Enjoy your drink. It's the last one I'll ever buy you."

27

Marquez woke to footsteps on the gravel, soft steps stopping near his truck before moving on. After whoever was there moved away he eased out of bed and very slowly clicked the deadbolt back and opened the door. Cold flooded in. A white moon was out over the water. He read the roofline of the marina building and saw part of the deck, but no one on the road. Another night he might have gone back to bed. He looked toward Perry and Torp's room, then dressed and slipped on his shoulder harness, felt the cold gun against his chest.

Torp and Perry's white van was still in front of the room they'd rented. The two rooms between theirs and his were empty. No lights were on. He didn't hear any sounds, and this was probably needless worry. He softly shut his door, threw the deadbolt, and then, rather than walk past Torp and Perry's room and down the road to the marina building, he went the opposite way up to the levee road.

Now he looked down on the roofs of the rooms Lisa rented and the big marina building, the boats docked below, the light on the river. He stayed in the shadow out of the moonlight and knew there was a footpath somewhere up here that led back down. It took a few minutes to find it. Then he climbed over the guard rail and dropped steeply on the path through mud and brush until he was down to where Lisa's car sat in a narrow carport.

He worked his way to the dark corner of the marina building. He knew he hadn't imagined the footsteps but wondered now if it had been Torp or Perry going outside for a smoke. He kept one hand sliding along the wood siding of the marina building as he worked his way around it, moving toward the river and the moonlit deck.

When he rounded the corner and was under the deck he heard movement on the deck. Soft footsteps. They stopped, then started again. He edged his way around to the river face of the deck, staying low, listening to a scratching noise, and then moved onto one of the deck steps and saw someone at the bar door, his back turned to him. He climbed the steps slowly and moved toward the figure, knew if the man turned he'd see him on the deck in the moonlight. It's Torp, he thought, looking at the back of him. Heard the faint rattle of the door lock, Torp trying to get the door open, and not turning around until Marquez was within ten feet of him.

"I'm getting a drink," Torp said, jumping back, startled and surprised.

"There's a whole river you can drink. Where's your friend?"

He saw a blur of movement or maybe he heard a chair scrape, or Torp was too quiet, too slow to answer. When Perry charged across the deck Marquez was already in motion. Perry's blade sliced through his coat, and Marquez swung a deck chair with his left hand, missed Perry but caught Torp in the face and broke a leg of the chair. He saw Torp go down moaning and faced Perry, was close to drawing his gun but swung the chair instead, kept Perry circling. Torp started to rise, and Marquez swung at Perry again, then kicked Torp in the head, watched him stagger, lie flat, and surprisingly start to get up yet again.

"Do him," Perry said and advanced on Marquez, the knife blade flashing in the moonlight. "Liam, shoot him."

Marquez swung the chair at the advancing Perry, and Torp was on his feet again. He reached into his coat, and Marquez jumped toward him with the chair and with a slashing swing forced him to block with his arms and jump back before he was hit. In the same motion he continued around with the chair and caught part of Perry. Then he was on Torp clubbing him to the deck, his big fist hammering down on the back of Torp's neck. Marquez pulled the gun from Torp's belt and aimed at Perry.

"Drop the knife."

"Are you going to shoot me, Fish Boy?"

"Right now."

He clicked the safety off, aimed at Perry's midsection, and heard the knife clatter onto the decking. He backed Perry up, picked up the knife, then walked them both up the road to the rooms and had Perry lie face down on the gravel near their van as a bleeding Torp staggered around getting their stuff out of their room. Then he had Perry get in and start the van. After they drove off he sat out in the cold for an hour and talked to Cairo, who was down the street from Crey's house where the lights were on still. He was still shaking from adrenaline.

"These guys are operating outside of Crey," Marquez said.

"You need to bag it and pull out tonight, Lieutenant. We can get a police cruiser to sit out there and watch the marina."

Marquez looked at the knife and gun, knew that they wouldn't be back tonight and that things were in motion now with Torp and Perry in a way that wouldn't stop until satisfied. He left it with Cairo that he'd find him around dawn, then went back into the room, lay down with his gun near him, his heart still pounding.

28

Around midday Marquez knocked on the door of Chief Bell's house. When Bell answered, his face was puffy, hair uncharacteristically uncombed, and he hadn't shaved in a couple of days. He wore jeans, a robe, no shirt, and tasseled brown loafers without socks.

"We haven't always gotten along," Marquez said, "but I want to say good-bye. I heard you're going east."

"I have a job offer." He stared as though daring Marquez to challenge the truth of that. "Come in, Lieutenant."

It was an invitation Marquez had never had. He'd attended a single backyard cocktail party, but only the catering company serving food had been in and out of the house that night. Guests had used the bathrooms in the cabana.

In the kitchen was a long plank table and a fireplace. Marquez took a seat at the bar counter, and Bell moved stiffly around to the other side to face him. He offered coffee.

"I'm sure you've heard the rumors about my wife."

"I heard you were served divorce papers at headquarters."

"Oh, I'm sure the story has made the rounds. Ellen ran off with a friend of ours. I couldn't count how many times he's had dinner here. This is a bastard I played golf with and thought was a friend of mine. I called him a day or two after she left to tell him because I needed somebody to talk to. When I found out it was him I had to lock up my gun. You can take that story back to headquarters, I'm sure they'll like that one too."

Marquez didn't know what to say to Bell. His pride was badly hurt, and Marquez didn't know Bell's wife, didn't know much of anything about their marriage. It made an awkward moment.

"What's the job in D.C.?"

Now Bell had to decide how much he wanted to say to this lieutenant who'd largely been difficult to manage. Bell had hobnobbed regularly with politicians, attended fund-raisers, made speeches about environmental preservation and gave of his time to different candidates. In the single conversation Marquez had ever had with Bell about those ambitions, Bell had been frank, said he felt his place was in the public arena. That's where his skills were best suited, and maybe that's what moving to Washington was about. He'd come out of a middle-class suburb, gone to UCLA, pursued biology and law, then served in the National Guard Reserves before coming to Fish and Game. He didn't have any children, was a hard worker and well liked inside the administration building, though disliked by all field wardens Marquez knew. Shauf had caught it best, saying when she was in his office she always got the feeling she wasn't supposed to touch anything or sit on the furniture, because Bell drew a clear line between the help out in the field and those who worked administration.

"I'm sure you'll be happy to see me go."

"You always had your reasons, and you always seemed to believe them. I thought someday you'd be running the show. But I came to say good-bye because we worked together for years. I figure to turn my own badge in when this operation ends."

"You don't mean that. What would you possibly do?"

"I don't know yet. What's the job in D.C.?"

"Lobbying for an environmental group at quadruple the pay I made with the department. I get a living expense, a car, and a credit card for entertaining."

The world didn't need any more lobbyists.

"When does it start?"

"Next week. My wife and I made several trips to Washington looking for a house to rent." Bell studied his face. "Lieutenant, I know it'll be a hard adjustment having the SOU close down, but you'll get used to a uniform again. Chief Baird has a place for you."

"I won't be taking it."

"It just takes some adjustment."

"Sure."

He shook hands with Bell and wished him luck in Washington. The divorce was a deep hurt for him, but he'd survive.

"One day I'm going to come home, turn on CNN, and there you're going to be," Marquez said.

That got a weak smile. Marquez had already turned to go, and Bell's voice caught him from behind on the steps outside, a quieter, far different voice. "Thanks for coming by, Lieutenant, and if there's anything I can do with the sturgeon, call me. Technically, I'm still with the department another two weeks."

"There is something, sir, but it means borrowing your house for a night."

"Okay, explain that to me."

Marquez walked back and laid out his request. When he left he drove back to the delta along a levee first formed naturally by debris and soil left in the spring runoffs and held in place by trees and brush and grasses. Before all the farmland, vineyards, and orchards, there had been tule and grasses and brush over the layers of peat. The natural levee had been scraped clean and built up with dirt and protected from the currents with concrete and riprap. The road he was on now was smooth and the river safely below, but like a lot of things the levees weren't what they appeared. They'd deteriorated badly. The severe long-predicted earthquake could cause all of this land to flood.

He went looking for Raburn, figured Raburn had his twenty-four hours to think it over, had time to sober up and cool down. He found him under his truck in the pear packing shed, changing out the master brake cylinder. Raburn got to his feet and dusted himself off.

"My brother is going to use the truck when I'm in prison." So he'd told his brother what was going on. "The brakes needed fixing. Pedal was getting mushy."

"That's touching, but here's the scenario I'm seeing."

"That reminds me of this detective I used to know. He'd stop in at Al Wop's in Locke and I'd sometimes meet him for a drink. His wife liked fresh fish so I traded him fish for drinks. He used to say all scenarios are bullshit."

Al Wop's still had peanut butter and pickles on the bar and served fried bread and steaks. He looked at Raburn and remembered the great trial lawyer, David Terrence Hayden, and the crowd that had followed him, stopping for a drink at Al Wop's after Hayden had turned a jury around and won a case.

"*Scenario* is a polite word for it."

"Sure, and *polite* is the word my father used to use before razor strapping Isaac and me to get the devil out of us. We ran away and survived here by picking pears and apples and fishing for dinner while living in a second-floor room of a falling-down building in Isleton."

"It just doesn't get easier, does it? If we arrest you it'll be for commercial trafficking. There'll be a conspiracy charge, which is a felony. There'll be multiple conspiracy charges because you sold to Crey as well. What will count in your favor will be whatever testimony you provide against Ludovna. You can turn state's witness against him."

"It's not going to happen."

Raburn wiped his hands with a rag, and through the big open door Marquez watched Shauf's van and Cairo's truck turn down off the levee road. The green pickup of the area warden was right behind them. Alvarez and Roberts followed. Raburn put his hands on his hips and faced the approaching vehicles. He tried to keep his face impassive.

"Don't arrest me yet."

"Then I've got to walk out and talk to them."

"They can't be here."

Marquez walked out of the pear packing shed, and the lead truck, Cairo's, slowed to a stop.

"He's changed his mind and wants to talk to me alone, so let's back away. He's particularly worried about the marked Fish and Game truck."

When Marquez walked back in Raburn was sitting on the raised metal blade of an old forklift.

"I know you caught me dead to rights, and okay, I admit I shot up my own boat, but you got to understand, Nick is like Isaac and me, he started with nothing, and he's not going to give it up. He's a hard guy, and you're not going to protect me from him."

"We'll take your testimony in the judge's chambers."

"He'll know where it came from, and he'll get me from prison."

"We're not trying to get you killed," Marquez said. "But we are going to shut down the sturgeon poaching."

Raburn shook his head. "You're not hearing me. Even if he went to jail it wouldn't be for more than a couple of years, and I'm more afraid of him than I am of you. You'll go on to another case, but there's more than just Nick and they'll start up again, and then they'll come find me. There was a guy named Chris Stevens. I used to fish with him, and he sold a couple of sturgeon to Nick when I was just getting started with the whole thing. We both sold to him, and Nick said to us, if you ever fuck with me, I'll kill you. Said it just like that, and Chris said, if you ever threaten me again, I'll go to the cops. About two weeks later Chris just disappeared. No one saw him again. The police said he probably got tired of his life and went somewhere to start a new one, but it isn't true."

"Did Ludovna ever say anything to you about him?"

"What he did was call me every day for a couple of weeks and we had the same conversation, you know. Like this. He'd ask, do you have a fish for me? If they were biting, then maybe I had one. If they weren't, then I said no. But if I said no, then he always asked why not, you're supposed to get me fish. Then he would ask, where's Chris, he's not calling me back? Have him call me today? Then it started to be more like, have you seen Chris, and I would say, no, and after a couple of weeks I could tell he was making fun of me by asking. He started asking if Chris had moved. Questions like, how come your friend doesn't call you anymore? I could always tell he knew where Chris was."

"Did you go to the police?"

"I went with Chris's wife and filled out a missing persons report."

"And he never turned up?"

Shook his head.

"Is his wife still around?"

"I don't know, but I have something in back."

Marquez watched him walk into the gloom at the back of the packing shed, heard the door creak open and saw light from the room. He walked back out with a piece of paper in his hand.

A color poster of the cheerful face of a blue-eyed man. In black ink at the top it read MISSING. There was a physical description of Chris Stevens and one of his car.

"Was his car ever found?"

"Nope."

"Is this number for her still good?"

"I don't know."

"You never liked Ludovna but you got involved with him."

"I had to have the money."

Marquez turned the phrasing of that in his head. Had to have the money. Different somehow than saying I needed the money. Had to have it for what? He laid a hand on a cardboard pear box with the yellow-orange script of Raburn Pears. A pear tree laden with ripe fruit was the logo, then he said, "I'll be back in a minute." He walked outside and called Roberts. She'd be the best one to get on a computer and phone and check.

"You'll have to go back in the newspapers, the public records," he said. "We might have to talk to some of the other orchard owners. There's something there. Maybe we need to talk to a banker in town."

"I'll get started."

Marquez walked back into the pear packing shed. He sat and talked half an hour with Raburn about Chris Stevens and then decided Raburn had suspected Ludovna but had never told a police officer. If that was true, he could only guess at why, but his gut said Ludovna had something on him. With Raburn watching he called Chris Stevens's wife. She still lived in the same house off Poverty Road in Ryde.

"I'm a Fish and Game warden. I'd like to come over and talk with you if I can about your husband."

"He's not home right now."

Marquez wasn't sure how to respond to that.

"Then maybe you and I could talk," he said.

"That would be fine. I've been waiting for somebody."

"I'll see you in fifteen minutes."

"I'll make some tea. You'll have to knock on the door, the bell doesn't work anymore. There are a lot of things Chris is going to fix, but he just never seems to find the time. Thank you for coming."

She hung up, and Marquez held the phone. He asked Raburn again.

"How long has Stevens been missing?"

"Three years."

"And when is the last time you saw Mrs. Stevens?"

"Not since he disappeared and we filed the report."

"If you came with me, would it help?"

"No, she hates me. She thinks I got him killed."

29

Amy Stevens invited him in, then seemed uncomfortable having him in her house. He got the feeling she lived quietly, unseen and unnoticed on this stretch of road. The house was too neat. The kitchen window stared out at rows of leafless vines. The kitchen table and surrounding counters were clean and empty. There were no magazines or newspapers, no fruit in a bowl or anything at all. After she suggested it, Marquez sat down at the kitchen table.

"I made tea. It's almost ready. I don't know when Chris will get home."

The mechanical way she moved, movements that started jerkily, then smoothed, the privacy invaded suggested grief and unanswered sadness. It said something about how alone she was.

"I work part-time as a librarian."

"You do?"

"Yes, but I haven't worked in a while. I was working full-time three years ago, but there have been cutbacks at the county."

"Cutbacks everywhere, I guess."

"At your department too?"

"Some cuts, yes."

She dropped the lid of the teapot and picked it up. Then she stood quietly at the stove.

"I don't know why it's taking him so long to get home."

Marquez nodded. He laid his badge on the table.

"I'm with Fish and Game, and we're looking at a sturgeon poaching problem. One of the people I've been talking to is Abe Raburn. Abe showed me the posters you and he put up."

"He didn't help me." She turned toward him, and there was another long pause. "If Chris had never gone fishing with him I don't think this would have happened."

"Can you tell me about that?"

"I already gave a statement. Haven't you seen it?"

"No, I'm sorry, I haven't."

"They met in a bar, of course. Where else would you find Abe Raburn? Chris came home late one night, and I knew something bad had happened. We always eat dinner exactly at 8:00, and he wasn't here. I sat down to dinner without him, and when he called he was on a slough road with Abe. Then he brought Abe here. They didn't get here until after midnight and sat outside drinking beer, if you can imagine."

"What time of year was this?"

"In the spring. They had both been drinking, and that wasn't like Chris at all. Abe is a very bad influence on him. I'm sure that's why he's not home now. Chris is very organized and very careful.

But Abe is just the opposite. They were probably sturgeon fishing and had engine problems with Abe's boat."

She placed tea cups and poured from the teapot, and he realized she'd boiled water but hadn't added tea. The hot water steamed in the cup. She sat down across from him, her eyes intently on him.

"You will find him, won't you?"

"I don't know if I'll find him. I'm trying to find out what happened to him."

"I was afraid the police had forgotten about him. I told them he went fishing with Abe, and I wish Chris would stop that friendship. He's gotten home very late a couple of times. The night he didn't come home at all I thought it was another one of those situations."

"Was he fishing with Raburn that day?"

"They were going night fishing for sturgeon. I think that's what Chris was planning to do. Of course, Chris may have left me. I can't have children, and we wanted children. I would have adopted, but he wanted children of his own. Maybe he couldn't live here knowing we'd never have any. You see, we both came from large families." She wrung her hands. "I love him so much, I just don't understand why he isn't home yet."

She began to get more and more agitated, and he got the feeling that every night as 8:00 approached she imagined her husband walking in the door. It was difficult and probably wrong to ask her questions, but he continued.

"Do you have a reason to think he was going fishing?"

"Yes, he took his gear. Abe told the police they weren't going fishing together, but I'm sure you know that already. He told the police he didn't see Chris that day and that they weren't mixed up in anything illegal, but I've been very worried."

"Were you worried he was mixed up in something illegal?"

"Oh, no, not Chris."

She took a sip from the tea cup, and Marquez nodded, listened to her description of Chris, the honesty, the gentleness.

"I'm very lucky. The police thought he left me, but he would never do that. They drove around and looked for his car but that was about it. I made posters and put them up and somebody tore a lot of them down, but Chris doesn't have any enemies. He's a very sweet man."

"Did he tell you he was going fishing with Abe?"

"He said he thought they were going to meet after Chris got off work down at the boat landing at the state park."

"Brannan Island?"

"Yes, and the police checked. Chris didn't go through the booth. You know, you have to pay a fee. No one knows where he went. He just disappeared with his truck."

"But he had his fishing gear with him?"

"Yes, he has it."

She folded her hands in front of her, and his heart went out to her. He knew what the police had likely alluded to, what they would have suggested without directly saying it. She needed psychiatric help in a big way, but he also guessed she knew Chris was never coming home again. Her instincts told her it had something to do with Raburn, which made him wonder why Raburn brought the poster out when he did.

"I don't know that I'll find out anything, but if our investigation overlaps anything to do with Chris's disappearance, I'll call you." He paused. "Do you have family in the area?"

"No."

"Any close friends?"

"Not since I went part-time."

"I think you need someone to talk to. I'm going to call somebody."

"I don't accept visitors unless it's about Chris."

She stood, and he put an arm around her shoulders, held her for a moment, thanked her for talking to him, and left. He didn't want to make any calls that triggered her ending up a ward of the state. She was obviously getting by somehow, feeding herself, must have some income. But she needed help.

He talked to the team, then started for home, didn't want to sleep in the safehouse tonight. On the run back to the Bay Area his phone rang, and when he saw the number he knew Katherine and Maria were home.

"We just got in and stopped at the store and picked up some food for dinner," Kath said. "Where are you?"

"An hour away and welcome home, but aren't you three days early?"

"Four."

When he got home it was tense between Katherine and Maria, though both were in the kitchen cooking. Kath's cool fingers laced through his, and he kissed her, saw fatigue on her face, disappointment in her eyes.

"How was it?" he asked Maria.

"It was great."

"How was New York?"

"Didn't I already tell you?"

A pasta was on the table, and the room smelled like bacon. Maria tossed lettuce with oil, vinegar, and an expensive French salt she'd been trying to get her mother hooked on. The dinner was stiff. He asked the only questions, and neither wanted to talk, begging off by saying they were jet-lagged, but obviously the decision to come home was unhappy. No great school had become the sweetheart hope, no mother/daughter bonding.

After dinner Marquez opened the heavy iron damper in the old stone fireplace and built a fire, an old defense for him. Wind gusted hard over the mountain, rattling the windows, and it took a while to get the fire to draw. The quiet coming off of Katherine was like a weight dragged around. The kindling caught and then small oak branches he'd been drying for a couple of years. He pulled a chair up close to the fire.

"I'm thinking of starting to serve tea at the coffee bars," she said, and he thought of Amy Stevens. "It may be too late since everyone knows them as coffee bars, but I'm playing with changing the store identity."

She'd made another tea to try a different flavor and offered him a cup. He adjusted a log, and Katherine launched into it.

"She was more interested in shopping in New York than looking at schools."

"I already got that part."

"But you didn't get it with attitude."

Marquez adjusted the fire again, liked the pungency of the oak. He got up and found the bottle of a Cuban rum he'd been given last spring. He loved the taste and smell of the rum and poured an inch. The windows rattled in the wind. Another storm was forecast to hit a few days from now. If it stayed on track across the Pacific it would drop several inches of rain and maybe a couple feet of snow. The rivers would swell, and the runoff would churn the bottom. Sturgeon loved the brown muddy water.

Katherine's cool fingers touched his right hand. She slid her chair over as Maria walked down the hallway.

"Dad, can I ask you something in my room? Mom, I'm going to bed."

Marquez set the rum down gently on the hearth. He walked down to the room he'd added on and still hadn't finished. It had been a year. The walls were sheetrocked and painted, but the trim work wasn't complete, and he wasn't a carpenter.

"What's the question?" he asked.

"Is my bathroom door ever going to work?"

He'd hung the door himself after watching a rerun episode of *This Old House* on a cable channel. The door latch didn't meet properly. He knew he was going to have to remove the casing and rehang the door, and he hadn't gotten to it.

"I talked to Mom on the way home, and she's afraid it's going to offend you if we hire a carpenter to finish the room."

Offend was not a word Maria would have used a year ago. Marquez tried the doorknob out of habit. It still didn't work.

"Will it offend you?"

"I'd still like to fix it for you."

"Dad, it's not happening, and Mom has plenty of money." She quickly added, "I don't mean it like that."

"Then don't say it that way. Tell you what, if I don't get it fixed in the next two weeks we'll hire a carpenter."

"The door swings open when I'm using the bathroom."

They'd had this conversation a few times. "Shut your bedroom door when you use the bathroom."

He thought of Raburn talking about the room he and his brother had rented in Isleton after they'd left home and moved to the delta. They were younger than Maria was now. Raburn had said the bathroom was downstairs and they didn't need a window because the wall was open to the back of the lot. The shower was a garden hose with a nozzle set on the spray function and held pinned in place by two nails. He and Isaac had gotten to be great fishermen just so they could eat. It was why Isaac wouldn't eat any fish anymore, or so Raburn said, and the more Marquez turned in his head the way Raburn talked about his brother, the more likely it seemed that Isaac knew absolutely everything going on.

Now as he got ready to leave her room, Maria said, "It's not my fault we came home early. We got in a fight, and Mom said there was no reason to stay. I made her sad. I'm a big disappointment to her. She wishes she had a different daughter."

That was a mix of childish and true and a way of getting it out.

"What were the schools you liked?"

"The University of Virginia and Boston College, but I won't get in to either."

"You won't?"

She explained as though it was obvious. It was all demographics, and she had nothing going for her. She hadn't excelled at a sport, didn't have any extra-currics. She'd done some community service but not enough. She didn't have legacy anywhere. You just about had to have better than a 4.0 GPA, and she didn't have that. You needed top SAT scores, and she'd taken them twice and said her combined total still sucked.

"What's your combined total again?" he asked.

"1305."

He'd graduated from high school, gone to a state college for two years, then two in the National Guard and back to college.

He'd met and married Julie, and they'd planned to travel the world for a year, finding work wherever they could. When Julie was murdered in Africa everything changed.

"I think what you've done is pretty amazing." She'd turned her grades around completely in the past two years. Kath had driven her to better herself, and the effort had taken root, but only because she had it in her. "You're too hard on yourself sometimes."

"Mom pretty much thinks I'm wasting my life."

"I've never heard her say anything like that. If you want to take a year off and work and earn money for college, go for it. But whether you go next year or the year after, you should get a degree and you should find something you really care about to learn."

"I know I'm just the ungrateful kid, and I should listen to both of you, and I don't know anything about the real world."

"It's got to be a conversation, Maria, not an argument, not a position statement, and I don't really need you to tell me how I think. I've got a pretty good idea already." He repeated it. "You and your mom need to try to have a different conversation. You need to give each other a chance."

"Tell that to her."

Then he was out in front of the fire again with Katherine. He took a sip of rum.

"What did she say to you?" Katherine asked.

"She feels like she's failed you and she's lashing out, but I also hear something I haven't before. She sounds afraid she's going to be rejected everywhere she has applied."

"Every kid has the same challenges and most don't have the advantages. It's time for her to grow up."

"It is time, but it wouldn't surprise me if that insecurity isn't figuring into saying she doesn't want to go to college."

"There's always another excuse." After a pause, Kath added, "I'm going to go unpack."

He stayed near the fire, drawing some comfort from it, his head not in the college issue. He heard Katherine unpacking in the bedroom and thought about the SOU ending, whether Baird would hold him to the Christmas deadline if they were putting together prosecutable cases. He added another small piece of wood, and the wind was a low moan blowing over the top of the chimney. Kath came back out, wearing only a robe now, sitting near him, the robe sliding off one leg, her skin golden in the firelight. He reached and touched her smooth thigh.

"How's your team taking the shutdown?" she asked.

"They're starting to make plans. Cairo is going to grow tomatoes."

"What about you?"

"I'm going to shut these guys down before I make other plans."

Her skin was very smooth. He closed his eyes a moment.

"It would sure be nice to see you more. Keep that in your plans, John."

"I will."

"My business really is growing. I know it sounds crazy, but you could think about it."

"Sure."

"I mean it."

He slid his hand higher on her thigh, felt the warm heat there. The way her coffee bars had taken with some good press had caught even Kath completely by surprise. They took all of her time now. Growing the business had become her main thing and maybe a way of dealing with loneliness when he was gone. Undercover had taken its toll, and they'd never talked about the fact that she made so much more money than he did. When she'd opened the first Presto he'd written her a check for all his savings, twenty-two grand, not much, but all he'd had. She'd opened the store with it, and no one could have predicted how successful the coffee bar would become. He knew that to some of her new friends his job was detached from normal life, and hers was not a situation any of them would want to be married into. And in some insidious way the new money was working against them, as well as providing great opportunities, like this trip she'd just taken with Maria.

Katherine would pay for Maria to go to college, and with his salary he wouldn't contribute much. Kath had no problem paying the money. In truth, she looked forward to it because it meant Maria would get a better start in the world than she'd had. She was looking at opening more stores, while he was fighting for enough time to finish one undercover operation.

"How would I fit in?" he asked.

"We'd have to come up with a role, but with your charisma you'd make a lot of things happen. And I'd get to see you a lot more. That would be good."

"Yeah, it would." He looked over at her. "Hey, remember where Maria was a few years ago."

"She put herself in that spot."

"And she worked her way out of it."

"I don't want to see her get in another rut. She works at the Presto on Union, and her friends come in and hang out for hours. Her picture of a good life is living with them in the city and going out clubbing at night. I'm around her, I know what I'm talking about. She'll be with a completely different crowd at college."

"What I remember of college is everybody having a good time, then working hard for a week or two around midterms and again at finals."

"It's not at all like that everywhere."

The fire burned lower. Colder air drafted from the thin window glass, and Katherine shivered. She drew her robe back over her leg and turned toward him. "I'm sleepy," she said and then put her head against his chest, and Marquez held her.

"I promise we could create a job for you that you would really like. I promise, and we would get to see each other so much more. You've given so many years already. You've done your share. We can travel like we've talked about."

He didn't answer but pressed her close, never wanted to let go of her. He saw Raburn's face in the last firelight, heard him say again as he held up the poster, "This guy disappeared." The look on his face like he couldn't believe it.

30

Sturgeons are toothless bottom-feeders that use long whiskers to feel their way along. Their backs carry armored sections called scutes, and they love churned-up water and feed on worms and shrimp kicked up off the bottom, yet they'll also rise to the surface to eat the bodies of salmon that have spawned and died upriver. Depending on how the storm went through, Marquez figured the bite would be on later today.

The rain started as he crossed the Antioch Bridge. Along the top of the concrete arc of the bridge his truck shook in sheeting gusts. The big SUV ahead of him swayed and overcorrected. He gave it more room and listened to a radio talk show host demanding that Congress force OPEC to bring down the cost per barrel of oil so gas prices would fall again at the pumps.

"We have to open the Arctic Wildlife Refuge to drilling," he said. "The namby-pamby, complain-about-everything environmentalists are destroying the country's strength."

Marquez knew the vehicle in front of him now on the bridge got no better than sixteen miles to the gallon. His team had used one for a couple of years. They were solid vehicles, but the low gas mileage was a problem, and it was hard to see how it was OPEC's problem that Americans had embraced gas-guzzling SUVs. Hadn't the great strength of the country always been in solving problems, rather than in biting accusatory whining or blaming someone else? We'd known for thirty years we had to build more efficient vehicles. After another few minutes he turned the radio off.

Dropping into the delta he called Ruax and continued up the river road past fields of cut sorghum and orchards of apple and pear, their branches near bare and black in the wet morning. Wind had stripped more of the last leaves. The Sacramento River was a dark green, pitted with rain when he turned down the fishing access entrance. He walked the line of cottonwoods and oak bordering the lot, then out to the river, and standing near the water spotted a pair of jeans that had washed ashore into the reeds and were half-buried in mud.

The jeans made a sucking sound as he retrieved them, and his shoes got wet. But that was the doubt still lingering in him. He knew Selke was almost certainly right; she'd staged her disappearance. He found a wallet in the jeans—amazing it hadn't fallen out long ago. Silt had worked its way between the plastic protector and the driver's license. He slid the license out and rubbed the mud off with his thumb. Buffington. John Buffington. He dropped the jeans in the trash can on his way out and dropped the wallet on the passenger seat. If he had time later he'd get a phone number for Buffington and give him the good news.

Continuing upriver he drove past redtail hawks hunkered down on the power lines. Rain dripped heavily from the eucalyptus, oak, and palm trees surrounding the big pink stucco frame of the Ryde Hotel. He parked next to Ruax's truck.

"Probably best if we go in two vehicles," she said. "I've got some other names for you also. They all have to do with the case we were building against Raburn. I should have turned them over last time I saw you. The pair we're meeting this morning I've bought from twice before."

Half an hour later Marquez counted out twenties to a couple of guys from San Jose who'd hooked a big sturgeon out in a hole in the river and then dragged it into the slough after jabbing it with a gaff. They were nervous and pushing to get the deal done. Marquez negotiated and recorded their voices and faces, pointed the fiber optic sewed into his sleeve at the face of one and then the other, recording their faces.

He called Crey and left a message that he had the fish, then went into Big Store in Walnut Grove to buy more bags of ice. Bought ten and packed them around the sturgeon, went back and bought another four, told the young guy working the cash register that he was getting a jump on a football party he was having this coming Sunday. He took a call from Roberts as he got back in the truck.

"I found something interesting going back in the newspapers. There was a Federal tax lien on Raburn Orchards, sixty-eight thousand dollars for unpaid taxes in 2001. I'm trying to find out now whether they settled it. I'll call you back when I know more."

She called back half an hour later and had gotten an IRS agent to confirm that it had been paid in full.

"Paid off in early November of 2001, including interest. One check paid off the whole thing?"

"So we know they were behind with their creditors."

"And there were other liens from suppliers."

She read off the liens. A farm equipment supplier. A firm supplying fertilizers. She'd found five liens by private firms and the IRS lien. He knew it was likely she'd uncover a state tax lien as well.

"Bottom line is Raburn Orchards had money problems in the summer and fall of 2001," she said.

"Call some of those firms," he said, "and ask if they ever got paid. You'll have to make up some sort of cover story. Maybe you're thinking of doing business with Raburn Orchards and the standard credit checks turned up the record of liens."

"I'm going to need a business and a name for it."

"Yeah, and I'll leave that to you. Ask if they got paid in full or whether it was pennies on the dollar, and would they do business again with Isaac Raburn."

An hour later he still hadn't had a call back from Crey. Fairly soon, he'd need a way to refrigerate it. He punched in Abe Raburn's number, talked briefly to him, then drove to meet him at the pear packing shed.

Raburn had built a wooden platform with slots that slid over the forklift blades the same as a pallet. He drove the narrow forklift around to the back of Marquez's truck, leveled the platform with the open tailgate, and they wrestled, slid the sturgeon out and onto the platform. In the room in back they slid the sturgeon onto his gutting station.

Raburn pressed the belly of the sturgeon. "You've got yourself a cow here."

They cut in, exposing eggs. For the millions of eggs a female produced, perhaps ten million in a lifetime, few offspring would come of them. Raburn lifted out a brown ovarian sack and carried it over to his screen. He mixed the salt solution, worked the eggs loose, and was gentle in the way he did it. The eggs were left in the 4 percent salt solution. Salt would penetrate and preserve them. They'd be stored at twenty-nine degrees.

There was little conversation between them, but there was a tension in the room. Marquez knew that with a motion he wouldn't have time to stop, Raburn could turn and drive the blade into his chest. Raburn's body language made it clear he wanted nothing more to do with him.

Marquez washed his hands after they'd cleaned off the table. Outside, it was still raining and the morning was dark. He walked back over to the bowl where the eggs were. From here you either ate the caviar or you needed a way to preserve it, a means of production, an understanding of preservatives, vacuum packing, pasteurizing. August wouldn't go for pasteurizing. There was a stigma about what that did to taste for the market he dealt with.

Marquez rested a hand on the bowl. He smelled the salted roe and dipped his fingers in, slid a few eggs out and tasted with Raburn watching him. The eggs burst with intense flavor.

"Is your brother here this morning?" Marquez asked.

"He took Cindy to the dentist. She has a bad tooth."

"Are the kids with them?"

"I'm supposed to drop them at school."

"Let's go look in a couple of buildings before you take the kids." When Raburn frowned, Marquez said, "I've got active search warrants in the truck, but I'm not asking to search."

Raburn had a hard time with that, especially after helping out with the big sturgeon. His wide face openly showed his bitterness.

"Never stops," he said, and they drove down to the equipment storage shed that Marquez had walked through once before. Roberts called as they came inside, and he moved away from Raburn to talk to her. He saw the same look of disgust on Raburn's face as he'd seen the night Raburn had booted the ovaries off the embankment.

"One of the fertilizer companies talked to me. They settled for sixty cents on the dollar on a nineteen thousand dollar debt. The woman I talked to gave me the name of their lawyer, and I called him. He told me the Raburns settled all their debts at once and told everyone they'd taken on another investor, but only the Feds and the State got paid in full. And you were right, there was a state tax lien as well. I'm trying to call the Secretary of State's office, but it's probably going to be easier to drive over there and see if anybody got added to the corporate documents."

"My guess is no."

"Mine too. I'll call you from there."

The equipment storage building had once been a barn and held more than equipment used to tend the orchards. Marquez walked around with Raburn, asked about the fertilizer stored here and the small repair shop and the tools. There was a greenhouse. They walked inside it, and the air was musty and damp.

"My brother is experimenting with growing mushrooms." There were flowers and other seedlings in the greenhouse, and Marquez slowed and looked at those before they moved to the door. "I've got to take the kids to school."

"I'd like to see the house."

"Do you have a warrant for the house?"

"I've got a warrant for all the buildings."

"Why are you such a hardass today? There's nothing in their house, so why do you want to look in it? If you thought there was anything there, you would have looked before now. Why invade their privacy? Besides, I've got to take the kids to school. I've got to get going."

In many ways Raburn was right: Marquez didn't know what he was looking for, and it was more about pushing Raburn to see what would happen. He'd thought over Raburn shooting up his boat and had decided there could easily be more behind it than just trying to get out of the deal he'd made with time. Or get away because he was afraid of Ludovna. So he'd gotten new search warrants. He was getting in Raburn's face. He pointed at the canning building. It was small, had cinder-block walls and a metal roof and door, no windows.

"All they do in there is apple and pear butter."

"Open it for me and go ahead and take the kids to school. I'm fine here alone."

Raburn unlocked the door, then strode in ahead of him and opened all the cabinet doors. The metal cabinets lined the walls, and their doors banged against each other as Raburn threw them open.

"What's the problem, Abe?"

"Oh, there's no problem. Look at whatever you want."

There were six- and eight-ounce glass jars with the Raburn Orchards label and boxes of jars for both apple and pear butter. Marquez picked up one of the jars, looked at the red-orange label, the color of the top similar to the burned color of the remaining pear leaves on the trees. He moved along looking in the cabinets. On the opposite wall there were four cabinets with locks.

"What's in those?"

"Same stuff, but they hire seasonal help and were getting things stolen so they bought locks for half the cabinets. Do you want me to go find a key?"

"Do you mind?"

"Hey, why would I mind, and why would the kids mind being late to school?"

"Where are you going to get the key?"

"I don't even know where one is, and come on, man, this is the canning room. If you're looking for some apple butter I'll get you a case. Do you want me to comp you a case of apple butter? Do you want apple butter for everyone on your team? I'll get as many cases as you want."

"Take it easy."

"What do you mean take it easy? I just cut up your fish for you, and now you're jacking me around."

"Where are the keys?"

Raburn shrugged, acting now like he didn't have any idea.

"Isaac can open it for you when he gets back. The key is probably in the house, and it's stupid for you and me to look for it."

"Let's open them now."

"Why can't it wait? I've got to drop the kids off."

"I'll walk down to the house with you."

When they got there Raburn remembered a key high on a shelf in the kitchen. Marquez walked back up the gravel road and opened the cabinets. Inside, he found more six-ounce and eight-ounce jars. Then he found the two-ounce glass jars he was looking for. The labels would go on later. August would put those on.

"Those are for pimentos," Raburn said, as he put his head back in. "He's got a friend growing pimentos and Cindy jars them for him. It's just another way to make a little money at farmers markets. I'm leaving."

Raburn walked away, and not long after, Marquez heard his truck idling outside. The oldest Raburn boy sat in the passenger seat and Raburn's niece in the jumpseat in back. Both kids stared at him, wondering who he was, and he waved at them.

"Better take them to school," he said.

"What are you going to do?"

"I'll be here when you get back."

Marquez picked up one of the jars and out of the corner of his eye saw Raburn back in the doorway, agitated, not wanting to leave him here alone. But he didn't find anything else in the cabinets. He went through each shelf carefully.

"How long will it take you to drop them and get back?"

"Ten minutes."

"Better do it."

"There's nothing more to see, and this is my brother's space. You don't need to come in here anymore. He's got his business, and he's not involved."

He drove off with the kids. When he did Marquez walked back to the cabinet that held the two-ounce jars. The jars were the right size. He looked around at the room again. Raburn hadn't wanted him in here and maybe that was his growing resentment, or he was emboldened, or maybe it was as simple as violating his brother's space. But his gut told him it was more than that. He'd watched the way Raburn threw open the cabinet doors. Making a show of it, but he couldn't hide his nervousness. He turned one of the glass jars in his hand and looked around the room again.

31

"You knocked out Torp's front teeth," Crey said.

"Yeah, he owes Lisa a chair."

"Man, you're too much. What did I say to you about working with my crew? This really screws everything up."

"He started to pull a gun, and Perry came at me with a knife."

"He was just trying to get another drink. He couldn't get inside. The door was locked."

"Tell him to drink out of the toilet next time he's thirsty. You and I know he was going upstairs."

"No, he wasn't, and you read too much into everything. At the most he was going to borrow a bottle of Jack Daniels."

"He had a gun."

"He's always got a gun. That doesn't mean anything. You think he was going up to do her, then what, the cops are there in the morning, and how long do you think it would take them to figure out who did it? He ain't that stupid, man, and the point is I asked you to work with my crew."

"I took a mask and gloves off him. He had a bottle of chloroform."

Crey was silent, then quietly said, "Lou didn't tell me that."

"Because Perry planned to follow him upstairs. They were both on the deck. Start meeting me yourself because I can't deal with them anymore. I've got a drop for you later today, and I don't want to see anybody but you."

"What time will you get here?"

"Before 2:00."

He hung up as Raburn came back from dropping the kids off. Marquez had left the canning room and walked the gravel road through the orchards back to the packing shed. He was at his truck when Raburn came up alongside him.

"I'm leaving," Marquez said. "The key is on the table in the room."

"When is all this going to end?"

"You know, that's a question I ask myself. How long is it going to take to shut these guys down?"

"What am I supposed to tell the kids when you're rooting through their family's business?"

"You could tell them that the man going through cabinets in the canning building is trying to keep Uncle Abe out of prison, and Uncle Abe still doesn't get it."

Marquez loaded the fish and caviar and left to meet Crey in Rio Vista. After the drop with Crey he'd continue on to Grizzly Bay to make another buy. He met Crey at the bait shop, and Crey wanted him to follow. They drove out to the end of the street and moved the sturgeon and caviar from Marquez's truck to Crey's. Almost nothing got said, and Crey was very jumpy. When

Marquez wasn't watching he'd dropped an envelope with the cash in it on the driver's seat of Marquez's truck. He pointed it out without identifying it.

"Is that money for me?"

"I gotta go," Crey answered.

"You okay with me counting it before you take off?"

Marquez lifted the envelope off the seat. He let the bills slide into his hand. But Crey had already turned and was getting in his truck. Without waiting for the money to be counted he drove away, and after he left Marquez had a quiet conversation with the team. Alvarez would go with him to make another sturgeon buy in Grizzly Bay, and the rest of the SOU would stick with Crey.

Grizzly Bay was the color of lead, then bright silver where the sunlight broke through onto the water. Marquez could remember when troops were trained here in preparation for fighting in the Mekong in Vietnam. He rechecked his directions, then pulled over on the shoulder 2.3 miles from the last stop sign. About twenty minutes later a couple of kids pulled up in a gray minivan, neither looking older than eighteen. The driver got out, walked up to Marquez's window, and then introduced himself. Julio Rodriguez. He was clean-cut, hair short and gelled, a cheerful guileless face. Marquez could tell the kid hadn't done this before.

"You want to look at the fish first?" Julio asked.

"Sure would."

Marquez got out and looked at the sturgeon in the mini-van. It was a decent size, over the slot limit by a foot. The kid was very proud, said it was the biggest he'd ever caught. The other young man stayed in the cab, looking around once but apparently just there to help lift the sturgeon, didn't have anything to do with catching it.

"How long have you known Abe?" Marquez asked.

"My uncle knows him. I don't know him."

Marquez counted out the bills, and Alvarez drove slowly past, videotaping the exchange of money. Julio couldn't have been more unaware. They moved the sturgeon, and Marquez questioned him.

"What are you going to do with the money?"

"I'm saving for college."

"You'll have to catch a lot of sturgeon to get through college."

"I've got two jobs."

"Yeah, where do you work?"

"In Suisun."

He kept talking. He played baseball and hoped to play in college. He lived in Suisun, so did the uncle who knew Raburn and taught him how to fish for sturgeon. He was the oldest kid in his family and had four brothers and sisters. He shook Marquez's hand before leaving, and Alvarez trailed him as he drove away with the money, said the kid never looked in the rearview mirror except slowing at stoplights.

"Looked to me like he went shopping for the family," Alvarez said later. "He went straight to a grocery store and then home. Must have been his brothers and sisters who helped unload groceries."

"Where's home?"

"A little asbestos-shingled house facing the water."

Marquez called Ludovna with this one and got told to bring it over to the Sacramento store. A couple of guys working for Ludovna helped him unload. The team was already jokingly calling today the "sturgeon derby."

At 2:00, Crey's boat left the dock with six sport fishermen and worked sturgeon holes around the Mothball Fleet and later went farther upriver and docked at the Delta Queen. After the sport fishermen filed off the boat and went into the bar, Perry and Torp drove up in their van. They boarded Crey's boat, then left again a few minutes later with a blue plastic cooler and drove to Weisson's Auto. Shauf and Roberts stopped a third of a mile back. Shauf radioed Marquez.

"What do we do now?"

"Stay with them when they leave there."

"Can we call the Feds?"

"I'll call Ehrmann and let him know we took it this far and we think caviar was delivered here. That's the cooler I delivered to Crey's Rio Vista house so we've already got it on tape."

Cairo sat on Ludovna's house, and late in the afternoon Cindy Raburn backed into Ludovna's driveway and stayed only as long as it took to load a cooler into her Volvo backseat. Hard to tell for sure, but it looked like the same blue cooler, and now Marquez came up alongside the Volvo at a stoplight. He looked down through the back windows and saw the Save Lake Tahoe sticker they'd put on the cooler.

"It's the same one," he said.

They followed Cindy Raburn back into the delta and home. But rather than drive her car to the house, she stopped at the canning building and lugged the cooler inside. They watched the lights come on.

"No wonder Raburn was so nervous this morning," Marquez said. "Let's let it unfold now. She must be in there to jar the caviar. They went to a lot of trouble to get it here. Let's see what happens and let's follow it from here."

He broke the team into shifts and drove into Walnut Grove with Shauf. There he bought bread, peanut butter, apples, a couple of candy bars, and filled a thermos with coffee before Shauf dropped him off along the southwestern side of the Raburn property. With Alvarez he came down the steep levee bank in the darkness and then out along the property line, following the edge of the trees. Shauf would stay with her van and watch the roads, and, with Alvarez, Marquez started through the orchards. The rest of the team would go to the safehouse, and they'd rotate in the morning.

Leaves stuck to his boots as they walked the mud between the pear trees. They worked their way closer. The Raburns didn't have any dogs, and it was unlikely anyone was behind a darkened window in the main house with night-vision equipment. The single light outside the canning shed door glowed yellow and hazy at this distance, but with light-enhanced cameras they could read the terrain, and the lines of the canning shed took form. Her car was still out front, Isaac's pickup near the house. Up on the levee road Shauf drove slowly past and on down toward Raburn's houseboat. She said the lights were off there, his pickup gone.

"Take a drive through Walnut Grove and Isleton and check the bars. Maybe you'll find him in town," Marquez said.

The cold deepened, and a few more lights came on in the main house. Marquez read Alvarez's face in the dim light from his cell screen, saw his breath cloud in the cold. The wind picked up. Cindy Raburn was still in the canning building at 10:00 when lights started clicking off in the main house. Not long after, Isaac stepped out onto the porch, and they watched him walk up the gravel road to the canning building.

"Bringing her dinner," Alvarez said, and it looked like he was carrying a plate.

Isaac stayed in the shed an hour then walked back to the house.

"We'll stay until she locks up and leaves," Marquez said. "She may be doing more than one thing in there. There may have been a whole other delivery we missed."

Traffic died off on the levee road, and the night quieted. Marquez talked to Shauf on and off. She was about a mile away from them off the side of the road.

"How is it?" she asked.

"Cold out here. It feels especially cold tonight."

"Yeah, it does, and you know, that's the part I'm not going to miss."

"We're getting older, I guess."

"Think we've made any difference?"

"Sure, we've slowed it all down. Some of those people would still be out there poaching."

Marquez talked with Alvarez about a case they'd never solved, a hunter who'd made it his mission to hunt down and kill mountain lions. As far as they knew he was still out there, and the rumor was he claimed his wife had been killed by a mountain lion. They knew he was from out of state and didn't know much more about him, except that he had a knack for tracking lion. At midnight Alvarez said he'd rather take the first than second shift.

"Then I'll see you at around 4:00."

Shauf picked Marquez up on the levee road, dropped him at his truck, and he told her to go on to the safehouse and sleep. He'd see the night through with Alvarez. He ran the engine long enough to heat the cab, plugged his phone in to recharge, lowered the seat, turned the radio on low, and listened to Lucinda Williams singing. It didn't take long for cold to seep back into the truck, and when he finally dozed he was listening to the wind high in the trees. He dreamed of a simpler time when he'd been much younger and the world had looked more open.

At 4:00, before hiking back out along the edge of the orchard to take over from Alvarez, he drank a cup of cold coffee. Then he made the mile walk from his truck. The cold wind had strengthened, and Alvarez said he'd been moving around to try to stay warm.

"She's still in there, Lieutenant."

After Alvarez faded into the pear trees Marquez repositioned himself. He zipped his coat collar up and about twenty minutes later saw headlights he recognized as Abe Raburn's slow on the levee road. Checked his watch, 4:22, thinking, okay, here we go, we're on. Shauf hadn't found Raburn's pickup when she'd checked the bars or his houseboat earlier, but here he was now. His headlights flashed through the bare orchard trees. He pulled up in front of the shed, parked, and went in. A few minutes later Cindy Raburn left the canning building. She hurried down the road to the house, and Marquez waited for Raburn to come out.

But nothing happened. Marquez had been close to calling the safehouse and waking the team, had expected him to load and go, but instead, the lights went out in the canning building and Raburn was still in there. Now, he came out and walked around on the gravel. It took Marquez a minute to realize Raburn was talking on a cell phone. Then up on the levee road a car slowed and turned down. Marquez read the profile as a Toyota hybrid, a Prius, as it drove past his position. It drove slowly along the gravel road until Raburn stepped out into the headlights and directed the driver to park near the canning building door.

The driver got out, and Marquez used the light-enhanced feature to tape boxes getting loaded into the rear of the hybrid. He called Shauf.

"Raburn showed up and took over for Isaac's wife, and now we've got a driver picking up a load of boxes. Looks like Raburn Orchards boxes. Get everyone up at the safehouse. We're rolling."

He called Alvarez and woke him as the hybrid started moving. Alvarez picked up the car as it climbed up to the levee road and then gave it a lot of room. Marquez hustled out and up to the road, and Shauf dropped him at his truck.

"She's going toward I-5," Alvarez said.

"You say, she?"

"Looked like a white female at the wheel when it passed me, but I'm not sure yet."

"How good a look did you get?"

"I didn't. The driver is wearing a cap. I'm running the plates right now."

"Good, because I didn't get them when it went past."

The hybrid got on 5 northbound and continued into the darkness beyond Sacramento. Cairo passed it and reconfirmed the driver was female and they already had a registration address in Thousand Oaks. Southern California.

"A long way from home," Marquez said, and thought of the car Ludovna had stolen and burned.

"Who's closest?" Marquez asked.

"I am," Roberts said, "and I like it. It's a nice color blue. I think it's an '05. I wish Detroit would get off its ass and start making a good hybrid. I'd like to get one of these."

"Keep working at headquarters," somebody said, and Marquez asked, "How can you tell it's an '05?"

"Some article I read, the detailing is a little different."

Marquez felt the subdued optimism running through the team. They were still in darkness but they had the car surrounded. They wouldn't lose it. He hadn't said so yet, but he'd also thought it was a woman who'd gotten out and helped Raburn load boxes in the rear. With night-vision goggles it was difficult, things bulked out, but in general men and women walk differently, not all, but most, and then something in the way she moved her arms, shifted to let Raburn slide a box in. You carry a memory of the way somebody moves.

Shauf and Cairo had to be wondering too. Marquez edged closer to Alvarez's truck, rode up near him and took over the lead at first light.

"What's the gas mileage on those hybrids?" Alvarez asked.

"Two and half times what we're getting."

"That's why I'm asking. I'm there. I'm at a quarter tank."

Alvarez pulled off at the Mobil, Shell, Chevron signs up ahead. He was just getting back on the freeway when the first sunlight came through the passenger window of Marquez's truck.

"Right lane at sixty-five," Marquez called out. "Sitting on sixty-five."

He felt sunlight touch his face and heard Alvarez say he'd picked up two cups of coffee. "One for you, Lieutenant, unless I finish this one before I catch you."

"Catch me, I could use it."

As the sun rose, Marquez dropped back, putting more space between himself and the hybrid, his mouth dry, heart racing, though nothing had changed in the last hour. But there was daylight now, the shape of a head, a cap coming off, Roberts said. Dark brown hair, and, from behind her, Roberts used her binoculars to look at the reflection in the rearview mirror.

"It's a woman, for sure," she said, and the focus on the gender was really only about one thing. "Want me to get closer?"

"Yes, but let's hang on a little longer."

The dark hair was right, head and shoulders were what he remembered, and Roberts was close to saying something. Up ahead was open country, soggy with the rains, fields brown and stubbled, hills in the gray early light in the distance. Before Chico there were olive groves, dusky blue-green, riding the hills off to his right, and Alvarez had closed in behind Marquez.

They made a quick stop, Marquez handing Alvarez a photo, a snapshot he'd run a copy of, and Alvarez handing him the coffee and pastry he'd picked up when he'd gassed up.

"That's her face?" Alvarez asked.

"Yeah."

The hybrid still rode in the right-hand lane, the blue color of the car bright against muted hills of olives, sky white since sunrise.

"I'm coming up alongside her," Alvarez said. "I'm tailing a pickup, and the pickup just passed her, and here I come."

Then he was silent, likely not sure yet or not wanting her to see him talking, not that it mattered like it used to, given all the "hands-free" devices.

"Okay, I'm past her."

"Did you get a look?"

"I got a good one, and I'm just double-checking now. I've got her in my mirror."

He knew Alvarez well enough, knew already from his tone. She'd gone as far as to ask him about what it took to become a Fish and Game warden, asking whether someone with her river experience and time outdoors could become a warden. He'd taken her seriously, told her he'd see what he could do to help. She'd burned him the whole way.

"It's definitely her," Alvarez said.

"Are you that sure?"

"It's her, Lieutenant, and yeah, I'm that sure. I'll move well ahead now."

Marquez fell farther back, and, briefly, it was almost as if he lacked the strength to push down the accelerator. He figured he'd seen just about everything in twenty years of undercover work and was surprised how much this affected him. He opened his log and found where he'd stuck Selke's card.

"Who's this?"

"John Marquez."

"I don't know anything new, and I'm in a meeting. Can I call you back?"

"We've just ID'd a female suspect we're following north on I-5, coming up on Redding."

"I can only think of one female suspect you'd be calling me about."

"You're right. It's Anna."

32

It was simple enough, wasn't it? They sent her in and she burned you. You were too eager for a lead and a break and didn't check her out enough. They stayed loosely with her now. Anna didn't push it, kept her speed steady. There was new snow on Mount Shasta and winds on the summit that blew streamers of powder off the cornices. The SOU leapfrogged, pulling off to get gas, use a restroom, then close the gap again. They drove through Yreka and neared the Oregon border, Marquez making the calls as they did to clear them to continue the pursuit. He talked to a sergeant he knew and liked on Oregon's Special Investigations Unit, told him what they had going on.

Anna's window was partway down, hair catching in the wind flowing in. Shauf passed and turned to study her, Shauf's face stolid behind dark glasses as she took her in and then talked to Marquez. He polled the team when they were well into Oregon.

"Alvarez?"

"I'm still good, but I'm hungry."

"You haven't slept."

"Yeah, I have. I slept for an hour or so right around Shasta."

A few laughs. "Cairo?" Marquez asked.

"I'm doing fine."

"Roberts?"

"I need gas and a restroom."

"I'll take point," Marquez said. "Go ahead and break off."

"Shauf?"

"I'd like to wring her neck. That'll keep me going another thousand miles."

"We'll be talking to her soon enough."

But it was Ehrmann he talked to next. He figured it was the right moment to push for information.

"We found Anna Burdovsky. We've followed her from the delta into Oregon. She picked up what we think is caviar in jars being moved in Raburn Orchards boxes. Four boxes were loaded into the back of a Toyota Prius a little after four this morning. She showed up in the delta at a building we had under surveillance. It's a southern Cal vehicle. Could it tie into what you've got going?"

"Read me off the plates."

Marquez read them off.

"Burdovsky has made deliveries for people working for her ex-husband, the Karsov we've told you about. It's possible this is the overlap we've been wondering about, Lieutenant."

"Is Karsov here?"

"Why are you asking that?"

"You said he travels, and obviously something is up."

"As a matter of fact he may be in the country. We've learned something this morning that suggests he might be. Under no circumstances should you make contact with Burdovsky."

Marquez knew that was coming. It didn't surprise him.

"We're going to join you following her."

"We don't want to lose track of what's she's carrying."

"I'm sure you'd like to have a conversation with her also."

"That can wait."

He gave Ehrmann their position, then hung up. Two hours later Anna finally pulled over for gas. "She's got an iron bladder," Shauf said, and they watched her move through the gas station store. She was in line at the cash register and came out with bottled water, hot chocolate in a white Styrofoam cup, and a sandwich. Her face looked calm. She chatted with the employees. You wouldn't know looking at her she'd been driving for eight hours. She yawned, talked to the kid who pumped the gas, and then got back in her car.

Marquez was across the street parked in a Burger King lot on the phone with Ehrmann again, answering more questions about how they found her. He was starting to figure out what Ehrmann wasn't saying.

"When did the FBI lose track of her?"

"A week ago."

Marquez watched her pull out and then back onto the freeway. They could expect to start spotting Feds any moment now.

"We'll take over when she gets to her destination," Ehrmann said.

Anna drove harder as they neared Portland, but when it started raining she slowed and not long afterward exited and drove up to a diner. In the diner it looked warm. The windows were steamed, and outside the rain turned to sleet. Roberts went in and ordered food to go for everyone, including the extra sandwich Marquez asked for and now took down the street to where an FBI agent had nosed his car in between trees. He got the agent to lower his window, but he wouldn't accept the sandwich, said regulations wouldn't allow it.

"No one will know," Marquez said. "How long have you guys been on her?"

"I don't even know who she is. Maybe you can fill me in."

"We're following her on a sturgeon poaching case, but you're on an organized crime car theft ring."

"I didn't even know that. They just gave me a list of vehicles to look for."

"Which one did you spot?"

He smiled. "Yours."

The agent was young, clean-cut, hard-eyed, wouldn't touch the sandwich Marquez had handed him until he was alone and driving. Marquez left him as Anna got up to leave.

It was a thousand miles from the Sacramento/San Joaquin delta to Seattle, but she didn't go all the way to Seattle proper. She held a cell phone to her ear as she veered from the far left lane over to the Seattle airport exit, then drove to the Southwest gate and pulled over at the curb and got out. Before an airport officer could tell her she couldn't leave her car alone a man stepped off the curb, took the keys from her, slid onto the driver's seat, adjusted the seat, and pulled away. The whole exchange took less than a minute. Anna headed into the airport, and Marquez watched the airport doors slide shut behind her.

"What do we do?" Shauf asked.

"We stay with the car; we follow the caviar."

33

Now they were parked down the street from a condominium project in Seattle. The new driver had glanced continually at his rearview mirror after he left the airport, boxing several streets when he left the freeway. Then he'd pulled into the garage beneath the condos, parked close to the elevator, and got on his phone. Two men came down the elevator. They unloaded the boxes, and the hybrid driver backed up, tires squealing on the smooth concrete of the garage as he started forward again and bounced onto the street.

"Let him go," Marquez said. "The Feds have him covered."

They watched the hybrid round the corner and disappear. The boxes went up the elevator. Both the garage and elevator had security cameras, so there were multiple shots of the two men and the boxes. But the information came secondhand to the SOU. The FBI asked that they not go into the building, said they were in contact with the building owners, who, after the first conversation, turned the situation over to their lawyer, waking him at home. They watched the lawyer drive up half an hour later.

"He doesn't look too happy to be here," Shauf said, and Marquez got out and walked up to within earshot. He heard the lawyer's peevishly aggressive tone as he informed the FBI agents what liability the government would take on if they interrupted any of the security cameras in operation. But the problem was the cameras were on a loop and eventually the tape would play over itself and the images of the men could get lost or become difficult to recover. The lawyer wanted everything to wait until morning. He wanted to go home, didn't want to deal with this tonight. No one had told him exactly what was in the boxes, yet they were clear they didn't believe it was stolen property or drugs, so why couldn't it wait until morning? And the building owners were opposed on principle to providing any information regarding the individual condo owners.

A manager showed up. He stood next to the lawyer and faced the two FBI agents. Marquez was called over to answer the lawyer's questions.

"How do you know they brought illegal substances here?"

"We watched it loaded and followed them from California."

"Did you see what was in the boxes?"

"No."

As he said that, Marquez caught a look from the apartment manager that worried him. The manager watched him intently as the lawyer launched into a quasi sales pitch.

"These are expensive units, and the owners are professionals who value privacy and security. Access to the building is restricted—"

"The security cameras show what floor they got off," Marquez said. "Why don't we knock on some doors? We know what they look like."

The lawyer looked like he'd swallowed battery acid. "That's exactly what doesn't happen here." He addressed Marquez now as though explaining manners to trailer trash. "Nobody knocks on doors here. People make appointments, and we can't begin to ask owners at this hour of the night, without any warrant or proof of anything illegal having been brought into the building, to open their doors." He really got warmed up now. "I believe this is still America and the Constitution is still in place."

The apartment manager drifted away, and Marquez watched him go in the keyed entrance and disappear into the building. He had a bad feeling about the guy, and the sense the opportunity was slipping away. The FBI agents continued to politely engage with the lawyer, but Marquez walked away. He pulled his cell phone and broke down the team, sent all but Shauf to go find food and a motel.

Shauf moved her van, reclined her seat, and closed her eyes while they waited. The lawyer had left. No one's privacy would get disturbed tonight. The street cleared off, and it started drizzling. He kept watching the concrete mouth of the garage on the possibility the men who'd taken the boxes up the elevator would come back down, ready to move them to their next stop. His bad feeling about the manager intensified, but maybe the guy was actually inside trying to figure out which unit the boxes had gone into. It became harder to look through the blur of the drizzle, and still, he continued to watch, turning over the things Ehrmann had told him as a way to stay awake.

Anna had done things here for her ex, though not necessarily willingly. Coercion and extortion were sacred values etched deep in the granite pillars of organized crime, so maybe it all strung together, Anna delivering stolen cars or running caviar a thousand miles because she felt she didn't have a choice. He debated what the implications were to their investigation. If there'd been any lingering question about Anna's compromising them, there was no question anymore, and he was mulling that over when Katherine called. She was so upset her voice quavered.

"Maria didn't come home after school and now she's called and says she's moving out."

"Moving where?"

"In with two of her friends who have an apartment in San Francisco. Wendy and Stacey. You've met them." He'd met them but wasn't sure which was Wendy and which was Stacey. "John, where are you?"

"In Seattle. We followed a suspect moving caviar from the delta." He sketched for her quickly how they'd gotten here, then said, "I'll call Maria, right now."

Maria answered on the third ring.

"I can't deal with it anymore."

"What can't you deal with?"

"Fighting with Mom, and I'm eighteen. I'm a legal adult. I can work and pay rent and still go to school. I can't handle it anymore, besides it's totally dysfunctional around there. You're never home, and Mom is always working too much because you're not home. It's time for me to make my own life."

"You need to finish high school first."

"I will. And I'll go to college when I'm ready."

He heard resolution in her voice that gave him hope, a fierceness that caused him to smile. Nothing was said for a moment, and he looked into the blank fluorescence of the garage, stripes painted on the floor.

"I'm at Wendy and Stacey's apartment." Then she added for no obvious reason. "And Shane is going to quit if Mom doesn't stop dissing him."

He knew Shane worked at the Presto on Union because Maria had talked about him. But don't question her about Shane. This thing has got to be unraveled a different way.

"Are you with Mom?" she asked.

"No, I'm in Seattle. We chased a suspect up here. Your mom called me a few minutes ago."

"Did you drive to Seattle?"

"Yes."

"That's crazy. Is this on the sturgeon thing? Is it really worth it?"

Marquez heard a young man's voice say, "Hey, babe, we got to go," and he realized whoever had said that was so nearby that he must have been listening in and there was enough push to the voice to show he wanted to control the situation.

"I have to go," Maria said.

"Don't hang up yet."

"Shane has to be at work early tomorrow morning. We went to dinner, and he just dropped me off. I'm at Wendy and Stacey's, and I'm fine here, dad. I just can't do it anymore."

"Where is their apartment?"

"In the Mission."

"What address?"

"You're just going to say it's a bad area."

"Have you ever heard me say stuff like that?"

She didn't answer. Behind her, "Come on, babe."

"I'm going to hang up, Dad."

He wasn't sure what to say to her. He was very surprised she'd packed and left, but he couldn't argue her home. He could order her home and she might obey, probably would, but it was already midnight and Katherine knew the two young women she was camping out with. This Shane figured in, but now wasn't the time to try to figure that out.

"I'll see you at home tomorrow night," he said.

"What do you mean if you're in Seattle?"

"We'll talk tomorrow night."

Not long after hanging up, Marquez had another conversation with the FBI special agents who'd given up on the lawyer and conferred with their supervisor, who'd then bumped the situation up to the S.A.C. running the Seattle Field Office. The Special-Agent-in-Charge was in contact with Ehrmann. The agent on the street with Marquez said, "You guys ought to pack it in. Looks like we're going to deal with all of it from here."

"Are you going to stake out the building tonight?"

"I'm going to do whatever they tell me. They're going to get back to me. The S.A.C. is involved now. You stumbled into a big one."

"We didn't really stumble into it, and we don't want to lose track of this caviar. If these two guys come down the elevator barehanded in the morning and drive off, you'll go with them."

"That's right."

"Can you get Ehrmann on the line?"

"No, he's talking to my supervisor and my supervisor is talking to the S.A.C."

Marquez had a pretty good idea how the fifty-six FBI field offices worked. Many decisions got made at the task force and supervisory level, and the S.A.C. got informed of the progress of operations and had to give approval for aspects, but he was also the bureaucracy fall guy if a fuckup had to be contained to a particular field office. That way the big guys back east were protected from blame. A great thing about the Bureau was if they really set out to make something happen, it went down fast, but most of the time when they started talking about supervisors and S.A.C.s you could forget about anything happening fast, particularly if you weren't talking about Federal violations.

"You understand the problem," the special agent said.

"Sure."

The guys upstairs might be tied into Ehrmann's larger investigation. They might go down on much larger violations than trafficking in illegal animal products. Sturgeon was very low on the list, but this special agent wasn't going to say it. The agent took a phone call and stepped away. When he walked back over he said, "Ehrmann will explain when you get back to California."

"These boxes may move tonight. How many people have you got?"

"We'll handle it from here. I mean it. The word is your team is to pull out."

"If it doesn't move tonight, we'll pull out at dawn."

"You're just going to make a problem for me and you."

Marquez was nonconfrontational but adamant. More phone calls got made and then it was agreed to. What could it hurt? He told Shauf to get some sleep and then sat awake in his truck. At first light it was still drizzling and the streets were dark and wet. The streetlight near the van hummed. Marquez got out and walked around. He knocked on Shauf's window and then went over to talk to the FBI before leaving.

Shauf followed him to the wharf. They found a place to eat, and Marquez ordered scrambled eggs with salmon and toast cooked dark and just barely touched with butter. Shauf ate a bagel and drank four cups of coffee. Then they woke up the team, and everyone headed south within an hour. As he left Seattle he saw the Olympic Range in his rearview, sunlight between the clouds reflecting off patches of snow high on the mountains. He drove slowly, fatigue heavy in him, and less than a hundred miles down the road he had to pull over and sleep.

Now he was driving again and approaching the Klamath River in southern Oregon. Ehrmann called and the reception was bad, but Marquez didn't expect to learn anything. Ehrmann's voice was dry, rasping, a cough interrupting sentences that crackled and stretched with the poor connection.

"We're with her."

"Is she in custody?"

"We're not bringing her in." Ehrmann coughed, and Marquez held the cell away from his ear. "We haven't found your caviar."

After hanging up, Marquez crossed the Klamath River, and the brief glimpse of the Klamath conjured memories of the largest die-off ever in the United States, thirty-two thousand Chinook salmon as a result of the ongoing struggle for water rights. Plenty of people on either side to tell you exactly why it happened and how the other side was in conspiracy to perpetrate a lie, but one truth that couldn't be argued very far was that the fall run this year of Chinook was down twenty-five percent. The biologists guessed it would stay down at least another couple of years. That assumed normal rainfall and no more water diversions that killed the young.

But even that was hardly news anymore. Perhaps we'd grow accustomed to eating salmon raised in pens. Only 2 percent of the salmon sold now was wild, and the pen farmers who fed their salmon dye to color it for market and fought regulating the antibiotics in the feed, they'd eventually get it figured out, wouldn't they? Salmon had once swum in every ocean, but it didn't need to be wild as long as we could build farms, pack them in ocean pens, and choose flesh colors like paint chips.

Besides, trying to live in balance with these wild creatures was a hassle. Farmed salmon was cheaper, simpler, and the only way to meet the demand. Problems of funguses and lack of musculature from living in crowded pens, those were solvable. Perhaps growth hormones would speed up the time it took to get them to market and bring the price down further. That should please the shareholders, and look at what the chicken farm factories and hog operations had faced and solved. Eventually, no one would remember what wild salmon tasted like anyway, or maybe they'd finally get sold on the idea that farmed salmon tasted the same, or even better. It was just a matter of the right ad campaigns.

The Lacey Act passed in the early part of the twentieth century was still the one law game wardens could count on, the strongest measure ever passed in the States to protect wildlife, but it hadn't come from Congress's desire to achieve a balance with the wild. It passed out of fear that we'd lose everything at the current rate of slaughter. We'd lose what we believed we rightfully owned, and maybe that view was a big part of the problem. We didn't really own the wild or the right to wipe out species. We'd beaten back our predators and just assumed the right to whatever we wanted with the rest of the creatures.

But fast forward a hundred years. A different battle was underway in the West for habitat and species survival. Whether it was economically feasible to preserve salmon runs for future generations, or fair to make hardworking businesses suffer to allow a species to survive, those were open questions. The debate wasn't so much about how to live in balance with nature, but whether it was worth the effort, whether the wild meant anything to us.

Let it go, Marquez thought. You think too much and you're beat. He put the Klamath behind him, remembering the rants of radio talk show hosts as the controversy was in full swing, radio hosts whose only real art was in turning issues needing discourse into venal political standoffs. It all took him down today. His usual resilience wasn't there, and when another call came from Ehrmann he let it go to voice mail and only took calls from the team. He told everyone to break the drive in half, find a motel, and finish the drive tomorrow. But he kept driving. When he was still three or four hours out he called Maria.

"I'm going to be late, Maria."

"How late?"

"I probably won't get home until after 10:00."

"Then I'm going to stay at Stacey's again. I'm at Stacey's, and I was going to leave pretty soon, but if you're going to be that late I may as well stay here." She sounded calm, said it without any attitude. "I'm here and working on my homework. I have another three hours of homework."

"Okay, stay there tonight, but understand it's not going forward this way. It's not okay to move out."

"I know everyone thinks I'm completely ungrateful, but Mom is the one who said the worst things."

What he felt like saying was knock it off, Maria, grow up and come home. You've got a pretty good life, a lot better than what your mom or I had at your age. But he held back. He'd see her tomorrow. He made two other calls on the way home, one dependent on the other, the first to his ex-chief, Bell, to reconfirm, then a call to Ludovna.

"I'm calling to invite you over the day after tomorrow. What kind of vodka do you like?"

"Cold." A laugh. "Hey, my new friend, whatever you like is good for me."

"Let me give you an address, and we'll meet right around dark."

When he got home it was nearly midnight. He found Katherine sitting in the darkness on the couch. The only light on was down the hallway. Her arms were crossed and she held herself. He touched her face, felt the wet streaks of tears, and her face was hot.

"I am so upset. I remember when her father left I promised her what I would do for her. She doesn't remember, she was too young, but it was about this time of year, and Jack hadn't had a job offer in eleven months. Then he got the offer from the security firm, and the only position they had for him was in Alaska. He had just one day to decide, and I think he was as relieved as I was. I knew when he left he wouldn't be back and that the marriage was over. I don't even know where he stayed when he got there, but I think he had a girlfriend later on and he didn't call very often. He never came home again."

Katherine was quiet, looking at him in the darkness. These were memories he knew she'd rather leave undisturbed, but she continued now.

"I let Maria sleep in my bed for six months. She turned inside herself. Her little smile went away. She used to smile all the time, and she stopped laughing. I made her promises then, one of those was that we would always be close and I would always take very good care of her. Do you know what she said tonight, John? She said she can't live around me. Sometimes I think she hates me."

"I think a lot of it is about struggling with herself. She's eighteen and wants to be independent but can't be. She's not financially independent, but if she was she might be ready to get out there on her own."

"That's ridiculous, she's in high school. When I was a senior in high school that would never have occurred to me, and of course I got angry with my mother, but wanting to move out of the house, I would never have thought like that. She says I'm a control freak and I've always micromanaged her life. Am I a control freak?"

"Sure."

"All I've ever tried to do is make sure she has the most opportunity she can."

"And you've done that. Now she wants to do it on her own."

"She doesn't know what she wants. She doesn't know what she wants to study or where to go to school."

"She'll figure it out."

"She's been eighteen for all of two weeks. She's just a girl still, so what are you saying?"

"I'm saying she wants to grow up, and the best thing you can do, or we can do, is show her a way to be. I was on my own as soon as high school was over. I remember what it feels like."

"This is my daughter, and she's still in high school. She's sleeping on a couch in some ratty apartment in San Francisco. Are you telling me that I should accept that?"

"No, I'm not."

"Then, what are you saying?"

"I'm saying talk to her as though she was thirty. She's not, she's just a kid in so many ways, but she's ready to step it up a notch."

"No, she's not."

"Try her."

34

Early the next morning he sat at the dining room table and wrote his report on his laptop. In a separate file he added what they'd learned in the past two days, and then he read through everything to date. He had coffee with Katherine. She left for San Francisco, and he was on the phone with headquarters and the team as they continued driving home.

Outside, the sky was white and smooth, and when he talked with Shauf she was still way up north but said it was the same blank sky. He made more coffee, grilled a cheese sandwich, cleaned his gear and guns, switched trucks, and drove into San Francisco to the FBI Field Office.

"I can only give you five minutes," Ehrmann said.

"My questions won't take long. You let us follow her all the way up there before backing us off. That's a long ride, Stan. Why didn't you tell me before you've had her under surveillance?"

"I did tell you. I said we lost her, and we're lucky you found her again."

"Why didn't you tell me last week she was alive?"

"Because we're very close to our takedown, and it's a very dangerous group we're targeting. You'd seemed to have already accepted the idea that she burned you. I had planned to brief you when the time came."

"You're putting a lot of energy into following her. You could pick her up but you'd rather follow her. You're hoping she'll lead you somewhere."

"We are."

"Where?"

"To more individuals associated with this crime ring."

No kidding, Stan, but what individuals? If he asked about Karsov again he'd get a blank answer.

"Why did she go to the trouble to stage her abduction?"

"We're not sure who she was trying to fool."

"Not us."

"No, not you."

"The FBI?"

Ehrmann shrugged.

"Make a guess."

"I can't do that for you."

Nothing about Ehrmann was squirrelly, but he was acting squirrelly, and Marquez felt like the guy in the room who was only getting part of the picture. He understood the Feds thought Anna might lead them to more players in this Ukrainian mob group they were targeting, but there were gaps, and he could tell he wasn't getting the whole picture. Maybe he wasn't asking the right questions. Ehrmann waited for the next one, and Marquez didn't ask it. Instead, he stood up. Ehrmann's five minutes was up, and if it was an hour it wouldn't make any difference today.

From his truck he checked in with the team. They'd started driving early this morning from the Oregon border and were still a hundred miles from Sacramento and the safehouse. He recrossed the Golden Gate, drove up the mountain, and waited for Maria to get home. She didn't have a sixth or seventh period today so was home by 2:00. She came in the door, then called, "Dad, where are you?"

"Back here working on your bathroom door. Do you want to take a walk?"

"Where?"

"On the mountain."

"If it's not a long one."

"We'll turn around when you say so."

They drove up to the lot across from Mountain Home Inn and walked the paved road past the ranger station and water tanks, then up the steep climb to the fire road before saying much.

"Here's the deal. As long as you're going to school and talking to your mom every day while you two work this out, you can keep staying with Stacey and Wendy."

"Mom's okay with that?"

"Yes, but the deal is you and your mom have to talk at least half an hour a day."

"That's weird."

"Not as weird as you moving out, and besides, what's weird about talking to your mom every day?"

"Why for half an hour?"

"So there's a chance you'll communicate."

"You mean it's my fault."

"I'm not interested in fault."

"Does Mom agree with this?"

"I wouldn't be telling you otherwise."

She thought on that as they came around another long rising curve, and Marquez looked out at the dark blue of the ocean. Maria's long-legged stride was like her mother's. He watched her pick up a piece of serpentine and flick it off the slope, send it over the manzanita and oaks. It made him remember her at nine, the way she used to race up here.

"So I'm supposed to go back to San Francisco tonight?"

"No, you're already here. I figured you and I could go see my fishing friend, and maybe we can grill some halibut or bass tonight. That sound okay?"

She was quiet too long. She sensed some trick in all this, or maybe it bored her to think about riding around with him and picking up fish from his friend. But then she nodded.

They ended up grilling hamburgers instead of halibut, and he left Maria and Katherine talking near the fireplace, the light of the fire catching their profiles. From the deck he called in and asked dispatch to help him check three hang-up calls on his cell, numbers he didn't recognize, two from the same spot.

"What you've got there are pay phone booths. The two that are the same are in Fresno. The next one is in Sacramento."

"Thanks."

The first calls were late this morning, ten minutes apart. The third must have come when he was on the mountain with Maria. A fourth came later that night after he was in bed with Katherine. She moved silently against him, only the rustle of sheets making any noise as her hand found his shoulder and moved across his chest, touched his face, his lips before sliding down to his groin and taking him in her hand. He turned, and the smooth warm skin of her belly was against him. She pulled him on top of her and her arms wrapped tight around his back, and later she laid her face on his chest and quietly wept for the loss of a dream of the way life might have been. It all came back to Maria. She was no longer the little girl who'd been Katherine's best friend in the years after her first husband abandoned them.

Late in the night the phone rang, and he walked down the hallway and outside with his cell phone. He slid the deck door shut, speaking quietly, wondering if the FBI was listening in.

"A lot of officers looked for you that night."

"I had to do what I did."

"Sure, and I know you must be very sorry for what you had to do to me."

"I am sorry, but the FBI promised to get my son for me and now they say they can't. Everything has happened because of that."

"When did they promise to get your son for you?"

"A couple of years ago, and I'm supposed to help them get closer to my ex. They'd like to lock him up for a long time."

"Where are you now?"

There was a hollowness to her voice that made him think she was in a pay phone.

"I'm in California. I'm not far from the delta, but I really am going to disappear, if they don't arrest me first. Do you want to meet me tomorrow? I really do care about the poaching and that's why I came to you in the first place. I know what they're doing and what their plans are. I wanted you to bust them. If you don't meet with me now, I'm afraid you might not get the chance."

"Why not tell me what you know over the phone? Why make a game out of meeting you?"

"Because they're probably listening to this conversation."

"Who is?"

"The FBI. I can meet you tomorrow. I can tell you where the caviar gets moved around. I can meet you where we met that first time."

"Okay, I'll meet you there."

He sat with the phone in his hands after hanging up. Agreeing to meet her was an impulsive move, and he should call Ehrmann. They'd been backed off any contact with her when they followed her, yet this was different. She'd called him. She'd made the contact. He made coffee and thought it over, read the papers, watched the dawn, and decided not to tell anyone on his team, not to jeopardize anyone's career.

Just before 10:00 he drove into the delta, looped around Sherman Island, backtracked, worked his way east, then cut across a levee island and came in the back way to the slough. He parked and did the rest on foot, keeping an eye on the vineyard roads as he walked toward the meeting spot. Across the flat water the skyline of Sacramento was visible, pale red-gold in the early light, the slough calm, grass and reeds yellowed and burned with fall. He rounded the next turn and saw her standing near the big oak she'd been at the first time. Her face had lost weight and left her gaunt looking.

"For years it's been the only way he'll let me see my son or talk to him."

"The only way who will?"

"Alex, my ex-husband. He's a criminal, and I deliver things for him. Like fly to LA, pick up a stolen car, and drive it to Las Vegas or someplace."

"Someplace like Weisson's Auto."

"How do you know that?"

"By following the sturgeon." He tried to read her eyes, couldn't tell if she was lying or not. "Are you saying you help his criminal network and in return he lets you communicate with your son?"

She nodded.

"Where is he now?"

"He moves around the world. He has a big yacht in the Med and a house in Switzerland and lots of different names."

"Does he ever come here?"

"They say he does."

"Did you ever go to the police?"

"Yes, and to the State Department. They said they'd work on it through channels and referred my case to the FBI. The FBI came to see me and interviewed me for two days. They're very interested in my ex. He's wanted for a lot of different types of crimes. He sells stolen weapons from the Soviet Union and other places. They told me about all the things he does and what I'm supposed to listen for. I speak Russian. I was a Russian; I am a Russian. His guys all know that. They all knew I was married to Alex once and they all knew the deal. They figured I wouldn't risk screwing it up."

"Then the FBI showed up."

"That's right, and they wanted me to keep on making deliveries and whatever Alex's people wanted, and they promised they would work with the Russians, find my son and bring him here."

"Last night you made it sound like the FBI came to you with the idea that you start doing deliveries for Karsov. Now you're telling me the deal was already in place. Which is the truth?"

"I had already made a deal."

"And they discovered what was going on and approached you."

She nodded.

"And now they've told you they can't get your son back, so in your mind the deal is off, but the problem is they already had the earlier evidence on you. What they'd gathered before they sanctioned your dealing with Karsov."

She nodded again.

"They don't usually back out of deals."

"They backed out of this one. For a long time they said they were looking for him and when I first showed the emails I sent to him and the ones I got back, they were sure they would find him. But they didn't and after the first year they said the emails were bounced around the world and they didn't even know if he was in Ukraine. They thought he might be in Switzerland. They kept making me promises, but I could tell they weren't trying very hard anymore. They said they weren't sure they'd be able to get him. When they said they probably wouldn't be able to and I was still lucky because they could have arrested me instead of making a deal, I guess something snapped in me. That's when I decided I was done acting like a criminal. I decided to fake the abduction so the FBI would think something had happened to me. They knew I'd gotten involved with Fish and Game because Alex's guys wanted me to. Then I got the idea it was the way I could fool everybody and disappear."

"Then why didn't you?"

"Because it didn't work out like I hoped. I didn't fool anybody."

"You fooled me. You had me racing to that fishing access. I would have gone a long time looking for you." She reached and touched him.

"They're going to make the sturgeon business work, so they're learning all about Fish and Game. They want to find out where the wardens live."

"We're not talking about the FBI anymore."

"No, we're talking about Alex's people, and the FBI knows who they are. I gave them the names, and I know they already knew some of them. But once Alex's guys know where you live, they'll come to you just like they do with a banker they want a loan from in Sacramento. They'll watch your wife or your kids and then one day one of them will call you and you won't know them but they'll offer to pick up your kids when they get out of school, and they'll tell you what time, where they get out, and what school. Then it's your choice, either you let them fish for sturgeon or maybe they'll pick up your kids and the next phone call will be to let you know you can still have your kids back. With the banker all he had to do was approve a loan. I know it doesn't sound real, but it is, and they're very patient. They want to know who they're up against, and that's why I called to meet with the SOU. They told me to meet with you and find out who you are. The FBI should have told you all this."

"You told me last night that you called because you cared so much."

"That's because I was afraid you wouldn't show up."

"What do you think I can do for you?"

"They're going to try to put me in prison because I stopped helping them and I'm still doing what Alex's guys tell me to do. I just delivered a stolen car. The FBI probably knows, and they warned me if I ever stopped working with them I'd end up going to prison for all the things I've done for Alex. But I'm not working with the FBI anymore because I think Alex's guys are suspicious of me. They must have found out something."

Marquez started to answer, then turned as he heard engine noise. He saw a blacked-out Suburban coming toward them on the slough road and another down in the vineyard.

"Oh, no, here they come," she said. "Please don't stop me."

She ran across the road and down the slough bank. But where could she go? Without slowing she dove into the water and swam to the other side of the slough, had climbed up the bank before the first Suburban reached him. The agents drew their guns as they came out of the Suburban. Two ran past Marquez, two others ordered him down. He saw the second Suburban down in the vineyard slowing to a stop as he dropped to his knees.

"Face down, arms out, asshole! Where is she!"

Marquez was belly down on the road, face pressed to the soft soil as his gun was stripped off him, a knee on his spine as cuffs clicked into place. An agent leaned over him.

"You're done, pal. You just fucked up big time."

35

The cuffs came off after the agent in the passenger seat talked with Ehrmann. But not before they'd driven hard for a little iron bridge over the slough, trying to cut her off, trying to figure out where she went. They hammered him with questions about where she'd gone. The agent sitting in the passenger seat turned to face him.

"You're not doing yourself any favors," he said. "You're only getting in deeper."

"Drop me here. I'll walk back to my truck."

"Where's she headed?"

"Hand me my phone and gun."

"You'll get everything back real soon. Whether you're going to need your badge and gun when this is over, that's a different question."

One of the agents handed him back his gun, phone, and badge, then asked him not to make any calls. The Suburban bounced hard in a rut. They drove too fast for the slough road, and Marquez knew the map showed a way to cross up ahead, but there wasn't one really.

Still, unless Anna had it very well planned she'd never escape on a flat levee island. Row after row of bare vines and no place to hide. He rubbed his wrists, wiped the dirt off his face, saw one of the agents smile.

"Why were you meeting her?"

Marquez debated talking to them at all, waiting for Ehrmann instead.

"She called with information for me on sturgeon poachers."

"So you sneaked out to a slough to meet her."

"It was a place we both knew."

"Sounds like you know her pretty well."

Marquez didn't bother with that. He stared through the window and listened to the radio chatter. They'd begun to worry she had an exit plan and had chosen this slough for a reason. The other agents had chased down the wrong vehicle, and he heard the frustration, one of them demanding over the radio, "Tell that Gamer his ass is fried if he doesn't come up with answers fast about where she is."

The agent in the passenger seat turned to Marquez, asked, "Where do you think she went?"

"I don't know but she can't be far away. Get a helicopter, the island is flat. Why do you need her so badly?"

He got handed off to another agent and driven into the Sacramento Field Office. Then he was informed that Ehrmann was on his way but that there were questions for him that would start now, and they led him to a room where three agents were waiting. Two men and a woman, the woman with black glossy hair and large eyes that bulged slightly, a way of cocking her head that made him think of a crow. A young agent who was probably undercover with the FBI, or maybe their Operation Russian Ballet was a joint operation with other agencies. He looked like he could be ATF, not quite cleaned up enough for the Bureau. The third agent was older, balding, probably a contemporary of Ehrmann, and didn't look concerned, didn't look like he'd made up his mind about any of this yet. He sat quietly, arms folded while the other two picked at Marquez.

"When did she call you?" the younger officer asked.

"Very early this morning."

"Exactly what time?"

"4:10."

"You were aware she was under surveillance."

"Yeah, I was aware you picked her up when we left her at the airport. We found her for you and handed her off in Seattle, and I figured you might show up this morning."

"Then why did you arrange a meeting with her?"

"She said she had information on sturgeon poachers, and I knew she was in trouble and thought it might be the only way to get the information."

"What information did she give you?"

"She told me the FBI had reneged on a promise to her and she wanted to escape the situation. She said the deal was her son would be brought to America and in return she'd act as an informant for you until you busted her ex-husband. According to her, a promise got made and broken by the Bureau. We didn't get much farther than that."

He took a harder look at the young officer and decided he had to be undercover. No names had been given, none of the three had introduced themselves. They were acting tough but looked worried. Whatever they had going on they were vulnerable to Anna, and he gathered they thought now they should have picked her up in Seattle rather than continue to follow her. Possibly worried she was angry enough to try to get even or double-cross them.

"Why did you meet her?"

"I already answered that. If you can't come up with new questions then let me ask some. Anna was a confidential informant for us, and we still have an operation under way against sturgeon poachers. I drove out to the delta to meet her today because she disappeared one night and I haven't talked to her since. I knew the Bureau connected to organized crime through her ex-husband and knew from Ehrmann you've been trailing her, but I didn't know until today you had a deal with her. Was she telling the truth? Did you have a deal? Was she working as an informant for the FBI?"

"You've got some balls on you."

"What's your name?"

"Peres, and my vote is we lock you up until we get the truth."

The woman cut in, cut them off, "You were told explicitly, no contact whatsoever, stay away, go home. Your scoutmaster was told the same thing."

"My scoutmaster?"

"Your Chief of Patrol, whatever. I can't keep up with these state agencies. Give us word for word your conversation with Ms. Burdovsky."

"I've already given it to you."

Another call would go today, of course, to Fish and Game headquarters, and the language would get a lot rougher.

"Do it again."

"She said she had information for me, and I took a chance she might help us. We've been looking at a Nikolai Ludovna, Don August, Abe Raburn, and Richie Crey. Do any of those names mean anything to you?"

"You were told no contact," the crow said.

"No, we were backed off a couple of times. Check with Ehrmann. We've been looking for Anna Burdovsky since she vanished."

"And you were backed off her when you found her."

"Yeah, after we found her for you we were backed off."

Now the balding older agent spoke for the first time. "There was really no choice with that, Lieutenant, but you know that."

"Yeah, but the story made more sense yesterday."

"The way I hear it you've already been allowed unusual access."

The crow cut back in. "Which you just abused. Listen to me, Lieutenant, a lot of people are at risk and this is not a game of who's hooking those bizarre-looking fish." Her nostrils flared. "If you aren't one hundred percent straight with us, you'll put agents at risk. I guarantee you, you'll lose your badge, your job, and your honor."

"My honor?"

"That's exactly right."

"Where's Ehrmann?"

"Unavailable."

Marquez looked at Peres. "Are you part of the undercover team watching Weisson's? I feel like I saw you in a window." Peres stared hard at him. "Am I right?"

Peres turned to his companions. "The only safe thing is to lock him up until this is over. We've got him up on a levee road playing James Bond, and I don't want to take this risk. Let's find her and let's hold him."

"You're making the risks," Marquez said.

Peres turned to the balding agent. "Who is this horse's ass?"

But the balding agent had a question now for Marquez. "What do you mean you saw him in a window?"

"He didn't see me," Peres said.

"We saw a surveillance team, and Peres here looks like the guy that was in the window. I looked at him with binoculars, but I could be wrong. We were checking out everything surrounding Weisson's because we'd followed two suspects there." The balding agent nodded. "Look, I'm sorry, maybe I shouldn't have met with her, but we're still trying to crack this poaching ring. She told me she had information on the poachers she'd give me today and I bit. I should have called you first."

He realized he'd started to get through to them and continued talking. The balding agent was Stan Sullivan. He introduced the crow. "This is Special Agent Walker," and Marquez gathered that she was out here from the East, possibly Quantico. She was dead serious as she faced him again.

"We have significant charges we're prepared to file against a number of people. I don't know the details of the promise made to Burdovsky, but I'm certain we haven't reneged on anything. We wouldn't do that. That's all I can say about it. I know about Seattle, and despite what you may believe, the Bureau is very sympathetic to what you are trying to do."

The door opened, and Douglas walked in. He took a seat and looked across the table at Marquez.

"John," Douglas asked, "did she tell you anything else?"

In this room full of people Douglas focused on him, was trying to communicate with him. He waited for Marquez to respond to the cue. Marquez told the story again. Left out nothing, added what he was saving for Ehrmann, that she'd asked him not to stop her from trying to get away.

"Why wouldn't you stop her? She burned you."

"She was three steps and in the water and there were two blacked-out Suburbans closing on me. I didn't see any reason to chase her." Then the last thing, what he was saving for Ehrmann. "She said you have another source inside this Eurasian crime ring and that you don't need her."

"She told you we have another source?"

Marquez nodded, added that he'd been waiting for Ehrmann to arrive.

Marquez heard Peres to the crow, "What did I tell you?"

Douglas silenced Peres with his hand.

"Did she name this other source, John?"

"No, and she didn't say any more than that."

"That's disturbing."

The room was quiet. The crow's stare had turned opaque. But the balding agent seemed to understand his holding out for Ehrmann.

"How soon is your bust?" Marquez asked.

"Too soon to have her running around." Douglas looked from Marquez to the balding man. "We need to get Ehrmann right now."

36

He was another hour at the Sacramento Field Office, and when he walked out he was no longer angry that he'd been hauled in. He knew what the hours before a bust felt like, the countdown after the hour was picked, the premeetings done, the safety talks, warrants in place, everything ready to go. Then something unexpected happens and you don't really know what to do with it, particularly at the Federal level where the momentum is harder to start and stop. Momentum acquired its own life as a big bust neared, and in the hyped-up, sometimes near paranoid state before a significant takedown anything could rattle you.

But he was disturbed by what he'd learned and what he was piecing together. They hadn't found Anna and were frustrated and surprised she'd eluded them. Ehrmann had walked into the room where Marquez sat with Douglas and asked, "Where is there to hide out there? There's nothing there but vineyards and orchards.

There aren't six buildings on that levee island. Is she scuba trained? Is it possible she swam out underwater in the slough? How could we lose her out there?"

Now darkness was coming. Ehrmann had made it clear they were going forward with the bust, and Marquez had guessed that explained Douglas's presence in Sacramento. Not even Douglas would tell him when the go hour was, but it wasn't hard to figure out it was within twenty-four hours.

He drove to the safehouse and continued on to Bell's house. Everything was in place for Ludovna's visit. Roberts would be his wife for the night. She had put on bright pink lipstick and cut up celery and emptied bags of baby carrots and potato chips onto a platter. There was a sour cream dip.

"I'm in here, honey," she called, and he heard Cairo laugh. "Would you bring me a martini?"

He walked into Bell's study, and they were arranging fishing trophies and had hung photos. In a loose way they'd decorated the house for the guy he was. Roberts smiled and batted her eyes at him.

"I forgot the martini."

"That's okay, sweetie, but do you think everything looks nice? Should I run out to the market and buy more potato chips, and do you think your friend will go through more than one bottle of vodka?"

"He might but we'll pour champagne first. He told me he's bringing some caviar."

"That's too bad, I thought we should poach our own sturgeon. I thought that's why you're late. Wouldn't the party be more fun that way?"

He smiled at her. "You look nice. I've been with the Feds and that's why I'm late."

"I went all out," she said, and she wore a tight black dress, her long legs stretching from underneath it. "I bet I know what you're wondering," she said. "You're wondering where my gun is."

"You're not wearing it."

"Not tonight. I have it here in the kitchen and I could change, what do you think?"

Alvarez would be on the street and Marquez wasn't worried, but he was jittery. He tried to lighten up and hook into the banter, but his mind was on the FBI bust. Ludovna connected to Weisson's via the sturgeon and that got talked about in the FBI Field Office. He'd sat an hour with Ehrmann at the long table there and ticked off the names again of the suspects in their sturgeon poaching investigation. Ehrmann had acknowledged that the Bureau suspected Ludovna was trafficking in caviar. But he wasn't concerned about Ludovna's animal trafficking. That was Marquez's to deal with. The conversation was all about Anna.

Marquez sat with Roberts before Ludovna arrived. He told her what had happened today, told her about the call from Anna, meeting on the slough road, the questioning at the FBI Field Office.

"They're getting ready to make a bust and they're not saying where or when, but it's very soon. I saw an FBI SWAT commander that I recognized come through the Sacramento Field Office while I was there, and they all have that feel to them. They're gearing up. What I'm not clear about is Anna's role. I think they were hoping she'd get some particular bit of intelligence for them. They hoped and she didn't deliver, and now they're not sure what side she's on. She's stopped cooperating with them. They've threatened her with new charges and that's frightened her even more. And, because they didn't find her today, they think she had help escaping."

"What do you think?"

"She might have had help. My friend Douglas showed up and that calmed things down, but they're wired up and ready to go." He paused. "I made a mistake meeting her this morning without calling Ehrmann first."

"Because she's trying to use you?"

"Or communicate through me. She knows I don't trust her, but she assumes the FBI is talking to me."

"Sounds like they did plenty of that."

"If by any chance her name comes up tonight, and there's no reason to think it will, play dumb with Ludovna."

"That's easy for me. No one has ever seen me with her. Not so easy for you if August knows Ludovna and they're talking."

"If that's the case, then Ludovna has always known who I am."

Marquez could see headlights out on the street. Wind picked up dry leaves from the gutter and sidewalk that flickered in front of the headlights as the BMW turned into the driveway. His cell rang. Alvarez said, "Your guests are here."

"Who's with him?"

"Nike Man."

The doorbell rang.

"I should get it," Roberts said.

"Yeah, it should be you. Remember he's still suspicious of me. He was an interrogation specialist, and he's here to find out about me. He may ask you a lot of questions, and he may try to get you alone to question you."

"And whatever else."

"Yeah, that too."

Roberts opened the door and said something that was supposed to translate as *Greetings! I welcome you*. She got it off an

Internet clip of *Voyager* space ship greetings in various languages, kept replaying the Russian one until she got it down. They moved into the living room, and Ludovna smiled at Marquez after he took in the room. He spread his arms.

"So you were fucking with me. You live like a king."

"I'd rather have that house of yours and what comes with it." He winked at Ludovna. "I'll trade you."

"How much is this worth?"

"Two and a half million, but we don't own it. We lease and it costs too much to do that, but to build a business you have to put a good face on."

Ludovna's gaze followed the skin high on Robert's thigh as she bent over and put down the plate of appetizers. Marquez opened the first bottle of champagne, and Ludovna made a present of the caviar he'd brought. He had it rolled up in a black cashmere scarf that he pulled from the pocket of his coat and unfolded, revealing the glass jar. He gave it to Roberts, taking her hand, pressing the jar into her palm.

"Better than gold," he said.

Marquez took the jar from her, made a show of trying to read the label while complaining about nearsightedness. Caspian label but he had to wonder if it was from Raburn's, and it would be like Ludovna to test him now. The vacuum seal on the jar made a low pop as he opened it. The cork came out of the champagne, and Roberts took the bottle from him, her eyes teasing him, saying, "That's my job."

She poured Ludovna's glass first, then Nike Man and came back to Ludovna because the champagne's foamy bubbles had kept her from filling the glass as high as she'd wanted. She was near enough to him for Ludovna to feel the heat off her legs, and later, after Marquez had toured him around the lower floor of the house and satiated his initial curiosity, and after Nike Man had gone down the hallway to use the bathroom and secretly look into the bedroom, after they had opened the vodka and drunk a couple of glasses, Ludovna took him aside.

"Your wife," he said.

"What about her?"

"Does she know about our business?"

"Yes."

"Sometimes I want you to send her instead of delivering yourself."

"She may not want to do that."

"But you'll ask her, okay, and then you get her to do that for me. I don't like the same people delivering all the time." Ludovna moved the air with his hand. "Too predictable."

"She likes to stay out of it, but I have a friend—"

"No friends."

"Look—"

"No, you understand, I don't want anybody more that I don't know, so send her sometimes. I'll tell you when."

Before the night was over Ludovna had held her hands, kissed the backs of each, and told her she was lovely and he wanted to see her again. He said good night to Marquez, but he thanked Roberts. After he left they rearranged the paintings, collected the trophies and moved everything into the garage as Marquez had promised Bell.

"I'm real surprised Bell let us use his house," Roberts said.

"He said it doesn't feel like his house anymore, and he's signed a lease on a house in D.C. You ready to get out of here?"

"Yeah, let's go."

Marquez turned off the lights, shut the door. He doubted he'd ever see the inside of the house again and wondered when he'd see Bell. He got in his truck, and Roberts pulled away ahead of him. He figured he'd call Katherine after stopping in at the safehouse and then make the hour-and-a-half drive home. Then, just before getting to the safehouse, he got a call from Ehrmann.

"Where are you, Lieutenant?"

"In Sacramento at our safehouse."

"I've been thinking about what happened today, and I'm sorry for the way it went down with you. Not all of the agents were up to speed on your team working with her. There was no reason to bring you in that way."

They were playing a game here. Ehrmann didn't owe any real apology and they both knew it, but Marquez went along.

"No, I shouldn't have gone out to meet her. I should have called you, but I've wanted to confront her in person, and she sucked me in with the promise of names of poachers. Have you found her yet?"

"No."

"Are you out there looking for her tonight?"

"Until we find her we'll be out there." There was a staticky pause, and Marquez realized they hadn't gotten to the reason for the call yet. "How far is your safehouse from our field office?"

He had no doubt Ehrmann already knew the answer to that, and he knew what was coming but wasn't sure of Ehrmann's reasons.

"About twenty minutes."

"Do you want to ride along with me tonight? There are people you might help us connect."

"So it's tonight."

"We're stacked and nearly ready to go. You and I won't go to the on-scene command post, but we've got a building we monitor from and afterwards you'll get a look at the suspects. We'd like you to listen in to the initial interrogations. With these Eurasian gangs we get a lot of partial answers, things alluded to but not said, and you may hear something said about sturgeon poaching and be able to help us with the next question. We're going to separate them and try to work a couple against each other. Some of these guys will get charged with enough to put them away for life."

"All right, I'm on my way."

He wheeled the truck around and accelerated. At this hour he'd probably get there in under ten minutes.

37

The FBI Sacramento Field Office kept a SWAT team, but Weisson's was big enough that they had probably asked for help from San Francisco, which had an Enhanced SWAT team, one whose training included hostage rescue. The Feds prided themselves on gathering and preparing and probably had a precise plan for the takedown. They'd have layout diagrams, blueprints of the building, the whole works. If there was going to be a dynamic entry, then it was likely to be on the front face. Their usual MO was to show up with overwhelming force, seal and contain, then call out the suspects, one team waiting on the back side, one on the front, an extrication team standing by.

And they had a predesignated location they were gathered at now, a staged location where the on-scene SWAT commander would run the bust from. Blacked-out Suburbans with their runners on were already lined up, stacked and ready by the time

Ehrmann had called him, and if they'd suspected him in any way, there was no chance the call from Ehrmann would have happened. He felt an odd relief in that.

Marquez waited now for the heavy steel gate to roll open. He'd heard the gate had cost eight hundred thousand dollars and could stop an eighteen-wheeler at fifty-five miles an hour. Ehrmann walked out as the gate opened and directed Marquez where to park. A few minutes later they left in Ehrmann's car.

"How many are in the building?"

"Five and some bodyguards, and then there's us."

He smiled over at Marquez, but Ehrmann didn't really have the demeanor of a field guy, and his joking lacked the feel of someone who'd been there. It made Marquez think of some of the new aspects of the Bureau. The weight had shifted from CID and criminal investigation into the still amorphous fight against terrorism. Taking on Eurasian criminal gangs required an international scope and understanding of elaborate computer crime and sophisticated networks overlapping countries. It took a different kind of breed. Ehrmann was probably very adept with a computer. He thought of what Anna had said yesterday about Karsov owning a yacht he kept in the Med and a house in Switzerland.

"Is Karsov here?"

"We hope he is, and we think we watched him arrive, though the vehicle's windows were tinted."

"What else do you expect to find in there?"

"Weapons that came in disguised as car parts."

"Is that what this has always been about?"

"Yes."

So it was all coming out now. Ehrmann was suddenly very upfront and nervous too. His hands moved constantly. A long investigation was coming down to a moment. Marquez listened to the back-and-forth radio chatter, listened to Ehrmann's responses. Weisson's had been color-coded by SWAT. The front was red, the back side black, the west end green, east blue, and the roof purple. The purple team would go in first and access the roof. A helicopter was on its way. They drove up to a drab building a good mile from Weisson's, and Marquez saw a line of cars and several TV vans. He had thought they'd be as close as the on-scene SWAT commander, and Ehrmann guessed what he was thinking.

"This is as close as we get."

"Is Douglas with the SWAT commander?"

"He is."

"He's been part of your investigation."

Not really a question. He just wanted to confirm it.

"Since the start, he's been part of this since day one. I'll tell you something else, when we take Karsov into custody tonight, the world becomes just a little bit safer."

"He's that big a deal?"

"He is. You ready to go in?"

When they walked in Marquez saw the media being briefed in a room out front. A spokesman for the FBI pointed at the class picture, the faces of the suspects they hoped to arrest, pinned up on a wall. A few heads turned their direction as they moved past toward the back of the building. Marquez could feel Ehrmann's pride as the FBI spokesman told the assembled press what was about to happen was "the most significant takedown of Eurasian

Organized Crime ever in the state of California, the culmination of an eighteen-month investigation spanning the West Coast."

Now they entered a room with a table and banks of surveillance equipment. It looked like a war room. Ehrmann explained the equipment and introduced him. SWAT didn't need to crawl up to a rolling door and snake a camera underneath to check out the interior ahead of the bust. It was all right here on the monitors.

"How many cameras have you got inside the building?" Marquez asked.

"Twelve. They're all up in the roof trusses."

They had audio, had bugs planted in the room where the meeting was under way right now. It was all a little amazing, but the Bureau was flush with cash. He guessed there was two hundred thousand dollars' worth of surveillance equipment in the room. Three TV monitors showed the face of the building from different angles. But it was camera angles inside, the on-screen views looking down and across the working bays at a glass-enclosed and lighted office, that really said it all. They were watching the meeting in progress inside the building, watching it and listening to it. Marquez read the shapes of five men, four seated, one walking around.

"That's the meeting room," Ehrmann said. "The man standing is Karsov. We just got a positive ID and he's not here for caviar or cars. When the price gets high enough he can't trust his guys and has to show up himself."

Marquez looked around the room again. His eyes were drawn back to the shapes of the men in the meeting. An audio tech took off his earphones, and Ehrmann put them on. Looking at the setup here, it was pretty easy to understand the disdain the agents who'd picked him up out on the slough road had shown for the SOU operation.

"Are you going to tour the TV people through here?" Marquez asked, and Ehrmann shook his head.

A radio crackled to life. The helicopter was less than a minute away, and SWAT started to roll toward Weisson's gate. Marquez heard the copter pass overhead and focused on the monitors that caught the front facade of Weisson's. One camera looked through the fence and rows of wrecked cars at the Mercedes and minivan parked parallel to the building near the rolling doors. Though he wasn't part of the bust, anticipation rose in him. The energy in the room was electric. Ehrmann couldn't stop moving.

"Three, two, one," someone counted, and the power went out along the front face.

"We have snipers on the roofs of two of these abandoned buildings," Ehrmann said. "And we're moving onto the roof of Weisson's. They'll go down the roof access door to the computers on the mezzanine level if the gentlemen inside don't come out as soon as we call them."

"Will they answer?"

"We think the individual we're calling will answer. We've been a steady customer for him, and the number showing on his screen will read as out-of-state. Unless the power outage spooks him, I think he'll answer."

They could hear the cell ringing through the bugs in place in the meeting room. It rang six times and went to voice mail. They called it again.

"Come on, answer your phone," Ehrmann said. But the phone abruptly shut off.

The SWAT commander decided to flash-bang a door and use bullhorns to call them out. Marquez watched onscreen as four of the SWAT moved between the old Mercedes and the minivan. He could barely make out their shapes, and he overheard that the reason the door wasn't being popped open with their "Peacekeeper" vehicle was that there wasn't enough room to get between the Mercedes and minivan. He looked away from that monitor to one that was hooked to infrared cameras and recorded the heat images of the men who'd been in the meeting room moving past its screen.

"They're out of the room," Ehrmann said, and an audio tech said he could hear SWAT loud and clear calling them out with bullhorns. "No way they don't hear that," Ehrmann said. "No way."

Then there was a rapid series of light flashes that the inside cameras caught and Marquez read as automatic fire. A shooter kept a steady stream of fire toward the door that had been breached, and then outside along the front there was a flash of light so brilliant the transmitting of it momentarily lit up the room here. There was a second bright flash and yelling and chaos as a fireball formed and rose where the Mercedes had been. It took a full second or two before they realized the cars parked out in front of Weisson's had detonated.

"Omigod," an agent to the left of Marquez said. "Oh, Jesus, no."

The SWAT commander whose voice was broadcast live in the room was yelling as he aborted the bust and called everyone back, and the extrication team started forward with the Peacekeeper's armored body leading. Then there was hesitation, fear of secondary explosions, and a couple of minutes lost before the Peacekeeper moved in through the fence. The helicopter's searchlight showed the two vehicles burning and nothing moving. Six of the SWAT team had been inside the fence. The helicopter's light swept the pavement looking for them, and the pilot's voice ended with the word "shit," and there was a loud bang.

The SWAT commander kept his cool, reported, "The copter's been hit. It's going down."

Then abruptly the helicopter showed on a monitor as it struck Weisson's high along the east corner. It was in flames, and the tail section folded as it hit the ground.

Marquez watched the extrication team move in and around the burning vehicles, and the only voice in the room was the SWAT commander broadcasting through one of the speakers. There was a moment where no one said anything or moved.

38

"It's all over CNN," Cairo told him about an hour later.

Marquez had moved outside. All visitors and nonessential personnel were out of the building, and he'd told Ehrmann he'd get one of the team to pick him up.

"Better come get me."

He gave Cairo directions, and as he waited learned that Douglas had taken a ricochet gunshot wound to the head while helping get the injured out. Now Cairo called.

"I can't get to you. They won't let anyone within a mile. Can you get a ride out?"

"No, but I'll walk."

He tried to get more information on Douglas before leaving. Cairo drove him to the field office, and it was difficult retrieving his car. They had to get a hold of Ehrmann to release it. From the safehouse Marquez tried to find out where they'd taken the wounded and gave up using the phone and listened to the TV, which seemed to be the best source of what was happening. CNN was calling it the worst loss of life during a raid in the history of the Bureau. Three suspects were at large. Karsov's face along with several of his aliases were shown on screen, and Marquez couldn't figure out how they got past the SWAT team along the back face. There were four or five FBI snipers back there, and if they'd fought their way out, then how could they escape by vehicle with all the helicopters in the air? An hour later CNN reported a tunnel had been found running from inside Weisson's out to a large storm drain, and it was believed they'd escaped through the tunnel and used cell phones to call in people to pick them up. TV coverage of Weisson's showed the carcasses of the vehicles that had exploded, an armored carrier on its side, the downed helicopter, the TV correspondent calling it a picture from a war zone, comparing it to images he'd seen in the Middle East.

"Seven confirmed dead," a reporter said.

When the hospitals where the injured had been taken were named, Marquez drove to Mercy Hospital. He found the waiting room filled with the families of injured officers, then got asked if he was family and shook his head.

"Then go home."

He drove back past Weisson's, listening on both police band and regular radio where the FBI director was making a statement, speaking first to the loss of life, then to the manhunt under way for the three men whose faces were now being broadcast nationally. Klieg lights cast a glow in the sky. The streets were blocked off, and he couldn't get to the command center where he hoped by passing a message to Ehrmann he could get word on Douglas. The director described elements of Eurasian Organized Crime, Russian mob elements in California they'd first identified through contacts in Brighton Beach, New Jersey. He sketched arms deals tied to Karsov and returned to answering questions about the dead and wounded.

Marquez drove past Ludovna's house. His headlights were stark on the bare trees, the dark lawns of the street. No lights were on in Ludovna's house, and he didn't see the BMW in the driveway. He drove back to the safehouse, brewed coffee, and called Katherine, who had gone to bed without knowing anything about a blown bust. She walked out and turned the TV on while she was on the phone with him.

"Why were you there?"

"It was a mix of things, some crossover of suspects I'm not clear about yet. Charles Douglas has been wounded."

"Do you know how badly he's hurt?"

"Not yet."

He talked another hour with Katherine, and the TV was on in the background as Kath came up to speed. She'd met Douglas but hardly knew him. She liked him, but he was yet another law enforcement friend of Marquez's, and she was more worried that he could have been shot himself.

When he hung up with Katherine he moved outside to the patio. There was nothing to do but wait, and periodically he went in and checked the TV. But he was outside at dawn watching the red-rimmed sky lighten and thinking about what was being speculated about on TV, that the cars were packed with C-4 or some similar explosive and that the criminal gang involved feared the FBI and had created the car bombs as a way to repel a SWAT team.

How anyone in the media had gotten this information Marquez had no idea. He couldn't see the Feds releasing anything at this point. Shauf found him outside on the patio.

"They've gone national with Burdovsky's face, and they're saying she's wanted for questioning in connection with last night," Shauf said.

"What are they calling her?"

"A person of interest. The other three are still at large."

"Is there more about that?"

"Some. They're replaying it every few minutes. Come in and watch it, and let's eat something. You look like you need it. I'll scramble some eggs if you make coffee and toast."

They put a breakfast together, and he sat with Shauf and drank several cups of coffee, thinking about torture killings he'd seen in the DEA. A snitch had his eyes removed and his testicles stuffed far enough down his throat for him to choke before he bled to death, but not before he was dotted with cigarette burns and his wife raped and killed in front of him. You found a way past those things by finding the explanation—the cartel wanted to make an example to frighten others. You never forgot the images but if you understood why they were killed, it was the first step to dealing with it.

He took a call from Chief Baird as they were cleaning up. It had been Marquez's plan to return to the hospital and try to get word on Douglas. After that, he wasn't sure. But now, Baird wanted him to come in.

On weekends Baird took his fourteen-year-old and twelve-year-old grandsons fishing on Buck's Lake where he had a small cabin. He often said he'd like to live at Buck's and forget about the rest of the world. He wanted to live the rest of his life simply, but Baird was anything but simple and had the gift of seeing things in perspective sooner than others. Marquez drove to headquarters and answered the chief's questions.

"Did they know it was the FBI?"

"They knew."

"And they went ahead and detonated these car bombs and then shot at those trying to help the wounded?"

"Correct. The shooting was probably to cover Karsov's escape."

"And these are some of the same people you've been watching?"

"Probably not. We've watched caviar delivered to and shipped back out of the building, but we haven't had any contact with anyone who was in that meeting room last night."

"Are you sure? The FBI has only identified three, and you say there were five. Could one of the men in the room be an informer for the FBI?"

"From the audio and visual equipment they had set up, I don't think they need an informer." But Baird was asking if one of the unnamed men could have been Ludovna.

"No, Ehrmann would have told me."

Baird pondered that and said, "I want you to go home. That's an order."

He called Katherine on the drive home. Now he looked at the fall light on the gravel beyond the front porch and walked through the house and out onto the deck. A cold wind blew in from the ocean, and he turned the idea that Katherine was right, it was time he turned in his badge. He'd be fifty in a couple of years, and watching that last night only brought home how precious life was.

Maria was almost grown, and they were getting older. Maybe he'd given his fair share to dealing with society's misfits and the backwash of the gene pool.

There were drives Marquez remembered, coming back from somewhere or getting an early start, dawn along the north coast when the ocean was silver-blue and the steep coastal mountains still edged with night. Or a full moon rising over the Los Padres on a dusky June night, or the first snow as he crossed Tioga Pass in October, the fall light on the eastern slope as the aspens turned, the Kern River, the Eel, and wading into the Sacramento above Sweetwater to fish for trout, and a morning in March in the desert when the spring flowers bloomed. What he remembered best was the light and the feel of the land, the long dark velvet of the ocean, and Katherine was right, he didn't have to give the rest of his life to chasing bad guys.

He was still sitting on the deck when Ehrmann called, and he knew two things as he heard his voice. Ehrmann was at an airport, which probably meant he was being summoned east, and two, Ehrmann had bad news to deliver. He'd heard the tone too many times before, heard Ehrmann sigh and explain, "I wanted to call you before it was public, because I know you were friends and they tell me you came by last night."

"Aw, don't tell me that, Ehrmann. Tell me something else."

"Charles Douglas died this morning at dawn."

Marquez laid the phone on the railing. He leaned on the railing and bowed his head into his hand.

39

Douglas had once made a cryptic remark to Marquez about religion. As they leaned against the metal railing of a boat and looked out at the clean sky above the water, Douglas had said he believed in God too much to ever sit in a church.

But a memorial service is for the living, not the dead. Douglas's was held in a chapel adjacent to the East Bay mortuary and graveyard where he was to be buried alongside his mother. A pastor who'd never met Douglas conducted the service. He quoted often from the Bible and gave no sign that he had any feeling at all for Douglas's life or death.

After the chapel service Marquez followed a line of cars up the long hill to the gravesite, where two men were at work adjusting a dark wooden coffin so it would lower properly into the grave in the steep manicured lawn. A second service began, and those in the audience were asked if they wanted to say anything. An old friend of Douglas's, a man who said he'd known Charles forever, said, "It was simple with Charles. You could always count on him to do the right thing. It didn't matter what it was, he would do it."

Marquez took a long look at Douglas's sons, square-shouldered and brave as Douglas would want them to be, though tears ran steadily down their cheeks. His wife, Amelia, sobbed as the moment overwhelmed her, and Douglas's brother pulled her close and held her. When the coffin lowered Amelia broke free and sank to the grass. She grabbed at the chains, tried to stop it from lowering, and a deep sadness came over Marquez. He felt the tears on his own face, couldn't take this one stoically. He wished he'd found the words to speak earlier and looked away now down the long falling slope and at the dark green of the big oaks and out across San Francisco Bay, at the whitecaps, gray-black clouds at the horizon.

He and Douglas used to talk about what they'd do someday when they had more time. Douglas wanted a house where he could have a big vegetable garden and barbecue on a back deck that looked out on nothing but hills. He'd move north until he could afford a good house, or inland if he had to. He was tired of the fog. He wanted to be where it froze at night in the winter, someplace north where you could toss a football around on New Year's Day and you were warm in the sun in a T-shirt, but where you knew there was winter.

"Do you think about what comes next?" Douglas had asked, and he'd been serious. "I mean after you get tired of chasing perps and the geeks stealing from our children's future."

When the crowd began to break up and move toward the cars, Marquez went to Amelia to tell her how sorry he was. He felt her desperation as she gripped his hands.

"My dreams are gone," she said. "I had so many dreams of the things we were going to do."

Marquez walked to his truck. Only as he unlocked it and was getting in did he become aware of someone behind him. A young FBI agent had come up behind him, and he turned to face him, wondering what it was. Another special agent, a woman, backed him up. She stood within earshot but out of the line of confrontation.

"What are you doing here?" the agent asked.

"Charles was a friend of mine."

"I don't think you belong here, and I'm not alone thinking that."

"What's that about?"

"Don't show up at the wake."

The agent waited for a response as though the statement warranted it, but Marquez turned back to his car and got in. He drove away without looking in the rearview mirror, but it had affected him. He did not attend the wake. He'd been unsure whether he would or not, and maybe he deferred to the agent's words.

An hour later he was on the sidewalk outside the Presto on Union where Maria was working this afternoon. As he came inside her elbows were on the yellow marble of the counter, two customers, two friends of hers he guessed, standing at the bar across from her, cappuccinos in front of them, as she leaned toward them, chatting. A young man with a goatee cleaned an espresso machine to the side of her. He had a feeling that was Shane. He read Maria's quizzical smile at his black suit and then saw her put it together and the smile vanish.

"Why don't you take a break for a few minutes and walk with me?"

They walked up Union Street, then climbed up toward Pacific Heights and walked along Broadway where the wind was stronger.

"Your mom told me she came to visit you last night."

"Only so she could tell me to come home. It wasn't like she wasn't waiting the whole time just so she could say that."

"She told me she didn't ask for anything."

"Lies like that," Maria said almost under her breath, the comment almost lost in the wind, her anger at her mother surfacing again. Marquez stopped walking when he heard it.

"Lies like what?" he asked.

"That's why she came by," Maria said. "She hates me."

"Or you're so angry you think you hate her. She's worried because she cares so much, and like any parent she doesn't want you to take a wrong turn."

"Like I'm the first person to ever take a break before going to college."

"She's afraid you'll end up without a college degree and working for minimum wage."

"My friends don't have college degrees."

"It's like a business card here, Maria. A degree is a bare minimum in a lot of places you might go to work."

"Well, I don't want to become a suit. I don't want to live that kind of life."

"It's not about what you don't want to be; it's about what you do want to be."

"Mom thinks I'm ungrateful, lazy, and selfish. She was disgusted when I said I want to go shopping instead of look at a college I could never get into anyway."

"Things get said, and you'd better learn how to forget, if you can't forgive."

"How about when your own mother says them?"

"My mother dumped my sister, your aunt, and me at my grandparents when I was nine and my sister twelve. She was going to come back when she 'got her head clear.' But we never saw her again. She got killed in a train wreck in India. She was on a spiritual quest going somewhere to find out about herself, and my father was always going to take us back from his parents and raise us, but somehow he was always in the process of getting his life together. The year before they dumped us we lived in a tent up the coast. I was almost two years behind in school when I started, and all I really knew how to do well was fight. Two years behind and big for my age."

"How come you've never told me about living in a tent?"

"It's not the kind of thing you brag about. The kids at the funeral today just lost their dad. I knew their father well enough to know they just lost the best friend they'll ever have. You and your mom are going to have to deal with what you've said to each other. The only way to do that is to keep talking and put the bad stuff behind you. It's time you come home."

She hung tough. "I've got to get back to work, Dad."

He walked down with her, then drove to the Humane Shelter and picked up the cat that Anna had abandoned and August had dumped on the shelter. Marquez wrote a check to the shelter, and the woman there found Bob's collar.

"Okay, Bob, you've got a new home."

He put the cat carrier on the passenger seat and crossed the Golden Gate in heavy traffic, feeling very emotional about Douglas's death. Then he took a call from Crey.

"My man," Crey said. "I was beginning to think someone mistook you for an FBI agent in a parking lot and blew your ass up."

"I've been laying low."

"Tell you what, dude, I would have bought tickets to watch that shit go down. I hate those fuckers. They put me in a little room and tried to tell me I was connected to some big-time drug traders and I was going to do twenty years unless I snitched people out. A couple of them were in the bait shop today."

"What did they want today?"

"They're everywhere asking questions about the Burdovsky babe. I thought she got smoked, but I guess she's alive and they're trying to find her." He laughed. "More than alive, she's on the wanted list."

"I thought it was Russians they were after."

"Right now, if you've got a V in your name they want to talk to you. But look, I'm calling because I've got an offer for you. I talked to the boys, and I think maybe your story is just about right. They were going upstairs, which isn't cool with me. I've got a proposition for you."

"Yeah, what's that?"

"You and me partner up in the business."

"Partners?"

"That's right, and I'm serious. I'm talking about fifty-fifty. I move it and deal with the customers. You do your end, and we split everything. I got the big boat, you got boats, and we work the delta."

"I might be interested. Let me think about it. But what about Torp and Perry?"

"There's some other shit you don't know about. I think it's going to catch up to them. They ripped a car off a girl they were staying with, and now I'm getting some calls, people wondering where she is."

"What's her name?"

"You don't even want to know. Think about it and call me."

A second later he hung up.

40

That night it rained hard, and in the morning the clouds were low and the wind blew hard over the mountain. Marquez listened to the rain lash the windows and made calls. He talked to his team about the Crey offer, then picked up a message from Raburn and phoned him back.

"This is one you might be interested in or not," Raburn said. "There's an old Mexican albino they call Whitey. He called me yesterday because he's got one."

"How long have you known him?"

"A while. He's into peyote and mushrooms and used to live down in the desert in New Mexico. Came up here about a dozen years ago. He knows how to keep a sturgeon alive. He's got one with eggs. I usually hear from him once every six months, but he called twice yesterday. He says he's up Razor Slough."

Marquez had never heard of sturgeon biting up Razor. There was little flow, it was shallow, narrow, and last time he was there it didn't look like either the Army Corps or the state had done any dredging or clearing of deadfall in years. Razor was out along the edge of the delta, deep in the Central Valley, and there was little up there but mosquitoes in summer and the rotted remains of an evangelist's attempt to set up an encampment. It was also too early, far too early for a sturgeon to migrate that far.

"He'll meet you there," Raburn said. "That's if you're interested."

"Do you believe him?"

"Wouldn't make any difference if I did or not. I got a number you've got to call back before noon if you're interested."

Marquez looked outside. Raining hard and his boat was at Loch Lomond. Wouldn't be easy to launch his boat and run it all the way up to Razor on just the possibility of a sturgeon. But something nagged about it. He copied the number he was supposed to call.

"I'm not saying he's really got one, but he never calls unless he does. Do you know how to get to Razor Slough?"

"I can probably find my way back."

"'Cause I can't go with you. I've got to meet my brother."

"How's the weather where you are?"

"The rain has let up."

"Razor is where the preacher left that mess?"

"You got it. One end is closed off, but you can't get in there unless you want to hike. You got to go by water, but you can't go the whole way. If I was you I wouldn't do it, but you wanted me to call you with every offer."

Marquez felt a vague unease. He hung up with Raburn and called Shauf to talk it over. There was a Zodiac they could borrow and put in well upriver. That would cut the boat time to forty minutes, and they'd still have the hike.

"Is it worth it?" she asked.

"If I partner with Crey it might be, and the storm is supposed to taper off."

Marquez looked at Bob the cat sitting on the fireplace mantel where he'd been sitting since last night. Katherine had fed him on the mantel. A little can of something called Fancy Food was sitting in front of him. He'd eaten out of the can without knocking it off the mantel. Marquez looked at him and thought about why he'd brought him home. Maybe because the way Bob had been abandoned angered him, or maybe because when he'd first met Katherine she and Maria had a cat they loved that had died of cancer about four years ago.

"If Raburn was going to set us up, Razor Slough would be the place to do it," Shauf said. "After what happened at Weisson's, if anything happened to us that sure would be the end of any undercover sturgeon operation. How close to Crey's call was Raburn's?"

"Close. What are you wondering?"

"Whether anybody is working together."

"Let's go take a look. I'll call and leave the message with this Whitey character that we're coming up early in the afternoon."

Razor Slough was worse than he remembered. Brambles and blackberries tugged at their clothes and scratched their faces. They left the Zodiac tied off on a tree and climbed up the bank. The mud was sticky, and on the hike in it rained on and off and was cold, though there were patches of blue sky now. Marquez pointed out where someone had used a machete to create a channel in the slough. Cuts on the tree branches overhanging the water looked fresh.

It was an hour before they saw the faded plywood structures of the encampment. Smoke rising from a hole in the roof of one of the buildings bent in the wind, and Marquez looked for Whitey. He saw his blue skiff but not him.

The preacher had his brethren carve a swath of earth maybe ten feet above the slough and then level back seventy yards to low hills. Marquez had heard it was a rancher, a follower of the evangelist, who'd allowed this gash cut into land he leased from the government. In the winter runoff silted into the slough, and he remembered something about a lawsuit getting filed. No one had lived here since, except drifters like this Whitey and people hiding out.

They headed for the blue smoke, but it was Anna they found in the shack, not Whitey. She'd set it all up; she'd asked Whitey to call and gambled Raburn would call him. She looked scared.

"You picked a good spot," Marquez said.

"I was hoping you would come. I was hoping Abe would get a hold of somebody at Fish and Game who would get a hold of you."

"Do you have any idea how many people are looking for you?"

"I want to turn myself in, but after what's happened I don't want to do it alone. I'm afraid of them."

"They won't kill you."

He thought about how they were going to do this as he looked at her. He saw the kayak covered with a tarp in a corner of the building.

"I hid it along the slough. I rode a mountain bike to it. I'm sure they found my bike."

She pulled a small radio from her pocket, showed it to him, and put it back in her pocket. She probably had some idea of how the FBI would view this meeting, as well.

She kept her eyes on him, the planes of her cheeks sharp, acne scars in the hollows of her cheeks, eyes bloodshot, nose too narrow for her face. She didn't seem to realize how deep she was in now. He looked around. The Feds couldn't land one of their helicopters here and wouldn't know how to get up the slough.

"We'll bring you out," he said. "Then we'll turn you over and you're going to need to get yourself a lawyer."

"I don't know anything about what happened. What I told you last time was the truth."

Shauf used the kayak, and Anna rode in the skiff with him. He figured it was the last opportunity to ask her what she knew about the sturgeon poaching, but he didn't ask anything. She didn't have much credibility with him anymore. As they reached the Zodiac it started to shower again, and he covered the phone as he punched in Ehrmann's cell. When he got voice mail he hung up and redialed. Same thing happened and he did it again. On the fourth try Ehrmann answered. "I'm in Washington, Marquez. I can't talk to you."

"Then tell me who to call. I have Anna Burdovsky with me."

"Where are you?"

"Coming out of a slough in the delta. I'll give you coordinates."

He read them off and gave Ehrmann the boat landing they were headed to.

"You'll get a call in a few minutes."

Marquez turned and asked her as he waited for the call, "When did you get into Razor Slough?"

"I had to paddle out into the river to get away and waited for dark, and even then they almost found me. Then I paddled all night. I had food stowed in the kayak, enough for a week."

"How did Karsov know the raid was coming?"

"They're always on guard. They got raided in LA a couple of times. They look for buildings they can defend. I told the FBI to watch out because they're always talking about what they'll do to anyone that comes after them."

"Did they ever talk about car bombs?"

"Never with me."

They turned from the slough into the river, and Marquez kept the speed slow so he could hear her answers. She'd stowed a kayak and mountain bike, and she had used scuba gear to swim out of the slough. She told him how she got away and that she'd stashed the equipment in case the FBI showed up.

"Seems like you knew the bust was going to go down," Marquez said.

"How would I possibly have known? That's ridiculous."

"You're up a slough hiding when the bombs go off."

"I was hiding because I knew they were using me like bait. I was afraid I was going to get killed, so I figured out a way to hide, and I didn't lie to you. I was going to tell you everything, but now after what's happened I don't want to say anything until I talk to a lawyer."

Another shower raked the water, and the heavy rain ended all conversation. Marquez pulled a hood over his head, and the Zodiac plowed through the waves. When the rain lightened they were in view of the boat landing and there was no more time to talk.

"Look at them all," Anna said, and one agent looked like he was ready to wade into the river.

"Anna Burdovsky, you are under arrest."

Marquez listened as she was read her rights and handcuffed. She looked small and scared as they took her away. She looked back at him once as though he might help her, and then she was gone, and once more the Feds were asking him what she'd told him and why she'd contacted him. They had a lot of questions, and they wanted him to come in.

41

Marquez cinched down the straps holding the Zodiac to the boat trailer, then checked to make sure there was nothing in the boat that would catch in the wind and blow out after they got on the road. The FBI was gone, the lot had emptied, and the rain had stopped. It was just Cairo, Shauf, and him. He cleaned mud from his boots and waited for Shauf to get off the phone. She'd drifted out into the middle of the lot. Cairo was near him, one foot on the boat trailer. Roberts was back in the Region IV office until either they resumed the operation or it was declared over, which was what everyone assumed would happen. Alvarez had gone home though he wasn't back in uniform yet.

The *New York Times,* citing sources high in the FBI, ran a front-page story this morning indicating that top brass saw the blown bust as a "failure of high-risk warrant service protocol." Translated to English, that meant they were going to blame Ehrmann. It struck Marquez that the cowardice of leaking information to the press first as a way of testing public reaction, a habit common to presidential administrations, was particularly unfitting for law enforcement. It had a permanent self-serving sleaze quality to it. TV pundits, including a retired FBI expert that Marquez had watched last night, said more patience was all that had been required. Ehrmann should have waited for the suspects to come out of the building. It was that simple, and it was always that simple. He should have run instead of passing on third down. And now these high-ranking officials on the east coast, guys who picked up their Starbucks lattes on the way into headquarters every morning, they were going to pass judgment on how the bust went down.

The subtext of their leaked message was that we have nothing new to fear. This was just a failure of protocol. The same as 9/11, right? We could stop it all from happening if we were just careful enough. Seal our borders and stick to the protocols. It didn't make sense that a guy as serious about law enforcement as Ehrmann was being set up for a transfer to North Dakota or the Middle East, or wherever the Bureau saw fit to banish him.

"You okay?" Cairo asked.

"Just thinking about things."

"What happens to her now?"

"They'll work her pretty hard unless they find Karsov first. She's lied to too many people."

"Where do you think we fit in?"

It wasn't fair to say, but Cairo's tone was almost one of curiosity, as if expressing interest, but with the understanding the interest wouldn't be pursued. At the last SOU dinner together at the safehouse Cairo's enthusiasm for dry farming tomatoes had lit up his face. He had one foot in the future, had accepted what Marquez couldn't yet.

"I think it was August who sent her to make contact with us. But it's possible the FBI knew she was living with August, in fact, it's likely, and it's likely they told her what she could and couldn't say to me. When she started to wobble on them, when it looked like the deal with her son might fall through and they were wondering what came next with her, they may have worried she'd pass on information that could compromise their operation. They didn't pick her up and bring her in because they were hoping she'd lead them to Karsov or someone that would get them closer. When she contacted me they were afraid she was going to tell me too much. At least, that's my guess."

And they'd question her now about the weapons they hadn't found in Weisson's. They'd question her for hours about those.

He put the boots in the truck and saw Shauf was off the phone. The FBI had requested that he come in this afternoon, and he'd agreed. But the question was where they were going now. Was Cairo flying to San Diego, then driving out to the desert to look at greenhouses, and was Shauf going early to spend more time with her nieces and nephews? They were at a cusp, and as Shauf walked back over, Marquez decided to put it to a vote.

"There's a news report they may have caught one of the three that got away," Shauf said.

"Which one and where?"

"Munoz. In LA."

Carlos Munoz, wanted for conspiracy trafficking of cocaine,

money laundering, murder. According to Ehrmann, Munoz operated out of LA. So it was believable.

When they made the ride out to the command center Ehrmann had ticked off details on Karsov as well. The passports he carried, aliases, fluency in language, a big plus for the modern-day criminal, black hair, blue eyes, Ukrainian national, six foot two, one hundred eighty pounds, kept himself fit. Karsov was wanted for arms trafficking, conspiracy murder, drug trafficking, grand theft, money laundering, RICO violations, a long, long list, Ehrmann said.

The third face they'd gone public with was Misha Filipovna. RICO charges, conspiracy to traffic in drugs, conspiracy murder (six), dating to 1995, five foot eleven, one hundred ninety pounds, built like a middle-heavyweight, brown hair, green eyes, a good-looking, confident face that was showing on CNN, FOX, and the rest.

Ehrmann put it flatly. By the rules of the game, Burdovsky had abandoned her son by leaving the country, and the boy had been legally adopted by a relative of Karsov's. Had she been in the country or had the Ukrainian courts found a way to contact her in the United States, which they weren't obligated to do, then she could have contested the proceedings. Now it was very difficult to unravel. The boy didn't know her and wanted to stay where he was, and the email contact she had with him was evidently more sporadic than she'd told the FBI. They didn't doubt she wanted her son back, but she hadn't been truthful with them either.

"Let's hope they get all three," Marquez said, then took the conversation to Crey. "Do I become Crey's new partner?"

He looked from Shauf to Cairo and wanted them to understand this was a decision they were going to make together. He knew Shauf had been on the phone to her brother-in-law. He knew Cairo had one foot out the door, but he also had the heart of an elephant and never quit anything. The assumption was they were down, it was over, the FBI investigation into whether the blown bust was preventable would include interviewing anyone with any contact with Weisson's, which meant they'd visit Ludovna and question him about selling illegal sturgeon. Cairo nodded, then Shauf spoke.

"I'm in. Let's partner up and play it out another round."

42

Marquez called Crey as he and Shauf pulled away with the Zodiac.

"I'm in, but we're going to have to talk about how to handle a couple of things."

"We'll get a drink and talk it out."

"I can't do it today, but let me ask a couple of things."

"Do it."

"The questions might make you a little touchy."

"Go ahead, my man."

"There are rumors about how you bought Beaudry's business. People say you stashed some drug money, retrieved it after you got out, then used it to buy the business. Are the Feds going to come after you someday for that?"

"Nope. Because those rumors are bullshit. I borrowed money from a friend to buy the business."

"Cool. That's what I wanted to hear."

"Well, you're hearing it, and you can tell anyone who says anything else to come talk to me."

"What about Beaudry?"

"What about him?"

"Is he completely out of the picture?"

"He's way gone, and no one is ever coming after him either, regardless of what you hear. All Beaudry ever did wrong was Fish and Game shit. You go out with the right party with him, and he didn't care what you caught. It got a little out of hand for a while, then he got scared Fish and Game was going to catch his ass. That DBEEP boat started watching him one afternoon. That about cured him."

"You were there?"

Crey coughed and cleared his throat. His impulse not to implicate himself in anything kicked in.

"I'm not saying I was there per se, you know, but let's just say I checked out the business before I made an offer."

"Okay, good enough."

"What else?"

"The pinheads."

"Like I told you, it would be just you and me. A detective called looking for them again yesterday and they're thinking about taking off until he stops calling."

"I don't want them coming back thinking you and me owe them something later because they helped you out."

"Not going to happen, man. I'll deal with them. It's cool."

"All right, partner, we'll figure out everything else over a drink."

The next morning Marquez was back in Beaudry's driveway. Beaudry's Chevy was parked in the shade with ice on the windshield. He climbed the stairs, knocked hard, and waited.

"Now what?" Beaudry asked.

"You never told us you ran party boats for poachers."

"That's a lie."

"I've got people who'll testify."

"Then get them to and I'll see you in court if I don't see you in hell first."

Beaudry started to shut the door.

"I think you'd better invite me in. You close that door and you're opening a case file."

Beaudry had a study, an office that smelled of dust caught and slowly burning in the coils of a portable heater. His website was up on two computer screens. A bloodstained FBI shield showed on the site, and Marquez recognized it from a news photo. Beaudry must have cut and pasted from a newspaper.

"I warned those fools thirty years ago they needed to be prepared for military-type assaults."

"You also looked me in the eye for years, and I have a hard time with that, Tom. You made the phone calls tipping us, and we thought you were a man of your word. Now it turns out you weren't."

"It's all a lie."

"Ludovna kept a record."

"Of what?"

Marquez studied him, saw his eyes drop to the desk, then gambled.

"Of everything." He pointed at Beaudry's computer screen. "What do you think the Feds are doing right now?"

"I wouldn't have any idea of what they're doing."

"Do you think they're sitting in the office wondering what happened? No, they're burying the dead and they're furious. They're going to find out who and how, so they're questioning everybody remotely tied to the Russian mob."

Marquez reached over and touched the screen.

"I was there when those car bombs went off." He turned his wrist to read his watch. "I'm going to give you sixty seconds to start telling me the truth."

He didn't take his eyes from Beaudry's face as he sat back down, but he knew Beaudry well enough to know he would let the clock run out, and he did. The sixty seconds passed without Beaudry looking up. But he didn't challenge Marquez either. Then he began to talk.

"It was because of gambling. I had a problem I couldn't control until I went through a program."

"You took fishing parties out and let them catch whatever they wanted as long as you got some extra money."

Beaudry nodded, said, "I'm sorry for it now. I'd take Ludovna and the people working with him out on the boat. They wanted sturgeon, and I know where to find them. We traded. He paid gambling debts of mine. The KGB sonofabitch had money when he landed here. He told me the U.S. government helped him move here. I think it was the goddamned FBI. Then, when my sickness was at its worst the people in Vegas I'd borrowed from wanted to collect everything. They wanted me to sell everything to pay them. They didn't want to wait anymore."

"Do you think Ludovna knew them?"

"I don't really know. If he does he's worse than I thought."

"So with him you only traded illegal fishing trips for cash. He serviced some of your debts for you."

"Yes, but when they wanted everything right away, I had to put the business up for sale. Then my sister died in a fire and left me life insurance money. I paid them with that."

"You sold the business too cheaply to Crey."

"How do you know that?"

Marquez played on Beaudry's fear of conspiracies now. Black helicopters, UN takeovers, FBI plots to overturn the Constitution, turn us into zombies with drugs.

"Because the FBI tapped everything. They listened to every sound you made."

"Then you know I didn't want to sell to him any more than I'd wanted to sell to the people I'd borrowed from in Vegas."

"Then why did you sell to Crey?"

"I was afraid not to. I knew the FBI wasn't going to help me after the way it ended with them, and Richie made it sound like his investors already knew about my business. I thought it was the Vegas money coming back, and they'd decided they were going to get the business after all."

"What did you think Crey was going to use the sport boat for?"

"For the same things I did."

"Poaching and taking out regular customers."

Beaudry nodded again. "Richie knew Ludovna. I knew he'd take him out."

"So you sold out knowing Crey was going to use your business to poach whenever he could, and that was okay because that's what you'd done all those years you were helping us."

"I am sorry."

"Are you?"

"Yes, sir, I truly am."

43

Baird came down from headquarters, met him on Ninth, and they walked across the capitol lawns toward J Street. There were school buses, children grouped out in front of the capitol building getting ready for a tour of the capitol, and after they'd threaded their way through the kids Marquez explained.

"Beaudry told me this morning he sold way too cheap because he was afraid he was dealing with the same guys he'd borrowed from to pay his Vegas debts. He thinks they scouted his business after he said he'd sell it to pay what he owed. On his own or with the mob, Ludovna bought Beaudry's business using Crey as a front."

"That's the way it strings together?"

"I think so. Ludovna went out on the boat enough times to decide he wanted the business. He knew Crey was an ex-con with no prospects so loaned him the money with a lot of conditions attached. Crey gets to own the business, but the catch is he's also got a debt to pay off to Ludovna and has to provide a steady supply of sturgeon. What we're selling Crey is making its way to Ludovna."

"But we can't prove that."

"Not yet, and we don't know whether Ludovna is tied in with this Las Vegas group either. When I've talked to the FBI about Ludovna they haven't been too interested."

"I remember Beaudry. Didn't he help us out? Didn't we give him CalTIP money?"

"Yeah, we did, and he turned in a few poachers. They were probably crowding his boat and taking all the good fish."

Marquez and Baird moved away from the capitol lawns, Marquez laying out what the SOU was doing now, partnering with Crey. At a street corner as they waited for the light to change, they overheard two young men, one asking the other, "Did you hear the FBI blew away one of those guys they've been looking for? Up in Seattle."

Marquez turned to the young men, interrupted their conversation. "When did that happen?"

"Like an hour ago. Not the Karsov dude, but the other one."

The light changed, and Marquez and the chief crossed. They walked on for another half hour, in part for Baird's health. Baird's doctor had him on a high dosage of statins and an aspirin a day. He'd been told to exercise regularly, so he walked. But now they ducked into a bar Baird knew had a TV. The bartender changed the channel to news, and they watched. It only took a few minutes to get the gist.

Rain slicked off the coat of the CNN reporter in Seattle. She interviewed a bystander who'd witnessed the gun battle with

Filipovna. Filipovna had attempted to shoot his way out when they knocked on the apartment door.

"They must have known where to wait for him," Baird said as they came back out into sunlight. He slowed and turned toward Marquez. "You got your three-week extension and now we're down to the last risks I'm going to okay. What happened to the FBI has shaken me. If we're dealing with any of the same people that's very disturbing, but I agree, we're at a crossroads where we either give in or stop them. I'm trusting your judgment. If you're wrong, God help both of us."

Marquez nodded.

"Make sure you keep me in the loop."

Marquez found Raburn on his houseboat, trimming out his new windows. He had a couple of sawhorses set up on the Astroturf. A gallon paint can of quick-drying primer and a brush were nearby. The Astroturf around the sawhorses was dotted with white paint drips, and Raburn dipped his hand into the river and scrubbed primer off his fingers.

"I was a lot happier before I got mixed up in any of this."

"Next time don't shoot your windows out."

"Next time don't force me to lie to a guy who wouldn't have a problem killing me."

"You may remember I asked you to stop working with him. I told you if he calls you and asks for sturgeon, you refer him to me."

"It doesn't quite work like that."

"Then you're not telling me what's going on. You're holding back. If you've been doing that since we got into this, then you haven't kept your word."

Raburn looked past him at some spot above the river.

"When did Ludovna last call you?"

"I don't know."

"You don't know?"

"No."

"In the last few days?"

Raburn didn't answer. Marquez studied him and the paint all over the Astroturf. He thought about Raburn shooting out his own windows. Beaudry was scornful of Raburn. Ludovna called him a drunk and a goof. Even Crey looked down on him, yet Raburn had managed to work with everybody, including the SOU. The guy was more clever than anyone gave him credit for.

"He called you, but you don't want to talk to me about it. Is that because you've played it both ways ever since we made the offer to you?"

"I've done everything you asked. I've taken you out to people I've bought from, I've cleaned sturgeon and made caviar. I've driven you around—"

"Yeah, and you helped load Anna's car in the middle of the night so she could deliver caviar. You help everybody. Tell your brother and sister-in-law I'm going to come see them tomorrow morning and have a talk with them about the canning room before they see charges filed. And I don't know if you know this, but in California, if they both go down on felonies the judge has the right to place the kids in foster homes. That's what you've got them into."

"There's something wrong with you."

"You're so sure you're going to beat us at this, you're willing to let them take big risks. Tell them I'm going to talk very frankly tomorrow and I'd advise them to do the same. I'm advising you not to talk to anyone else about any of this. Something is going down now that I don't think you want to be a part of."

He left Raburn standing near his sawhorses, then he met Crey at the Bighorn in Rio Vista and drank several beers. Afterward they walked the ten blocks back to the bait shop, and Crey unlocked the door and fired up a joint that he smoked alone as he showed Marquez his sport boat schedule and pored over a navigational map, pointing out sturgeon holes. He got a bottle of Jack Daniels from the back room and two short glasses.

"That girl that works for me is coming back here in an hour." He winked at Marquez. "I've got a bunk on the boat, and she's bringing Chinese food."

"How long have you known her?"

"She just about came with the place."

They drank to the new partnership, and he should have realized then how hard Crey was working to find out where he'd be later tonight.

44

The next morning Marquez met Shauf at Mel's in Walnut Grove, where they got coffee and sat in his truck and talked before heading toward Raburn Orchards. They drove slowly up the river road.

"Think anyone will be there?" she asked.

"Sure, they'll be there and we may get another confession out of Raburn as he throws himself on the tracks to try to save his brother."

"You really think he cares that much about his brother?"

"I do."

When they turned off the road and came down the steep drop to Raburn Orchards Marquez spotted Abe's truck under the high gable of the packing shed, so they went there first. The driver's door was open, the truck parked at an odd angle, but no lights were on in back and they couldn't find Raburn.

"His keys are in the ignition," Shauf said.

"Let's drive down to the house. They must be waiting down there."

Isaac's big dark blue Ford F-350 and Cindy's Volvo were there. Marquez pulled in alongside the Ford.

"Cold this morning," Shauf said as they got up on the porch of the main house and knocked.

The sky was white, and the lights glowing from inside the house gave the porch a feeling of dusk, though it was just 10:30. The kids would be at school. They knocked on the door again and waited for the sound of creaking boards as someone came to answer. Shauf's breath clouded the air in front of her as they talked.

"Beautiful old house, but it sure needs work. Almost easier to tear it down," she said, then asked, "Do you think he's blowing us off?"

They checked the outbuildings and the rows of trees, looking for Isaac through the bare limbs. They checked the equipment shed because they'd seen day laborers come and go out of there. They drove down to the canning building, and the door was closed but the deadbolt not thrown. Marquez knocked and then pushed on the door. Behind him, Shauf spoke quietly.

"We ought to be careful how far we take it. We don't have an active warrant anymore."

The canning room door swung open, and Shauf's questions died in her throat when she saw what he was looking at.

"Why the children?" was all that came from her.

Marquez reached and stopped Shauf and then walked over to their bodies. He didn't really need to. He could see they were dead, but leaned over and touched Isaac's throat and then the girl. He went back for a flashlight and shone it into the pupils of the boy and then Cindy. They lay side by side, lined up, he thought, made to lie that way. Blood had dried, crusted in their hair. He moved the flashlight from one to the other, then turned it off.

Abe had several high wounds on his back as if he'd ignored an order and started to rise after they'd all been made to lie down. His brother had a wound at the temple in addition to two in the back of the head. All five of them had been shot in the back of the head. He moved toward the door, went to the truck and the radio, then changed his mind and flipped open his cell phone. He found Selke's number.

"Great minds think alike," Selke said as he heard "It's John Marquez."

"I was going to call you this morning. We've ID'd the body in the refrigerator. Her name is Sherri La Belle. I want to meet with you this morning, and I'll come to you. Just tell me where you are. Where did Torp and Perry lose her car? Was that at the chop shop where the bust went down?"

"Selke, hang on, I'm at Raburn Orchards. Do you know where that is?"

"Sure."

"One of the outbuildings here has a canning room. One of my team, Carol Shauf, is with me. We arrived at approximately 10:30 expecting to meet with Raburn, his brother, Isaac, and Isaac's wife, Cindy." He felt compelled to give Selke facts he could start with, some framework. "But we've just found their bodies as well as those of the two children in an outbuilding where they do canning. They've all been shot twice in the back of the head."

There was a quiet, a rustling like leaves, and then a much quieter Selke.

"Are you absolutely certain they're gone?"

"They're gone."

"Have you touched anything?"

"Isaac's throat and the girl's, feeling for a pulse. The door was ajar. I pushed it open, saw them and walked over to make sure." He did not want to stay on the phone. "We'll be out front."

It felt much colder than it had earlier. He stood near his truck looking out across the bare orchards, and Shauf tapped him on the arm, said, "I'm going to let everyone know."

Don't assume the killing is about sturgeon, he thought. It could be an old debt, anything. He could not comprehend killing the children if it was about sturgeon. The boy was older, fourteen is what Raburn had said, wearing the same clothes he'd probably gone to school in yesterday, jeans and baggy T-shirt, but no shoes, no heavy sneakers. They were used to seeing him with his iPod, and he guessed now it happened last night before the kids had gone to bed. The girl was no more than eight or nine, long straight hair blown back alongside her head into pooled blood.

Marquez turned and looked at the door he'd pushed open. He saw the girl lying inside and knew the door had been open long enough after she was killed for her hair to blow into the pooled blood. The girl wore a sweatshirt. Someone at her school would remember what she'd worn yesterday. Someone had seen them yesterday.

Isaac's arms were along his side. The right side of his face rested in blood. Marquez looked from Isaac, to Abe, to the boy on the far end and couldn't say why, but saw Cindy and the boy shot first. Shot before anyone knew they were going to die. Then questions asked of Isaac and Abe. Cindy's hand looked as though it might have rested on her daughter's back and slid off. Why the kids? On the risk that they'd overheard something?

"John, you look rough," Shauf said. "Maybe you want to sit down."

"This happened because I leaned on him."

"Then he called somebody."

"Yeah, he probably did."

"I know it sounds hard but that's one more mistake he made."

Except that we don't really know, he thought. He felt sweat start under his arms and along his spine. He was sure this had happened because he'd cornered Raburn and forced him to it.

"If we'd just taken him down like you wanted to, this never would have happened," he said, then turned and asked her, "Where's your camcorder?"

With Shauf he videotaped the scene inside the canning shed. He heard sirens now, heard leaves rustling in the wind through the grove, smelled the heavy mineral blood smell seeping from the door, and took everything he knew about the operation, Raburn's face yesterday, a fleeting look of shame at shooting out the windows of his own boat. He saw August with his fine Italian leather coats, his black driving gloves, the meticulous Porsche, the goatee trimmed to try to make him look hip.

"They're here," Shauf said. "They just turned off the levee road."

Marquez walked out in the road and caught the eye of the lead driver, stopped him from getting close to the canning room. He watched an ambulance turn down, then an unmarked county unit and a detective getting out. The detective had talked with Selke. He was waiting for Selke but walked in to view the bodies. He set up a perimeter and took statements from them.

At dusk, hours after the coroner had come and gone, Marquez drove away with Shauf. He drove home and plugged the camcorder into his TV and made two tapes. Later, in the middle of the night when he couldn't sleep, he watched the tape again. Cindy's long hair had blown the same direction as her daughter's, and that fit the wind out of the east. The door had been open, the wind blowing, and Marquez could almost hear voices, the questioning. Not caviar though. Not this kind of killing. What possible threat were the Raburns? Not Cindy. Not with her routine of kids and school and work. Not Isaac who almost lived among his trees. It was Abe. What did you see, Abe? Was it something you saw, and you made the mistake of telling somebody or threatened to tell us? You called somebody after I came by, didn't you? What did you say to them that brought them out last night?

45

In the late afternoon Marquez waited for Selke on the deck of Raburn's houseboat. He looked through the windows and saw the same disarray as last time, a man of modest means living alone with his habits. The bed was unmade. Magazines and fishing lures covered the table. A green Heineken can sat at one end. In the kitchen, smoked fish rested on a plate. A big pot sat on the stove, and he remembered Raburn talking about making chili. He'd never finished trimming the windows, and the same can of primer sat under the sawhorse. Paint had dried on the brush. *Honest Abe* hadn't been bailed since the last rain and sat low in the water. It was impossible to look at the scene without wondering how much of what had happened was set in motion the rainy Sunday when they'd offered Raburn the deal.

The last sunlight was a pale gold-white on the water when Selke came down the path. Marquez got up from the chair. The cold had never let up today, and he felt it in his feet and hands.

"Raburn had keys in his pants. I forgot to bring them," Selke said.

They didn't need keys. He'd watched Raburn lift the door, then slide it over. He'd said the lock was a pain in the ass anyway, and people in the delta, or at least the old-timers, all knew each other and didn't worry about theft.

They went inside. He wasn't sure what he could do for Selke here but was in no hurry to go anywhere else, and there was a chance Raburn had written something down.

"A name you'll recognize and I won't," Selke said as they searched. He added, "I'd like to find something that helps us get a warrant for Ludovna's house, but we're not exactly going to find a diary, are we? Did Raburn have any girlfriends?"

"None that we ever saw."

"What about boyfriends?"

"I don't think so. He talked about different friends. A lawyer here in the delta that he threatened us with, but I don't know whether that was real or not."

"I'd like to talk to this lawyer. There's got to be an address book or something. We didn't find anything in his pickup."

"I think he was close to his brother and otherwise largely a loner."

The pot on the stove did have chili in it. There was more beer in the refrigerator and a vodka bottle, ice, and wrapped cuts of fish in the freezer.

"He didn't own much in the way of clothes," Selke said. "There's no desk or anything. He had a cell phone on him, and it's beeping that he's got messages. I won't know who those were from until tomorrow. I'd like to get from you a list of all the contacts he introduced you to."

"Sure."

"Who do you think killed him?"

He'd already answered this question earlier, told Selke that he thought Raburn had called the wrong person, that it somehow came back to the meeting that should have happened this morning with both brothers, Cindy, and Shauf and himself.

"His brother had unpaid debts and old debts that got negotiated down to pennies on the dollar after a near bankruptcy. You need to look there too. Let me ask you a question. Why would anyone kill the children?"

"Children are hard," Selke said softly. "They're hard. I've only seen it a couple of times in eighteen years as a detective, and both of those were for the same reason, a divorced husband deciding his ex wasn't entitled to remarry and start a new life. But that's not what we have here." Marquez didn't respond, and Selke said, "You're quiet."

"Like you say, the kids are hard."

Selke found an address book and flipped through with Marquez watching. Mostly initials next to numbers. He talked as he examined the pages.

"The FBI will take this case. This is execution-style murder, and given what's happened in the last week I'm surprised they haven't already showed up. It's got a caviar connection, and it's too close in timing to Weisson's. If we don't solve it tonight, they'll step in by noon tomorrow, and I don't think we're talking about a joint investigation either."

He was probably right. Selke found the light switches and turned them on. He stepped out on the deck and came back in.

"We've got sightseers," he said, and Marquez glanced up toward the eucalyptus and saw a handful of people, probably neighbors. By now, the word would have gotten around. The river darkened, and the riprap, the rock lining the opposite bank, lost its reflection.

"The boy was barefoot," Selke said. "Somebody walked him and his sister down from the house, possibly the wife as well. I'm guessing there were at least two shooters. From your end, what are the possible reasons to kill the kids? I mean from a poaching angle?"

"To get information."

"Threaten to kill the kids if they don't talk?"

"Something like that."

"Do you think Raburn would hold back confessing he was working with Fish and Game and let the kids get killed one at a time?"

"Not a chance. He'd give the information up right away."

"Even if it was going to get him killed?"

"He'd push it as far as he could."

"He pushes it and, bang, one of the kids gets shot."

Selke knew it was Ludovna who Raburn claimed to be afraid of. He knew Nike Man had shown a gun the first time Marquez had gone with Raburn to make a sale to Ludovna. They'd been over these things earlier in the afternoon, and Marquez didn't feel like he had anything new to add. He watched the light leave the water and was sure the chain of events started when he decided to flip Raburn. He'd been wrong about Anna. He'd been wrong here. Shauf had argued against flipping Raburn, and maybe it was more than not trusting Raburn. Maybe it was intuition. He didn't burden Selke with that theory, instead moved over as Selke began to look at photos on a laptop he'd powered up.

"Jesus Christ, this keyboard. Did he use this thing for a place mat?"

He poked at something stuck between the A and S keys. Looked like tuna fish mixed with mayonnaise and dried, but Selke had been able to open photos Raburn had downloaded onto his computer.

"I've seen him take photos with his cell phone," Marquez said.

There was a photo of Ludovna, Nike Man, and a black Mercedes in the background. A blurry shot, but it was them. Photos of the delta bridges. Drawbridges with concrete pilings and painted steel frames. A photo of Mount Diablo at the far end of a slough, the slough flat and still, the colors of sunrise above the mountain. Anna with sunglasses on and her hair blowing back, August alongside her with an arm around her shoulders.

"That's Burdovsky," Selke said. "She's gone on to celebrity status. Where do they have her locked up?"

"Keep going."

Another shot of Nike Man and an odd shot down an embankment along a river or slough, a small man bent over holding his face.

"The man in the photo is bleeding," Selke said, and Marquez told him the story of the Mexican fisherman and the treble hook. Then they both studied the photo in silence. Now a photo of Sacramento Fresh Fish and one of August Foods, and a topless shot of Anna sunbathing, lying on her back on boat cushions, dark nipples. Two shots of Crey. One on his sport boat with the captain's hat. It looked like Crey had posed for the photo, whereas the others looked like they'd been taken without the people in them necessarily knowing.

"You've found his log," Marquez said. "How'd you get past the password?"

"I tried his brother's name for the password and it worked."

Selke clicked to the next one. "That's the DBEEP boat and its crew. Jo Ruax is at the wheel," Marquez said. "Looks like he was on the water when he took it." There were two more of the DBEEP boat and a close-up of Ruax's face. "They may have questioned him on the water and he pretended he was on the phone."

"Give me a reason why?"

"Ruax may remember this and I'll ask her. Maybe he took this close-up of her to email someone who wanted the faces of the local law enforcement."

"So are we going to find you in here?"

"Keep going."

There were various photos of sloughs. Photos of Raburn Orchards as the pear leaves turned with the fall. August's Porsche outside the packing shed. A shot across vineyards to a sky-blue Victorian-style house. Two fishermen in their boat.

"I recognize those two. Raburn took me to meet them. Ruax knows that slough and she's got a name for it, Camp Sturgeon."

"These are guys he bought from?"

"Yeah."

"It's not about a debt his brother owed, is it?"

"No."

Individual shots of Perry and Torp. Perry leaning against the Le Mans. Then another shot, this one of the two of them.

"Bingo," Selke said, and clicked to the next photo, a dark-haired woman trying hard to smile for the camera. Marquez didn't recognize her. "Sherri La Belle," Selke said, "and now I'm going to tell you something you can't talk to anyone about yet." He clicked back to Torp and Perry. "I'll have murder warrants on these two tomorrow. I know where they got the refrigerator and what banding tool got used. They stole more than her car."

Marquez answered the question before it came. "I don't know where they are, but you know who to ask."

"I do, and Richie Crey is going to find out he could end up back inside if he obstructs."

They looked at the remaining photos and then returned several times to three shots, all taken through fog and with no way to make out the location exactly, but it was Anna's car, a parking lot Marquez knew was the fishing access, then a second car, a white BMW, and a shot of a man standing near a woman who was probably Anna. The photos were taken from above, probably from the levee road. The tall man near her was not Ludovna, August, Nike Man, or Crey. Well, he might be Crey, he conceded, then added, "But I don't think he is."

Selke's phone rang before he could answer. Marquez watched him study the number on his screen.

"That's the Feds," he said to Marquez. "They're going to take my case away."

He walked onto the deck to talk to them, and Marquez could hear enough to know that's exactly what was happening. When he heard Selke describe what they'd found on the computer he backed out of the photos and clicked onto the Internet. Raburn was on dial-up, had a power and telephone line strung from the roof of the houseboat to a tree on the shore. The dial-up was slow, and he heard Selke starting to wind down the conversation. But now the Net came up, and he attached all of Raburn's photos, then emailed them to an address he used only with the SOU. The file was still sending when Selke hung up and came back in.

"What's the story?" he asked Selke.

"They want that computer tonight. They want me to bring it to them and there's something more going on. It's more than the Raburn murders."

Marquez looked down at the laptop, saw the last green bar fill, and the icon disappear. He clicked out of the Net as Selke walked over.

"Want me to turn it off?"

"Yeah, go ahead."

Marquez shut down the computer.

"I emailed myself the photos."

"I figured that's what you were doing. I want you to copy me."

"Give me an address."

He waited now as Selke wrote it down ayzSelke@yahoo.com. So Selke wasn't going to chance sending it to the county either.

46

The next morning he rode into San Francisco with Katherine, and it was nice to be together. They were out of their routine for once. He looked at Kath's face, her profile, the ghost streak of white hair along the dark hair at her temple. They drank cappuccinos, sitting at one of the marble tables at Presto on the Wharf, the new one, and he watched her with her employees, the deft way she communicated.

Then he took her car, because Maria was going to pick her up later. He drove over to Golden Gate Avenue to FBI headquarters, where Ehrmann was waiting for him. Marquez had three of the photos with him and more copies of those at home. When he'd left Selke he'd called a photographer friend in Oakland, then emailed the three fishing access photos. His friend ran them through his software program. You could read the faces now on the man and woman in the parking lot. You could read the license plates on the cars. He'd run the plates on the BMW and gotten the name Sandy Michaels and the same southern California address as the Cadillac that Ludovna had burned. He rode the elevator up and then waited as the duty officer found Ehrmann.

Marquez couldn't remember a face that had changed more than Ehrmann's had in less than a week. The skin under his eyes was very dark and sagged. He had a cup of coffee on his desk, but his movements had slowed.

"Lieutenant, do I look that bad?"

"You look like you're carrying it all. You couldn't have known."

"They moved those two vehicles every day. I made an assumption I shouldn't have made about why they were there. We could have gotten someone in the night before to check them out. Those agents are dead because of my failure, but that's not what we're here to talk about today, and I don't want to talk about it. There are several people who are going to sit in with us, and I'd like you to take us through it, including any theories you might have of your own about the Raburn murders."

They moved to a conference room, and Marquez recounted his conversation with Raburn the day before. He gave them the approximate time of that meeting and knew they'd gather Raburn's phone records and go through his computer and determine who, if anyone, he contacted after Marquez had left. Then he related driving out there the next day with Shauf and finding the bodies.

"They would have done them in the house," Ehrmann said, "if it was a straight execution. They wouldn't have walked them down there without a reason."

"The door wasn't locked or latched, but it binds on the jamb and was closed enough to be stuck shut. I pushed it open. But I'm saying this because the wind was out of the east that night, and one thing that struck me was that Cindy Raburn and her daughter, who both had long hair, had pools of blood around their heads and must have bled before the wind blew their hair into the blood."

"What's that mean to you?"

"Only that whoever killed them didn't just walk in, shoot them, and leave. Makes me think there was questioning going on, and if the killings had to do with sturgeon poaching, then it's very possible it all comes back to Raburn's working with us. If it looks like an organized crime–style killing to you, could that mean it was somehow retribution for the Weisson's bust? What I'm wondering is if someone thought Raburn knew something, had information they could get out of him. Since we did connect sturgeon traffic through Weisson's, it's possible that Raburn let slip that he was working for us, and they tied the bust to him and killed him out of retribution."

"Highly unlikely."

Something Marquez had said caught the FBI's attention. It didn't matter whether they told him or not. All that matters is that they find who killed them. He pulled out his photos, had planned to show them only to Ehrmann, but what difference did it make? He kept them face down and then slid the lone shot of Anna's car across the table to Ehrmann.

"Where did you get this?" Ehrmann asked.

"Off Raburn's computer yesterday. I met the county detective there. Someone I know was able to improve the quality. That's Anna Burdovsky in the fishing access lot she staged her disappearance from. This next photo seems to have been taken after another car pulled in alongside her."

Marquez slowly flipped over the photo with both the BMW and Anna's Honda. The cars were side by side. With a magnifying glass you could now read the license plates.

"The BMW is registered to a Sandy Michaels, which as near as the county detective can tell may be a fictitious name. We followed Nikolai Ludovna in a Cadillac with the same registered owner. The Cadillac was allegedly stolen and burned. I say allegedly because we think he had it stolen. The point is both are registered to Sandy Michaels."

He waited. The first two photos were slid around the table. It was obvious they'd already seen them, and no one looked surprised. Instead, they watched him as he flipped over the next one. Again, he slid it to Ehrmann.

"I think the photos are sequential. This is after the BMW pulled in and they both got out of their cars."

"Okay," Ehrmann said. "Any others?"

"One. I asked a photographer friend what he could do with the profile of the man and then to compare it to Karsov."

Now he had their attention. He slid the enhanced headshot and the computer profile comparisons onto the table for everyone to see. "Who's this photographer?" someone asked, not Ehrmann, but one of the others.

"With our Fish and Game surveillances we're often taking photos from a long distance, so I've paid attention to the advances in improving the quality of photos, particularly digital."

Marquez did not give the name of his friend in Oakland. Nor did he get asked again.

"My friend seems to think that's a match. He downloaded Karsov off your Most Wanted List on the Field Office website."

"It is a match," Ehrmann said.

"I'd like to ask a couple of questions."

"Go ahead."

"Did the FBI ever have any contact with Abe Raburn?"

"No."

"Did you take over from the county because you suspect the Raburn killings were an organized crime hit?"

"It has those earmarks, but that's as far as it goes right now."

"Okay, then let me ask it this way, could this in any way be connected to Karsov smuggling arms?"

"It could."

"Then I have a question about Nick Ludovna."

"Go ahead."

"When he immigrated to this country was the FBI in some way his sponsor?"

Marquez caught the reaction of the man across the table. But Ehrmann answered matter-of-factly.

"He was a Special Interrogator for the KGB, and we were very interested in talking to him and in getting him to talk to us. Specifically, in his KGB role he had interrogated some of the criminals we were pursuing and a few we're still pursuing."

"Karsov."

"Yes, a younger Karsov was incarcerated for a year." The photos had all made their way to Ehrmann's end of the table. "We'd like to hold these," Ehrmann said, "and John, I'd like to talk to you alone before you leave."

When he did, it was to reiterate how vital it was Marquez didn't talk to anyone about any of this. "Not even your wife."

Marquez drove home with it all turning in his head. He found Bob the cat outside on the back deck. The idea was to leave him in the house for a week to get used to his new surroundings, but he'd pushed his way out through a kitchen window and was sitting in a chair watching the birds in the brush below. Marquez sat down in the chair next to him and got up again when he heard a car in the driveway. To his surprise it was Chief Baird.

"You change vehicles so much I didn't know if you were home. I was going to leave a note. I'm down here for a conference."

"Do you want to come in and talk, Chief?"

Marquez offered him a beer and asked if he wanted to stay for dinner, but Baird said his wife was with him, at the hotel right now. They were making a little getaway out of the two-day conference, or at least out of the nights, going out to dinner, and the city was decorated for the holidays so it was particularly nice to be here.

"What's the chance of you and Katherine getting away for a few days?"

"Probably not much chance of that right now." He added, "Katherine just got back from a trip."

"She likes to travel though, doesn't she?"

"Loves to."

"It might do you some good. I heard about the Raburn murders this morning. I tried to call you. Did you get my calls?"

"I've been with the FBI, Chief. I just got home. I was going to call you this afternoon. Why don't I make some coffee?"

Marquez made coffee, standing in the small kitchen. The chief took his with a lot of milk. Marquez poured himself coffee and told Baird about finding the bodies, then Selke and now the FBI taking over. He talked about Crey.

"He offered me a partnership, and I took him up on it."

Marquez sensed that what the chief really wanted was to say

now was, "We aren't going to do anymore in the delta right now about sturgeon poaching." But he was too tough for that. He wanted Marquez to volunteer it instead, and when he didn't, Baird slid into the future.

"When this is over I've got a new role for you in the department. I want you to train wardens in undercover work. It's a position we can afford and the best way to make use of your experience. And you're due for a promotion."

"If I make captain then I'll be behind a desk and never run the SOU again."

"The SOU will go down until there's new money budgeted for it."

Nothing was said for a minute. Marquez watched a squirrel run along the deck railing outside.

"I'm going to give you some time to think it over, but I want you to stay."

"Thank you."

"You don't like my idea."

"It's a fine idea, but I don't see myself behind a desk writing training programs. I belong in the field, or maybe it's time for me to call it."

Baird ran out of time and had to get to the city and meet his wife. On the way out the door he paused, turned, took in the big frame of Marquez blocking the light, sun-gold hair with gray in it, the broad face.

"I have not forgotten why we are here, Lieutenant. I will never forget."

They stood looking at each other a moment. Then Baird nodded and left.

47

They'd told him one other thing when he was at the FBI, that Anna had hired an expensive lawyer. Jack Batson. Marquez knew of Batson and had read about his plush below-ground office on Montgomery Street the press had dubbed "The Bat Cave." That was where he wanted to meet Marquez when he called the next morning. They agreed on the delta instead, and Marquez got there early enough to walk the trail out to the water and find the place up on the levee where the photos of Anna and Karsov had been taken.

A BMW dropped down from the levee road, and he recognized Batson at the wheel. Batson's car was a BMW M5, an older model, dark blue. Batson got out, looking like he was dressed for a safari, and maybe that's what coming out here meant to him. The delta reached back into a different time and didn't have the fast roads the high rollers needed to get from place to place. BMW seemed to be the car of choice this week, though this older model was probably not his regular car. Not with the money he was making. But give the guy a break. He's just another lawyer.

"Lieutenant, thank you for meeting me, and I know you've been through a lot and my client feels deeply responsible."

"She should."

They shook hands, Batson with a firm grip, warm brown eyes, eyebrows like Bin Laden.

"This is where she faked the abduction," Marquez said.

"Faked may not be the right word."

"It may not be, but I don't know what she was thinking. I'm just speaking from my point of view. Her car was right about where yours is when I pulled in."

"She didn't want anything to do with it. Are you familiar with the Patty Hearst syndrome?"

"Is that what you're going with?"

"We're going with the truth."

Marquez nodded. "Well, the truth sometimes works. It's at least worth a try."

"She was forced to deliver a stolen vehicle to Las Vegas. That's where she went from here. I doubt the FBI has told you that. She left her car and drove that car to Vegas, as she has done other things to protect her son."

"Well, I don't have anything I need delivered, so what can I do for you today?"

"Karsov forced her into all of this, and instead of following through with the deal the FBI cut with her in return for her help bringing him down, they're now trying to bring murder charges against her. They're claiming she was part of a conspiracy to commit murder. They're not interested in justice, only revenge for their officers killed. Anna has asked me to approach you and see if you're willing to help."

"What could I possibly do for her?"

"On the stand you could counter the manner in which the FBI will paint her character. She's not a killer, and they're going to frame her. At the moment she just wants to talk to you. She did help your team before all this happened."

"Not really."

"You encouraged her, you told her she did."

Marquez couldn't believe it was possible but had to ask. "You do know she burned us, right?"

"No, she did what she had to. She didn't burn your team, and she shares the same intense feelings about the land."

Marquez thought, forget it, what a waste of time meeting Batson. He took the conversation back to the car.

"So she picked up a car here?"

"That's right, her instructions were to leave her car and call you. One of these mobsters was waiting here with a stolen Hummer that she then drove to Las Vegas. His was the voice you heard. She was used, extorted, if you will. It's gone on for years, and the Bureau has essentially participated in it. There's an around-the-clock suicide watch on Anna. She needs your help."

"I would like to talk to her again. Tell her that."

He watched Batson drive off. Then he drove to meet Crey to talk about the Raburn killings, how it might be a business opportunity for them. They spoke out in the bait shop lot. He told Crey he'd been the one to find them, because somehow it was going to come out and he didn't want Crey to discover it later.

"They took me in and questioned me all day and almost all night, really tried to mess with my head. The wife ran the caviar making out of that shed. You knew Cindy, right?"

"Yeah," Crey said. "Nice little ass on her."

"She did some work for me through Abe, and I don't know how they found out about it, but they were trying to tell me I offed the family." Marquez held his hand out, fingers spread, his big scarred hand riding a few inches above the bar. "They wanted to test my hands for residue, you know, wanted me to volunteer to let them. I did the lie detector test, residue test, all that shit, but I passed everything."

"What were you doing out there?"

"Trying to find Abe. He owed me a hundred bucks."

That made Crey laugh. Raburn dying and getting away without paying just fit perfectly.

"That's just perfect," Crey said.

"I collected."

"What? You got in his wallet when he was lying there?"

"No, man, but I went down to that canning room for a reason. I stepped over them and grabbed a stack of labels and jars before calling 911 to report they got smoked. I'll show you what I got. It's the official stamp, the whole thing. There's more stashed out there. I couldn't hide it all in my truck."

They moved the conversation from the parking lot to a bar now, walked up Main Street, and the bartender brought a gin and tonic for Crey. He brought a beer for Marquez.

"I've got to make some calls but it's possible we can get something going tonight.

"Want to play a little poker tonight? There's some guys that might show up who I've done business with before. They're interested in talking about doing more together. I figure it's a good time to introduce you."

"How do we know they'll show up, because if it's just poker, I already went to high school."

"I'm going to make some calls, then I'll call you later. These guys could be good for like a hundred grand a year."

Marquez nodded, didn't believe any of it, though he'd call and talk it over with the SOU. It sounded like more Crey bullshit until the last line.

"There's a guy in San Francisco with a store," Crey said. "He's got another one in LA and one in Seattle, and he sells all kinds of caviar over the Net, only not on English websites. These guys supply him. Goes from the water through us to them to this dude in San Francisco. We're not going to get the business right away, not with Raburn getting offed, but after things cool down. Tonight is the night to meet these guys. I'm going to make the call, then call you." He grinned. "How's poker sound now?"

Marquez smiled back at him. He killed the draft beer and stood up.

"Okay, call me."

48

The poker game was at a house a few miles outside Rio Vista. A long flat driveway led to a detached garage. Little light seeped from under the garage door and the window on the side, and it didn't feel right as he walked down the driveway with Crey. Crey turned to reassure him.

"This guy's wife bitches at him all the time. Wait until you see what he's got set up in here."

"Where's the wife tonight?"

"Fuck, who knows, just be glad she's not here."

Marquez glanced at the house. No lights. An SUV was backed up against the garage door, and he listened for voices and didn't hear any as he followed Crey over stone steps alongside the garage. There was a door, and Crey waited for him to go in first. As he stepped inside, Marquez felt a gun press into his back.

"We're going to keep this fair," Crey said from behind him and then stripped Marquez's Glock. "Pretty interesting piece you got here."

"I took it off a cop. What's the deal? Why are you doing this?"

"Sure, you took this gun off a cop. What cop was that?"

Perry aimed a shotgun at Marquez's gut. Torp was the only other person in the room.

"We've got a little plan," Crey said. "We're going to take a ride together."

"No poker?"

It was the best answer he could come up with, but what he felt was fear. Perry and Torp were very quiet, anticipating, and Crey was methodical.

"Take your shoes off," which was not something he wanted to do since his left shoe had a telelocator in it, a device that would let his team track him. He untied his shoes and was slow getting out of them.

"Where are we going?"

"Where we can settle this."

"That could affect our partnership."

"Yeah, it's going to fuck with it, but I don't know how many more partners I need anyway."

"Since you've already got Ludovna."

"See, there you go. That's probably why I don't like you, and shit, these two hate you. Lou here can't wait. Put your hands behind your back."

And he moved his hands slowly, had no doubt Perry would pull the trigger. Torp moved in and brought a blade to Marquez's throat as Crey clicked on plastic handcuffs.

"Just like they used to do to me, man."

The blade cut the skin under his chin. He could turn his head fast, kick out at Crey, and hope Torp didn't run the knife into him and Perry blow him away. Or gamble the SOU was able to follow wherever Crey took him. A kind of calculation flowed through his head and went nowhere. His mouth was dry, heart pounding, and he resisted the order to get down on his knees. When he did, the knife drew real blood, left a sharp stinging burn along his throat, and he felt blood trickle toward his collar. He got on his knees, and Crey's boot pushed his shoulders down, his face onto the cold concrete.

"If you kick me, I'm going to stick a knife up your ass," Crey said. "I'm going to hook up your ankles, and then you're going to fucking hop to the truck."

"Where are we going?"

He hopped to the SUV, and they loaded him into the rear and covered him with a blanket. Now he had to count on the SOU, but it was Katherine and Maria he thought about as they drove. He heard the tires hum over the metal plates on the Rio Vista Bridge. He felt the curves of the levee road and wondered if he could talk his way out. They left the paved road and were still running hard, rocks pinging off the underbody and Crey giving directions, a left turn, a right turn, another mile straight ahead, then slowing to a stop. The back opened. The blanket got jerked free, a slide racked on a gun, and Crey leaned over him.

"Don't move," Crey said. "Lou, slide the lock down alongside his ankle and then lock the chain and the cuff together and give me the key."

Cold metal slid along his ankle between the skin and the cuff. He heard the rattle of a light chain and a lock snap into place.

"Getting you ready, my man," Crey said. "Then we're going to undo the cuffs on your legs and settle this man-to-man."

Now he got jerked out the back of the truck, heard Torp and Perry laughing as he bounced off the bumper and landed hard on his side. He checked the horizon for headlights and saw nothing but darkness. The ankle cuff was still on his left leg. A chain was attached to the ankle cuff and he saw the chain snaked around to the front of the truck. Lying on his side he followed the chain to where it hooked to a tow ring. Crey put a boot on him, leaned over, and cut his shirt off.

"In a couple of minutes I'm going to undo your handcuffs, and we'll flip a coin to see who goes first. I'm going to give you a knife and then you're going to fight."

"Why am I chained and they're not?"

"Because I want it finished here. I don't want you running away and I don't want to have to shoot you in the back."

"You don't want to do this, Richie. There's no happy ending."

Crey's cell phone rang, he stepped away, and Marquez got to his feet, his hands still cuffed behind him. The Blazer's headlights shone on a clearing and on rows of vines. On the road in here the team could run without lights. Shauf won't mess around. The signal from his boots still came from the garage, but she would have seen the Blazer leave the driveway. Probably didn't see him get loaded in back, but one of the team would have followed the Blazer.

Crey rubbed his face as he talked. Torp and Perry watched him, didn't like the delay, and Crey didn't like the phone call. He argued with whoever was on the other end. He looked down the dirt road, then at Marquez. When he hung up he was suddenly in a hurry and walked over to Marquez, waving Perry forward as he did.

"Turn around and I'm going to free your hands."

When the cuffs fell away Marquez started rubbing his wrists to get circulation. Crey laid a four-inch knife on the hood.

"That's yours," he said. "Since they don't have your reach I'm keeping it fair by giving them bigger knives. Rules are we're going to go one at a time." Crey had moved back beyond where the twenty feet of chain that held Marquez could reach. "Pick up your knife. Everybody get ready for the coin toss. This here is the Super Bowl of knife fights."

He flipped a coin that flickered through the headlights and landed in the dirt of the clearing. Leaned over the coin, then grinned at Torp.

"Your lucky night, Liam."

"Crey, these guys are already going down. You don't want to tie yourself to them."

"Are you going to beg now, man? You going to piss on yourself or be a man? The knife is on the hood with your name on it. Pick it up because the rules are fight to the death."

Crey scratched out a half circle in the dirt with his boot.

"That's as far as he can reach with his chain, so the rules are no one leaves the circle unless the other man is dead. If Liam kills him, it's over. If John wins, Lou, you're up next."

Marquez picked up the knife.

"Okay, here we go," Crey said. "I'll take it down from one minute starting now." He held his watch in the light. "Thirty seconds to go." He smiled at Marquez. "Ten seconds." He nudged Torp. "Get in there and make the fucker pay. You're fighting for your honor, man."

Torp crossed over the line and moved to Marquez's left, talking as he did. "When I get you down I'm going to pull your teeth out one at a time before I kill you."

"Take it easy," Marquez said. "You look better than you did and your breath is a whole lot better."

Crey and Perry laughed as Torp slashed at him. Marquez jumped back, and Torp tried to corner him, get him out on one end of the chain, but Marquez kept the truck at his back. He blocked the left headlight, felt the heat of the headlight low on his back and lifted his left leg just high enough to grab the chain. He hoped Torp didn't see that, hoped that without the headlight Torp's view was restricted, and when Torp slashed at him again he barely moved and the blade caught skin on his right side. A line of red erupted, and Torp lunged in again. As he did, Marquez swung the chain, throwing a long loop, hooking Torp's head for a moment, then his arm. He jumped sideways and spun the chain around Torp's arm before he could pull back.

Torp jerked back hard, trying to get his arm free, diving for the outside of the circle and tripping. He lost his knife. He got to his knees and almost got away before Marquez caught up to him. Part of Marquez's mind registered Perry lifting the shotgun and Crey pushing the barrel up as he brought the knife down in a hard cutting slice across the back of Torp's foot. He felt it slow, then go through the Achilles tendon. Torp screamed, twisted, and the blade slid free.

Now Torp curled outside the circle, grabbing his ankle, calling for help as Crey got the shotgun from Perry. He heard him tell Perry, "We're doing this like we said. We're doing this fair." He pushed Torp with his boot. "Get your ass back in there."

Then there were headlights coming toward them, and Crey stopped prodding Torp, and Perry ignored the lights. He quickly stripped off his shirt, picked up a knife, and moved into the light in front of Marquez. Marquez watched the way he crabbed and moved forward and knew he was in trouble.

"You're gone," Perry said and moved sideways, was trying to grab the chain, then tried to step on it. The knife snicked off the hood, and a horn sounded, and Ludovna's car drove into the clearing. He drove straight at Perry, who dove out of the way. Ludovna hit the brakes and jumped out of the driver's side with a gun aimed at Crey.

"What did I tell you?" He kept the gun on Crey. "Come here. Unlock him."

Crey didn't argue, leaned over near Marquez's ankle, and freed the cuff.

"You, come here," Ludovna said to Perry, and, to Marquez's surprise or maybe because Perry was too far from the shotgun, he came over. He stood near Crey, and Marquez edged away from both. There was something more to happen here. Ludovna had Crey toss the keys to the Blazer to him, and he swung the gun over at Marquez.

"Don't move any farther."

The gun swung toward Torp and Perry.

"The fucking detective came to my house today."

He pointed the gun at Torp's head, and Marquez knew one of the team had to have followed the Blazer and must have seen Ludovna's headlights come down here.

"He came to my house asking about Sherri who used to come see me." He waved the gun toward Torp and Perry again. "These fucks killed her. He's got murder warrants. They sold her car, and no one told me." He stared at Crey. "You know what you're going to do now. You come here. The rest of you lie down."

Marquez didn't lie down, knew where this was going and knew it was going to happen fast. Crey had the boat, and he'd borrowed money from Ludovna, so it wasn't easy to get rid of him. He had a future utility. But not the rest of them, not Torp, Perry, or himself.

"Let me talk to you alone," Marquez said.

"Get the fuck down."

He pointed the gun toward Marquez, fired wide, and Marquez didn't move. Ludovna walked toward him, closing the distance, pointing the gun at his head, Marquez speaking quietly as he got close.

"I'll do it," Marquez said. "I know what needs to be done. They were going to kill me so I have no problem with it. Get my gun back and give me the keys to the Blazer, then leave, and I'll deal with it."

"Get down! Get the fuck down!"

Marquez pointed at Crey.

"He won't do it, but I will." Marquez whispered. "Tell him and see what happens. He'll make an excuse. He'll argue with you."

Ludovna's eyes narrowed. "Richie, come here."

Ludovna stepped away with him. They talked, and Ludovna kept the gun aimed at Perry. Then Crey retrieved Marquez's gun and the shotgun. He handed Ludovna Marquez's gun and the Blazer keys. He leaned the shotgun against Ludovna's car. Marquez knew Crey had a handgun as well, but this was the boldness of Ludovna. He had Crey stand next to him, then handed Marquez his gun and pointed at Perry and Torp.

Now, Marquez walked them out at gunpoint toward the darkness of the vines. Torp had to lean into Perry. He could barely walk and left a trail of blood. He whimpered in pain, and any second Marquez expected Perry to shove him away and run. He figured Perry was waiting to get outside the headlights.

"No farther," Ludovna called.

But Marquez pushed Perry, said very quietly, "Don't say anything. Do exactly what I say and maybe there's a way out of this. Lay down."

He brought the butt of the gun down across the back of Perry's head and clubbed Torp to his knees, then kicked him in the head and fired a shot into the dirt an inch from Torp's ear. He blocked Ludovna's view and brought the gun down hard on Torp's scalp. He made sure Torp bled enough to look like he'd been shot.

"Making it real," he whispered to Perry. "You've got to look dead," and brought the gun down as hard as he could against Perry's skull, fired twice near him.

Behind him Ludovna's car started. Its headlights shined this direction, suddenly brightening the ground, lighting the bare vines. Marquez turned to Crey walking toward him, carrying the shotgun, coming out to kill me, he thought. He saw Crey start to raise the gun, and Marquez shot him first. Crey's shotgun discharged and the blast went high as Crey fell. When he did, the Cadillac backed up fast but didn't leave yet. The passenger window lowered, and Ludovna watched as Marquez walked up to where Crey lay on his back. He leaned over him and fired twice. He stared at Ludovna and yelled at him, waved the gun.

"Get out of here," he yelled. "I did it, now get out of here."

And he watched Ludovna drive away. He walked back to Crey, who'd been hit high on the shoulder and already lost a lot of blood. He staunched Crey's bleeding, found a cell phone in the Blazer, and got a hold of a Sacramento County dispatcher. He held Perry and Torp at gunpoint as Roberts and Cairo made their way to him. They'd been on foot less than half a mile away when the gunfire started. They cut through the vines to where he was, and Marquez told them the new plan.

49

Sacramento County deputies took charge of the Chevy Blazer, and two ambulances followed police cruisers out the vineyard road. They took Crey out first, loaded Torp into the second ambulance, and Selke confirmed that Ludovna had returned to his house. An unmarked had picked him up as he came through the delta. He showed Selke where the fight had gone down in the clearing and then made his proposal as they drove away.

Down the highway they pulled off on another road, and Marquez waited with Shauf, Roberts, and Cairo. Cairo found him a sweatshirt. They all waited as Selke talked to his captain and ran the idea by him. He was a long time on his phone in his car. Then he walked back to where they were standing.

"You're insane," Selke said, "but my captain is willing to go along with your idea. We'll call the *Sac Bee* and the TV stations, but there's no guarantee. They don't like this kind of stuff because they think it makes them look bad later, and we can't just lie to them. Also, no one is going to hold the story forever so it'll all have to go down fast, but everyone agrees it's worth a try. You really think Ludovna was upset over La Belle?"

"I think so, but I think the real reason was you coming after them with murder warrants. He's afraid some part of it will reach him. If Crey had killed me I think he would have shot Crey. Right now he's probably thinking about how to deal with me. What's going to happen with Crey, Perry, and Torp?"

"Well, it's interesting. I called the Feds, and they've got a way to treat them and keep them away from phones and anybody they can talk to. They're suddenly very interested in what Ludovna's doing."

"Get the TV stations to go along, and I think it has a chance of working. Ludovna has the TV on all the time."

"We'll see what we can do."

The morning news reports were less than six hours away. Selke looked at his watch and shrugged. He was for trying the idea but not overly hopeful. Seemed like a long shot to him.

"Let's get out of here," he said.

Six hours later Marquez called Ludovna's cell and told him to turn the TV on to KMAX. He added, "I should have had a shovel."

Marquez watched the KMAX report. Three dead of gunshot wounds in a vineyard in the delta, a winery superintendent finding them this morning. Selke was interviewed as the detective in charge. On TV they were saying only that the bodies were Caucasian males approximately thirty-five to forty years of age. He watched the report and waited for Ludovna to call back. When he didn't call right away, Marquez called him.

"Did you see it?"

"Yes."

"No one is going to care about these guys. When they figure out they're all ex-cons they'll assume it was a drug deal gone bad or something. Everyone will say good riddance."

"Don't talk on the phone. You meet me at Raburn Orchards."

"Are you kidding? Why there? Anywhere else but there."

"There's no one out there. The police are finished."

"So what? I don't want to be seen around there."

"Meet me there."

At noon Marquez met Ludovna in the packing shed at Raburn Orchards. He wore a wire. Ludovna got there ahead of him and was parked near the main house.

"What if someone shows up?"

"I already talked to the bank. I want to buy this property. It'll be months before all the probate bullshit is done, but if a cop comes he can check with the bank."

"Why are we here?"

"Because Torp and Perry and Crey killed them, and I have a gun I want you to put on Crey's boat today."

"What gun?"

"The one he used here."

"I'm not tracking you."

"He killed the Raburns. He killed them with the other two. Torp brought the kids down. The kids could have stayed in bed, but they brought them down to make the parents talk. They didn't know anything. It was the goof, Raburn, who knew things and he tried to stand up, and they had to kill him before they could get the questions answered. It was all fucked up. It was all a waste."

"How do you know all this?"

"Crey told me, okay." Ludovna stared hard at him to make the point that it was the truth. But Marquez didn't believe him.

"You killed three men last night. They would give you the death sentence, right? But only I know."

"What's that mean?"

"It means you do what I say this afternoon. You take the gun that's here and put it on Crey's boat before the detectives go there today."

"Where is it?"

"In the building over there." He pointed at the equipment building.

"How do we get in?"

"I have a friend at the bank, so I have a key."

"The guy has been offed, and I'm going to walk down the dock, get on his boat, and plant a gun?"

"This way the murders here get solved. They find the gun and figure it out."

"I don't want to take a hot gun anywhere."

"It won't be so hard. You're his friend, you're coming by. People know you're his friend." Ludovna pushed keys into Marquez's palm. "These are all of his keys. Someone asks you just say he's your friend and you have a key. Lose the keys in the water after you put the gun on the boat. Okay, then like you say, it's simple. The detective has his killers of Sherri. The FBI solves the case here, and when they go through the van Perry and Torp have been driving, maybe they find another gun that was used here."

"Is that what's going to happen?"

"What did I tell you Torp did here?"

"He walked the kids down and shot them."

"With his gun, and his friend must have helped. Crey told me while we were waiting for you."

"Right, while I was out in the vines shooting the idiots, Crey was confessing. Bullshit. And you sent Crey to kill me."

"No, I sent him to check on what happened, to make sure you were okay." Ludovna got close to Marquez, stood inches from his face. "You murdered him. I saw you murder him. I saw you murder three people. It cost me money because Crey owed me money, and now he's not there to run the business and pay it back, so maybe you run the boat and the bait shop, or you hire someone and then pay me back."

"I'm not running any bait shop."

"You owe the money he owed me, and last night I let you take care of them. Now you owe me. If you have a problem with that, then we have a problem."

They walked over to the equipment building, and Ludovna opened the door. The orchard machinery was neatly organized inside, and Ludovna led him to one of the tilling machines.

"You have to crawl under. He told me it's taped under one of these machines."

It didn't take that long to find, and now Marquez tried to figure out a way to avoid touching it and contaminating the evidence. He stared at the gun and called back to Ludovna.

"I don't see it."

"Okay, check the next machine."

He checked three machines and then questioned Ludovna. "When did he say this?"

"Last night."

"Maybe he got confused."

"He was very specific. He knew the police would find the bodies of Torp and Perry and then they would find Torp's gun. There were two guns used, this one and Torp's. Even before you murdered them he knew because of what I said about Sherri La Belle. She used to come to my house once a week. She's a prostitute. I was a client, okay, and the police found her book with my name. I told this to the detective, but Crey didn't know until I came out and saved your life last night."

Marquez stalled. He scowled, wanted Ludovna to repeat it for the wire.

"I still don't follow you."

"The detective has murder warrants for Torp and Perry, okay. Then they'll go through the van and find the gun used here. They're not stupid. They'll figure it out, and when they find the gun you hide on the boat, then they have both guns used here."

"Why did Crey kill the Raburns?"

"It was about money."

Ludovna got in his face again now. He got close when Marquez was too quiet.

"This is what you're going to do because I tell you to and you owe me. I saved your life last night. He chained you so he could drag you with the truck if you won the fights. Then to make sure, he said he was going to run over your head and leave you. It was all because you fucked with his guys, the same as Raburn fucked with him. Look what happened to Raburn. So you owe me your life. Find the gun. I know it's there."

"How do you know?"

"You fuck with me and we're going to have a real problem." Ludovna pointed to the tilling machine the gun was under. "Check that one again. I don't want to have to get my coat dirty."

This time Marquez found the gun and a gas rag in the equipment shed to wrap it in. They walked back to Ludovna's car.

"I'm going to want you to work sturgeon the same as you have. You'll take over the boat and the shop and keep what else you have going. I'll tell you how many pounds of roe we need a week, okay? You set it up and run it. You get 30 percent of what we make. Your job is just the sturgeon but sometimes I'll ask you to make other deliveries for me. Sometimes you'll take your boat out on the ocean and pick somebody up. You'll get paid for that. I have other people I work with, but you won't talk with them or ask them any questions. You understand?"

"It was Crey's shop. How do I take it over?"

"I'm a partner. I have the majority, okay. In a couple of years when everything is going well no one will remember what happened last night." He tapped his chest. "Even I will forget, but first we get everything working." He got in his car and lowered his window. "Go put the gun on the boat. Everything will be fine."

"Sure, everything will be great. You have a good day," Marquez said and watched him drive off.

50

But Ludovna didn't have a good day. Marquez got a call from him around dusk. His voice was tight, uncomfortable, perhaps sensing something deeper was wrong.

"There's nothing on the TV," he said. "They're just talking about steroid baseball. Did you go to the boat?"

"Yes, and there was no problem."

"Did the detective call you?"

"No."

"Turn on your TV."

"Turn my TV on?"

"Turn it on the Sacramento news."

"Why?"

"Because there's nothing on about them."

"So what, maybe this morning is all they're going to report. Now you're the one who needs to relax."

"There's something wrong."

"What could be wrong?"

Ludovna hung up, and Marquez called Selke.

"He's getting nervous. He's looking for more news."

"He's not going to get it. The media wasn't too wild about the whole idea. It took a call from the Feds to make it work." He added, "They've started surveillance of Ludovna, and there are two special agents here with me."

"Are you with Torp?"

"No, with Perry. Torp got out of surgery a couple of hours ago, but he's not talking. He wants a phone and a lawyer."

"Has anything been said to him about the Raburns?"

"Not yet. Perry's here in an interview box, and he's wobbling. He may rat out his friend if a deal can be structured. The Feds have looked over what I have on Sherri La Belle and agree, better to try to get a confession before anything is said about the Raburns. Get the confessions, lock them up, then the Feds can go to work on them." Before Marquez could ask about Crey, Selke answered the question. "He's still on the table. The bullet shattered his shoulder, and he was pretty dicey from loss of blood when they got him in here, and it turns out he's anemic and doesn't clot worth a shit. The bastard is trying to die on us."

"I'm supposed to take over his business anyway."

Selke chuckled. He'd already recounted the conversation at Raburn Orchards for Selke, but Selke surprised him now.

"There's a better life out there than dealing with these punks. My brother has a cabin up along the Boundary Lakes in Minnesota. It gets cold, the black flies are a bitch in the summer, but it's beautiful. A guy like you could run a sport boat and when you think about being out on the bay on those warm still nights in the fall and the moon rising, a scotch in your hand instead of trailing these lowlifes." He sighed, exhaling into the phone. "What they did to her with a knife I just can't believe, and if Torp and Perry weren't stupid we wouldn't be catching them, but I tell you, I'm tired of this. I talk to my brother, he's up there fishing, he's happy. Anyway, I'll call you as it changes here. FBI got to you yet?"

"They're on their way."

Marquez sat in the front room of his house with two FBI agents. The gun he'd placed on Crey's boat had been recovered, and they had more than enough to take Ludovna down, but without saying so directly, they indicated that the Bureau was waiting for something more. They were somber and quiet and watched as Maria came in the door and had an awkward but friendly exchange with her mother. Then Maria and Katherine drove down to Mill Valley to do some shopping after Marquez explained he'd have to talk to the agents alone.

It was dark now and cooling down in the room. Marquez turned on another lamp, asked the agents if they wanted anything to drink. No one wanted coffee, water, anything except to hear again Ludovna's last instructions.

"He said that occasionally I'd have to take the boat out in the ocean and pick up a passenger."

"How far out?"

"Didn't say."

"How are these passengers supposed to get onto the boat?"

"That one sentence was all he said, but I had the impression Crey had made similar trips. He thinks Crey is dead, and I'll step into Crey's shoes and do whatever Crey did for him. Ludovna put the money up for Crey to buy Beaudry's business, and it's understood that I'm assuming Crey's debt. He made it clear he's got the leverage of being a witness to the murders."

One of the agents spoke now. "He ought to be worried you're going to take him out."

"He made it clear he's got other partners, and he seems to think it's all going to be worth it for me and that I'll like the deal once I get dialed in."

"Is that what he called them? His partners?"

"Yeah."

The agents on the couch glanced at each other. Marquez looked from one to the other. The Feds hadn't said anything about what they'd found or not found at Weisson's. If they'd found sturgeon or caviar, no one had told him. Nothing had been in the news, other than Karsov was a known arms trafficker and there were national security issues.

"Are you going to pick up Ludovna tonight?"

"No."

Torp would have a lawyer by tomorrow, but that was about Sherri La Belle, and Torp wouldn't be calling Ludovna anytime soon to chat. Neither would Perry or Crey.

"You're waiting for him to make a phone call."

One of the agents nodded. Marquez got up and made coffee. The agents stood. They were almost done here, and now everyone watched as Marquez's cell phone rang and he checked the screen. "Selke," he said to the agents as he answered.

"We just got a confession from Perry on La Belle, and he says he was there when the Raburns were killed but did not participate. The charge will get cut to manslaughter for Perry on the La Belle murder, and he's going to testify that Torp stabbed her to death and cut her up. Perry helped Torp dispose of the body."

"Who killed the Raburns?"

"He claims the shooters were Torp and Ludovna. Ludovna shot Abe. Torp shot the kids, and I can tell you Perry is lying, that he was part of the Raburn killing, but we'll get that from the others. But get this, he says he doesn't know why they killed the Raburns. He says for Torp it was just about money. He got paid for it. I'm going to throw something else at you. This is from piecing together what Perry told us. I think Crey knew his 'boys' were going to get offed out in that vineyard and he came up with you as a lure to get them out there, but that pissed off Ludovna, who just wanted them driven out there and shot. That's why Ludovna was angry when he drove up and found you chained to the Blazer."

The pager of one of the agent's went off, then a cell phone. Marquez hung up with Selke, and the agents thanked him and were suddenly more forthright as they were leaving.

"It'll be no later than tomorrow," one of them said.

"Are you hoping he'll try to contact Karsov?"

"We are. We're sorry we couldn't tell you before. We've monitored every call Ludovna has made for the last year."

51

DBEEP picked Marquez up at the Benicia dock the next morning. They glassed a couple of fishing boats out along the Mothball Fleet then rode up the San Joaquin River before back-tracking and going up the Sacramento with a strong wind at their back. Marquez and Ruax compared notes, looking at fishing holes and sloughs and docks and boat launches they'd determined had been used by poachers. They rode past Raburn's houseboat. They pooled their notes on who was left, talking above the wind and boat noise and much more quietly as they docked and dropped Marquez in Walnut Grove.

The day was bright and clear, the sky wind-scoured. He bought coffee at Mel's and waited outside across the road looking down at the river, the coffee keeping his hand warm. DBEEP was gone, and the SOU operation was basically done, though it felt unfinished. He turned as Shauf and Cairo drove up, and they bought a couple of sandwiches and sodas and sat and talked about where they were at with everything. With the exception of August, the players they'd tracked were going down or had gone down, but in some larger sense the importance of stopping the poaching had been subsumed by human crimes. The Raburn murders. The grisly killing of Sherri La Belle. The deaths of the FBI agents and the intrigue still surrounding what the Feds were after. It left a disturbing sense of incompletion or imbalance.

Shauf drove Marquez into Sacramento, and he picked up an old Ford Explorer, one of the early models before they'd become so large. He liked the vehicle and hadn't driven it in a while. He made sure it still started and then walked over to Shauf's window.

"Time to go see your niece and nephew."

"I'm leaving tonight. What about you, John?"

"I'll be home."

And he would have been, but for taking a call from Ehrmann. The call could have come from another special agent in the Sacramento Field Office, and it wasn't clear from the questions he'd asked yesterday that Ehrmann was still part of the investigation. He'd gotten the impression Ehrmann might be on involuntary leave.

"Ludovna made a call we were hoping he'd make, and we're going to take him down tonight," Ehrmann said.

"I'd like to be there."

"Sure, if you want."

Ludovna was at a girlfriend's, a woman who lived alone not two blocks from his house. She was very surprised when she opened the door. It was all very polite. There were eight of them and one of her. Two agents went in and buttonhooked left with their guns drawn, two went right, and four straight ahead. Ludovna was in the shower. When Marquez saw him, Ludovna stood naked and handcuffed on the tiled floor of the kitchen. He'd come out of the shower and tried to get a gun from near the bed, and they'd taken him down on the bedroom floor. Water dripped from the dark hairs of his chest, abdomen, and groin. Ludovna's eyes focused on Marquez.

"You're FBI?"

Marquez shook his head, showed his badge. Special Operations Unit, Department of Fish and Game.

"I should have killed you," Ludovna said, and an FBI agent cut him off.

The last Marquez heard was an agent telling Ludovna they were going to unhook him so he could dress. They'd already read him his rights, and he was demanding a lawyer. Marquez walked outside with Ehrmann.

"I'll drop you back at your car," Ehrmann said. As they drove away he added, "I guarantee you he won't be buying fish for a very, very long time."

52

And that was the way it ended, except it wasn't the end of everything. There were the poachers they tracked down that came from Ludovna's list of contacts, and with Baird's approval Marquez was still chasing those after Christmas. There was enough in Ludovna's computer to bring trafficking charges against August, though what came later far surpassed those. It was the end of the SOU, or the end until new money was found in the state budget. It was the end of Sacramento Fresh Fish and Beaudry's Bait Shop and Sportfishing, and the end of August Food's caviar line.

Torp and Perry got charged in the La Belle killing, and Ludovna, Torp, Crey, and Perry in the Raburn slayings. The FBI had other pending charges against Ludovna that Marquez was told might eventually include arms trafficking but definitely included further counts of murder, auto theft, RICO violations, and drug smuggling.

Marquez didn't doubt that August would hire the best lawyer. He laughed when he heard it was Batson, but it didn't surprise him. It was also the end of Anna's ability to pay Batson when the FBI located, and was able to get a judge to freeze her access to, a Cayman Island account.

Maria moved back home on Christmas Eve, walked in around dusk carrying a bagful of presents, and rode with Marquez a couple of days on his trips into the delta, said she wanted to understand better what it was he did. She was with him this New Year's Day morning, and it was one of those California winter days when it was bright and clear and warm. The light shone like polished gold on Suisun Bay, and the sturgeon bite was on.

He figured the kid, Julio, would be out, guessed he'd think he was clever getting out early New Year's Day and fishing for sturgeon when everyone was recovering from last night. Marquez knew Julio had taken more sturgeon since he'd last bought from him. He knew from talking to him where he liked to fish, and they went there now after buying coffees at a convenience store.

"This coffee is terrible," Maria said.

"Not to your refined tastes."

"I don't see how you can drink it."

Marquez drank it anyway and then carried the Styrofoam cup as they walked along the shore. He glassed the few boats out there and found Julio.

"This guy I may bust is about your age," he told Maria. "He's got a fish, but I don't know what it is yet."

He felt the sun on his face and watched the kid bring the fish in, then work a gaff. The gray armor of a sturgeon rolled in the water. He'd brought a pair of binoculars for Maria, and she watched Julio secure the sturgeon, and now they trailed him toward the dock. At the dock a couple of Julio's friends were there to help. They carried the sturgeon up to a pickup and covered it with a tarp.

Marquez looked at Maria holding small binoculars to her face, hiding the binos with her hands. Julio wouldn't be armed, and his friends were gone. He was alone and back down at his boat, tying it off. He might have a place he needed to deliver the sturgeon to, but they weren't going to follow him there.

"Let's walk on down there," Marquez said, and Julio smiled but was leery as they approached.

"Do you recognize me?" Marquez asked.

"Sure, I sold you that one that time."

"That's right. Is this your boat?"

"My uncle's."

"The uncle who taught you about sturgeon?"

"Yes."

"Where's he at today?"

"Home."

"How's that college account coming along?"

Julio hesitated at the change of subject, then pride got the better of him.

"I got in," he said, and his eyes were full of hope and light. "I got the scholarship, and I'm earning the rest. I'll be the first one ever in my family to go to college. But how come you remember all that?"

Julio looked to Maria's face for the answer, then back at Marquez.

"Maybe because Maria has applied to colleges. This is my daughter, Maria. We saw you wrestling with the fish, and I recognized you. We watched your friends help you load it into the pickup."

"Do you want to buy another one?"

"No, but I want to talk to you. Why don't you walk with me a minute?"

"What for?"

"Because I don't want you to sell it to anyone, and I think I can convince you."

Marquez showed him his badge, and the kid's face fell as they walked down to the end of the dock. He told Julio what he could cite him for and what that might do to the scholarship, told him the sturgeon had been here two hundred fifty million years, but it was going to take the ones like the fish in the back of the pickup to keep the species going.

"I'm sorry," and he was a big strong kid but close to tears. "I'm really sorry."

"How about you give me your word you'll do something to make up for it, and I don't bust you on the first day of the year you start college?"

Of course Julio gave him his word, gave it immediately, and Marquez got his full name, wrote it into his notebook. Julio Rodriguez.

"I'm letting you go on this because I think you're good for your word."

Julio was scared but trying to face him. He squared his shoulders, looked Marquez in the eye, then looked away.

"I can't remember the last time I let someone go who has taken as many as you have."

"I'll never do it again."

"Everyone says that, but make that the truth, and I want you to tell your uncle what happened out here."

"Yes, sir."

"Last time it was Abe Raburn you called. How did you meet Raburn?"

"Isn't he dead?"

"He is."

"I met him through my uncle. We delivered a couple of fish to him."

"To the orchard? Was there a packing shed or did you take them to the houseboat?"

Julio didn't seem to know either of those places. He shook his head, then described a two-story blue house out in vineyards and another man who was also there and talking in a foreign language his uncle said was Russian.

"What town was it in?"

"It was up from Courtland in the delta. We followed Raburn there."

"How far off the levee road?"

"Like a mile or so."

"And when you got there the Russian guy was there?"

Julio nodded.

"Would you recognize him if I showed you photos?"

"Maybe."

"Okay, I've got some photos in my truck."

Julio looked at a stack of photos that included August, Ludovna, Crey, Torp, Perry, and six other poachers they'd taken pictures of.

"I don't know."

"Fair enough. How long ago was this?"

"Like four months."

"Okay, look at these photos and eliminate the people you know it isn't."

Julio laid the photos on Marquez's hood in the sunlight, and the air was just gentle enough today to where they didn't blow off. He began to take away photos. He picked up the shots of Crey, Ludovna, a couple of sturgeon fishermen and put those in a pile by themselves. He hooked a fingernail under the prison mug of Torp, and then Perry, uncannily pairing the two before moving them out of the way.

"Not one of those two?"

"No."

"And Raburn led you out to this house?"

"Yeah, we loaded in someone's car there." He remembered more about the property now. "You drive through a lot of grapevines first."

Now there were only four photos left, and among those remaining, August was the only one fluent in Russian. Juio concentrated on each photo, his eyes moving from one to the next and back. He remembered his uncle had caught a sturgeon in San Pablo Bay. He'd called Raburn from his cell, and when they'd gotten to Raburn's houseboat, Raburn was already up under some trees near his truck waiting. He'd given Uncle Carlos a beer because the day was hot. It was dusk when they drove out the road to the blue house, and there were a couple of cars there. His uncle drank the beer as they drove, and dust blew in the windows because they were following Raburn. He remembered the house because it was blue like the sky, and now Marquez thought he knew which house it was. One of the photos Raburn had downloaded.

Julio had heard the man talking, and his uncle said it was Russian he was speaking to somebody else inside the house. The man came outside in the heat, looked over the sturgeon, and paid Raburn, who then paid his uncle. They moved the fish from their pickup to Raburn's.

"Raburn was going to clean it," Julio said, "but he had to show it to the man first."

"So you were just there a few minutes?"

"Yes."

"Did you see any other people?"

"Just the other cars."

There were four photos left on the hood, and Marquez pointed at them.

"And you think that man might have been one of these four?"

"Maybe one of them."

"If you had to pick one, who would you pick?"

He didn't pick August, picked a carpenter instead, a guy who was working on a Fish and Game building.

"I may need to speak to your uncle later today. If I do, I'll call you this morning, but we're done here. You can go."

When they got in the truck Julio was back down at his boat. He kept his head down as they pulled away.

53

"Are we going there, Dad?"

"Yeah, if you're okay with it we're going to take a ride into the delta and look for this house."

"That's fine, and it's really pretty out here today."

"Do me a favor." Marquez handed her his phone. "Scroll through the address book until you find SEH. Right above it will be SEC. It's a guy named Stan Ehrmann. He's with the FBI. The H is for his home number."

"Clever."

"Yeah, I know, and I try so hard to be cool."

"Okay, I've got it."

Marquez held the phone to his ear, and a teenage boy answered. He said his father had gone to find a store that was open to "get something for my mom."

"Tell him John Marquez called. Here's my phone number. Will you tell him I need to talk to him this morning?"

The road was empty and clear, and Marquez drove hard. He waited for Ehrmann to call back.

"That guy was so up about college," Maria said.

"Yeah." He glanced over at her. "You heard where he's coming from."

She didn't say anymore about it, and they crossed the river and came up past Poverty Road and the pink-stucco Ryde Hotel. People were starting to get out into the day. There was traffic and a long line of motorcycle riders going past from the other direction and a few boats out on the river. They were already to Isleton when Ehrmann called.

"You shouldn't be calling me," he said. "I have to refer the call to my S.A.C."

"When you talk to the S.A.C. tell him I only want to talk to you." He recounted the conversation with Julio. "Raburn should have led us to this house, but he never mentioned it. There's a sky-blue house like the one Julio described among those photos Raburn had stored."

"I remember a few photos of houses. We haven't been looking for a house in the delta, but sure, it's worth checking out. Do you think you can find this place?"

"I'll know soon."

"I'll make some calls in the meantime."

He hung up with Ehrmann.

"What's that about, Dad? How come you're calling the FBI?"

"Because we followed a lot of people and none of them ever went to this house Julio is describing."

"But is that really any big deal?"

"Probably not, but it's worth checking out. Raburn had downloaded photos he was saving. Some of the photos he might have taken on the sly, and the FBI has been looking for other connections. Still, it probably doesn't mean anything."

There was one house he had in mind and could see now. He'd found it after he'd looked at Raburn's photos. It wasn't that far upriver from Raburn Orchards. They rolled down a lightly graveled road for almost a mile, and there weren't any fresh tire tracks ahead of them. He could tell, driving in the long straight road through the bare vines, that no one had been here through several storms. When they got there the house still looked empty. No other cars.

It was an older Victorian raised off the ground in what had been a delta habit to avoid yearly floodwaters in the years before the levee system was completed. It sat high on a thick concrete foundation, stood six feet off the ground like a house trying to get a view of the river by looking over the levee road a mile away. He looked at the faded blue siding, at the porch Julio had described, then at Maria.

"What do you think?" he asked.

"Sounds like what he described."

"I'm going to knock on the door and take a look."

When no one answered the door he walked back to the truck and gave Maria his keys.

"Sit in the driver's seat and we'll talk by phone as I walk around the back."

"That's pretty paranoid."

"So if anything happens, you head for the road. You call 911."

"What?"

In the back of the house he saw locks and the heavy-gauge steel doors covering an entrance to the big basement space created by raising the house above the floodwaters. He'd seen enough houses raised a similar way, but none with the basement locked up like this. He kept an eye on the windows of the house as he looked at the quarter-inch steel doors and the locks and chains. It would take two men to lift a door.

"Maria, I'm going to hang up. I've got to call the FBI back."

Lift one door, then the other, and you'd walk down four or five steps and be in a storage room under the house. He got Ehrmann's son again when he called.

"Dad said you should call him on his cell phone. He's got a new one. I'm supposed to give you the number."

Marquez copied it down. The kid was as efficient as his father. He called Ehrmann.

"I'm on my way to you," Ehrmann said, "but there are two agents who'll get there in a few minutes, and if anything looks suspicious, just wait."

"Why did you decide to start driving here?"

"Something fit with a piece of conversation we eavesdropped."

"This is one of the two things I really like about the Bureau."

"What's that?"

"When you decide to move, you don't waste time."

"And what's the second thing?"

"You don't seem to need to ask anyone anymore before going in to look at something. I'm here with my daughter. No one seems to be home at the house. There are heavy steel doors and hardened steel chain and two padlocks like you don't see often around here.

Someone wants to restrict access to the basement. You'll need tools to get in, if that's what you decide to do."

It was half an hour before the first government sedans came through the vineyard. It was another hour before they had the tools to break in. Then the doors got opened.

Maria was in the truck cab on the phone to her mother. Marquez left her and walked over as the first of the FBI went down into the basement. He knew from their voices they'd found something, and looking down the steps he saw them squatting near long metal boxes. Behind the boxes he saw hundreds of guns.

"Kalashnikovs," Ehrmann told him, and then walked a distance away with him. "This is it, Marquez. This is what we were looking for. A whole lot of people are on their way here now."

"What else is in there?"

"Handheld missiles. Some other hardware. They're going to chase you out of here."

"That's okay." He looked at Ehrmann. "Are you sure it's what you were looking for?"

"Yeah, we've got a printed list. We've been a buyer, but someone here in the States had outbid us for some of this."

"The handheld missiles?"

"Yeah, somebody really wanted them."

"And you don't know who that other buyer is?"

It was a stupid question. Obviously, they hadn't found the other buyer, and no wonder they were so anxious to find the arms cache.

"Would Karsov have come back for these?"

"Probably. Eventually. He had the other buyer; he'd try to make it work. It's all about money."

They watched more cars come down the road, and then a couple of special agents started toward them. Ehrmann pointed at a car pulling in.

"That's our S.A.C. I've got to go talk to him."

Marquez stayed where he was and waited for the special agents to walk up to him.

"You've got to back away, sir," one of them said. "Your daughter and you will need to leave the premises now. We're closing off the area."

"Yeah, Stan just told me."

Marquez felt the tension coming off them, and they were trying to be nice. He started toward his truck.

"They wouldn't even let me move," Maria said. "I wanted to come over to where you are, and they told me to wait here. What's over there?"

"Come have a look."

The first FBI agent who spotted Marquez and Maria walking back knew it was Marquez who'd found the house. He hesitated, and it was the next two who moved to block them.

"She's going to see this, and then we're gone," Marquez said.

"No, she's not, sir."

"This is the world she's inheriting, and I want her to see it."

One of the handheld missiles had been carried up into the sunlight, and the box opened. Marquez used his bigger frame to shield Maria's approach and repeated they were just going to take a look and leave. She got a look and a glance down into the basement.

A few minutes later they were in the truck, driving back through the grapevines. From the levee road they could still see the government cars down in the field in the distance. Off to their right the river was running hard. Does the way we treat other species say a lot about our chances of making peace among ourselves? Marquez was pretty sure it did. He was thinking about that when Maria spoke again.

"It's weird that a sturgeon is how we found those," Maria said. "Don't you think that's kind of weird?"

ACKNOWLEDGMENTS

Once again, many thanks to Kathy Ponting, patrol lieutenant of the SOU, and to Nancy Foley, whom I first met as a member of the SOU and who now is Chief of Patrol, head of the law enforcement branch of California Fish and Game. It's probably quite lucky for wildlife in California to have a Chief of Patrol who once ran the undercover team. Thanks also to Lieutenant Troy Bruce, SOU, George Fong, Supervisory Special Agent, FBI, and a gifted writer, whose novels I'm sure we'll all be reading should he ever retire from the Bureau.

Thanks also to Patsy for the Klamath stories, Lisa Stouffer for loaning her marina, Adrian Muller, Jennifer Semon, Tony Broadbent, Paul Hansen, Andrew Livengood, Kate and Olivia, Greg Estes, Branch for reading the first draft, Lydia McIntosh, John Buffington, whose wallet blew out the back of the boat and perhaps came to rest along the river bottom with the sturgeons. Anyone who has ever had Philip Spitzer as an agent knows a conversation with Philip can be like a good drink that leaves you happy and looking forward to the future. Many thanks to my tireless editor, Jay Schaefer, and to all at Chronicle Books who have worked to make the crime fiction line happen. And, Judy, always and forever you.

I've written three Marquez novels with the belief that if I wrote a good enough story I could help those who have devoted so much to saving open country and the wildlife in it. I hope in some small way I've done that.